SHADOWRUN:
WOLF AND RAVEN

BY MICHAEL A. STACKPOLE

SHADOWRUN: WOLF AND RAVEN
By Michael A. Stackpole
Cover art by Damon Westenhofer
Design by Matt Heerdt and David Kerber

Some of these stories were previously published in other venues:
"Squeeze Play" first appeared in *Challenge* #44
"Quicksilver Sayonara" first appeared in *Challenge* #46
"Digital Grace" first appeared in *Challenge* #47
"Numberunner" first appeared in *Challenge* #50
"Fair Game" first appeared in *Challenge*, #62-63
"If As Beast You Don't Succeed" first appeared in *Kage*, #11-12.
The character of Dempsey is copyright © 1990 Loren K. Wiseman, and is used with his permission.

Published by Catalyst Game Labs,
an imprint of InMediaRes Productions, LLC
7108 S. Pheasant Ridge Dr. • Spokane, WA 99224

CONTENTS

INTRODUCTION

I never thought I'd live long enough to be writing memoirs. Hell, I never thought I'd learn to write well enough to write memoirs. One of the things about associating with Doctor Raven is that you end up doing a lot of things you never thought possible.

In my case, that includes surviving into my thirties.

Anyway, the adventures I've written down here all took place back in the dawn of time—back a good six, eight years ago. Not very long in calendar days, but a lifetime when measured in physical therapy sessions and reconstructive surgery. Much of this will feel like ancient history to most of you.

I'm hoping it will seem like that to me, too, one of these days.

—Wolfgang Kies, Seattle, 2059

SQUEEZE PLAY

ONE

As the door shut behind me and the bar's natural atmosphere raped my nostrils, I had a sudden urge to remodel the place with a flamethrower. From the outside the boarded-over windows and plywood framing for the weatherbeaten door suggested someone had already tried that with "the Weed," as its denizens affectionately called the place. I had to agree with the name—nothing in here a load of Agent Orange wouldn't improve. The Weed was the kind of bar that aspired to be a dump when it grew up[1].

I hadn't liked Ronnie Killstar when I'd spoken with him to set up this meeting. After seeing the place he chose, I liked him even less. *Easy, Wolf,* I reminded myself. *Raven gave you this job because you've got more control than Kid Stealth or Tom Electric. Don't let him down—you already owe him too much.*

Against my better judgment, I crossed the short distance from the door to the bar. A small, Hispanic-looking bartender wandered over to where I'd elbowed in between two other patrons. His voice sounded like a ripsaw tearing into sheet steel. "Waddalya have?"

I squinted against the burning smoke from my neighbor's Saskatchewan Corona Grande and shrugged. "What's on tap?"

The bartender shook his head.

"Great. Make it a double."

He stared blankly at my attempt at humor. "Waddalya have?" he rasped again in a gravel-croak.

I glanced at the cooler. "Green River Pale. No need for a glass."

As he pulled the beer out of the cooler and brushed the ice off onto the floor, I pulled a roll of corp scrip from my pocket. He twisted the cap off and I started peeling bills off the roll. I slowed when I

---

[1] Oh, this is what a footnote is. Slick.

got near what the beer had to cost, then stopped when he started to move the bottle forward. He glanced up at me, shrugged, then gave me the drink. I could have used a credstick to pay, but in a place this archaic and seedy, crumpled paper seemed the way to go.

I carried the drink toward the corner nearest the door. The beer tasted like his voice sounded, but cold, and I set it down quickly. I slid into a booth, then unzipped my leather jacket and settled in to observe the bar and its patrons. I kept the beer in my left hand while letting my right rest near the butt of my Beretta Viper 14[2].

My new vantage point allowed me a fuller appreciation of the Weed's decor. The plastic baby doll heads and high-heeled shoes hanging from the ceiling somehow made sense, especially when seen within the larger context. Most of the light came from sputtering neon signs begging patrons to drink exotic brews the bar no longer stocked. Silvery tinsel and some flashing lights left behind during some long-ago Christmas mocked the moribund setting, but somehow brought gaiety to the expression of the plastic, safe-sex doll floating above a busted pinball machine.

The place oozed atmosphere.

I used my beer bottle to smear a six-legged piece of that atmosphere across the table.

About the only normal portion of the bar lay kitty-corner across the room from my position. Three jack-tables, the cocktail model, sat up against the wall. Only one wirehead was using the Weed's facilities. The 'trode halo circled her ebony brow, and the light from the unit's display washed in rainbow waves over her face, but she didn't notice. Whatever graphics were flashing across the screen were for outsider consumption only—she was jacked in deep and playing her own little games.

I caught the scent of dead flowers all mixed up into a noxious blend that made the Weed smell worse and was trendy enough to cost 150 nuyen a milliliter. The stink came to me about a second and a half before I heard the *click* of Ronnie Killstar's wrist spur.

Large as life—or at least as large as he could muster—the pasty-faced street samurai slid into the booth across from me. The jaundiced light from the bar skittered across the razored edge of the curved metal blade jutting out from his right wrist, and a red light glowed in his eyes.

---

[2] Sure, the Beretta Viper 14 is old. So's gravity, but it still works. Nice thing about the Viper is that I have a bullet, I have a target, I pull the trigger, and the gun does all the math for the hit. And with the Viper, I never have batteries go dead on me in the middle of a firefight.

He sneered at me. "You oughta get your eyes done. I can bull's-eye a rat's ass at a thousand meters in the pitch dark. I saw you come in and I saw you sit down. I can see in here plain as day."

That being the case, I saw no reason to mention he'd just wiped the sleeve of his white jacket through cockroach paste. I sniffed the air. "I don't need eyes to find you."

Two large men appeared from in back where Ronnie had been waiting and stood on either side of our booth. They were both built like those smiling Buddha-type statues you find down the coast in Tokyo West, 'cept these two wore more clothes, didn't smile, and didn't look like they'd give you good luck if you rubbed their bellies. Still, if they were hanging around with Ronnie it meant they had to be losers—which also explained why they looked so much at home in the Weed.

His intimidation batteries in place and ready to fire, Ronnie reinforced his sneer. "I didn't figure the great Dr. Raven would trust Wolfgang Kies with an assignment of this importance."

I smiled. "TM."

"Huh?"

I smiled more broadly. "I said, 'TM.' You forgot to add the trademark to the phrase, 'the Great Dr. Raven.'" I shook my head ruefully. "That's why he sent me. You've got no manners and no sense of propriety. You wouldn't expect him to come to a place like this, would you?"

Clearly, any space in Ronnie's monosynaptic brain devoted to humor was overloaded by my effort. His eyes flashed on and off as he got angry and his concentration broke. Suddenly, with a metallic *snap* that sounded like a pistol being cocked, a twenty-five-centimeter icepick blade shot out from between the middle and ring fingers on his right hand and he lunged forward. The tip touched my throat right above the silver wolf 's-head totem I wear and drew a single drop of blood.

"I don't need your static, you drekling! Raven sent word that he wanted to make a deal with La Plante, not the other way around. We're not doing you a favor—it's you that wants one from us." Killstar's dark eyes narrowed. "I want Raven!"

With great effort I killed the urge to lunge forward and bite his face off. I swallowed hard and felt the icepick brush against my Adam's apple. "I wanted La Plante. I would suggest we're even."

I forced my eyes open and got the surprise reaction I expected as Ronnie looked into them for the first time. With the anger rising in me, I knew they'd gone from green to silver—that change is not all that rare. Ronnie got an added treat, though, as a dark circle surrounded each iris with a Killer Ring. *Your augmented eyes may let you see in the dark, but they can't do this. It's something you've got to have inside—not an option you get to tack on aftermarket.*

Ronnie leaned back, but left the stinger extended.

"Maybe we are even. What are you offering Mr. La Plante?"

I ignored the question as a droplet of sweat burned into the pinprick at my throat. "I want proof she's still alive."

The punk snapped his fingers and one of the Buddha brothers produced a portacomp and slipped a small optical disk into the unit. I took it from him and hit the Play button.

The LCD screen flickered to life and I saw Moira Alianha standing calmly before a wall screen trideo display. She moved back and forth in front of it, and I concentrated on how her long black hair trailed out and through the image. If they'd recorded her moving before a blank screen, then masked in a recent program to make me think she was still alive, the process would have broken down on those fine details.

It looked clean to me, but I didn't want to give Ronnie the satisfaction of knowing I thought he'd actually done something right. "A simchip would have been better."

It was an effort for him to roll his cybereyes to heaven. "And we could have brought her here with a brass band and an army of grunges[3], but we don't think we're gonna recover our overhead on this one. Satisfied?"

I tapped the Disconnect and pocketed the device. "She's alive."

Ronnie smiled like a gambler holding four of a kind. "Mister La Plante has a client who has offered us a great deal of money for Moira Alianha with her maidenhead intact. How can Raven make it worth our while to turn her over to him instead?"

I tried to suppress the wince, but the additional construction on either side of Ronnie's smile showed me I'd failed. Dr. Raven lost no love on Etienne La Plante, but recovering Moira and returning her to Tír Tairngire meant he had to suppress his feelings and deal with the man. As Ronnie's smile cooled into a smug look of superiority, I decided Kid Stealth might have been right in the first place: bring the whole crew in and take La Plante's crime empire apart.

"It won't guarantee we save the girl," Doc had told him.

"Yeah," said the Kid, "but it'll feel gigabytes better than helping that slime."

I rested my elbows on the table and steepled my fingers. "I have been authorized to offer you the Fujiwara shipping schedule for the next six months in return for the girl. We can make the exchange tonight."

---

[3] Yeah, I know grunge is fairly vulgar slang for ork, but the term applied to the orks who worked for La Plante. I think he found stupid ones, then fed them paint chips to dull down any native intelligence they had. Since he used them mostly as mobile weapon transport and trigger fingers, brains weren't vital. As we used to joke, to work for La Plante, you took an intelligence test: if you failed, you were in.

For all of ten seconds Ronnie got that divine-revelation look on his face. Suddenly, he realized just how big a game he was involved in, and how small a player he was in it. Then his eyes hooded over as the little maggot figured out how important Moira Alianha had to be for the Doctor to offer that kind of hot-byte data for her. A thought shot off on the wrong branch of his neural network and he began to believe in his own importance.

He scoffed and began to ease himself out of the booth. "Maybe. I'll talk to La Plante and let you know. You can wait here until then."

My right leg swept out and hooked up between his legs. I drew my knee up, jerking him and his squishy parts against the edge of the table. That knocked the wind out of him and made him jackknife forward. I grabbed a handful of his stringy blond hair with my left hand and tucked the barrel of my Viper in his left ear.

A Killer Ring stare kept the karma twins at bay. "That was a wrong answer, Ronnie." I eased the hammer back on the Viper 14 even though that was unnecessary on the double-action pistol. "Mr. La Plante, I know you'd not be who you are if you let an idiot like this conduct your negotiations for you without keeping tabs on him. I'd guess you've bugged Yin and Yang here, unless you tricked this dolt into carrying a set of ears on himself."

A glint of gold from the cloisonné orchid pin on Ronnie's lapel had given him away. "Very good, Mr. La Plante. Your gang's trademark pin is a listening device. I salute your foresight. I suggest your chauffeur pull the limo around so we can discuss things in private, say, in five minutes. We'll take a spin around the block and then you'll drop me back here. If not, I'm going to decorate the Weed's ceiling with something that'll add some real color."

The Coors clock on the wall ticked off four and a half minutes before the door opened. The Chauffeur[4], dressed in a spiffy uniform with creases sharp enough to cut like razors, nodded to me.

I patted Ronnie patronizingly on the head. "We'll have to do this again some time, when I have more time to play."

Whatever Ronnie replied, it wasn't very polite and I put it down to his discomfort as I leaned heavily on his head while working my way out of the booth. The twin pillars of Eastern wisdom let me pass, and I made it to the doorway unmolested.

---

[4] I've always thought The Chauffeur was a dumb street name. Usually you want a handle that suggests you're on top, like Tiger or King Cobra or something slick like that. Wolf, maybe, even. But The Chauffeur? I guess he liked it because he thought it made him sound like he was going places.

I handed the Viper to The Chauffeur and stepped into the street. The white Mitsubishi Nightsky stretch limo looked as out of place on the litter-strewn street as a wharf rat in the mayor's office, but that didn't stop it from being there. I waited as The Chauffeur scanned me with whatever he had for eyes behind those dark glasses of his, then smiled and entered the limo's dark interior.

Having grown up among the concrete alleys of Seattle, I thought of class as something you escaped from during the day. Despite my absolute loathing of anything and everything Etienne La Plante did and was, I still had to admit he looked classy. His double-breasted suit was cut from cloth of silver, yet—if possible—did not look ostentatious or flashy. His wavy white hair had been perfectly cut and combed, giving me the impression that I'd stepped into a boardroom for a long-planned meeting.

I settled into a velvet seat so comfortable I could have died happy in it, especially if the woman seated next to La Plante gave me another one of her I-want-to-have-your-baby-or-at-least-try-hard-at-it smiles. In the armrest at my left hand sat a frosted mug of beer—the half-empty bottle next to it proclaimed it to be Henry Weinhard's Private Reserve.

Very good, Etienne. My favorite. Is it true that you bought the brewery because you heard one of Raven's men loved the stuff?

La Plante refrained from offering me his right hand, but I didn't mind. If there was any flesh and blood left to it, the silver carapace hid it completely. I noticed, as he picked up his own mug of beer, that the hand articulated perfectly, but then *he* could afford perfection. I'd not heard of any assassination attempts against him, so I had to assume he had voluntarily maimed himself.

"I would apologize, Mr. Kies, for my underling's actions but, you understand, that was a test." He shrugged wearily. "After the bad blood between Dr. Raven and myself, you can hardly forgive my being suspicious."

I gave him a quick smile that broadened as I looked at his companion. "You can call me Wolf." I directed the comment more to the woman than La Plante, and waited a half-second for a similar offer of intimacy from the crime boss or, more specifically, *her.*

I continued when he ignored me—she was just being coy, I could tell. "When Dr. Raven was informed that you had become the custodian for Ms. Alianha and was called upon by her elven guardians to get her back, he was forced to make some choices. I am sure you can understand that that negotiation was not the most popular course of action suggested."

La Plante nodded sagely. "Former employees can be so, ah, vindictive, can't they?"

Sure, especially when you try to plant them in the harbor with their feet bound in a block of cement. No one would have figured Kid Stealth would blow off his own legs to escape that little death trap, but he did and survived. When your time comes, the timekeeper will be wearing shiny new legs and will move faster than even you remember.

"You heard our offer. You get the Fujiwara shipment schedules for the next six months in return for the girl. We'll burn you a chip. We can do the exchange tonight."

La Plante's nonchalant expression remained rooted on his face. "You have a decker good enough to get into Fujiwara that quickly? We're talking layers of protection—psychotropic IC, defensive and offensive knowbots, expert constructs, you name it. Enough ice to give anyone a case of terminal frostbite."

I smiled confidently. "This decker is so hot the only way to stop her is to dunk her in liquid nitrogen and hit her with a hammer. We'll get the schedule for you."

He hid his excitement at the offer well. "How do I know the data will be good?"

I sat up straight. "You have Dr. Raven's word on it."

Where Ronnie Killstar would have answered with some inane barb, La Plante just nodded. "Very well." He leaned over and whispered something in the redhead's ear. As she reached over and picked up my mug, he spoke. "You've not tried your beer. I assure you it has not been tampered with."

She sipped and returned the mug to its place on the armrest. As she licked her lips I felt an urge to procreate, then counted to ten—no, fifteen—to regain control.

"Sorry," I said, and smiled, "but after the Weed, drinking in here just wouldn't be the same. You understand." For her benefit I added, "Maybe another time..."

The door opened again. La Plante's chauffeur hovered by the door with my gun in hand. "Tonight, Mr. Kies, at warehouse building 18B, on the docks. We will give you the southern and western approaches. I would prefer this to be an intimate gathering."

"My feelings exactly. You bring a dozen of your grunges and I'll consider it even." I succeeded in getting myself perched on the edge of the seat. "And leave Ronnie at home..."

La Plante waved my last remark off with a silvery flourish of his right hand. "Do not concern yourself with him. He has been assigned new duty. He'll be feeding fish for the foreseeable future."

The Chauffeur handed me the pistol, then swung the door shut. I smiled at him, and his plastic mask of servitude cracked. "Someday, Wolf, it will come down to you and me. I'll make it quick. I want you to know that."

I met his mirror-eyed stare with my number two nasty glare. "Good, I like that. If a fight goes on too long, the bloodstains set and then you can never get them out..."

His plastic mask back in place, he turned and walked away. Though every olfactory nerve ending in my nose protested mightily, I reentered the Weed. My beer still waited on the table, but Ronnie Killstar and the Wonton boys had vanished. I waited and sniffed, but I couldn't smell the mulch drippings that passed for Ronnie's cologne. *Given how that stuff smells and sells, the Weed could bottle its mop stoppings and make a fortune.* I shook my head. *Never happen–they 'd actually have to mop this place.*

Instead of returning to my table, I walked over to the jacktables. I pulled the bug from inside my jacket and tossed it on the black woman's deck. "Did you get it all?"

Valerie Valkyrie, Raven's newest aide, gave me a smile that made me forget La Plante's taste-tester. "Everything, including your pulse rate and blood pressure when she sucked on your beer." I felt the burn of a blush sweeping across my face, and it grew hotter as it pulled a giggle from her throat.

"We'll discuss how much of that makes it into the report for the Doctor later. Right now we've got work to do."

TWO

"All right, Zig and Zag, let's go through the drill one more time."

Zag frowned and the razor claws on his left hand flicked out, then retracted with the speed of a snake's tongue. "We've got names..."

I raised myself up to my full height, which put me a centimeter or so taller than the smaller of them. "And right now they're Zig and Zag. You're local talent and I'm your Mr. Johnson. Now, you claim you want to join this elite circle? Fine, this is a tryout. Try living with new names for a second or two, got it?"

Zig elbowed Zag and they both nodded. For street samurai they weren't bad. Zag had gone the obvious route of adding chrome in the form of razor claws grafted to his hands and some retractable spurs that popped up from the top of his feet. He'd replaced his right eye with a rangefinder modification linked to the scope on his autorifle. He'd gone a bit far, in my mind, by having a fluorescent orange crosshairs tattooed over that eye from hairline to cheekbone and ear to across his nose, but it came close enough to warpaint that I could understand it. Still, I knew if I was on the other end of a sniper rifle, that would make a real nice target.

Zig had been more discreet. He'd gone in for body work. From the way he moved I knew he'd had his reflexes cranked up to move with the speed of something between a Bengal tiger and a striking cobra. I didn't see any body blades, but he was a bit more subtle than his partner, so he might not have flashed them. I also got the impression he'd had some dermal sheathing implanted to protect his vital organs—a wise choice. One never knows where those replacement organs were grown, and the failure percentage on cut-rate Khmer hearts made having a Band-Aid slapped on the old one look like a good bet for survival.

"Val and I are going to jack into the Matrix. No one should be able to track us to where we're going, but we can't be a hundred percent certain of that. I need you two to be alert and careful because when we bust the system we're going after, things could get messy. What do you do if there's trouble?"

Zag grumbled and walked over to where my MP-9 submachine gun[5] rested on the bed. "We slap the 'trodes off you and hand you this toy. Then we get the wirehead out of here."

Val didn't notice the rancor in Zag's voice at having been shot down earlier. When he'd asked if she would be interested in a little horizontal tango to "relieve the tension," she'd looked at him as if he were a deck with Made in UCAS stamped on its side. Zig and I shared a smile as Zag's anger deepened when Val continued to ignore him.

"Good. That's it. You get her out and get her to the place she tells you. Don't worry about me. I'll be fine."

"Or dead." Zag hefted one of the spare mags for my MP-9. "Freaking nine-millimeter toy and you've got silver bullets? Who do you think you are, the Lone Ranger?" He thumbed one bullet from the mag and tossed it to Zig.

Easy, Wolf. Better this tough guy act to hide his nerves than him falling apart on you. "I think I'm your Mr. Johnson—and a superstitious one at that."

Zig looked closely at the silver bullet in his hand. "Drilled and patched. You got mercury in there to make the bullet explode?"

I shook my head solemnly. "Silver nitrate solution. Physics is the same, the result is nastier. Burns as it goes."

Zig tossed the bullet back to his partner. "You planning on hunting a werewolf or something?"

"Were you in Seattle during the Full Moon Slashings?" The mention of that series of killings tore Val away from her deck. "A half-dozen years ago? That was the first anyone had heard of Dr. Raven, wasn't it?"

"Yeah." I let that one-word answer hang there long enough for all three of them to realize I wasn't going to say anything specific about that outing. "After that I've carried silver bullets. Never want to be without them if you need them."

Val shivered. "Viper, too?"

"Amen." I forced myself to smile and break the mood. "You got that Hibatchi chip encoder prepped yet?"

Val scolded me. "Hitachi, Wolf, and you know it."

I accepted a 'trode coronet from her slender fingers and pulled it onto my head. I adjusted it so the electrodes pressed against my temples and ran back over the midline of my skull. Val reached over

---

[5] Yeah, yeah. It's another antique gun, but it shoots straight, which is all I ask. Stealth keeps my guns as well tuned as my mechanic does my Mustang, so they work. Besides, the MP-9 is considered such a toy by most gillettes that they don't see it as much of a danger until one of its bullets is finished making an exit wound.

and tightened the band to improve the contact, then she clipped the dangling lead into a splice cable. She slid that jack into the slot behind her left ear, then flipped a switch on the deck.

I winked at her. "Let's do it."

She winked back and hit a button on the keyboard. "Play ball."

Doc Raven had warned me that Valerie Valkyrie was special, but until we plunged through that electric aurora wall of static and into the Matrix, I had no idea how special. I'd jacked into the Matrix before—who hasn't—but it had always been on a public deck where I ended up inside an entertainment system. Moving from game program to game program, I caught glimpses of the Matrix through the neat little windows the programmers had built into their systems, but I'd never had any desire to go out adventuring on my own.

Before, the form and shape of the Matrix had always been decided by the local network controllers. Here in Seattle the RTG resembled a vector graphic of the urban sprawl it encompassed. Well-fortified nodes were surrounded by fences and walls, and Matrix security teams patrolled the electronic streets like cops cruising a beat. I'd heard it had been designed that way because it made the casual user feel like he was in familiar surroundings, and thus easier to find his way around.

As things got strange and the world shifted, so did the Matrix. When a user entered the Chinatown area here in Seattle, for example, the buildings melted away and the nodes took the form of mahjong tiles. Deckers claimed that made it easier to pick out unprotected nodes, but I don't know about that. I've heard it said, and can believe, that no one goes near the nodes represented by dragons.

But that's the way of the world. Steer as clear as possible from dragons—words to live by and advice it'll kill you to ignore.

I've heard decker tales that if a decker got good enough, they could impose their own sense of order on the Matrix. With enough skill, they could make the Matrix appear the way they wanted it—free of extraneous data. Another urban legend born in the Matrix.

Valerie Valkyrie was a legendary decker.

After only two seconds, the landscape construct shifted. Gone were the clean lines of glowing, lime-green streets and shining white buildings. Suddenly I found myself standing beside the pitcher's mound in a monstrous baseball stadium. Val, outlined in a neon-blue that matched her eyes, pulled on a baseball cap that materialized from thin air and gave me a broad grin. The cap had a Raven patch on it.

"Sorry if you aren't used to this, Wolf." The shrug of her shoulders told me she wasn't sorry at all, and that my surprised reaction made her day. "Warping the Matrix to my conception of it gives me a home-field advantage."

Within the solar yellow of the glove on her right hand, she twitched a ball around and got the grip she wanted on it. From a dugout over on the third-base side of the field a smallish man walked up toward the plate. Behind and above him a scoreboard flashed to life and spewed out all sorts of information in hexidecimal.

I pointed up at the display. "Can you translate?"

She looked at me as if I'd disappointed her, then nodded. Suddenly the scoreboard flickered and the handy notation of baseball replaced the curious array of numbers and letters. Coming up to bat was Ronnie Killstar's personal file. The count was zero balls and two strikes, and the scoreboard reported his batting average as .128. He batted right-handed.

Val licked her lips as a catcher and umpire materialized behind the plate. "Can of corn." A green ball appeared in her left hand and she spun it around until she grasped it between her thumb, index, and middle fingers. Rearing back, her azure outline blurred and she delivered the pitch. It arced in at the plate, then dropped a full fifteen centimeters below Ronnie's futile swing.

"Yer out!" screamed the umpire.

All sorts of data poured out onto the scoreboard. It was a bit more nasty than one might expect to find on the average baseball card, but it still bespoke nothing more than a mediocre career. A quick comparison of his successful stolen bases versus times caught out in the attempt confirmed that he was an unsuccessful small-time thief before La Plante had taken him on as a leg-breaker.

As the record of his most recent telecom calls started to flash up on the scoreboard, I looked over at Val. "You can cut this any time you want. He's useless, and now he's dead." I glanced over at the number of the last call he'd made. "Hope it was to his mother."

Val wrinkled her nose. "I was unaware anyone had taught Petri dishes to answer the phone." She caught the ball the catcher threw back at her. "That was just a warm-up. I shouldn't have used a forkball on him—that was overkill."

Certain things started to click into place for me. Cracking systems required a vast array of ice-breaking programs. Most deckers used commercially developed software and, consequently, could only break into the most simple of bases.

True artists like Val modify and write their own wares. I once talked with a decker who went by the handle of Merlin who'd named all of his ice-breakers after spells. "It helps me remember what's what. When some system's trying to flatline you, you want to be able to react quickly with a codebomb that will do the job." Val, with her passion for baseball, had designed and named her ice-breakers for pitches.

"Let's get on to the main show, okay?"

"Roger."

Val concentrated and slammed a fist into her glove a couple of times. I noticed some subtle changes in the stadium as the Fujiwara system came into range for us to access it. "Okay, we're ready to begin. Kind of like robbing Peter to pay Paul, isn't it?"

I nodded. Fujiwara Corporation was a legal shell that laundered money for a yakuza group based further down the coast in Tokyo West. Whereas La Plante was a broker who facilitated the movement of things from one party to another, Fujiwara actually brought contraband materials into Seattle from all over the world. On a scale of one all the way up to Hitler's SS, both groups ranked fairly high, but Fujiwara exercised a bit more restraint in how they dealt with rivals.

That meant they preferred a single yak hitter to a mad bomber. La Plante did too, until Kid Stealth had had the temerity to defect to Raven. Neither group played nicely with their enemies, and this little Matrix run was about to deposit us on Fujiwara's bad side.

The butterflies started in my stomach as a behemoth stepped from the dugout. He looked like something from a cartoon. He had tiny legs and a narrow waist that blossomed up into immensely powerful arms and shoulders. The bat he carried looked like it had been cold-hammered into shape from the hull of an aircraft carrier, but he wielded it like it weighed no more than a spoon.

The field changed abruptly when he stepped into the batter's box to hit right-handed. Runners appeared on second and third and the count stood even at 0 and 0. The batter's name appeared on the scoreboard as Babe Fujiwara, and his batting average stood at a whopping .565.

I swallowed hard. "Why do I get the feeling this guy is the All-Star team all rolled into one?"

Val wiped her brow on her sleeve. "That's because he is." Then she shot me a winning grin. "But that's okay, baby, because I'm Rookie of the Year."

"Play ball!" cried the umpire.

Val's fingers twitched as she toyed with the ball hidden in her mitt, then she reared back to throw. The fastball sizzled yellow and gold as it streaked toward the plate. Babe Fujiwara swung on the pitch and missed, but not by much. From the look on Val's face, she'd expected a larger margin of victory.

Her cerulean eyes narrowed. I saw her grip the now-green ball in the same way she'd done to deal with Ronnie. The forkball shot from her hand at medium speed, then dropped precipitously. Even so, his bat whipped around and he hit the ice-breaker solidly. Suddenly it shifted color from green to red and rocketed back onto the field.

It hit me in the left ankle and fiery pain shot up my leg. The ball popped into the air as I dropped to the ground. Val sprang off the mound, gathered the ball up, and tossed it over at Babe as he lumbered up the baseline toward first. When the ball hit him in the shoulder, he exploded into blue sparks.

Gasping against the pain, I looked up at her. "What the hell was that?"

Val's nostrils flared. "Fujiwara's put some cascading IC on line. The fact that you got hurt means it's blacker than La Plante's heart. I managed to flip a couple of bits into that program and used it to destroy the ice layer that spawned it, but I'm not sure I can do that again."

I got an uneasy feeling in the pit of my stomach. "We're in a bit deeper than we want to be, aren't we?"

She looked over at the runners on second and third. "We got a pass on the first two layers of ice. We would have wasted time and broken them, but I thought speed was of the essence. Fujiwara gave them to us to make it difficult for us to get out of here..."

I raised an eyebrow as I massaged my ankle. "You mean we're trapped in the Fujiwara system."

She shrugged. "It's a matter of perspective."

"Well, try it from my perspective, one of pain."

"We're trapped." She must have seen my icon begin the fingerwork for the spell that would deaden the pain. "Don't waste the effort, Wolf. That stuff doesn't work in this environment." Her fingers convulsed, and a blue mitt appeared on my left hand. "Just use this to block anything they hit at you, and it should protect you."

I looked at the mitt and pounded my right hand into its pocket. "If I get something I just put the runners out?"

She nodded. "Don't tag them. It'll destroy the ice layer, but you don't want to be that close when it goes."

"What happens if they score?"

Val's smile died. "Don't ask. This is the big leagues."

"Got it."

The next layer of ice materialized as a somewhat smaller batter dubbed Mookie Fujiwara. He took position to bat left-handed, and I saw that did not please Val at all.

The ball in her hand took on a bright orange color. She wound up and threw. The whirling screwball arced in and broke toward Mookie, jamming him on the fists. He fouled it off.

Up on the scoreboard his batting average went from .500 to .375 and I took heart in that. It cheered Val up as well. She prepared another program, and the ball coalesced into an opalescent sphere. Her knuckles rested on the seams, then she started her motion and threw.

The program flew slowly toward the plate. It spun not at all, but floated and dipped erratically. It dove toward the ground as it neared the plate, and Mookie missed it with a clean cut. Another strike toted itself upon the board and his average fell to .175.

Val shot me a wink. "The knuckler always works on these cascaders—it reverses the value of the variables they use to get better, making them weaker. Better yet, it never shows them enough for them to create a countercode quickly."

I smiled reassuringly. "Gonna use it again?"

"Nope." She studied the scoreboard and shook her head. "Do it again and I give it a chance to react. Got something else for this ice."

A white ball formed in her hand. Val grinned cruelly and delivered the ball with a half-sidearm motion. It jetted in, then broke at the last second. Mookie swung and missed and the umpire called him out. He vanished, and I heard a couple of voices cheering.

Turning around I saw a couple figures in the grandstands. One looked like a glass spider and another wore the form of a black cat. "What the hell?"

Val waved at them. "Just some other deckers come to watch the fun. The Tarantula and Alley Cat are two locals I've met before."

That weird feeling ran up my spine again. "This was supposed to be a shadowrun, you know. What if Fuji learns we're here?"

Valerie fixed me with a stare that made me want to hit the showers. "Wolf, just because you're a 'trix virgin doesn't mean you have to show it. We've had an audience in the owner's box ever since we started. Blowing the cascading IC likely tripped some alarms, too, but they were here long before that. Looks like the yaks at Fujiwara have a line into La Plante's operation."

I filed that information away for future use as the final batter stepped out of the dugout. Whereas Babe had looked like a cartoon, this layer of ice manifested itself as a long, lean player with incredibly thick forearms and wrists. His flesh had a grayish, metallic tint to it, and his head metamorphosed into that of a horse. His name appeared on the scoreboard as Iron Horse Fujiwara and his batting average registered as .957. He batted lefty too, and the glint in his eye was nothing short of pure evil.

Val's skin took on an ashen hue. "Damn it, I didn't think it would be this tough. I'm going to have to doctor some stuff here." A white ball appeared in her mitt, but as her fingers worked on it, bloody tendrils shot through it.

Satisfied, but not looking as confident as I would have liked, she watched the batter, then let the ball fly. It cruised in at medium speed, then broke sharply as if it had fallen off a table. I looked for hesitation in the batter's eye, but I saw none and braced for disaster.

The Iron Horse's bat whipped around in a buzz-saw arc and smashed the ball back at the mound. Halfway there the ball burst into flame, but the line drive didn't slow at all. Val raised her glove defensively and managed to get it into place to stop the ball from hitting her in the face. Her glove burst into flame and she spun to the ground, but the ball hung there for a second, defying gravity.

I lunged at the ball. My glove boiled off and I felt as if I'd reached into a barbecue to barehand a glowing coal. "Help here, Val!"

How she did what she did I don't know, but the flame died and the ball took on a blue tint. I flipped it over to my right hand and saw the runner on third make a break for home. I drew the ball back to my right ear and threw it as hard as I could.

The blue ball shot through the base-runner like a searchlight through fog. It flew on beyond him and into the dugout. A volcano of sparks shot from there, and the baseball stadium began to crumble. In an eye-blink we were back in the city-map Matrix for Seattle, and the third floor of the Fujiwara tower exploded.

Then that imaging system failed me as well. I found myself floating in a sea of data. Waves of telecom numbers crested up over me and drove me down toward spreadsheets and cost overrun statements. Just as I felt as though I were drowning in a vast inventory system, a hand grabbed me on the shoulder and the safehouse room with Zig and Zag swam back into view.

Val watched me closely, and I knew Zag would have died to have her looking at him with such concern in her eyes. "Are you okay?"

I thought about the question for a second, then nodded. "Yeah, I think so. What the hell happened?"

Her eyes narrowed. "I can't be certain, but I think whoever programmed Fujiwara's IC built himself a back door. That blue ball was a simple virus meant to pump spurious data into the system so quickly that things freeze up and give me a chance to react with another program. You tossed it through one of the layers we bypassed and right through the back door into their system. That stopped the Iron Horse on his trip to first, and I used my own little ALS virus to dust him."

"Did we get the information we needed?"

On cue, the Hitachi deck's EPROM platform slid out from within the black case, offering the computer chip onto which the Fujiwara information had been burned. "Looks like it." Her smile lessened a bit as she looked at me again. "What else?"

I frowned. "Something's digging around at the back of my brain." I shrugged it off. "I guess I just want to be in an arena where I can shoot anybody who looks like the Iron Horse. It's the warrior in me."

"Pity," she said with a laugh. "You've got a future as a decker."

THREE

"What's he doing?" Zag asked as I started preparing to go into combat. Val frowned at him and remained quiet as I closed my eyes and reached inside. I pressed my hands together and touched the wolf's-head amulet at my throat. Using it as a focus, I let my mind touch the Wolf spirit dwelling in my heart and mind.

I saw it as a huge beast built mostly out of shadows except where lurid red highlights rippled across its fur. Lean and hungry, it still contained incredible power. When it felt my caress, enthusiastic fires burned in its eyes, but they dulled to a bloody color when it sensed my hesitation.

"*Is the time come, my son?*" it asked in snarls and growls.

"Yes, Old One. I need your speed and your sureness of movement."

It regarded me with the same disdain Val had shown in the Matrix. "*Let me deal with everything, Longtooth. You need not these machine men or the witch of the thinking machine. You will not need your guns. My way is pure. You know I am correct. Why do you resist me so?*"

I didn't want to go down that road of discussion because I knew what a dark and dangerous path it was. "I need what I need."

The old wolf lay down to mock me. "*I grant you what you need. It will not be long before you and I will have this conversation again.*"

I shook my head. "Seven days. I'll be clear of Seattle by then."

The wolf howled and the sound echoed through my head as I opened my eyes. I heard the hissed sizzle of the spells trail off and found Zag staring at me with new respect and a bit of apprehension in his eyes. I could smell his nervous sweat even over and above the tangy sea scent and musty mildew odor hanging over the dock area. I smiled and nodded. *All set now. Let's hope La Plante hasn't gotten stupid.*

Zag swallowed hard. "Look, Mr. Kies, I'm sorry about any static I gave you before. With your rep and all, I figured you were like us." He held up his right hand, and the razor claws flicked out at the tips of his fingers. "I didn't realize you weren't chromed."

I read the confusion in his eyes like a banner headline on a news service monitor. I was known to be quick and nasty in a firefight. I was the chummer who'd survived the most adventures with Dr. Raven— and that was no mean feat. To gillettes like Zig and Zag that meant I must be heavily cybered. The idea that I might be someone who used magic to augment their skills hadn't occurred to them. And, because they had chosen a route that virtually barred them from using magic, the magical arts baffled and scared them.

Zig handed me a small stick of black grease paint. He'd darkened his face all over, then erased out two downward-pointing triangles with dots in the middle. "Symbol of the Halloweeners over in the Green River District."

"I know." I put the face paint stick down on a crate. "I don't paint up."

That seemed to surprise them almost as much as my having used magic. After the Ghost Dances had worked and killed lots of folks, many people had traveled out to the reservations and swelled the population of what are now called the Native American Nations. Some later left because the lifestyle didn't suit them, but those who stayed contributed to the polyglot make-up of the tribes. Consequently it wasn't completely strange to find a white man who knew Indian magic, but it was weird to find one who didn't go the whole way and paint up before battle—though I saw going "native" like that too showy for my tastes.

Like the folks you scrag will care what you looked like while doing it.

I broke the tension. "I don't paint up for something I hope won't be a battle. I'll be out there getting the girl, so I'll be naked-nude anyway." I pointed to the Kalashnikovs they carried. "Those AK-97s look like old friends."

Zig patted his automatic rifle affectionately. "Sighted at four hundred meters for close work like this. Stood me in good stead during the Triad War out on the Strip."

"Good." I gave both of them one of my I-have-confidence-in-you smiles. "The drill's the same as earlier today. You get Val and Moira out. La Plante uses his grunges for muscle. If things get nasty, pop one or two of them, then see-saw your way out of there. If you burn a mag, I expect all the shots to hit a grunge, or you'd best be shooting at me. Hit and move—we can't win a war of attrition."

Both of them gave me a thumb's-up, so I turned to Val. "Sure you don't want a gun?"

She shook her head with disgust. "You've got me bundled up in kevlar so tight I can barely breathe. The last thing I want to do is make myself a target so they'll have cause to shoot me."

I chuckled lightly. "Okay. Moira is your charge. Things get nasty, you get her out of there. Zig and Zag will keep the beasts at bay."

Val nodded. "You got the chip?"

I patted the pocket of my jacket. "Check." I hefted my MP-9 and let it dangle by the strap over my right shoulder. "Let's do this clean and all go home healthy. Places, everyone." I filled my lungs with air and calmed my racing heart. "It's showtime."

I stepped from the warehouse into a dock area that had been cleared of anything approximating cover. Lit by bright halogen lights that held the night's darkness at bay, the open arena was defined on two sides by crates and loading machinery and on my side by the warehouse I'd just left. The fourth wall, the one I faced as I slipped between some crates, had been formed by another warehouse. The large doors stood open, and La Plante's limo had been parked in it so the hood and tail of the vehicle almost appeared to be holding the doors back.

A dozen grunges sporting various styles of submachine guns stood dutifully behind the limo and pointed their weapons in my direction. I held my hands away from my body and kept them open, but I knew my magically enhanced reflexes would allow me to shoulder the gun and snap off a half-dozen rounds before they even saw me move. In three seconds I could clear the mag and draw the Viper from my waistband to finish the job...

Back off, Wolfgang. It's the Old One's meddling that's making you think that way.

The Chauffeur appeared in the middle of the line of grunges. "Drop the gun, Kies."

I barked out a sharp laugh. "Dream on. You've got me covered a dozen ways to Sunday."

The grunges La Plante had hired began to hoot and twitter like the half-witted beasts they were. Ugly as sin and more stupid than even Ronnie, they were drawn from the ranks of those who didn't take their "goblinization" at all well. After their hormones kick in they start thinking a lot less, and make perfect little automatons for someone like La Plante to exploit. Of course, that's not to suggest they couldn't be cunning little beggars and get themselves into plenty of trouble, but it generally takes someone with an IQ in at least the low eighties to whip them into a destructive frenzy. The ork community tried to do all it could to save their less fortunate brethren from connivers like La Plante, but a helping hand isn't as attractive as a hand filled with nuyen.

I pointed to myself. "I'm going to walk out to the middle of this area and you'll send the girl to me. Then I'll turn over the chip to you. Keep your fingers off the triggers and this might just go down well."

I didn't hear what The Chauffeur said to the grunges, but their gibbering stopped. I crossed to the center of the arena, using my magically enhanced senses as best I could to see if I'd just walked into a massive trap. The halogen lights were a problem because they left the tops of the warehouses in an impenetrable darkness that did nothing to make me feel at ease. I had to assume La Plante had people up there securing the high ground, but the fact that the only grunges I saw were leaning on his ride did not reassure me.

When I reached the middle, I stopped. The passenger door of the limo opened and a slender woman of indeterminate age left it to stand beside the vehicle. She didn't look like the simsense I'd seen of her—yeah, everyone says that about sim shot of them—but I knew instantly that she had to be Moira Alianha. The pale dress she wore was fashionably short and revealed legs I was almost willing to die for, but she quickly cloaked herself with a dark wool blanket to ward off the chill air.

With her head up, and just the tips of her ears peeking out through the long veil of her midnight hair, she walked toward me. I gave her a smile intended to inspire hope and confidence, but she ignored me and only saw the black and red raven patch on the shoulder of my jacket. She blinked twice, and then I thought she was going to faint.

I reached out and steadied her. "Easy now, Ms. Alianha. We're almost home."

She touched the patch with incredibly slender fingers. "My husband sent you?"

I frowned and figured she was confused. "I work for Richard Raven."

Moira smiled. "Yes, my husband to be.[6]"

I almost swallowed my tongue. "Huh? Say what?" She just looked at me with vibrant green eyes. Suddenly everything seemed to run to chaos in my head. "Does anyone else know who you are to Raven?"

Moira shook her head. "No, not here, why?"

I let her question drift by unanswered. "Don't tell anyone, period." *If anyone finds out she's close to Raven, her life won't be worth a melted sim, and she could be used against Raven when dealing with scum like La Plante.* His aides, folks like me and Val, accepted the dangers connected with belonging to Raven's group. Moira was lucky La Plante had no idea of her true value, or this little exchange would be lots more rude.

The Chauffeur shouted at me. "Let's save the tea party and true confessions for later. We want the chip, now!"

Carefully, slowly, I reached into my jacket pocket. I withdrew from it a white piece of plastic about three centimeters square. The chip itself showed up in sharp contrast to the snowy plastic wafer to which it had been mounted. "I'll just put it down here..."

---

[6] This was a shocker. I didn't even know Doc was dating. Turns out he wasn't, but that's a story for another time.

I felt the plastic quiver and the chip explode as the bullet shot through it at Mach 4. The booming, rolling echo of the gunshot followed the bullet by a split-second, but I'd already turned and started to push Moira to safety. My right hand dropped the piece of plastic and enfolded the MP-9's pistol grip. I swept the gun around and snapped off two shots, one of which sent a headless grunge pitching back to the warehouse floor. I heard the staccato roar of Zig and Zag's AK-97s and saw three more grunges drop out of sight amid sparks lancing from the limo's armored frame.

Gunmen hidden on the rooftops slowly stood and their weapons lipped flame as I dragged and pushed Moira out of the killing zone. With so many people concentrating on just the pair of us I was sure we'd be blasted to ribbons before we'd gone a half-dozen steps, but the men on the roof started shooting at La Plante's grunges. The confused orks returned the fire, but did so ineffectively because of the wealth of targets and the babble of orders being shouted by The Chauffeur.

I'd just propelled Moira through the narrow warehouse doorway when a bullet finally caught me. It blew into the back of my left thigh and ricocheted off to the left after shattering my femur. It ripped free of my leg five centimeters left and seven below the entry point, tearing a chunk out of my femoral artery as it went.

I screamed, but as the echoes of the scream died in my head I heard the howl of a wolf rise in their place. Stumbling forward, I spilled onto the warehouse floor. My left knee hit hard and sent another shock wave of pain through my leg. I tried to choke back another cry, but it came out as a lupine yelp.

I rolled over onto my back and pulled the MP-9 to me. "Move it, campers. Get Moira out of here."

Val stared at the hole in my leg. "You're hit!"

I bit back the pain. "Yeah, my days in the big league are over. Maybe you can retire my uniform." I looked up at Zig and Zag. "Move it! I'll hold them off if I can. It's got to be Fujiwara yaks out there shooting the grunges up. That'll buy you some time, and I'll buy you more. Go!"

Zig made for the back door, but Moira shook her head and knelt beside me. "No, I'm not going. You need help."

She started making all the hand motions for a spell, but I closed a bloody hand around her fingers. "Save it, sister. You'll need all the magic you can muster to get the hell out of Seattle. Val, get her out of here."

Valerie crossed to Moira and rested her hands on her shoulders, but the elf shrugged her off. "No. I can save you. I can fix your leg."

Inside my head the Old One growled seductively. *"Let her fix you. Let her fill you with magic. Do as she asks, and I assure you the others will not follow."*

"No!" I shouted at both of them.

Her eyes flashed with an anger that told me my stay of execution had been denied. "Wait." I pulled the Viper from my belt and tossed it to Val.

She stared at it as if it were commercial software. "I don't want this."

I swallowed hard. "You might." I reached down and dipped the fingers of my left hand in my blood and painted twin parallel lines beneath each eye and across my forehead. "Do this, Moira, and then leave. All of you, get out of here. Don't look back, no matter what. Don't go looking for me. I'll find you, when I can."

Zig and Zag stared at me as if I'd gone mad, and Val shivered. Moira ripped my pants away from the wound and pressed her hands to it. She subvocalized a chant, but I felt warmth and a tingling flow from her hands into my leg. Almost instantly it nibbled the pain away. The energy continued to build and tissue began to heal, my body motivated to restructure itself at a rate that should have taken months. Even so, I knew the spell she'd cast was more than I needed.

And it was more than I could control.

I gritted my teeth and shoved her away. "Go, go!" I snapped at them. "Run!"

They vanished from sight just as the first tremor hit me. I shrieked as fire filled my ribs with molten agony. I heard the crack as my breastbone parted down the middle, thickened and broadened to accept the new angle of my expanded rib cage. I gnashed my teeth at the pain and the growing canine teeth split my lower lip.

"Don't fight it, Longtooth. It won't hurt so much," the Old One whispered.

Gotta retain some control! Can't let you run wild!

My long bones telescoped back down, shortening but strengthening my limbs. The muscles flowed into protoplasm as the transformation continued, then congealed into new muscles with new insertions able to exert more powerful pressure and leverage than before. My fingers and toes likewise shrank—the latter far more than the former—and organic claws grew to give me some new weaponry.

My head felt as if it were exploding when my jaw and facial bones broke. My whole face grew into a muzzle, and my tongue lengthened along with it. The top of my head flattened somewhat and my eye sockets sank back to a more protective position. According to the only person to watch me go through this lunacy, my eyes do not lose their silver color or the Killer Rings.

The bodily transformation almost complete as my pelt thickened and ears lengthened, I felt the Old One begin to gnaw on my resolve and humanity. I clung to the image of Dr. Raven sitting across from me as I changed and the sound of his voice telling me how to concentrate so I would not surrender to the beast inside me: "You have been blessed *by Wolf, greatly blessed, but that blessing will be a curse if you surrender yourself to him."*

The Old One whimpered with disgust. *"Someday Raven will fail you and you will become mine."*

Stuff it, you mangy mutt. I've won this round.

The advent of three grunges storming through the warehouse door precluded any remark the Old One might have made. I gave them a toothy grin from the shadows. "My, my," I growled in a voice that even grunges knew to fear. "What fine little piggies we have here.[7]"

It took a bit more than a fairy-tale huffing and puffing to blow them all down, but the grunges didn't offer much more than that for a fight. They've never been much for hitting a moving target, and in my more compact wolf form I don't stay in one place very long. I left them in a broken heap on the warehouse floor, then dashed out into the kill zone, doing my best to spit out grunge blood.

I couldn't have been much more than a gray blur as I streaked across the opening, but I felt The Chauffeur's eyes on me the whole time. I paused for a second at the place from where the rifle shot had come, but a yakuza forced me to tear out his throat before I had finished nosing around. I almost lost control with that kill, but, fortunately, the yak had some sort of augmentation that meant I got hydraulic fluid in addition to blood when I took him down.

Despite that hardship, I learned what I wanted to know and took keen delight in watching The Chauffeur shudder when my joyous howl filled the warehouse district like the fog rolling in from the coast.

---

[7] Okay, right, everyone knows there's no such thing as a werewolf. And a hundred years ago there was no such thing as a dragon, too. Raven's explained it all to me, that the Wolf spirit picked me special to grace me with abilities and all. Doc's smart, but he's never been through this transformation, and even Native American traditions tell of skinwalkers. The Old One and I know what I am, which means you don't want to invite me to any Full Moon parties you'll be having.

FOUR

Ronnie Killstar's eyes grew as wide as the hole in my leg had been when he heard me release the charging lever on the MP-9.

Seated in his favorite chair, nestled deep in the shadows of his unlit living room, I spoke to him in a husky whisper. "Close the door. Sit down at the table."

"What's this?" He stared blankly at the little repast I'd prepared for him while I waited.

I smiled. "That's your last meal."

The punk stared at me. "Milk and cookies?"

I shrugged. "It's the perfect thing for a little boy who doesn't know when he's not supposed to play adult games. If you'd have been content to just sell us out to Fujiwara, that would have worked fine."

He tried to look offended, but his nervousness betrayed him. "I don't know what you're talking about."

"Can it, joeboy. Val and I cracked your personnel file and it concluded with the last telecom number you called. Later, when we broke into Fujiwara, I recognized the number. There was a connection."

Ronnie straightened up in his chair. "Circumstantial evidence."

I shook my head. "It would have been if you could have kept your ego in check. In the Weed you told me you could 'bull's-eye a rat's ass' at a klick in the dark. A chip's got to be four times the size of your average rat's ass, and the range wasn't nearly that long." I sighed. "And to top it off, you were still wearing that cologne of yours."

It suddenly dawned on him that I was going to kill him. The color drained from his face and he looked at me with big puppy-dog eyes. Yet before they could have their full sympathetic effect on me, his features sharpened and a bit of the old defiant fire returned. "Wait a minute. I destroyed the chip you never really wanted to give to La Plante anyway. That's gotta count for something!"

I hesitated for a second and hope blossomed on his face. Then I shook my head. "No, it doesn't. Dr. Raven had tipped Fujiwara about what we were going to do anyway. Fuji's programmers put a Trojan horse carrying a nasty virus in that chip that would have destroyed La Plante's computer system. The ambush—which didn't include your shooting of the chip—was just to make sure La Plante bought the whole thing as genuine."

Ronnie sank his head in his hands. "Go ahead, shoot me. I deserve it."

I lifted the MP-9's muzzle to the ceiling. "No, I think I prefer letting you wallow in your own mortification. Word to the wise, kid," I shot back over my shoulder as I crossed to the door. "Remember that you're not as tough as you think. Don't let your delusions of adequacy get you in over your head...again."

On the way out, I stopped The Chauffeur from going in. "Don't bother."

The plastic-faced man stared hard at me. "I didn't hear a shot."

I gave him a wolfish grin and licked my lips. "You never do." I patted his cheek. "*Ciao*—no pun intended. Until it's just you and me."

QUICKSILVER SAYONARA

I normally define a "rude awakening" as any that takes place before noon, but Kid Stealth gave that phrase a new depth of meaning. Stealth would maintain it was my fault because I was the one dreaming about cuckolding a chrome-fisted underworld kingpin when the Kid clapped his own steel hand over my mouth. The kiss of cold steel against my lips is not something I enjoy at the best of times, and two hours before dawn is seldom one of those.

My eyes focused on Stealth, and his identity registered in my brain a half-second before my finger tightened on the trigger of the Beretta Viper[1] I'd snaked from beneath my pillow and pressed to his side. Stealth gave me a satisfied grunt and dangled the gun's magazine from his flesh and blood right hand. He pulled his metal hand away from my mouth and flipped the mag back to me. "Good instincts."

I pulled myself up into a sitting position, letting the sheets slip down from chest to waist. I pulled the slide back on the pistol, and one bullet popped out into the bed. "I keep one in the chamber."

Stealth nodded in the half-light, the laser sight built into his right eye making a small cross on his pupil. "I know. Nine-millimeter, silver bullet with inertial silver-nitrate explosive tip."

The matter-of-fact tone with which he delivered his assessment of the bullet that had been aimed at his stomach somehow robbed it of all its deadliness. I'd survived six years with Doctor Richard Raven, and I'd seen aides come and go, but Stealth had to be the strangest of them all. The bullet in my gun, he had decided, could not punch through the Kevlar clothes he wore, nor get through the dermal plating that protected his body.

---

[1] Thing I like most about the Viper, as old as it is, is that I get fourteen in the clip and one in the chamber. Not that I need that many shots, mind you, but you never can tell when something will just be too stupid to die.

That, or he didn't care if it could.

"What the hell's going on? Is Raven back from Tír Tairngire?"

Stealth shook his head. "Still there. No word on his return."

I fed the loose bullet back into the mag, then reloaded the pistol. "That answered the second question. What about the first?"

"La Plante."

That one name, spoken in a sepulchral whisper like the rustle of a sidewinder slithering across dry gravel, answered lots of questions. Etienne La Plante was the local crime boss who'd played a cameo role in the dream I'd been enjoying. I'd recently helped liberate an elven princess[2] from him. Unbeknownst to me until the middle of that little adventure, it turned out that Moira Alianha was betrothed to Dr. Raven. Raven had returned her to Tír Tairngire two weeks ago, and then had been summoned back there again after the Night of Fire and the battle for Natural Vat. That meant he'd left Kid Stealth, Tom Electric, Tark Graogrim, Valerie Valkyrie, and me to watch the store while he was away.

La Plante held a special place in Kid Stealth's heart. Stealth had first come to Seattle to work as La Plante's enforcer. Inevitably, La Plante had assigned Stealth the job of killing Raven. Stealth was good enough to get two of Doc's chummers—my head missed being mounted on his trophy wall by a stroke of luck or two—before La Plante decided to put a pinch-hitter in for Stealth. That individual, known on the streets as The Chauffeur, had fitted Stealth's feet with a large pair of cement blocks, then dumped him into the Sound.

Setting the pistol on my nightstand, I threw the covers back, then turned on a light. "What did our friend do this time?" Naked—'cept for the silver wolf's-head amulet worn at my throat—I padded to the closet as Stealth puzzled over how to answer that question in his customarily taciturn manner. I looked at the clothes hanging there and almost chose a normal t-shirt and pair of jeans.

You're going somewhere with Kid Stealth.

I opted for black pants woven of Kevlar and a heavy Kevlar sweater with trauma pads over my chest and back.

"I don't know. An ear says a VIP is sprawling, and La Plante's calling in some heavy favors to make him happy." Even as he spoke, Stealth moved his head back and forth, his cybernetically augmented senses scanning for the sound of anything out of the ordinary. I silently hoped the Blavatskys down in 2D didn't decide to play "I've-Been-Bad, Teacher" while Stealth was monitoring the area.

---

[2] I don't know that Moira was really a princess per se—the elf I know best is Raven, and he's not much on hereditary titles. Anyway, she was pretty important, and after her rescue Doc had been bouncing back and forth 'tween the Tír and the sprawl. I gather there was a lot of palavering going on, but about what I had no idea at the time.

"Your street source didn't know who the VIP is or why he's here?"

Stealth answered me with an exasperated expression that said, "If I knew that, I would have told you."

I refrained from answering with my you-never-know-unless-you-ask shrug and zipped up my pants. "La Plante had been holding Moira for some Mr. Johnson from out of town. I bet there's a connection—I bet this VIP's the one who wanted her."

Kid Stealth's eyes narrowed for a half-second, and I knew he'd filed away both my conclusion and the fact that I'd made the connection. As tough as he was, and as much of a perfectionist as I'd seen him be, Stealth seldom advanced theories on his own. He'd study a situation and offer his observations, but he left the guesswork up to others. He'd made his living dealing in dead certainties before joining Raven, and since becoming one of the team, he'd found plenty of people to jump to conclusions for him.

Most of Stealth's body part replacements and modifications were made by choice, to eliminate as much uncertainty as he could. His mechanical left arm—the original, I gathered, he'd lost in an old accident—was tricked out with a gyromount that locked a sniper rifle in place rock steady and soaked up all the recoil from a shot. It could also punch through concrete blocks, but that was a bonus that came from its design specifications. Stealth's eyes had been modified to include a rangefinder, low-light, and thermographic vision—all the stuff any well-heeled assassin would love to have. I knew for certain he had some smartlink gizmo in there, too, which fed him data ranging from the time of day to the distance to targets—I think he could also pick up Seattle Seadogs[3] games if he wanted to. He'd probably have replaced his right hand, but he needed it for the "touch"—be it to squeeze a trigger or throw one of the many stilettos hidden on his body.

He'd even gone so far as to have the upper left lobe of his lungs replaced with an internal air tank that eliminated his need to breathe when lining up those one-klick assassination shots. That special option had saved him the day The Chauffeur dumped him into the Sound—La Plante hadn't paid for it, so he didn't know about it. It had given Kid Stealth ten minutes to figure out how to get his legs out of a rock or become fish food.

On my list of things to do with a spare ten minutes, having to figure a way out of a deathtrap did not rank real high.

I pulled on a heavy nylon jacket with Kevlar and shock pads sewn into breast and back. "Where?"

When I saw that hint of a smile on his lips, I felt an immediate urge to dive back into bed. "The Rock."

---

[3] Sure, they're really called the Mariners still, but only if you want to suck up to management.

I let my jaw drop open. "The Rock? Did they do a good-sensectomy when you went in for your last lube and tune?"

The Rock was the nickname for what had formerly been a seaside resort hotel La Plante had "acquired" when his organization had cannibalized another criminal cartel. It had previously served as a notoriously hedonistic retreat for criminal megabyters and corporate warlords deciding to "do the sprawl." After word of Stealth's survival leaked out, The Chauffeur, at La Plante's request, had fortified the place and made it into an open challenge to the local government, Stealth, or Dr. Raven to close down.

Stealth looked at me as if I were the one operating in an alternate reality.

I raised an eyebrow. "We do have Tom Electric going with us, right?"

He shook his head. "He's *visiting.*"

I hesitated. Tom occasionally dropped out of sight, and that generally meant his ex-wife had come to Seattle. The six months between her visits were enough to let Tom forget why they'd gotten divorced, and the week he spent with her always made him more than happy that they had split up.

"What about Valerie or Tark?"

Another shake. "Val's great, but she's a decker and doesn't like guns. Plutarch is still nursing the chest shot he took in the Night of Fire. His ork chummers are reluctant to put him in the line of fire for something that doesn't directly benefit them, so he's out." Stealth forced himself to give an especially broad smile. "I did leave a message for Raven in case he gets back, and I decided not to call La Plante to tell him we were coming."

I exaggerated a sigh. "Thank God for small miracles."

His grin became purely evil. "It gives us the element of surprise."

That and an army division might get us in. Divine intervention and an army division might get us back out again.

Stealth tossed me the key ring from the top of my dresser. "You're driving."

"Guess again, Stealth." I shook my head and batted the flying keys onto the bed with my hand. "The Fenris is brand new, and I still remember what you did to the upholstery in the Mustang IV."

Stealth squatted down in that peculiar way only he can, but didn't look the least bit contrite. "I'll be careful." Balancing on his left foot, he extended his right leg and plucked the keys off the bed with his claws. "Besides, you have that new radarbane paint job and a sunroof."

I took the keys from his foot's titanium talons and suppressed a whole-body shudder. In that ten minutes at the bottom of the ocean, Stealth could only see one thing to do—aside from dying, that is. He'd used his belt and shirt to tie tourniquets around both of his legs above the knees. Then he pulled some plastique from a compartment in his left arm and created some very small shaped charges, which he fastened to his own legs. He set them off and managed to make it to shore.

Raven had found him and kept him alive. Both of Stealth's legs were gone from the knees down. He'd taken lots of other damage—his left arm showed scarring from a shark hit—but he refused to die or surrender to the depression that would have swallowed anyone else. Though he never said much during that time—or since—I knew it was his hatred for La Plante that kept him alive, and his awe of Dr. Raven that kept the rest of us alive.

Stealth had worked with Raven to design himself a new pair of legs. The original humanoid design was abandoned when Stealth located a better one while scanning some chips on animal biology. Wearing an expression I've only seen on the faces of lottery winners or the criminally insane, he pointed it out to me. "*Deinonychus,*" he said, reverently chanting the word like a mantra. "Terrible claw."

It took some convincing, but he prevailed on Raven to help him. Human thighs grafted down into titanium shins and feet. Birdlike in construction, his new legs featured the elongated foot bones that made it look as if his leg had an extra joint. Each foot had a dew claw and three toes—the innermost of which was truly a thing to behold. Both stronger and larger than the other two, it had a huge sickle-shaped claw that pulled back toward the ankle while Stealth ran. It turned funny-looking legs into razorhook-equipped limbs capable of slicing through foes and, in Stealth's case, let him climb incredibly sheer walls like a fly on a pane of glass[4].

No, he hadn't ripped up the upholstery in my Mustang.

The claws just dripped blood all over it.

I tied some rubber-soled black shoes on my street-legal feet, cocked the Viper, and stowed it in my pants at the small of my back, then followed Stealth out to my living room. He leaned over the back of the couch, then turned and handed me my MP-9 submachine gun[5] and a satchel bulging with magazines. I felt the weight of the ammo pouch, then shook my head. "Planning quite the little war, aren't we?"

He shrugged. "We'll have surprise, but I don't know for how long." He pointed at the satchel. "I hand-loaded your silver bullets, but

---

[4] Raven did insist on making Stealth a pair of normal legs, so I know he can swap the nightmare pair out for regular legs whenever he wants. I've never seen him when he's wanted to—or he's never let me see him when he was running around on normal feet. That ability to go unnoticed, given his trade, is a useful one.

[5] Stealth would prefer it if I would get a "real" submachine gun instead of this HK antique. I think he thinks my weapon choice reflects badly on him. Of course, since he's Kid Stealth, if anyone did think less of him for it, they wouldn't say anything—at least, not in public, and not for long.

used mercury instead of silver nitrate. I wanted to try a silver-nitrate suspension in a gelatin of my own manufacture that approaches the viscosity of mercury, but I couldn't finish it this quickly. I also boosted the powder up to six full grains so your bullet will have the velocity you need to make a mess of the target. I hope you don't mind."

I felt an odd chill run down my spine. I realized he was speaking about loading bullets for maximum effect in the same voice my mechanic used to describe tuning the Fenris' twelve-cylinder engine.

I headed for the door as Stealth shouldered his Kalashnikov[6], carefully avoiding any bump or jarring to the boxy rangefinder mounted on the barrel. When activated the laser would send out an invisible, ultraviolet beam that would paint a dot on the chest or head of a target. With his eye, Stealth just locates the dot, then pulls the trigger and puts a bullet through it.

I let him precede me from the apartment and locked it. As we worked our way down to the basement garage, Stealth paused on the second-story landing and stared at the door to 2D. "You've got strange neighbors, Wolf..."

I shrugged. "The Blavatskys have hired a tutor."

Stealth's eyes grew wide. "They have tutors for that stuff?"

I waved him forward. "Get your mind out of the gutter. I think it has something to do with the new math."

Stealth remained silent until we reached the basement and stripped the cover off my Fenris' body. The sleek vehicle lacked the sharp angles and lines of a Porsche Mako or a Ford Astarte, but it still looked as though it were moving at Mach 1 while standing still. The flat black finish absorbed the garage's meager light and flashed none of it back. The Fenris might as well have been built out of shadow, so well did the radarbane coating Raven had given it prevent the reflection of electromagnetic radiation.

I unlocked it and climbed into the driver's side as Stealth folded himself up and dropped into the passenger seat. I slid the MP-9 into the door holster on my side. Stealth laid his Kalashnikov gently in the area behind our seats and produced an ugly little Ceska Black Scorpion machine pistol to use if we ran into early resistance.

I reached over to punch in the ignition commands, but Stealth wrapped his metal hand around my right wrist before I could do so. I looked over at him and frowned. "You should have gone when we were upstairs..."

That got to even him, and his fierce expression lightened for all of a nanosecond. "We might run into some difficulty before we get there." His eyes shut for a second, then popped open again. "There,

---

[6] Frankly, I think he could do better than an AK-97, but he's jazzed that baby up so it does everything shy of cooking hot meals for him.

I'm geared up for anything now. Don't you think you better do your stuff?"

I hesitated. Kid Stealth, being an amalgam of all the best technology money could buy, prepared himself for combat by opening circuits and running diagnostic programs mated with his brain. In literally the blink of an eye he went from being an abnormally vigilant and quick-reacting individual to someone who could move faster and accomplish more in a single heartbeat than even most other augmented people. He was that good—probably the best—and going from idle to overdrive was nothing but a change of perceptions for him.

Me, well, I'm not augmented in a mechanistic way. Growing up in the Seattle sprawl of gray canyons and trash-strewn alleys, I never had the resources for even the most basic of modifications. In a day and age when almost any street tough has razor-claws that pop out from under his fingernails on command, or an eye that can see in the dark, I was left to what the gods, in their perversity, had given me at birth. In a world where ManThe-Tool-Maker took great delight in making himself into Man-The-Tool, I was consigned to the slender side of natural selection known as extinction.

I had nothing.

Then I'd discovered the magic.

Actually, the magic discovered me. From the time of puberty, in which the monster inside me festered and grew, to the day I met Richard Raven and gained control over it, my life was indescribably interesting. Street toughs learned quickly that he who assaulted me during daylight hours would end up a bloody smear along an alley at night. Those who lived—the majority, in fact—gave me wide berth, which made life a bit easier; but the blank times of which I remembered nothing made it a living hell.

I gave Stealth a hard stare. "I don't like driving jazzed."

Stealth shrugged philosophically. "You might not get the chance later."

Reluctantly, I nodded. I settled myself comfortably into the seat and let my head drop back against the headrest. The fingers of my right hand drifted up and unconsciously caressed the silver amulet at my throat. Drawing in a deep breath—and savoring what I feared would be the last of the new car scent from my Fenris—I cleared my mind and started the journey within.

Six years ago, a series of savage murders had most of Seattle's citizens cowering in fear. They had been tagged the Full Moon Slashings by the NewsNet pundits, and the fact that I couldn't remember where I'd been during the killings had preyed on me. Actually, waking up bathed in blood is what had scared me the most, and it was about that time I heard that the elven High Prince had sent some of his heavy-hitters into town to clean up the problem.

Fortunately Raven had found me before the elven Paladins did. He taught me that the beast within me was not always the enemy, but a gift from what I thought of as the Wolf spirit. He talked me through one of the changes I underwent when the spirit becomes overwhelming, and he taught me how to control it. He also prevented the Paladins from murdering me while I learned how to master my inner self, then the two of us, to the Paladins' dismay, brought the real Slasher down by our lonesome.

Deep inside myself, I stepped through the black curtain sheltering the Wolf spirit from everything else that I am. As black as the Fenris, the spirit let a low growl rumble from his throat. Bloody highlights flashed across his glossy coat, then evaporated like scarlet fog. *"You come to me at the behest of the Murder Machine?"*

I smiled, which increased the growl slightly. "Yes, Old One. Kid Stealth sends his love."

The old wolf lifted his head as if sniffing the air. *"Had you let me take control of the situation, that machine would never have gotten your friends."*

Ice water gurgled through my guts, but I turned my anger and fear back on the Old One. "No, Stealth might not have gotten them, but I might well have done his job for him."

The Old One shrugged. *"I am, you are, we are a predator. Prey is ours to take, and our skills are to be employed in its taking."*

"Then lend me those skills, Old One. Stealth promises plenty of good hunting."

The wolf dropped its lower jaw in a lupine grin. *"Strike swiftly, Longtooth. I will make your strike sure and deadly."*

I opened my eyes and instantly my magically enhanced senses reported a world I had been oblivious to only moments earlier. From Stealth I smelled machine coolant, cordite, and anxious anticipation without a hint of fear. As the Fenris' engine roared to life, my head filled with chemical scents, and the desire to be out under the open skies almost overwhelmed me. Slipping the vehicle into gear, I drove it out into a nighttime that, while dark, held few secrets from me.

The arc-light glare of the Fenris' headlights burned the hopeless expressions on the faces of the street people into black masks of despair. Some shrank back from the harsh light as if it were a laser vaporizing them, while others shuffled forward zombie-like, and raised grubby hands in mute pleas for some kindness. Their hands fell slowly when the afterimage of the vehicle faded from their sight.

A tiny knot of razorboys from the local ork gang called the Bloody Screamers scattered as if I'd launched a grenade into their midst. I fought the Old One's attempt to drive the Fenris straight through them. As soon as we sped past, the gillettes slithered from the shadows and taunted us with the insane yelps and howls that were the gang's trademark. Stealth glanced at the steering wheel and then the closed sunroof, but I shook my head. "Not worth the time it would take to mop up the blood."

Speeding through the streets, I interpreted Stealth's occasional grunts or nods and steered accordingly on a course he had chosen. I knew where The Rock was, but Stealth had picked out a route that would both be safe and would let us determine whether anyone was following us.

Finally, he told me to stop the car, and I found myself parking in the shadow of the old Kitchner Fish Cannery—a property that abutted The Rock's fenced-in territory on the north side.

I turned the car's dome light off before either one of us opened the doors. As we alighted, we left the car doors open. Just as we didn't need the light to announce our arrival, we decided we could do without the sound of the doors slamming shut. Stealth's feet made less noise on the gravel outside the car than mine did, but I slid the MP-9 from the door holster more quietly than he pulled his Kalashnikov from behind the Fenris' seats.

To the south, I could see the pink glow of The Rock's night lights. I figured the distance we'd have to cover at something just under a kilometer, and that began to worry me. Stealth can hit targets at twice that range with ease, and I half began to imagine him up in the cannery giving me all the covering fire I could handle while I went in alone. I turned to confront him with this startling new conclusion, but he held up his left hand to forestall anything I might say.

He seemed to be listening to something in the distance, then he spoke. "Copy that, Outrider One—our back trail was clear. Bring it in. Let's do it, my friends."

I instantly knew he was using his headware to stay in contact with confederates who'd been watching our approach, but before I could draw any conclusion about who they might be, a door in the cannery slid open and a weak, yellow light silhouetted a dozen figures of various sizes and shapes. Almost instantly, above the fish smell, I caught the scent of one or two orks, and the hackles rose on the back of my neck. *Who...what?*

Then it hit me, and I turned to Kid Stealth without trying to hide my anger. "You didn't tell me you'd brought the Redwings in on this..."

Stealth's head came up and he unconsciously let himself rise to his full 2.3 meters of height[7]. "I need you, Wolf, to bring this off. I also need them. Bury the hatchet. The enemy of my enemy—"

"—is still not anyone I'd want marrying my sister," I finished for him. Stealth had developed a habit of doing anything he could to annoy La Plante after they'd parted company. One of those things was to rescue other La Plante loyalists who had somehow run afoul of the

---

[7] Sure, the legs may look goofy, but when he needs to stand tall, they certainly do the job.

chrome-fisted Capone. Bloody-handed butchers and petty criminals alike, Stealth pulled them out of whatever terminal situation they found themselves in and had formed them into a band who called themselves the Redwings—a not-too-distant allusion to Raven's crew. I hadn't liked them from the start, because we'd tangled over their excessive use of violence in certain situations. While Raven left it up to Stealth to keep them in line, and Stealth freely offered their assistance whenever we needed some added talent, I preferred selecting my own gillettes from the over-abundant supply lurking in the Seattle sprawl.

I spat the sour taste out of my mouth. "Well, at least I'll have no trouble with target acquisition."

Stealth smiled in a most grimly amused manner. "I also got you some back-up. I hired Morrissey and Jackson—they're on the inside, and will take this section of the warning grid down for us."

I frowned. "Morrissey and Jackson?"

Stealth settled back down on his spurred haunches. "The two street samurai you used to rescue Moira Alianha. You know, the two who called us in on the Nat Vat thing?"

I laughed, letting some of my tension go. "You mean Zig and Zag." I nodded with satisfaction. "Good. They shoot straight and fast."

"Glad you approve. When your two boys take the fence out, we go in hot." Stealth pointed off to the seashore. "La Plante tends to concentrate his guards on the wet side because he expects me to bob up out of the water and come at him from that direction. We'll go in at the other end and just start ripping things up."

I tossed Stealth a quick nod and he signaled the Redwings to move forward. The light from inside the cannery went out, and the men deployed themselves with quiet efficiency. I followed behind Stealth and hunkered down when he did as we approached the twelve-meter-tall cyclone fence topped with thick coils of razor-wire.

Two figures silhouetted themselves against The Rock's glow as they sauntered toward our position. Stealth moved his head back and forth a couple of times, then allowed himself a grim smile. "A bit late, but it's them." He moved forward and I joined him at the fence.

Zig, a solidly built razorboy sporting a longcoat and an AK-97, gave me a nod of recognition. "Sorry we took so long, chummers. The VIP yacht arrived late at the docks—only about an hour ago. Assignments got scrambled. It looks like something is going down very shortly—the yacht's owner and La Plante wandered off for a heated chat."

Zag—bigger than his Caucasian partner and wearing an orange and black gang jacket with the Halloweener insignia torn off—fished a remote control device from his pocket. He pointed it at the section of fence and hit a button. "There, it's down. I hope this thing is reporting back normally the way you said it would. If not, we'll have more trouble than we need in about two minutes."

Stealth answered eloquently by reaching out with his right foot and clawing away some of the fence. In a half-dozen passes—unaccompanied by warning sirens or the shouts of guards—he opened a hole large enough for us to drive the whole cannery through. I crossed over first and took up a forward position with Zig and Zag as the Redwings followed. "Zig, tell me more about this yacht."

He shrugged. "Don't know that much about ships. I make it thirty meters long at least and capable of transoceanic travel. The crew are wee little brown guys who find things like razor claws and the like to be amusing. I suspect they're like you—they rely on magic instead of chrome. All of 'em carry nasty-looking daggers, but they're not strangers to guns."

I turned to his partner and gave the black man a gentle elbow in the ribs. "Yacht have a name?"

Zag shrugged. The red light in his right eye flickered as he tried to remember if he'd seen any name on the ship's hull. "Nothing I saw, but it did have some funny writing where I would have expected the name to be. And in one of the cabins, there were no pictures, only geometric designs."

I frowned. Funny writing and geometric designs meant only one thing to me: Moslems. Growing up, I'd known a family that ran a restaurant down on the strip. They claimed their people had come to Seattle before the Awakening from a place called Syria, and they used geometric designs and Arabic for decorations on the menus. I knew that country was some place on the other side of the planet, and I knew Islam was widespread enough to make the ship's point of origin any place from Spain to Indonesia. Even with that wealth of information, however, I couldn't puzzle out what someone from so far away would want with Etienne La Plante.

Stealth crouched down behind me. "Heard the questions and answers. What do you think?"

I swallowed hard. "I think someone has gone to an incredible expense to get something from La Plante. If we assume that something was Moira Alianha, we can explain the visitor's anger. La Plante probably would have apprised his client of the problem only shortly before the visit, so the fact that they're talking means La Plante must have offered something as a substitute."

"Logical." Stealth gritted his teeth. "Conclusion?"

I shook my head. "Finding out who the client is would probably be good. If La Plante has offered a substitute for Moira, it might be another individual, in which case I can see a rescue being in order."

Stealth nodded and called one of the Redwings over. "Grimes, you and the boys will go in as planned. Start at the east end of the complex and work west, but stay away from the docks. Go for lots of pyrotechnics, and don't start blasting civilians."

Grimes looked a bit crestfallen at the last parameter of his mission, but he accepted it. Stealth turned back to Zig, Zag, and me as the Redwing slunk away. "We'll go in by the docks and recon the area. We'll see what we can see, then, if needed, make our moves when the party begins at our backs."

The Redwings took off and headed away from the ocean. Stealth stalked forward and took on the role of point man for our detachment. We crested the rise leading toward The Rock, giving me my first view of the resort. Even in the dark, the long building with five stepped levels did look interesting. I found it very easy to mentally impose bright banners on the balconies and put bathers around the pool. At the same time I deleted the barbed wire strung around the perimeter and the razor-wire awnings above the balconies.

Off to my right, toward the ocean, I saw the massive clubhouse and marina area. From in between a couple of boathouses I caught a glimpse of the yacht riding the ocean's gentle swells. The ship's design and flying forecastle made me think of a shark cruising through shallow water—it had a real air of menace about it.

The Old One's voice echoed up from deep inside. *"There lairs a foe who could challenge even your Raven."*

Great! Homicidal maniacs to the east of me and sociopathic grunges[8] *straight ahead, and now there's another player who could challenge Dr. Raven.*

I glanced over at Stealth. "Anytime you want to tell me this is all a dream and wake me up, go ahead."

Stealth raised an eyebrow. "What?"

I shivered. "Nothing, just let's be careful. Something isn't right about that ship or the person it brought with it."

Zig and Zag both did a quick double-check of their combat systems, but Stealth just took my warning in stride. "Let's find out if you're right." He set off down the slope at a quick pace, and his bobbing gait almost succeeded in making him look funny. I say almost because just as I thought of the phrase "bunny-hop" to describe how he moved, stray light glinted from the sickle-claws—ruining an accurate analogy.

I dashed after him, and the two razorboys followed quickly. Though we couldn't keep up with his pace, Stealth waited at important junctions until we caught up, then headed off to secure the next point along our path. Twice, we found dead guards with thin stilettos buried

---

[8] So, okay, maybe all the orks working for La Plante weren't sociopathic. Fact was, though, that their employment contracts paid bonuses for antisocial behavior committed upon intruders like me, which colored my perception a bit.

in their throats. Neither of them had managed to get off a shot, but with their silenced weapons it would have hardly mattered.

Stealth finally stopped behind the nearest of the two boathouses. The windows of the building were completely blocked with packing crates—telling me La Plante was using them for storage. Between the first building and the second I saw a scattering of other crates, or parts thereof, and got a clear view of the boat Zig had described earlier.

Stealth pulled me down and cupped his hands over my ear. "I mark seven crewmen on the ship. Cross-correlation of their conversation pegs their language as Malay with a heavy Arabic influence. And you're right—there's something strange about that ship. It's all lit up, but I can't hear any engines."

I sniffed at the air. "No gas vapors." I turned to Zig. "Did they refuel?"

"Not so's I noticed, chummer."

The intrusion of voices ended our whispered conversation. Appearing on the sea side of our hiding place, Etienne La Plante strolled along with a man who Zig silently indicated was the owner of the boat. From the top of his white-haired head to the tips of his black shoes—and for the length of the perfectly tailored, double-breasted black suit he wore—La Plante looked every bit an aristocrat from the days before the Awakening. Only the silver of his artificial right hand seemed out of place, but it didn't break the image—it just dented it a bit.

His stocky guest stood a bit below average height, but the Old One growled a warning that prevented me from dismissing the man outright. As I studied his olive-skinned, hawk-nosed profile, I caught his dark eyes darting warily about. The man missed nothing and stroked his black mustache and goatee thoughtfully while La Plante babbled on. I saw no obvious signs of chroming, which meant the man had to be taken very seriously.

I always take spellworms very seriously.

Following La Plante and his visitor at a discreet distance, The Chauffeur affected the air of a jilted lover or a young sibling aching for the adult privileges his older kin had been accorded in the family. I could read his concentration as he struggled to overhear any and all remarks that passed between his boss and the smaller man. The ship's lights glinted from the slender man's sunglasses as he turned and once again commanded the cadre of grunges and razorboys behind him to keep silent.

The grunges simpered and groveled when scolded, but the razorboys met The Chauffeur's looking-glass stare with glares of their own. The two gillettes in the middle were supporting a young woman who marched along as if drunk. Her head lolled to the side and I saw a flash of red hair as she pulled free of one man and tried to escape the other. Her remaining captor just tightened his grip and a grunge tackled her. She cried out in despair, but grunge laughter quickly swallowed the sound in huge hyena-gulps.

Suddenly, the sound of an explosion behind us heralded the start of the Redwing assault. La Plante dropped to one knee and covered his face with his metal hand. The guest darted toward the gangplank of his ship while the crewmen scrambled down below decks. The Chauffeur barked orders at his minions, and they instantly deployed into defensive positions.

Abandoned by her captors, the girl got up and began to stumble away toward the second boathouse. The Chauffeur pointed at her, dispatched a razorboy after her, and signaled him by drawing a finger across his own neck. Ten-centimeter talons sprouted from the street samurai's fingertips as he rose to go after his prey.

If I'd stopped to calculate my odds of success, I'd have failed. "She's mine!" I shouted as I vaulted the crate in front of me and set off. With my reflexes jazzed, the world around me moved at an unbelievably torpid pace. As my feet hit the ground, I snapped off a shot that hit the gillette in the left shoulder, slowly spinning him to face us. Stealth's shot followed immediately and jackknifed the street samurai like a tanker-truck on ice.

Three steps into the open ground between the two boathouses, and only the closest of the grunges had seen me. As he turned and started to bring his Ingram up, everything above the bridge of his nose vanished and his body toppled back as if its bones had become water. As if I needed confirmation of what had happened, the report of Stealth's Kalashnikov echoed back from the ship.

Zig and Zag added their firepower to Stealth's effort by the time I'd closed half the distance to the girl. La Plante had already spun and dove toward the edge of the jetty. Bullets savaged the wooden decking all around him, but the silver-handed man lived a charmed life and avoided Stealth's retribution. A slug from someone's rifle blasted The Chauffeur to the ground, but he kept moving and scurried to cover. I couldn't smell blood because of the cordite filling the air, but I figured him to be smart enough to be swathed in Kevlar, the same as me.

A gillette stood up right in front of me. I could see from the way he moved and reacted that he'd not seen me at all and had been angling a shot at one of my compatriots. I shoved the MP-9's snout into his stomach. Because of the speed at which I was running, he folded around it like a knight skewered on a lance, so I kept my finger off the trigger and sprinted the last three steps to the woman.

Stealth screamed something at me, but I lost everything except his urgent tone amid the gun-battle's thunder. I saw flickering movement and light over by the ship, but I was so intent on the woman, it didn't register fully. Even the acrid, oily scent didn't trigger any emergency alarms in me.

Traveling at roughly Mach 2.086, the bullet smashed into me between the shoulder blades, just to the right of my spine. Even though the Kevlar of my coat snared the bullet before it could penetrate my hide, and the trauma padding absorbed some of the projectile's energy, it still packed quite a punch. It lifted me off my feet like a leaf in a cyclone and tossed me forward. My left arm scooped the woman to my chest as the MP-9 went flying. A heartbeat later I twisted in the air so my back hit the boathouse and shielded her from the collision.

Suddenly a dragon's-tongue of fire flickered out through the space we had occupied before the bullet gave my feet wings. Without thinking I drew the Viper and pumped two rounds into the grunge wearing the flamethrower. The first bullet drilled an ugly hole into his right thigh, dropping him toward the ground. The second bullet took him high in the chest, and his dead body rolled to the foot of the gangplank.

Before the body had expended all of its momentum, La Plante's visitor appeared at the head of the gangplank and gestured toward the wharf area. In a flash of blinding gold-white fire, a monstrous figure appeared—a creature utterly out of proportion to the rest of us. With golden skin and eyes to match, the heavily muscled cat-thing laughed in a hideous voice as a grunge whirled and emptied his Ingram into it. The bullets ricocheted off in a puff of gold dust, leaving faint freckles on the creature's chest.

In return for the decoration, the lion wearing a woman's head playfully swatted the grunge with its right paw. When the body hit the ground and stopped rolling, its chest sagged like the roof of a fallen-in building.

The torpedoes in La Plante's employ immediately threw their weapons down and lit out for the marina clubhouse and parts beyond. I would have joined them except that the conjured beastie stood between me and that possibility.

Kid Stealth, firmly gripped in his own form of battle madness, vaulted over the crates he'd been using for cover and attacked the lioness. His leap carried him five meters into the air and nine forward, with sickle-claws glittering like stars in the night sky. The Ceska Scorpion in his left hand sprayed gunfire over the left side of the human profile, then his claws hit. The metal-on-metal scream ripped through the night, then died as a feline roar of pain accompanied the gold curlicues Stealth tore out of the monster's left shoulder.

The creature dropped away from Stealth and rolled quickly onto its back. Stealth retracted his claws and jumped free to avoid being caught and crushed beneath it. In doing so, however, he hung motionless in the air just long enough for the cat's right paw to bat him out toward the bay. He arced over the yacht's prow and I heard a splash, but could not see anything to determine if he lived or died.

The creature pulled itself into a sitting position. Its tail swished back and forth, knocking the grunge with the flamethrower into the water. Despite wearing a woman's face, it licked at the wounds in its shoulder like a cat and briefly stemmed the flow of molten, golden rivulets running down its left foreleg. When I moved forward to put myself between it and the woman I'd rescued, its head came up and it hissed at me in a nasty fashion that had the Old One urging me to give myself over to his control.

The wizworm who'd conjured up the creature looked down at me from the ship. "My sphinx seems to have cleared the battlefield of friends and foes alike, excepting yourself, of course." He squinted at me, then a most evil smile curled his lips. "Is it possible you are the Wolfgang Kies mentioned as the person who took the elf, Moira Alianha, from La Plante?"

I nodded and stood slowly without dropping my pistol. I waved both Zig and Zag back with my left hand—I knew that with the sphinx between them and the magemaggot they couldn't get a shot off at him. I also knew that if the sphinx was powerful enough to kill Stealth, it would make catnip out of those two, so I didn't want them shooting it. I smiled as graciously as the Old One's nattering would allow. "You have me at a disadvantage."

The little man brought himself to attention and bowed his head. "I am Hasan al-Thani. I have been sent to obtain the woman La Plante had for us. Though we preferred the elf, we will accept the flame-haired woman with emerald eyes."

Something about Hasan irritated me, much like the wet sucking sound of a nasty chest wound. In mid-sentence his lips and words began to move out of synch and I got the feeling that I was hearing the words more in my mind than with my ears. I shook my head to clear it, but between his monologue and the Old One's continued war-chants, I found it impossible.

I stabbed my left hand into the air and shouted at both of them. "Hold it! Are you telling me that you want me to just hand this woman over to you so you can cart her off somewhere?"

Hasan smiled woodenly. "We do not see that you have any choice." He gestured toward the sphinx. "If you do not, we will kill you and take her anyway."

I brought the Viper around and pointed it at the unconscious girl. "So if I blow her away, you'll just leave?"

Hasan's eyes grew wide with shock, then narrowed to a more thoughtful size. "We do not believe you would do that. We call your bluff."

I dropped to one knee and triggered the remaining dozen bullets in the Viper. Spent shells rained over the wharf like cylindrical hailstones. Hasan ducked back by the sixth shot, but did not realize until later that he'd not been the target of my assault.

Stealth's shots, and those fired by the grunge, had only blown fragments of metal from the sphinx because they attacked the creature on only one level of its existence. They hit the shell it wore when summoned to the material plane. While they could damage it or even cripple it, they couldn't kill the creature itself. Even the rents Stealth had carved into it with his claws had started to heal over.

My silver bullets, I was pretty sure, could affect the monster on the metaphysical plane. Silver has magical properties that make it perfect for killing all sorts of things like shapeshifters and vampires. It's been considered sacred and necessary for countless rituals down through the ages. As the Viper's slide snapped back for the final time, I just knew I had to be right.

I wasn't.

Sure, I'd done some damage. The sphinx had recoiled from my barrage and the silver bullets had indeed hurt it. I'd centered the shots on the face, and the dozen silver projectiles had savaged the creature's nose by blowing its tip off. The sphinx's reaction was sluggish and it appeared to lose its balance at one point, but it recovered before it could pitch over backward into the bay.

Hasan reappeared on the ship's bridge and glared at me. "You leave us no choice. Kill him."

As the sphinx got up on all four paws and stalked toward me, I realized where I must have gone wrong. Shapeshifters and vampires might have some natural aversion to silver—an allergy to it, if you like. But the sphinx was neither. It was a summoned spirit, which meant I needed something else to kill it. Being plumb out of sphinx leukemia virus, and suddenly regretting the loss of the flamethrower to the bay, I tried to remember if I had life insurance and if whoever I'd named as beneficiary really deserved the money.

"No matter," I muttered as I tossed the Viper aside and backed up slowly. "The Mr. Johnsons at Kyoto-Prudential will figure my tackling this to be suicide." To kill this thing would require attacks on both the material and metaphysical planes. I toyed with the idea of letting the Old One have his way with me, but I knew I'd end up like that grunge and Kid Stealth. It had to be something magical and physical, but with a creature this size, it also had to be big.

Really big.

In fact, it had to be as big as the black coyote that materialized out of the shadows above and around me. For a half-second I thought the Old One had managed to manifest outside my body, but his howl of outrage at being seen in the form of a coyote quickly disabused me of that notion. The canine beast sheltering me growled in a low voice, then lunged forward at the sphinx, its ebon teeth gleaming with the light of the fire the Redwings had started.

As the two titans nipped and swatted at each other, I dove over to where the woman lay. A second or two later Zig and Zag joined me.

Zig grabbed my shoulder. "Raven's here—he got Stealth's message. He said to get her out as fast as possible. Says he can't be sure how long he can hold the sphinx back!"

I lifted the girl into Zag's arms, then gave Zig the ignition sequence for the Fenris. "Get her home or to a hospital. Go, go—the car's back at the cannery."

Zig hesitated. "Raven said to get you out of here, too. He said there's something very wrong here."

"He's got that right. Go on. I'll catch up with you later." I massaged my left leg for a second, and I saw them both shudder as they recalled the last time I'd sent them away.

The pair of street samurai vanished into the shadows, and I turned back to find Raven. With the Old One's help—he let me see Raven through his eyes—I spotted the Doctor up on top of one of the crates near the first boathouse. Wreathed in the golden nimbus of a defensive spell, he looked magnificent. Incredibly tall, even for an elf, he looked very much a human because of his powerful build. His coppery skin and high cheekbones bespoke the Amerind heritage he was likewise heir to, and the sea breezes lifted his long black hair back from his well-muscled shoulders. Fists thrust into the air so he could channel more energy into the coyote he had created, he looked every bit a god.

Opposite him, now standing on the yacht's bridge, Hasan came into view. The Old One showed me a purple glow surrounding Hasan. Sweat beaded on the mage's forehead and pasted his black hair against his pate. He also held his fists aloft, but I noted a tremble in his limbs that I had not seen in Raven. Hasan, powerful though he might be, was not Raven's equal in skill or magical energy. The battle would not last long.

The sphinx jumped back on its hind feet and slashed with a paw at the shadow coyote. The golden claws sliced through the canine's snout like sunlight streaking through boarded-up windows, but the wounds sealed themselves quickly enough. The coyote responded by lunging in and catching the sphinx by the throat. The attack bowled the feline over, but it managed to twist free, leaving the coyote's black teeth stained with gold.

A new surge of magical energy swept forward from the ship, making my hands and feet tingle as if I'd stepped on a live wire. The sphinx's wounds healed over immediately, then the creature became half again larger. I shot a glance at Hasan, but instead of seeing a man crippled by the effort, he looked as if he'd been rejuvenated in the process. The purple glow now stained the ship's bridge and forecastle and Hasan stood invincible within its cocoon.

Raven's limbs quaked with the strain of sustaining the coyote. The defensive spell around him shimmered, then died because of the lack of energy to maintain it. Raven's lips peeled back from his white teeth in an angry snarl as he redoubled his effort. The tremors in his limbs ceased, but the pain on his face told me he wouldn't last much longer.

I have to do something. I'd tossed down the Viper, so now I looked around for any other weapon I could find. I spotted and scooped up my MP-9 and cocked it.

Recalling the special loads Stealth had made, I drew a bead on Hasan. *Maybe the silver will get the bullets through the spell, eventually, then the mercury loads will do him. Something for magic, and something for flesh.*

It hit me like a virus wasting a database. I shifted aim and squeezed the trigger. As soon as I burned that mag, I jammed another one home and let it rip. *Something for magic, perhaps, and definitely something for flesh, especially if it's gold flesh! Poor pussycat.*

The mercury loads in the silver bullets bonded instantly with the gold of the sphinx's flesh. The silver bullets themselves did a great job gnawing into the beastie. The result manifested itself in a bizarre display of feline leprosy. Silvery gobbets of demon-cat splashed to the wharf. The beast whirled to snarl at me and I let a burst go that ate away half its lower jaw.

The coyote hit it hard on the left flank. The sphinx twisted back, but its hind right leg gave along a line I'd scored with several shots, crashing the beast down on the docks. I directed a stream of fire at its spine, burrowing in just at the base of its neck, while the coyote distracted it with lunges and feints. Once my fire severed its spine, the creature lay still for a moment, then evaporated into mist.

I ran over to Raven as the coyote likewise disintegrated. Raven had slumped to his knees on the crate and held himself up from total collapse on his hands. His chest heaved and the black curtain of his hair hid his face from me. Sweat glistened on his arms and shoulders and I saw droplets stain the wooden crate.

I reached over and squeezed his left shoulder in congratulations. "We got him, Doc. We got his monster."

Raven shook his head and looked down at me. "He's not defeated yet." He pointed back at the yacht, purple highlights being etched onto his face by the glow still surrounding Hasan. "He's getting an energy boost from the ship. It's an ally spirit of incredible power and it's using him as a conduit. Whatever summoned it must have been unbelievable."

The same voice I'd heard Hasan use before now burst into my brain without the sham of having the man's lips move. *"It is true, Richard Raven. What summoned me was beyond your mortal ken to understand. You have interfered with the mission given me by my master, and now you must pay! But first, you will see this one of your friends die because I relish the pain it will cause you!"*

I felt magical force begin to gather around me, then tighten like a chain wrapped around my chest. It crushed in from all sides and I wanted to scream, but I could get no air from my lungs. I wanted to beg Raven to destroy the ship, but I realized that was impossible. How do you kill a thirty-meter-long ally spirit?

The burning agony drove me to my knees. The Old One howled in pain and fought to win my release, but even it was helpless against the power that held and crushed me. Sparks began to float before my eyes, then great shimmering balls of light sizzled across my field of vision.

I knew the end had come.

I felt certain the explosion I heard was my heart bursting, and the sudden cessation of pain only meant I'd died. I could smell death in the air and I recall having been disappointed that it did not smell differently when it came for me. I waited for the blackness to steal my sight, but it did not. In fact, the light grew brighter and I laughed that death was not so dark and grim after all.

Then I realized I'd heard myself laugh.

That meant I wasn't dead.

I scrambled to my feet just in time to have a second, larger explosion blast me back into the boathouse wall. Whereas the first explosion had only torn a small hole at the base of the ship's superstructure, the greater blast punched fire out through all the portholes below the main deck and pulsed a flaming corona out over the deck itself. Then the whole superstructure lurched to port and dropped down a deck level. The ship listed to port and started to take on great floods of water.

High on the superstructure, the purple glow imploded. A column of fire whirled up into the air and Hasan combusted instantaneously. I saw his skeleton outlined in black against the golden fire, then it too vanished.

The ship screamed, then sank from sight in a steaming caldron of bubbles.

By the time Raven helped me to my feet and we then picked our way through flaming debris to the edge of the wharf, Stealth had managed to awkwardly haul himself up out of the water. His left arm hung limply from his shoulder and showed where most of the working parts had been crushed when the sphinx had batted him out of the air. Water poured from the arm compartments where he carried plastic explosives, and his talons gouged into the decking to steady him.

Raven and I exchanged smiles while Stealth turned and nodded grimly at the burning ally spirit. "Underwater I could see no props or jet nozzles—the ship had no natural way to move. I figured that made it very special, therefore I resolved to destroy it. Then a grunge corpse strapped to a flamethrower drifted down from the surface, so I improvised a bomb. Not much can stand up to a combination of napalm and Semtek."

His mention of the flamethrower brought my earlier encounter with it back to mind in full sizzling detail. I shifted my shoulders around to ease the soreness in my back. "By the way, that was pretty tricky shooting you did when that grunge popped up with the torch gun."

Stealth nodded solemnly. "He was half hidden so I couldn't go for a head shot. A body shot would have ruptured the tank, and that would have roasted you alive." He shuddered and glanced at his tattered left arm. "Burning to death isn't something I'd wish on anyone."

I turned to Raven. "You should have seen it. He nailed me in the back and knocked me forward into the woman I was trying to save. That blasted us out of the way of the flamethrower." I looked back at Stealth. "It's a good thing you remembered I was wearing Kevlar."

The look of surprise on his face took a second or two to die. I felt a chill pass between us, but it drained away as Kid Stealth punched me lightly in the shoulder and gave me a genuine smile. "Yeah, I'm glad I remembered, too..." *

DIGITAL GRACE

ONE

Given that I didn't know where I was when I woke up, I figured still having my clothes on was a plus. I mean I can remember similar incidents when I thought otherwise, but I hadn't been tied up in those situations. I also didn't have a kid sitting on the end of the bed pointing a pistol with a bowling-ball bore at me.

"Kyrie, he's awake." The little albino showed me his teeth in a feral grin and held the heavy revolver with pale, unwavering hands. "Do anything, Kies, and the last thing going through your mind will be a bullet."

Great, I thought, *I'm being held by some psycho punk who's been downloading intimidation lessons from Kid Stealth.* "No problem, ace."

I took a moment or two to assess my situation. Because of the thick blue and red Amerind blanket drawn up to my neck, I couldn't see my hands, but it felt like the kid had used hawser to bind my wrists together. The cable had been knotted tight, but my hands weren't tied behind my back. Whatever spark of hope that little gift inspired died in the railroad tunnel at the end of the gun barrel staring at me.

The old, metal-frame bed had been painted enough times for me to see a rainbow of colors where chips cut through to bare metal. Off to my left, just on the far side of the doorway, I saw a table and two chairs. My leather jacket hung over the back of one of the chairs and my shoulder holster, complete with pistol, lay on the table itself. The room, from the cobwebs in the corners to the cracks in the plaster, had seen better days, but it was still habitable. The bedding looked fairly clean, but the scent told me it had been a week or two since it had been washed.

Using my elbows and heels, I slowly pushed myself back and up into a sitting position. I clamped down on the blanket with my chin, pulling it up with me. Bending my knees and digging my heels in, I popped the blanket up into a little tent and watched the albino over the artificial horizon stretched between my knees.

"So, tell me, do you have a 'Preferred Guest Rate' or am I being soaked for full fare during my impromptu stay?" The albino's pink eyes watched me without blinking. His white hair had been shaved into a mohawk and stiffened into a bristle of porcupine quills. Aside from the reddish cast to his eyes, the only color on him came from the dirt beneath his fingernails and the little creases at the corner of his thin-lipped mouth. His jaw showed white wisps of beard-to-come. His Maria Mercurial t-shirt and synthetic pants matched the dingy gray walls in hue.

Before he could answer, or pull the trigger, a second person entered the room. She was a pretty little elf, if a tad on the lean side. She had fire in her dark eyes, though she seemed to take care to hide it when she looked at the albino. She wore her black hair very short in a boyish cut. That, and her slender figure made it easily possible for her to pass as a young man—a wise thing to do if, as was my guess, we were in the Barrens and this was where they lived. She wore mostly synthleather—standard for the sprawl—though hers was of browns and tans that would have seemed more appropriate in the Tír.

"How are you feeling?" Kyrie leaned on the foot of the bed as she asked the question. "Are you hurt?"

I shook my head casually. "Tongue feels thick. I could use some water."

She turned to leave, but the gunboy snarled at her. "Overruled. You'll get water when I say you get water."

"Albion, he's not an enemy."

"He's not a guest either, Kyrie. He's a hostage." Albion locked his serpent-stare on me again. "You're Wolfgang Kies, right?"

My eyes narrowed. "Cut to the chase."

"My game, my rules, my speed."

"Okay, if that's the way it is. Yes, I'm Wolfgang Kies." I pulled my head up and back, pressing it against the wall behind me. "Next?"

"You work for Dr. Richard Raven, right?"

That question, combined with calling me a hostage earlier, started alarm bells going off in my head. I knew that Etienne La Plante, a big Seattle crime boss, had a standing reward for the delivery of Raven's head in a sack. I didn't think these kids were setting a trap for Raven with me as bait, but anything was possible in the sprawl. As desperation finds plenty of prey in the Barrens, that might be exactly what was happening.

"Yeah, I work for Raven."

Immediately Kyrie's expression brightened. Albion remained stone-faced, but tipped the pistol up toward the ceiling. Some of my anxiety drained off as the pistol ceased its violation of my personal space, but I knew lots more was going on than I could read.

Two more kids entered the room, and the second I laid eyes on the smallest of them, how I got involved in this mess came flooding back with a clarity that caused me to blush. I'd just come out of Kell's over between First and Second, down by the Market. I'd been drinking a bit, but not much because I was more interested in watching the Seadogs[1] in their fight for the pennant than I was in getting drunk. Jimmy Mackelroy salted the game away with a three-run homer in the ninth, so I left and headed out toward Stewart to get my Fenris.

I should have known better, but in the alley between Kell's and the Gravity Bar I heard someone crying. I pulled my Beretta Viper 14[2] and thumbed the safety off, then glanced around the corner of the alley. Aside from two rats perched on the rim of a dumpster and the usual accumulation of trash, I saw nothing out of the ordinary except a tiny humanoid form.

Its head came up and revealed the most cherubic little face I'd ever laid eyes on. Because of the multiple layers of clothing swathing the child, I couldn't tell if it was a boy or girl. It took one bold step toward me with its left foot, then hesitated and let its right leg drag shyly in behind the left. With the length of cuff overhanging its right hand, the child swiped at the tears on its grimy face, then smiled at me.

"Ah you Woofgang Kies?" it asked in an innocent, mush-mouth voice.

I slipped my Viper back into the shoulder holster I wore under my leather jacket. "Yes." I stepped into the alley and approached the child.

"And do you wook for Docto Waven?" it followed up in a voice rising with expectation.

---

[1] The Seattle franchise for major league baseball is officially still called the Mariners, but pretty much everyone who isn't under contract to them calls them the Seadogs. About ten, fifteen years ago they had a really bad streak—stats just weren't clicking the way they should, so everyone started calling the team the Dogs. Then this guy—an ork related somehow to Plutarch Graogrim, another of Doc's chummers—gets this idea about turning out Seattle Seadogs merchandise, including caps and shirts, and all with a great pirate-hound logo. Everybody started getting into the whole charade, with a local radio station even doing play-by-play of fantasy dog-day games. The Mariners tried to sue, but when fans stopped coming to games in protest, the suit was dropped, and the Seadog name has been a thorn in their sides ever since, even though the team has gotten good.

[2] I hasten to note that even some newer, wizzer gun wouldn't have kept me out of this situation.

I dropped to one knee and held out my left hand. "Yes. Are you lost?"

It smiled as agelessly as a Buddha. "No." It held its hands out to me. As it did so, a mist sprayed out from its left sleeve, while the little figure clapped its right sleeve over its own nose and mouth.

The neurotoxin stung my eyes, but before I could even think of running, I'd pulled enough in through my open mouth to drop me on my tail. I coughed weakly, then lay back. As consciousness drained from me, I remember praying for one thing over and over: *Please, God, if I have to die, don't let Stealth find out how I got it.*

That same little boy now disengaged his hand from that of the fourth member of the youth assembly and approached the head of the bed. "Ah you okay?"

The hurt and fear in his small voice prompted an instant smile of reassurance on my part. "I'm fine."

The albino looked over at the other girl in the room. "Sine, get Cooper away from him. You're supposed to be watching out front."

The blond flipped her long hair back from one shoulder with a contemptuous toss of her head. "Load up Reality 1.0, chummer. These are the Barrens. There's nothing out there, and no one will find us here. No one but that damned preacherman." Still, despite her defiance, she held her hand out to the little boy, and Cooper took it. His other hand came up to his face and his thumb disappeared within his mouth.

"Okay, chummers, what's the scan?" I put a nasty-face on and centered my attention on Kyrie. "You tagged me good, and you've got me here. You want something, that's obvious, or I'd have woken up dead. Slot and run. I've got places to go and people to see."

"You're going nowhere, Kies." Albion began to get antsy with the gun again. "We want Raven to do a job for us."

I shook my head. "Is that all? A job? Fine, let me call him."

"Nope." Albion dropped the gun toward me and sighted a pink eye down the barrel. "He won't do it on your say-so. He's legal—he's got a System Identification Number. We don't trust anyone with a SIN. The only way Raven will work for us is if your life is on the line."

"That six-shooter has more bullets than you've got brain cells." I looked over at Kyrie. "You're an elf. You could have gotten word to Raven through the Tír and he'd have helped. You must have thought of that."

"Overruled," snarled Albion.

I felt my anger rising, and along with it came the howl of a wolf in the back of my mind. "Overruled, Albion, because that was a bad idea, or because you couldn't control the situation then?"

"Overruled because we don't trust anyone legal." He opened his arms wide. "We're a family. We all do for each other, and can trust each other because we're all alike. You SIN, and all sorts of laws start kicking in. Folks get worried about covering themselves in legalities. Not us. We just want to be left alone—and that's what we want Raven to get for us."

"Okay, if that's what you want." I snorted a little laugh. "I think you're making a mistake, however. I think Doc would prefer working with folks who sought his help openly, not coerced it."

"My rules, remember?"

"You might want to reconsider." I pulled my hands from beneath the blanket and shook the frayed hawser from them. "I think he'd frown on having me tied up, too." Looking past Kyrie and Sine, I smiled. "Isn't that true, Doc?"

The kids spun toward the doorway faster than a pedestrian hit by a Porsche Mako going full open. Albion's jaw hit the floor, followed a second later by his pistol. Kyrie leaned back against the bed's frame. Sine sat down hard in the chair with my jacket on it, while Cooper just stared wide-eyed and continued to suck his thumb.

Doctor Richard Raven more than filled the doorway. Tall, even for an elf, his head towered above the top of the door. His broad shoulders tapered down to a narrow waist, slender hips, and powerful legs in a build more typical of humans than elves. His coppery skin, high cheekbones, and long black hair bespoke some Amerind blood, though his white shirt and khaki canvas slacks were the latest in corp casual.

Somehow, though, his size and mixed Amerind/elven racial characteristics were not what surprised them. His eyes held their attention. Red and blue ribbons of color wove through their black depths in an aurora-like display. Half terrifying and one hundred percent fascinating, his gaze swept over them, then he nodded solemnly.

"I thank you for finding and taking care of my friend. When the emergency locator beacon built into his belt buckle went off, I became understandably concerned."

I kicked the blanket off and brushed the remnants of the rope from the sharpened edge of the buckle. "Did that thing get activated again?" I shrugged. "Just as well, I suppose, Doc, because these kids want to hire you to do a job for them."

Raven smiled easily as I crawled out of bed and slipped my holster back on. He looked at Albion. "How is it that I can repay your kindness to Wolf?"

Albion swallowed hard, bringing a little joy to my heart. "You know Reverend Dr. Lawrence Roberts?"

I tugged my jacket out from under Sine and recalled her earlier remark. "The television preacher?"

Albion nodded. "The same." He looked around, silently polling Kyrie and Sine. They gave him nods. "We want you to kill him."

TWO

As I headed my Fenris sports coupe out from the garage beneath Raven's headquarters I found myself silently agreeing with Kyrie's final comment about Reverend Roberts—it didn't make any sense. What the kids had told us defied logic in the way only insanity or divine inspiration can possibly manage. Had control of my life suddenly been threatened that abruptly and radically, I'd have wanted the man dead, too.

Reverend Lawrence Roberts, Doctor of Divinity by some ROM-staffed diploma mill, had decided to make that band of kids his own little project. He wanted to redeem their lives. Not only did he intend to baptize them into his particular sect of Christianity, but he wanted to get them System Identification Numbers and bring them back into the mainstream of society. He wanted to create in them an example of a way Christians could fight back against Satan's rule on the earth.

Raven had Tom Electric run a sample of one of Roberts' services by me. It was part of a simsense chip package that Roberts' ministry offered. Being a male in my twenties, I got version 20M. The simsense would feed back the emotions of a person recorded observing the service, so matching me with the appropriate version was vital for me to get the full impact of the good Doctor's presentation.

I pulled a trode rig over my head and started it running. As the static wall thinned and evaporated and the simsense began to roll, the Old One growled in disgust.

The preacher oozed charisma from the top of his thin, blond hair to the Italian leather loafers on his feet. Clutching a battered Bible, he looked out from his lectern like a prisoner about to confess before a jury. One amid thousands, I felt my heart begin to pound with anticipation.

"Yes, my friends, the things you have heard about me are true." Reverend Roberts began in low, embarrassed tones, but I sensed he was in control of the whole situation at all times. "Fifteen years ago I was nothing but a con man, and one of the most vile stripe. My partner and I used to read the newsfax to see who had died, then we'd print up a customized edition of a Bible. It would be inscribed from the deceased to whoever his closest survivor happened to be." He showed us his well-used book. "This was the last of the Bibles we ever created.

"We knew no shame. We'd go to the bereaved and ask for the deceased. When we were informed of the death, we would act embarrassed and eventually confess that the deceased had special-ordered the Bible. He had paid only twenty nuyen of the one-hundred nuyen it cost, and had gotten it specially for the person to whom we were speaking. We would say we were sorry for bothering them in their grief, and then turn to leave."

Roberts' eyes flashed down at the ground as a blush rose to his cheeks. He stared at one of the many carnation bouquets surrounding him. "Of course, the bereaved would stop us and give us the eighty nuyen remaining on the book. We would hand it over, having earned an easy seventy-five nuyen profit. It was an easy life, for anyone would pay gladly for that last piece of their departed loved one, and we talked ourselves into believing that we were really offering them another chance to say good-bye—manufacturing memories the people so dearly hungered after."

Roberts' brought his head up and steel entered his spine. I knew, aided by the digitized emotional feed coursing in through the trodes, that Roberts had somehow been motivated away from this evil path. He smiled and confirmed my belief.

"Then, one night, my partner and I were heading out for what would be our last attempt. God and the Devil came to us, and each showed us a vision of what we would reap in the afterlife. My partner held his hand out to the Devil and was taken to hell right then and there. I looked upon the face of God and chose the path of light. Praise Jesus, I was saved!"

Thunderous applause washed over me and I found myself mouthing the word "Alleluia!" I pulled the trodes off in disgust and let the Old One's growl rumble from my throat.

Raven looked over at me and smiled. "What do you think, Wolf?"

I patted my Beretta Viper. "I've got a love offering for the good Reverend, right here."

Raven decided that might be a bit extreme as our first effort at contact. He gave me the address for Roberts' ministry headquarters. I changed into a corduroy suit jacket, button-down shirt, and tie before I headed out, deferring to Raven's sense of decorum, not mine. The clothes hid my silver wolf's-head pendant and my Viper, but I didn't so much mind that. When entering the lion's den, it's best to dress like a lion.

THREE

Roberts' personal secretary was pretty enough that I would have considered converting were she willing to do some missionary work with me. She flashed me a smile as I came up the stairs to the third-floor foyer, but she kept getting distracted by the big goomer seated on the edge of her desk. He was clearly intent on ministering to her, but she looked like she wanted him exorcised faster than you could say "Amen."

I cleared my throat and quickscanned her nameplate. "Evening, Miss Crandall. I'm Wolfgang Kies. I called ahead for an appointment with Dr. Roberts."

The big man moved off the desk as she positively glowed at me. "Yes, Mr. Kies. Six forty-five and you're exactly on time." Her smile carried right on up into her blue eyes and clearly irked the other man.

"Do I get points for punctuality?"

"With me you do, Mr. Kies." She looked up at the man. "Brother Boniface will take you to Dr. Roberts."

Boniface looked like an ape that had been given one of those all-over bikini waxes or a troll that had been cold-hammered into a smaller shape. Either way, he did not look happy to be in a suit and sent on a mission that would take him away from the charming Miss Crandall. As a result of his discomfort, somewhere inside his tiny skull one electron collided with another and all of a sudden he had a thought. It was too much for him to contain, and he made his move to frisk me.

The Viper's barrel made a *thunk* as I drew it in one smooth motion and poked a Mark of Cain in the center of Brother Boniface's forehead. He retreated a step and raised both hands to cover the bruise. "Ask and ye shall receive, Boniface. Presume, and I'll make a martyr out of you."

I let the gun slip forward and hang from my index finger by the trigger guard. Boniface made a grab for it, but I ducked it under his hand and slid it onto Miss Crandall's desk. "Keep it warm for me."

"My pleasure," she cooed. The gun slipped from sight beneath the level of her desk.

Boniface slunk forward and led me down a short hallway to Roberts' office. He only opened one of the two oak doors, but it was double-wide anyway and provided a stunning panorama as I entered. I didn't feel slighted only getting the single-door treatment because I got the distinct impression that even if Jesus returned for an encore he wouldn't get a two-door salute.

The very first thing I noticed in the room was the expensive wooden paneling on the walls, and the stunning number of leather-bound books lining the bookshelves. Reverend Roberts had laid out significant nuyen to splash old-world respectability around his office. The west wall was made entirely of glass, with a view of the Sound that impressed even the Old One. Shown a picture of this place and asked to choose whether it belonged to some highly placed corpgeek or a preacher constantly crying poormouth, I'd have been wrong even with two free guesses.

It took me about two seconds to scan the place and get the Old One's howl to vet my opinion. By that time, the unearthly scent of hundreds of carnations assaulted my nose. Save for the top of Boniface's head, every flat surface in the room boasted a vase jammed with carnations of various colors. I recalled the riot of flora surrounding the Reverend on the simchip, but 3-D reality was another order of magnitude above even that.

The gaudiest of the carnations resided in the buttonhole of Roberts' lapel. Standing behind his desk, he nodded to me and extended his hand. "Welcome, Mr. Kies." I accepted his hand and found his grip disturbingly firm. I normally judge a man by how he shakes hands, but Roberts' grip felt *too* right and practiced. The difference might have been subtle, and I could have put it down to my general dislike of him, but I got the feeling he was playing at being a regular guy.

"I thank you for agreeing to see me on such short notice." I dropped myself into the chair in front of his desk. Boniface drifted over to stand right behind me, but I chose to ignore him. "I apologize for any inconvenience to a man with your busy schedule."

Roberts nodded and gave me a reassuring smile. "How could I refuse to see you when the message said you were interested in those children in the Barrens?" His smile grew and his hands spread wide apart. "Of course, I've heard of your Dr. Raven. Though I've never had occasion to use the services of an individual in your trade, what I have heard about Dr. Raven has been very encouraging. The respect in which he is held by some of the lower classes will help ease concerns about possible sinister motives on my part. I must admit, however, I had not expected Raven to join forces with me in this matter."

I leaned back in the padded leather chair. "I hate to burst your bubble, Reverend Roberts, but I'm not here to offer Raven's help concerning the children. As you know, homeless children in the Barrens are legion, and most would welcome your aid. These kids don't want it. We want you to leave them alone."

His head came up, and a bit of light reflected from his scalp despite the thinly sown rows of blond hair transplants. "Leave them alone? How can I do that, Mr. Kies?" His wounded tone began to parallel the tape's parable preamble, but I could do nothing to deflect him. "Those children need help, and I hardly think they're in a position to determine what's best for them. They need good food and schooling and direction. They cannot be allowed to waste away on the dung heap of society. We must take them into our fold to encourage others to do the same with similar tragic cases."

"Dr. Raven agrees with you in that regard, Reverend." I held a hand up, sending a quiver through Boniface. "He's already running full background checks on all the children in that house, using resources you don't command. He will find out who they really are and will get them help. We can get them protection in the Barrens, and we can ensure they receive the aid necessary for them to rise above their beginnings."

"Can you, Mr. Kies? Can you expect me to back off when what you suggest is making them fit fish for that small pond, whereas I will take them away from the Barrens and make them productive members of society?"

I didn't like the reproving tone of his question. "The people of the Barrens are capable of taking care of themselves. Betty Beggings and others work to form meta-family groups and to give people a solid base from which to operate."

Roberts smiled like a shark. "But they do not have the resources at my command." He stood and indicated the opulence of his office. "They can command tribute from others in the Barrens, dividing and subdividing a very small pie into yet tinier morsels. I, on the other hand, solicit money from the rich and well-to-do in this society. I get in single contributions more nuyen than Betty Beggings and all her ilk see in a lifetime. I can do for these children what no one else can."

"But you do it at the cost of their freedom. They don't want your help."

Roberts batted my objection aside contemptuously. "They are without proper documentation. They don't know what they want. The law says they must have custodianship, and I have decided to be their benefactor. In following my example, other members of my flock will adopt other children from the Barrens and we will rebuild this society."

My eyes slowly shifted from green to silver as my anger rose. "You will remake these children in your image?"

The good Reverend ignored my question as he walked toward the wall of windows in his office. He stood with his back to me, the dying sun making him a silhouette outlined by a red corona. The shadow narrowed, then expanded again as he turned to face me. "Do you believe in God, Mr. Kies?"

"I fail to see what that has to do with the matter at hand."

"I'm sure you do, and I will accept that as a 'No,' for the sake of what I am about to say. You see, I *do* believe in God. I believe in a merciful and forgiving God, but a God who demands his people work for their salvation. Once upon a time I was like those children—wild, abandoned, and angry at society. Then God gave me a choice: Eternal Damnation or life with him forever. For the first time, I looked beyond my next meal and chose a course for my life."

The silhouette hung its head wearily. "My choice is not without its price. My God demands I do all I can to help lead others to him. The Kingdom of Satan started its millennial domination of the Earth in 2011—the first dragon was seen in Japan to herald this change. All this magic is merely Satan's will made manifest. It is my duty and my calling to do all I can to bring Satan's reign to an end, and I *will* do it."

The strength in his voice spoke to me of a fanatical devotion to what he saw as his divine calling, but somewhere, deep down, I sensed I was being conned.

"I don't think we have anything more to discuss, Reverend Roberts." I started to rise from my chair, but two heavy hands jammed me back down into it.

"You don't go until Reverend Roberts says you can go."

Deep inside, in the lightless cavern where the Wolf spirit dwells within me, the Old One howled bloody murder. Insistently he demanded I let him have control. He promised to reshape me into an engine of primal fury. "*I will show them a justice and righteousness that predates their tree-hung godling by eons!*"

I forced myself to be calm, but I let some of the Old One's anger enter my voice. "Larry, do you practice faith healing?"

Roberts stiffened at the tone of my words, then nodded. "I do."

"Good. Brother Boniface has three seconds to stop this laying-on of hands, or he'll need all the healing you can give him."

The Brother's hands tightened.

"Two."

Roberts waved Boniface back, and the pressure eased. The Reverend returned to his desk and seated himself. "Brother Boniface can be overzealous, but that might be said of all my Warriors for Christ." Though he smiled benignly, the implied threat was not lost on me.

I stood slowly and straightened my jacket as Boniface retreated and opened the door. "You may not believe this, Larry, but I actually do respect those who listen to the message from the Prince of Peace.

I think, however, that the words you're hearing are a bit garbled. Let me make this very clear: leave those children alone."

Roberts smiled and laid his right hand on the Bible I'd seen him thump in the tape. "I understand your words, Mr. Kies, but I cannot be deflected from my course. On this very Bible I swore I would help them. I cannot go back on my word."

I snatched the Bible from beneath his hand and saw him blanch as I started to flick the pages open. I saw that the liner sheet backing the cover had popped free. Amid the glue stains I glimpsed a curious collection of strange symbols, but they were as much gibberish as the Greek passages on the facing pages of the book. The flyleaf had been inscribed, "*To my darling Tina, I will love you for eternity. Andrew Cole,*" but that made even less sense than the other cryptic stuff.

He made a grab for it, but I held it back, frustrating his effort. My stare met his and he flinched. "Consider this a reading from the Second Book of Revelations: And the Wolf saith unto the Preacherman, if you want Apocalypse, stay your course."

I tossed the Bible onto the blotter and plucked a carnation from the vase on his desk. Stuffing it into the buttonhole on my jacket, I turned on my heel and left him scrambling to clutch the Bible to his chest. I headed straight for the door, but Boniface grabbed me and spun me around to face him before I could leave the office.

"This is not over between us." Though his back was to the window, the solar effect did nothing but make him a big-eared shadow. The threat in his voice made him into big-eared shadow clown.

I nodded slowly and carefully, letting the Old One fill me with the strength and speed I'd need. "You have a point there, Boniface. What do say we take it outside?"

His smile widened his cheeks enough to nearly eclipse his ears. "Yeah, outside."

My hands shot up into his armpits and boosted him back toward the window before he could so much as yelp with surprise. The glass shattered in halo fashion, starting with the area around his head, then fragmented into a million pieces. The glittering glass shower rained down as Boniface disappeared from view. A second later, a vase of carnations I'd pulled from a table near the door followed him to the street.

I wiped my hands off on the drapes. "Sorry about ruining the view. Good day."

Outside, after I'd shut the door behind me, I noticed Miss Crandall was having a hard time keeping a smile from her lips. She slid my gun across the desk to me.

"Much obliged."

Her blue eyes sparkled. "My pleasure, Mr. Kies. God be with you."

"Thank you, Miss Crandall. I'm sure one of them is."

FOUR

I got back into my Fenris and punched in the ignition code. The scream of an ambulance siren started the Old One howling triumphantly in my head. I pulled away from the curb and got off the road before the DocWagon careened around the corner, lights blazing. It headed for the alley into which Boniface had plunged while I started down Fifth Avenue.

The meeting with Roberts left me angry and not a little puzzled. I had hoped that explaining to him that the kids didn't want his help and assuring him they would be taken care of would be enough to deflect him. Raven had dealt with other "do-gooders" in that manner, and they were usually content to let shadowfolk take care of their own.

I had believed I could accomplish my mission until Roberts asked the stopper question: "Do you believe in God?" I'd known other preachers, and found them all quite capable of rational thought and logical analysis of a problem. Like Roberts, however, when a discussion took them into a realm where they had no expertise or facts to bolster their argument, they resorted to the divine shield. For them, and for him, the ultimate refuge boils down to this: "We might not understand it, but it is part of God's plan, and we must do what we can to empower it or Satan will win."

I was willing to grant Roberts his supposition that Satan had taken over the Earth in 2011, when magic had returned to the world. At the risk of being seen as a heretic, I also acknowledged that the reemergence of magic in the world had done virtually nothing to change the lot in life for most folks. Yes, the few lucky ones who could wield magic were able to turn that talent into a career, but it did nothing for those who were magic-blind. Giant corps still controlled the economy, and most of them controlled cadres of spellgrubs as well.

I recognized that my mental discussion was doing several undesirable things. First, I had half a mind to turn around and defoliate Roberts' boutonniere with 9mm weed-killer. I realized that particular half of my mind had been taken over by the Old One, so I tucked the Homicide Hound back into his little box. I also saw that I was heading south toward the Barrens, and I knew I wouldn't feel good unless I was sure the kids were safe.

While Roberts seemed very earnest and directed in his Christianity, the theatrical bits layered on top of it still made me uneasy.

More than any of that, though, it dawned on me that I was hungry. I scanned the street and slid the Fenris into a parking place just up the block from a Dominion pizza joint. Even with an armed escort, the place would never consider delivering to the Barrens, so I went in and ordered five pizzas, including two vegetarian specials just in case Kyrie was not a carnivore.

While waiting for my order I decided to call the office. Valerie Valkyrie answered and got Raven for me immediately.

"How did it go, Wolf?"

"I discovered that Roberts' bodyguard can't fly." I grimaced and chewed on my lower lip for a second. "Roberts appreciates our concern, but he says he's made the kids into a centerpiece for a drive to encourage his flock in helping the disadvantaged. He sounds sincere, but something deep down inside me doesn't like him, and I agree."

Raven asked some pointed questions, and I reported the meeting back to him as completely as I could. He sounded most interested in the Bible, its inscription, and the sigils, but my momentary glance at them made the information I gave him fairly useless. I promised I'd try to duplicate the symbols for him when I returned to headquarters, and told him I was taking some food to the kids.

"Good idea, Wolf. Valerie has turned up some interesting information on Roberts, but we've yet to find anything truly sinister. I'll have her working on this Tina and Andrew Cole. Maybe we'll have something when you get back here."

"Good. I'll be back early, I think."

I hung up and discovered, to my surprise, that my order was ready. I took the pizzas out to the Fenris and belted the stack of boxes into the passenger seat. As I got the car on the road, my stomach growled more fiercely than the Old One had ever managed.

Kid Stealth would have questioned the wisdom of bringing my Fenris within a nautical mile of the Barrens, but then he thinks he's traveling in a kiddie-kar unless the vehicle is armored and has a .50 caliber machine-gun mounted in a turret on top. I parked right in front of the crib that had been my temporary home and set the anti-theft system on "maim." With a stack of pizzas precariously balanced on my left hand, I used the other to knock on the door of the ramshackle townhouse.

Kyrie answered the door and didn't recognize me by what little of my face showed over the top box. "You've got the wrong place. We didn't order any pizza."

I lowered the boxes and smiled at her. "Not to worry. This is Dominion's new service. We drop pizza off and you pay for what you eat. You're a test market."

She laughed lightly and I saw true happiness in her face for the first time. "Smile like that more often, Kyrie, and I think you could convince Dominion this service is more than worth it."

Her dark eyes glowed with a more mischievous light. "I'm sure Dominion would just love to give me an endorsement contract. We eat pizza fairly often, and it's usually theirs." She stepped back away from the door. "C'mon in before the neighborhood catches a whiff of that stuff."

Albion met us halfway to the kitchen and I dealt him a box off the top. Sine splashed a bucket of water over a soapy collection of plates and glasses in the sink, then wiped her hands off and took a box from me. With one broad swipe of the box, she cleared some old paper plates and styrofoam soyburger cartons from the table and onto the floor. When that earned her a reproving glare from Kyrie, her next pass was less swift and more silent.

Cooper came clumping up the steps from the basement and shut the door behind him. He looked at me and smiled. I presented him a box with all the ceremony of Seattle's governor bestowing a citizenship medal on someone, and his smile broadened to show me all of his teeth. He scrambled up on a stool beside Sine and pried his box open.

I handed Kyrie the next to last box, leaving one for me. "Help yourself. Raven doesn't often cater his jobs, but when he does, the food is good."

She smiled and looked down timidly. She started to say something, but Cooper's surprised shout cut her off. "This ain't pizza!"

"Sure it is, Cooper. I just got it myself from Dominion. Eat it and you'll grow up to be big and strong like Jimmy Mackelroy."

The little guy shook his head adamantly and jammed tiny fists against his hips. "Nope, it's not pizza. It doesn't have pizza stuff on it." He glared at me, his lower lip thrust out defiantly.

I frowned and looked to Kyrie. "Pizza stuff?"

She blushed. "You don't want to know. We do most of our food shopping in dumpsters." She set her pizza down on the kitchen shelf and squatted beside Cooper. "Listen, Coop, this is *special* pizza, that's why it doesn't have pizza stuff on it. You don't have to scrape it off, see?"

Cooper's eyes flashed warily. "Special?"

Kyrie nodded emphatically. "It's birthday pizza. Today is Wolf's birthday, and he's sharing his birthday pizza with us."

Electric excitement lit Cooper's face with neon intensity. "Weally? It's yuar biwfday?"

I tossed him a wink. "You bet. That's why I have this flower on. Now eat your pizza so I'll have a good birthday, okay?"

"'Kay."

Kyrie walked back over to me and glanced at my lapel. "A carnation. You went to see Roberts, didn't you?"

"Sure did." I started to reach for some pizza, but the worry in her voice cut my hunger. "I tried to explain to him that you wanted to be left alone, but I don't think he got the message. Still, his bodyguard will be recovering from a test of faith so we might have bought some time. Don't worry, you'll be fine."

I wanted to reach out and take her in my arms just to reassure her, but she held herself back and I instantly knew why. Accepting a hug would have showed weakness, and that she could not allow. Albion styled himself the leader of the little band, and probably did motivate them to get lots of things done, but Kyrie certainly held the group together on a daily basis. If she gave him any opening, he would lead the group to ruin because of his bitterness and anger.

Cooper hopped down off his stool and came over to take her hand. "Don't wowwy, Kywie. Mista Wolf and Hawse will pwotect us. I pwomise." As if that affirmation had set all right with the world, he smiled and returned to smearing more pizza sauce over his face.

In a quiet voice I asked, "Hawse?"

Kyrie licked her lips. "When we scavenge, we sometimes have to leave Cooper here all by himself. Harse is his imaginary friend. He says Harse is guarding the house, and it helps keep Cooper calm, so we don't discourage him. Everybody has imaginary friends when they're young. He'll outgrow it."

"Or write simsense scripts about it and get rich. Listen, Raven wants me back at headquarters so we can figure out what we're doing next. I'll take a look around the area just to make sure nothing strange is going down, then I'll take off." I folded one piece of pizza over on another and saluted the assembly with it. "Thanks for sharing my birthday pizza, gang. See you later."

The second I stepped out of the slice of multiplex that housed the kids, I knew something was wrong. The Old One kept a growl simmering in the back of my mind and the hackles rose on my neck. The Barrens is, even at the best of times, a lawless battle zone that makes all but the irredeemably insane feel insecure. This time, however, it felt malevolent.

I bit off some pizza and chewed as I started a circuit around the block. I reached inside and demanded that the Old One lend me his heightened senses. He did so, but the garlic in the pizza quickly erased any advantage the Old One's olfactory abilities might have given me. Still, his increased night vision did help me pierce shadows, and his hearing made audible everything from rats scrambling inside walls to lies whispered passionately in one of the upper-floor apartments across the street.

I definitely heard something out of the ordinary. It started with the slushy, muffled, sucking sound a boot would make when slowly drawn out of mud. Along with that came the crunch of beer-bottle glass being ground against stones and a metallic clinking like links of a chain striking a post. And yet, as clearly as I heard what I have described, I heard much more as those sounds played in concert with others.

Above and beyond that I knew two other things. Had I tried to point those sounds out to anyone without hypersenses, they would have thought me crazy. The sound had no rhythm or repetition and thereby it avoided classification. It could have been a figment of my imagination, but given my other realization, I was uncomfortable in dismissing it as much.

It was stalking me.

That's not a conclusion I drew without benefit of experience. I've been stalked by some of the best. Two of the elven High Lord's Paladins had come after me during the Full Moon Slashings. Back before he became one of us, Kid Stealth had done his best to put my head on his trophy wall. Each and every time the uneasy feeling coiling in my guts tells me I'm one rung down on someone's idea of the food chain and I don't like it.

I swallowed and the pizza spiraled into the knot that had once been my stomach.

I turned toward the place from which the sound was coming, but I saw nothing huddled in the piles of debris between two buildings. I tossed the pizza away and drew my Viper. I hunkered down behind the burned-out hulk of a Ford American and suddenly found an acrid, bitter odor dissolving the garlic and carnation scents from my nose. Whoever or whatever was coming after me had bizarre ideas about personal hygiene.

Waiting behind cover irritated the Old One no end. "*Do not slink here like a coward, Longtooth. Let me help you. I will destroy this thing that hunts us. Leave it to me.*"

I shook my head. Though the scent had grown strong enough to be completely distracting, I concentrated beyond it. I heard a different sound: running feet. They were approaching from my back. I whirled and jammed my Viper toward the car's rear bumper.

Cooper stopped short and looked at me with eyes full of innocent hurt. "Mr. Woof?"

I swallowed hard. "Cooper! What're you doing out here?"

His smile cracked caked tomato sauce at the corners of his mouth. He extended a newspaper-wrapped bundle bound with string. "Biwfday pwesent."

Somehow, as if his words were a magic spell, the sensation of being hunted vanished. I slid the Viper back into the shoulder holster and accepted the little, pencil-thin package. I carefully tugged the string off it. "Did you wrap this yourself?"

He nodded proudly.

"You did a good job, Cooper. Why, what is this?"

As I peeled the paper away, I knew exactly what his gift was. The slender item was a credstick. They came in one of two flavors. A personal or account credstick has a microchip in it that can be encoded to take care of credits and debits—as convenient as cash and no problem with arguing about whether a corp's scrip is good this month or not.

The second type, of which this was one, is a bearer stick. It has a set amount of credit burned into the chip.

When that is transferred into a banking account or into a person's credstick, the chip melts. Some corps mass-produce them for petty funds expenses, but those sticks are generally of low credit value. The chief benefit of the bearer stick is that it can be used to transfer large amounts of funds without their being immediately traceable. Bearer sticks are small, unmarked bills in a much handier package.

The bearer stick Cooper gave me had been broken in half. The break, which rendered it useless, was jagged so I assumed it was an accident. I fingered both halves, but couldn't make heads or tails of the coloring scheme on them. I looked up to see an expectant expression on Cooper's face. "Thank you very much, Cooper."

His voice sank into a whisper. "The othews look fo da longa ones, so I decided to give you two of da small ones." He clapped his hands. "You and Hawse will keep us safe."

I tousled his blond hair. "You got that right. Harse will have to watch you right now, because I've got to go talk to Raven. Thanks again for the present."

The little boy beamed, then turned and ran off into the shadows. I noticed he headed straight for the area from which I had earlier heard the sounds, but he disappeared before I could warn him away. Using the Old One's ears, I heard him giggle happily and I envisioned more pizza leftovers peeling off his face.

Hopping into my Fenris, I made a quick circuit of the area, then left the Barrens to ward their own.

FIVE

The scowl on Valerie's face meant only one of two things. Either the Seadogs were losing, or she hadn't been very successful in collecting data concerning the Right Reverend Roberts. "What's the score?"

She shrugged. "Roberts one, me zippo." Her frown darkened her café-au-lait skin, but only intensified the azure fire in her eyes.

Raven came down the stairs and gave Valerie an encouraging smile. "I'd not say that, Val. You've pulled plenty of data on all the Andrew Coles who've ever lived in Seattle." He tapped the hardcopy report in his hands. "This stuff on the kids is very complete. You've also given us a rundown on Roberts' empire. As soon as your other search knowbots report back, you'll have everything you set out to get."

Val shrugged. "I know, but something is wrong with that report on Roberts. I know it's been tampered with."

"Mycroft?" I asked, naming another wiz decker I knew.

Valerie wrinkled her pretty nose. "No, if it were Mycroft I'd have to dissect it with a scalpel. For this one I need a chainsaw. If I had to guess, I'd say it's got a government mask running over a transcription program."

Raven's head came up. "Assuming you're right, how tough would it be for Roberts to find out the government is tapping his accounts to keep track of him?"

"Not that hard." Val half-closed her eyes as she concentrated. "Jack could spot it, and maybe the Glass Tarantula. And maybe a half-dozen other deckers in the sprawl, but the preacher's network goes all over. He could have deckers from New York or Dallas checking his stuff."

Doc nodded thoughtfully. "Wolf, did you learn anything from the children when you went out there?"

I seated myself on the edge of a chair. "No, not really. Most of the food they eat is scavenged, but I think I knew that all along the way." I plucked the carnation from my lapel and tossed it into the trash. "Wait, I did get something."

I reached into my pocket and pulled out both halves of the broken credstick. "Cooper gave this to me as a birthday present."

Raven took the two halves and fitted them together. Wetting the tip of his finger with his tongue, he washed away some of the mud and got a clear look at the colored markings on it. He stared at it for a second, then turned to Val. "Cross-correlate Cole, Andrew with Kensington Industries." He studied the stick for another second. "Backdate the search from fifteen years ago to 2005. When you get a match, give me resident data for the house the kids are squatting in for the month on either side of Cole's death date. I'll also need a full file on the house's resident at that time, starting with Lone Star data."

I managed to pick my jaw up off the ground by the time Raven looked back at me. "What are you looking for?"

"I scanned the Cole data earlier and I seem to recall an Andrew Cole working for Kensington Industries. The color coding on this credstick is the type they used for a period between 2005 and 2035, before their merger with Saeder-Krupp."

I nodded. "Didn't Kensington get into money trouble, so Saeder-Krupp came in like a white knight before Beatrice-Revlon could snap them up?"

Raven smiled. "I'm surprised at your knowledge of Seattle's financial history, Wolf."

I said nothing. I wasn't going to tell him the story had been the subject of a trid docudrama I'd once seen.

"Home run, Doc!" Valerie's enthusiastic shout saved me from any chance of Raven testing my command of mergers and acquisitions among megacorps. "Cole, Andrew, married to Tina, died 14 March 2034. He worked in their accounting and disbursement division and was under suspicion of having embezzled 500,000 nuyen in bearer credsticks. Tina died just last year, but Kensington gave her a clean bill because she never spent a dime that couldn't be accounted for by her income. Insurance paid Kensington/Saeder-Krupp off after her death."

"And the resident of the house where the kids are?"

"Thomas Harrison lived there from June of 2033 to March of 2034. The house was reported abandoned after some food riots in the area. Officials list it as ASC-1, but no one has filed a claim on it, so it technically remains in the hands of the city. Harrison himself was a small-time hood and conman." She spun in her chair. "He has a list of bunko arrests longer than Mackelroy's hit streak!"

I blinked twice. "Wanna bet Harrison was the unnamed partner the good Reverend claims the devil took away?"

Raven nodded. "They went to work the Bible scam on Tina Cole after her husband died. She doesn't buy into it, but confesses to these two obviously godly men that her husband has been stealing from his corporation."

"Yeah, Doc, yeah. She's afraid for his soul, so they offer to return the credsticks to Kensington anonymously. That way her husband gets eternal salvation, and his terrestrial reputation doesn't take any hits either. Harrison and Roberts have 500,000 nuyen in credits to split and Harrison skips with them?"

Raven shook his head. "I doubt it. Harrison would have gone through 500,000 in sixteen years. Given Roberts' success in that time, I would have to assume Harrison would return to blackmail his former partner. I'm certain Harrison is dead, and that Roberts killed him in a rage after Harrison said he'd hidden the loot."

"I don't follow."

Raven folded his arms. "The Bible Roberts uses is left over from the scam they tried to work on Tina Cole. I suspect Harrison hid clues to the location of the credsticks in the Bible. The symbols you saw on the cover liner could well be a code that leads to them. The glue finally gave way, exposing the secret, and Roberts has deciphered it."

I frowned heavily. "I've been to his office. What's 500,000 nuyen to this guy?"

"Curve ball, wait, two curves," Val announced as her computer beeped at her. "To answer your first question, Wolf, 500,000 nuyen is the cost of getting out of Seattle and living comfortably. The government has a lock on all of Roberts' accounts pending an investigation of fraud on his proposed Jesusville amusement park and devotion center."

"What else?"

"Second curve. Roberts has filed to take possession of the house under an ASC-1 action. He found some judge to give him custodianship of the kids in a phantom hearing, so he's got the Abandoned/Squatter Claim filed in their names. Lone Star is supposed to be heading out there to help him serve the papers right now."

Raven tucked the credstick pieces into his pocket. "Val, file an ASC-1 counterclaim on the property." He tore a sheet from the hardcopy file he'd been reading. "Use this name if the computer will take it. Otherwise file it in my name and we'll fight it out later. Wolf, let's move."

The Fenris left two blackened patches on the floor of the garage and part of one on every curve we took as we headed toward the house. I didn't just break speed laws, I smashed them to up-quarks. We surprised the hell out of some Ancients as I took a shortcut through part of their turf, but the elven bikers abandoned the chase when they realized by my driving that I wasn't in the mood for games.

Standing on the brakes, I swung the Fenris wide around the last corner and brought it smack up against the curb just at the edge of the street light's circle of illumination in front of the house. Further up along the street I saw a Lone Star car with the driver's door open and light strobing. Beyond that, Reverend Roberts stood in the shelter of his limo.

The Lone Star cop looked over as Raven and I exited my car with our hands up. "Just get back in your car, Wolf, and leave. We have enough trouble without you here."

"Not much for gratitude, are you, Braxen?" I let my hands drop slowly and closed my door with a hip-check. "Doctor Raven is helping these kids, so just chill."

The ork cop scowled. "Raven, I can run you in as easily as I can the kids. Roberts owns this place free and clear, and he's their guardian." He raised his voice for the benefit of the kids inside as well. "If they don't come out, I'm going to splash the loudmouth with the gun, then bring them out in handcuffs."

Raven raised a hand to hold the children back and another to calm Braxen. "Officer Braxen, no violence is necessary here. I believe, if you check your onboard computer, that the Reverend's claim to this property is in dispute."

That bit of information brought a sharp yelp from Reverend Roberts. "Get thee behind me, Satan!" He marched forcefully forward, brandishing his Bible like a sword. He came to confront Raven, but still kept the Lone Star cruiser between him and Doc. "You are meddling in good work being performed in the name of God."

Raven's head came up and a sardonic smile twisted his lips. "I was unaware that 'God' was a synonym for greed, Lawrence Roberts. I'm certain Tina Cole would be shocked at how you betrayed her trust."

In the half-second Roberts' terrified gaze swept from Raven's eyes to mine, I knew everything Raven had pieced together about him was true. He started to stammer a denial, but an unearthly roar cut him off. Cooper came running through the front door, and Braxen hunkered down behind his car door with gun drawn.

Surging up and forward through the front yard I saw the thing I had heard and smelled before. More formless than humanoid, it writhed forward like an amoeboid centaur. A vast skirt of mud and gravel and debris swirled around to form a conical base that supported a lumpish torso with multiple arms. At the top of the torso I saw a shape that could have been described as a head, and when some of the slime dripped down I knew I saw bone.

The Old One howled out a challenge that had my skull bursting. I drew my Viper and snapped a round into the chamber, but couldn't see any spot to shoot the thing that might hurt it.

Cooper looked over at me with horror on his face and shouted, "Wolf, no!" He glanced at the creature and repeated the cry. "Hawse, no!"

The creature went straight for Roberts. Multiple bubbles burst from the area of its chest as if the creature were trying to speak, but any sound it made was drowned out as Roberts held the Bible up and shouted something. The creature kept coming and, to my eye, picked up some speed. The good Reverend tossed the book at the monster, missed high, then turned to run toward his limo. Harse shifted left, tracking accurately, even though I couldn't see anything on it even approximating eyes.

Over the acrid burning stench of the creature, I caught a whiff of Roberts' flower and knew how Harse had tracked him. It had to be orienting on the carnation. I'd been wearing one earlier, and it had come after me until Cooper proclaimed me a friend. Now it was going after Roberts.

I briefly considered shouting a warning, then dismissed the idea. Whatever would happen to him, Roberts had brought it on himself. It was time for the moneychanger to be cleared from the temple.

Roberts screamed incoherent prayers as the monster chased after him. He cut back and forth, trying to shake it, but had no success. Harse tracked Roberts like the best cyberbacker going after the bitcarrier in cyberball, closing with each turn Roberts took. The creature slid forward on a pool of mud and oily scum, cutting Roberts off from the limo.

His gun shaking like a china plate in an earthquake, Braxen looked over at me. I turned to Raven for guidance, but the Doctor just shook his head. He glanced at the children huddled around Cooper, then back at Roberts. Something in his eyes told me he wouldn't have stopped the creature even if he could have.

Denied his escape, the Reverend dropped to his knees. Screwing his eyes tight shut, he clasped his hands together and prayed furiously. I don't remember the words he shouted exactly, mainly because they all sort of ran together, but they amounted to a confession of his sins and a promise to sin no more. Mind you, this is just a layman's opinion, but his catalog of sins was quite enough for several lifetimes.

He begged for God's absolution, and Harse made sure he was shriven.

The creature slammed into him like a mudslide into a house. One second I could see Roberts, and the next he was covered in oozing muck. The Reverend half-stumbled to his feet, literally knocked back by the monster, then fell again as his legs melted away. The creature's acidic touch peeled Roberts' flesh off and smoked his clothing away. He tried to scream, but could only vomit mud.

His body slumped face-first onto the ground, and Harse covered him with a cairn made of garbage. The tentacle arms dissolved into nothingness and the molten mound stopped moving. A small dust-devil danced up and away from the pile as if carrying off Harse's spirit.

Braxen slowly stood from behind his cruiser and the kids left the safety of the front stoop. Cooper tried to dart forward, but Sine held him back. I took one last look at the barrow, shuddered, and put my pistol back in its holster. The Old One barked out one final challenge, then retreated to his den.

Harry tipped his hat back. "What the hell was that?"

"Justice?" Raven, on one knee, examined the Bible Roberts had thrown. "This, along with Roberts 'deathbed' confession, indicates that he murdered his partner Thomas Harrison for a fortune in bearer credsticks. Roberts buried Harrison in the basement here. Apparently the ghost remained quiescent until Roberts took an interest in this place. His hatred for his old partner was strong enough for him to fashion a new body out of debris found in his grave and elsewhere."

Cooper sniffed. "I used ta bwing Hawse t'ings."

I walked over to him and knelt down. "Don't be sad, Cooper. Harse—Harrison—protected you just the way you wanted him to. He's gone, but he's happy now. You want him to be happy, don't you?"

"Yes."

"Good." I stood slowly. "Well, Braxen, I think you can ignore the claim Roberts filed for this place."

The ork frowned. "I'm afraid I can't, Kies. That claim is part of Roberts' estate."

Raven scooped the Bible up and tucked it under one arm. "Actually, Officer, I think you'll find that the counterclaim filed against the property is valid. After all, Kyrie has been living here for the requisite time to make a claim."

Kyrie stiffened.

Braxen shook his head. "Nice try, Raven, but she's SINless, so she can't own this place no matter how long she's lived here."

Raven turned and stared at Kyrie. "I did some checking, Salacia. You might have tried to run away from your family, but you are legal. The house is yours under the squatting statutes. Pay the back taxes on it, and you own it free and clear."

"Go for it, Kyrie," I said. I turned to the Lone Star. "Harry, how much to claim this place?"

The ork shrugged. "Ten grand, I think."

Kyrie's jaw dropped. "Where am I going to get ten thousand nuyen?"

Raven tossed her the Bible. "Five hundred thousand nuyen in bearer credsticks belonging to the Koshiyama Insurance Combine is hidden in a place indicated by the code on the cover-liner. Standard recovery fee is fifteen percent, which should buy you the house and plenty of the things Roberts would have offered you."

Sine picked Cooper up and hugged him, then he turned in her arms and gave Kyrie a kiss. "It's oar house now."

"Yes, it is, Cooper, it's ours."

"Fine, take the house and everything," Albion snapped bitterly, "I'm outta here."

"What?" The hurt in Kyrie's eyes slashed through me like a monofilament whip.

"You've got a SIN. We don't trust anyone who's legal." He slapped Sine's shoulder with the back of his hand. "C'mon, Sine. She owns the house now, so we're leaving."

Sine shook her head. "I'll stay."

"Great. Hope the lot of you rot." He whirled around and ran smack into me.

"You and I need to talk in my office." I grabbed him by the back of his neck and force-marched him to the street. "Has the glue you use on your hair gone straight into your think-box or what?"

He stared at me sullenly when I released him. "She's legal. I don't trust anyone who's got a SIN."

"Think for a minute, will you?" I pointed back to where Kyrie and the others were studying the Bible's clue page. "She's had a SIN for the whole time you've known her, but she's pretended not to. Why do you think that is?"

"We'd kick her out if she told the truth."

"Listen to yourself. You know as well as I do that she could head out for the Tír and get help from the elves down there. She doesn't need you, but you need her. Cooper and Sine need her. Kyrie hung in here because she didn't want the group to be torn apart."

He spat on the ground. "Good for her."

"They also need you. You provide the drive so things can get done."

Albion folded his arms across his skinny chest. "Great, fine, well, someone else can give them the kicks in the pants they need, not me. I'm outta here." He turned and walked away into the darkness.

I wandered back to the others. Kyrie looked up at me expectantly, but I just shook my head. "Sorry."

Cooper blinked his eyes as he turned to me. "Is Albion coming back?"

"I dunno, Cooper, I just don't know." I gave him a half-hearted smile. "Say your prayers, and maybe he will."

NUMBERUNNER

I felt like I was trapped in one of those math problems: Wolf, sprinting south through the alley at 40 kph, has 50 meters to the street and safety. The car, going south at 100 kph, is 100 meters from the street in the same alley. How long will it be before a steel-belted massage ruins Wolf's day?

Leaping over a grease-stained box oozing something noxious at the corners, I figured that my speed meant I was traveling 40,000 meters per hour, or 666.6 meters a minute, or 11.1 meters per second. That put me approximately 5 seconds from Westlake and a vague chance at being able to walk home under my own power.

The Acura Toro cruising down the alley behind me, with a piece of newsprint fluttering from its radio antenna like a flag, boasted 100,000 meters per hour. That put it at 277.7 meters per second. Roughly translated that meant it would be through me faster than the curry I'd eaten the night before—a distinctly unpleasant prospect.

The calculations checked and left no doubt. That's why I hate math.

That's why I like magic.

The Old One howled with glee as I let him share his wolf-born speed and strength with me. I stooped in the middle of the alley and yanked up the heavy bronze manhole cover. The driver, thinking I meant to drop into the sewer to escape him, punched the accelerator and centered his slender sports car on me.

Like a matador with a metal cape, I cut to my right, but let the manhole cover hang in space where I had been. The lower edge hit the windscreen about halfway down and shattered the glass like it was a soap bubble. The disk began to somersault, end over end, doing its best to turn the hardtop Toro into a convertible. It had better success with the driver, ensuring that while he might have lived fast and died young, he would not leave a pretty corpse.

The Toro hit the alley wall pretty hard. Sparks shot up from where the fiberglass body scraped away to metal, then the scarlet speedster rolled out into traffic. A Chrysler-Nissan Jackrabbit hit it going east while a Honda truck rolled over its nose. Nothing exploded and no flames erupted, but the Jackrabbit's driver did vomit when he yanked open the Toro's door. I think he wanted to give the Toro's driver a piece of his mind, but ended up getting pieces of the driver's all over his white pants.

I took one last look at the Acura as I left the alley and turned down toward the Sound. I didn't recognize it nor the half-second glimpse I'd had of the driver's face while it was still in one piece. It wasn't the first time a professional had come after me with intensive homicidal mayhem on his mind, not by a long shot.

It was, however, the first time it took less than a full day for someone to decide to off me.

New records like that tend to make me nervous.

Cutting back and forth through the streets gave me the time I needed to make sure no one was following me. I did see another Toro, which spooked me a bit, but only because it was white and looked like a ghost of the car I'd killed. Other than that my trip through the heart of Seattle's urban gray jungle showed me nothing I'd not seen a million times before.

My haphazard course brought me into what that had once been my old stomping grounds. Normally I'd avoid that area if I were traveling with anything less than an army, mainly because the local gang and I did not get along too well. The Halloweenies—*Homo Sapiens Ludicrous*—were led by Charles the Red, but he'd been feeling poorly for the latter half of the summer. That allowed me to go where I wanted without being hassled.

As I entered the old neighborhood, I suddenly found myself wishing for the return of hostility. A stretch of Westlake from Seventh Avenue to Sixth Avenue had gotten a significant toasting during the Night of Fire. I remembered the blaze rather well, as I relive that evening in more nightmares than I care to count. Every fragment of that frightful landscape was burned into my memory in exquisite detail.

Standing at ground zero, I couldn't recognize a thing.

All the burned-out cars had been moved. Buildings had been refaced and the tarmac was more level and pristine than I'd ever seen it. Old, boarded-up apartments had been refurbished and, if the window decorations were any indication, already occupied by tenants. All the little grotty businesses on the street level had been replaced with sharp-looking boutiques with awnings.

And not a single street light had a hooker grafted to it.

Looking at the place where I'd grown up I finally understood the meaning of the word desecration.

From deep inside me, in that lightless cave where the Wolf Spirit chooses to dwell, the Old One growled deeply. *"Now you know what I saw in the Sleeping Time. Your people, Longtooth, they destroyed the lands I loved. They crushed my people and savaged my world. And for what?"*

"So you can complain."

"Excuse me, young man?" An old woman with a dowager's hump stopped in front of me and let her little metal grocery cart come to a rest. "Did you say something to me?"

I smiled at her. "No, I'm sorry. I was talking to myself."

She squinted her eyes and I half-expected her to recognize me. Something did flash through her eyes and I desperately searched for a name to attach to her face, but I came up a blank. She, on the other hand, pointed at my tie. "We owe you a great vote of thanks."

I cocked an eyebrow. "Excuse me?"

She jabbed my tie again. "You do work for Tucker and Bors, don't you?"

For at least this week, if I survive it. "Yes—sorry, I just started with them."

"Oh." She smiled in a kindly way. "Your company oversaw the rebuilding of this neighborhood. Did everything very fast. You'd never know it to look at it, but this place used to be horrible."

"I can believe it." I smiled at her, then stepped into the street. "Good evening, ma'am."

My smile grew as I saw a familiar narrow doorway with a pumpkin glaring down at me from above it. Tucker and Bors might have renewed this bit of urbanity after the Night of Fire, but some institutions were too sacred to be touched and too disgusting to die. The Jackal's Lantern was one of them.

I pulled open the door and reveled in the wall of smoke that poured over me. True, I'd never liked the place when I lived here, and the Halloweeners would have cut my heart out for invading their stronghold, but the Lantern was a life preserver to a drowning man. I let the door swing shut behind me and rubbed my hands together. Who says you can't come home again?

Well, whoever said it was right. The Lantern might have been too sacred to touch and too disgusting to die, but apparently it wasn't that hard to buy out.

The smoke didn't cling to my flesh like a toxic fog because it came from a smoke machine. The only light in the place still came from orange and black plastic pumpkins, but the wattage of the bulbs had been upped so you could see more than a few steps into the bar. They'd left the car fenders wrapped around the pillars the way I remembered, but all of them sparkled with a new coat of chrome. Barbed-wire jewelry still adorned various parts of mannequins, but all the rust had been polished off it and the razor wire was duller than your average chiphead's sense of reality. They still used cable drums as tables, but thick coats of epoxy sealed them, fossilizing graffiti left behind from when real people used to populate the place.

A fresh-faced girl walked up to me and smiled. The two dark triangles surrounding her eyes pointed down and an upward-pointing one hid her nose, but they'd been drawn in a dark green make-up, not the black the Halloweeners demanded. Her clothing, while stylishly tattered, had obviously been washed within the last week. Instead of looking like a zombie summoned from beyond the veil to serve in the Jackal's Lantern, she looked like a creature from the Casper-the-Friendly-Ghost school of haunting.

She smiled. "Welcome to Jack O's Lantern."

Something inside me died. "Jack O's Lantern?"

"The very same. Table for one?"

I blinked twice, then shook my head. "I'm meeting someone. A guy, mid-forties..."

Her nose wrinkled in distaste. "In the back. He's nursing a beer."

I smiled. "Bring us both another."

Leaving her to traipse through the corpgeeks in synthleather trying to look tough at the bar, I made my way toward the back. Even though I didn't like the changes, I had to admit the added light was an advantage. I'd never noticed how big the place really was, or how tall the scarecrow crucified on the back wall. Of course the smiley face didn't really suit him, but not many people got this far back.

I slid into the booth and noticed my name was still carved into the table top. Even the nine lines beneath it had been left intact. "Hi, Dempsey. How's it going?"

Dempsey gave me a shrug. He's one of those guys who looks like absolutely everyone else in the world—you'd forget him in a second if you had no reason to remember him. That, and the fact that he knows people who know just about everyone or everything in the world, make him very good at what he does. Dempsey is a private eye and for someone who's got no magic and no chrome, he's lasted a lot longer than he has any right to.

"Life goes on."

"Easy for you to say." I laughed lightly. "Dropping cold into the corp world means I have to wake up during this thing called morning."

Dempsey kept both his hands wrapped around his sweating beer bottle and appeared not to hear what I'd said. "I've done some checking, just like you asked."

"And?"

Another shrug lifted the shoulders of his Kevlar-lined trench coat. "There are plenty of folks who'd love to take a shot at Tucker and Bors for what they did to the Lantern here, but no one has anything that suggests TAB is angry at the Ancients. Moreover, there are no anti-metahuman groups with ties into TAB. This city positively stinks with Humanis Policlub members, but TAB is as clean as can be in that department."

I chewed my lower lip. "What are the chances some snake is living under a rock you haven't overturned yet?"

Dempsey showed no concern over my having questioned his ability. "Slim and none. The word whispered in some high dark places is that Andrew Bors had a daughter who goblinized right after the Awakening. Her daddy got her out of Seattle and has her staying in a mansion up on Vachon Island. After that, employees were screened for their attitudes toward metahumans through their employment questionnaire. You show signs of being a bigot, and you're out."

"Damn." I'd been inserted into Tucker and Bors because the Ancients had gone to Doctor Richard Raven with their suspicions that TAB was backing gangs making attacks on them. As the Ancients are a rather powerful and militarily adroit street gang, the invasion of TAB headquarters was a distinct possibility, and Raven started to work on the problem to forestall that from happening.

The waitress arrived with our beers, and I handed her some corp scrip. She looked at it and laughed. "You should've told me you're one of us."

I frowned. "Come again?"

"You're a TABbie, just like me. Tabbies get a discount." She scooped up the bill and headed back toward the front.

The Old One did not like being called a tabbie, but I managed to keep him in check. "Dempsey, I need you to keep digging on the policlub angle. This whole thing smacks of race hatred to me. Something has to be there."

He nodded. "Anything else?"

"Yeah. I need you to find out if anyone has a hit out on me."

"You mean besides La Plante?"

"Yeah, besides La Plante." It was an open secret that Etienne La Plante had a contract out on Dr. Raven and any of his associates. It was also well known that hurting a single hair on any of our heads would set Kid Stealth on the assassin—proving once and for all that capital punishment, if applied quickly and without mercy, could be a deterrent to crime. "Some gillette in a Toro tried to interest me in tarmac fusion. I declined, and he flipped his lid and had an accident."

Dempsey took it all in stride. "Do I still relay information through Valerie Valkyrie?"

I thought for a moment, then shook my head. "Takes too much time. If you get anything on the hit angle, call TAB and ask for Keith Wolverton."

"And if Mr. Wolverton is not at his desk and I want to leave a message?"

"Say a relation is coming to visit. The greater the danger, the more distant the relative."

Dempsey's eyes focused distantly, then came back with a twinkle in them. "So if I say Adam and Eve are coming to see you..."

"I'll know Stealth is freelancing again." I glanced at my watch and slid out of the booth. "Stay and have another if you want. I've got to go meet Raven."

Dempsey shook his head and left the booth. "If I stick around here, they'll come by and give me a new trench coat."

"It's hell being a fashion trendsetter." I looked at the refurbished bar and shuddered. "I think this is the first time I've been in here and not felt like taking a bath afterward."

"It's the only time I haven't needed a bath afterward," Dempsey replied. "Those were the days."

I signed for the tab up at the front, then walked a couple of blocks to the parking garage where I'd left my Fenris. The black coupe waited for me in a darkened corner of the basement like a feral creature hiding from the light. I disarmed the anti-theft devices—you only forget to do that once—and climbed in. I punched in the ignition code and cruised out into the light evening traffic.

The trip to Raven's headquarters took longer than it should have because of the series of turns and cutbacks I used to make sure no one was following me. After Raven and the rest of our crew had done various things to anger some of the more powerful individuals in the sprawl, paranoia had become a survival trait. Just because Kid Stealth would descend like a bloody avenger on anyone bothering us did not mean we were inviolate. Insanity becomes a courtroom defense because lots of folks do irrational things, and I had no desire to have bits of me in baggies labeled Exhibit A.

I parked the Fenris in the basement garage below Raven's brownstone, then took the stairs two at a time as I climbed to the main floor. Adjusting my tie and rolling down my sleeves, I marched straight to Raven's office and paused in the doorway. "Would have been here sooner, Doc, but someone wanted me to play immovable object to their irresistible force."

Raven leaned back in his black leather chair, pressed his hands together and rested his index fingers against his lips. Seated there in a custom-built chair, behind his individually hand-crafted desk, he looked normally proportioned. The pointed tips of elven ears jutted up through his long black hair as the only clues to his heritage. If not for that, his coppery skin, high cheekbones, and broad-shouldered, muscular build would have marked him as an Amerind.

His dark eyes focused above and beyond me, but I found myself entranced by their steady gaze. The blues and reds weaving through them in an aurora-like fashion flickered past in what I imagined was a mirror of how quickly thoughts strobed through his brain. The lights slowed, then he closed his eyes and I felt myself in control of my own mind again.

"Interesting." His hands fell away from his mouth as he leaned forward and stood. "I will want a full report later, of course, but I should introduce you to our clients. This is Sting and her lieutenant, Green Lucifer."

Elven women are often described with plant imagery, but with Sting you'd have to make that an industrial plant. Sure, she was long and lean like most of them, but you could only describe her as willowy if you thought rebar swayed in light breezes. I'd heard she had a temper to match her fiery mane, and her yellow Opticon eyes certainly reflected none of the warmth in her soul—if she even had one. She had an edge to her that made it clear why she was running the Ancients, but likewise told me why, though she was attractive, I didn't find her seductive.

"My pleasure." I smiled but didn't offer her my hand. I knew her street name had been earned because of the metal claws that could shoot from the backs of her hands and rake through flesh like it was water.

"So you're Wolfgang Kies. Makes sense, I guess."

Before I could even begin to work my way through the maze of tone and inference in her words, the nearly imperceptible stiffening of her partner drew my attention to him. Unlike Raven, Green Lucifer had the typical starveling build of an elf. His chin, or underabundance of it, suggested a character flaw that the burning light in his gray eyes used as fuel. Green Lucifer clearly did not like the fact that Sting had paid me any notice at all, and he was aching for any opening to exert his territorial rights. That told me they were more than just partners in power, and that Green Lucifer was the jealous type.

I immediately put him on the list of folks I didn't want in possession of a chainsaw while my back was turned.

"Mr. Kies, or 'Mr. Wolverton,' " he began with mock sincerity, "what have you learned?"

I stared at him for a second, then turned to face Raven. "I spent most of the day getting situated. Valerie's transferring Mike Kant to Shanghai was accepted without question, as was my being sent in to replace him. Ms. Terpstra acts more like a school marm than a supervisor, but Bill Frid is helping me get squared away in Kant's office. In fact, I've not really had to do anything because Frid did it all while showing me what I'm supposed to do."

Raven sank back in his chair again. "Good. What about this attempt on your life?"

The mention of an assassination attempt caused the fourth individual in the room to take conscious notice of the conversation.

Kid Stealth, sitting back on his haunches, turned his head to watch me. The light flashed off his Zeiss eyes and his brows nearly touched as they pointed down at his nose. I knew better than to think he was concerned about me—he could see I'd survived—but his concentration came from his desire to hear how a rival assassin had failed in his job.

Having Stealth crouched behind Green Lucifer and Greenie surreptitiously trying to keep an eye on him made me feel loads better.

"I found a couple of things in some files and made copies of them. I tossed them into my trash basket, then bagged the litter and dropped it in the disposal chute. After work, I went back around to the alley and fished the bag out."

I reached into my back pocket and retrieved the folded-over papers. "They're several pages of receipts Kant got while, as nearly as I can figure, making money drops to the folks fighting the Ancients."

Green Lucifer's face darkened. "That's hardly a substantial amount of evidence, Mr. Kies." Scorn rolled from his words like crude oil off a duck's back.

I continued to speak to Raven alone. "It has to be something, because a razorboy in an Acura Toro mistook me for an on-ramp."

"Did you get anything from him?" Raven asked.

"Sorry, Doc. The dead don't like talking to me. Chances are my cover is blown. I think we should consider taking me out of there."

Raven nodded solemnly. "If you think it best."

Green Lucifer hammered a fist into the arm of his red leather chair. "This is too important and has taken too long to set up just to let him drop it like this. We're being systematically exterminated. Order him to remain in place."

Raven leaned forward and rested his forearms on the desk. "Being new here, you do not understand—"

"I understand this human operative of yours has no stake in or concern about elven lives being lost." Green Lucifer gave me a gray-eyed stare that started the Old One growling defiantly in the back of my mind. "He's your employee. Order him back in."

"You do *not* understand," Raven repeated slowly. The threat arced like lightning in his words and anger reverberated like thunder in his voice. "These people are not my employees. They are my aides, my companions, my friends, and my allies. They work with me, not for me. What they do, they do because I ask, not order. I have never found myself called to doubt their judgment or their courage or their compassion. If Wolf believes his life is in danger, then I believe that as well."

Green Lucifer managed to hold his composure better than the other half-dozen people I'd seen invoke Raven's wrath like that. He settled back into his chair like a steel beam being bent by the inexorable progress of a glacier, but his defiance did not drain away. Still, he knew better than to open his mouth.

His tone lightening only slightly, Doc continued. "Wolf is fully cognizant of your situation. He knows that your alternative to a peaceful solution to this problem is for the Ancients to wage war with Tucker and Bors, and that is not likely to be pretty. It is for the sake of your lives, and the lives of the innocents who might be caught in any crossfire, that we began this investigation. Wolf knows I would not ask him to return there unless I believed the risk was justified, but if he chooses to decline my request, I will think no less of him, and my confidence in him will not diminish."

I'd have said I was leaving Seattle for Japan if I thought it would deepen the scowl on Green Lucifer's face, and I knew Raven would back my play unquestioningly. I started piecing together the perfect way to drop that bit of information on Greenie, but I caught Sting's eye and saw a hopeless determination in her expression and shifting posture.

I knew the Ancients had gone through a nasty battle recently with another street gang. The Ancients, supposedly under direction from someone in TAB, had tried to expand their territory into the turf held by the Meat Junkies. The battle had gotten nasty fast, and looked really grim for the Ancients when an ork sniper killed their leader. At that moment, however, Green Lucifer smoked the sniper and used his rifle to ace the Meat Junkies' top dog.

Both gangs retreated to lick their wounds, but over the following weeks other gangs had taken shots at the Ancients. That wouldn't have attracted any attention except that no one was picking on the similarly weakened Meat Junkies, and the Junkies themselves started sporting very new and very expensive guns and bikes. As TAB had stopped bankrolling the Ancients, anyone with more than two working brain cells could deduce a shift in corporate policy that was not beneficial to the elves.

Sting clearly knew her gang had to deal with the problem of TAB's shifting loyalties or the Ancients would become fodder for the "Obits and Old Bits" newsfax files. If Raven couldn't help her—and looking for outside help, even from another elf, showed how desperate she saw the situation to be—she had to go to war. Given that TAB, like any other multinat, had its own army, long odds for betting on the gang were not hard to find.

Even knowing that, she would have no choice. If she didn't go to war, she'd be replaced by someone who would. The outcome would be the same, but when you whisper "I told you so," from inside a grave, very few folks listen or care.

"Actually, Doc, I have Dempsey looking into the contract angle. That could be a shortcut to whoever is ramrodding this campaign. If I bow out, the bait will be gone. I'll just be more careful." I glanced over at Sting. "As I'm replacing Kant and he appeared to be the bossman's courier of choice, I should see some action soon. If we let it slip that you're bidding on a shipment of arms coming into Seattle, our man should move to procure that shipment before you."

Raven smiled. "If someone wants you dead, Dempsey will find out. Good choice, Wolf."

I painted a wide smile on my face and proudly displayed it for Green Lucifer. He started to get a bit restive in his chair, but Stealth's flesh and blood right arm snaked over the back of the chair and his shoulder. Pointing in my direction, it stopped just short of Greenie's face. From the sleeve of Stealth's waist-cut coat, a blocky little derringer slid down to fill his palm. The delivery device retracted silently, then Stealth arced the gun across the room to me.

I caught it gingerly. "What's this?"

Stealth didn't exactly smile, but his expression grew as pleasant as I've ever seen it sans anyone actually dying in the vicinity. "Richard said he found your being unarmed disturbing. I customized a design based on a Remington Double Derringer[1]. I expanded the caliber to .50 and have crafted some of your 'silver' bullets to fit it. It is single action. You get two shots."

I turned the pistol over in my hand, then slipped it into my pocket. Getting it into TAB would not be a problem, and I could feel safe even without nearby manhole covers. "Thank you, maestro."

I knew it was loaded because Stealth wouldn't have it any other way. The Old One knew it too, and snarled something derisive about my dependence on the tainted and artificial when his tools were so pure and natural. The only problem with the Old One and the abilities he lent me in times of need was that I couldn't always be certain I would remain in control of my actions. In light of that, using a hand-detonated nuclear bomb could be seen to have an upside.

"So, what is your next step?" Green Lucifer leaned forward and leaned his chin on his right hand.

"Well, tonight I'm going to go check on a former client, Lynn Ingold. That's a very important part of this case." I saw Raven suppress a smile. Lynn Ingold was a woman we had rescued from La Plante earlier in the summer. She and I had begun seeing one another and I'd been planning to take her out to a Seadogs[2] game well before the TAB problem came up. "Then, tomorrow, I return to work and wait."

---

[1] Because Stealth knows I like using a Beretta Viper and an HK MP-9—both of which he thinks should be in a museum—he's decided I can't really handle any weapon crafted for use in the twenty-first century. Taking the specs for a derringer from some docudrama about the old, old West (I think it was called Deadlands), he manufactured the gun for me. I mean, I was glad to have it, and even happier that he had a hobby, but I kind of wished his hobby was more benign, like model trains. Then again, I didn't really want to see what the Murder Machine would do with model trains.

His face screwed into a sour expression, as if he'd been sucking sulfur schnapps through a straw. "We can't afford to wait long."

Raven looked over at Stealth. "Kid Stealth has agreed to let it be known that he and his Redwings are just waiting for someone to start shooting at you so they can raid undefended territory. Again, this steps up the pressure on TAB, and will make it easier to find out who is behind all this."

"Fine, Raven, just so long as you know we won't wait until forever." Greenie leaned back in his chair and steepled his fingers. "You have until Fri..."

Sting laid her right hand on his left arm. "You have as long as you need at this point. If things change, I'll let you know."

Greenie didn't like that very much, but he and Sting exchanged a pair of glances I can only describe as cobra and mongoose. I smiled broadly at his discomfort, earning myself a big jump on his enemies list, I do not doubt, and nodded to her. "We'll get you results."

"Good, Mr. Kies." She looked me up from my toes to the tippy-top of my head and back down. "Just so you know, if they do get you, Stealth will have all the help he needs in avenging you."

Damn, I just love it when women talk lethal.

Lynn didn't talk lethal to me, but she did say some other things that made me think I'd died and gone to heaven. I was tired enough in the morning that I almost slay-tested Stealth's pistol on my alarm clock. I refrained because I was too lazy to want to patch the hole I knew a bullet would leave in my wall—and that of the other two tenants on this floor—and dropped back to sleep for another half-hour.

The Blavatskys downstairs woke me up for the second time with a loud discussion of things that shouldn't be mentioned in daylight. After a quick shower and shave, I headed downtown to Tucker and Bors. I arrived ten minutes late and, as an afterthought, I considered what a good idea that might have been. Whoever had set me up to be killed would probably faint when he saw me come strolling in.

In fact, the only person who seemed to notice me was the matronly Ms. Terpstra. She stared at me hard enough to melt my brain, but I scampered to my cubicle too quickly for her to properly focus her powers. On my monitor I read the note she had sent me at precisely 9:00:01: *Punctuality is a virtue, and the virtuous are rewarded.* ~~Those without virtue face perdition.~~

---

[2] I had gotten the feeling, at the time we rescued Lynn, that she was special. The fact that she was a Seadogs fan proved it. And I do mean she was a Seadogs fan—I don't think I ever heard her call the team the Mariners.

Bill Frid appeared at the doorway to my private domain and handed me a steaming cup of soykaf. "I see you got a perdition memo."

I accepted the soykaf and sipped. "Is that bad?"

"Naw, wait until you get an 'eternal damnation' note. That's bad. She's been in a bad mood since Reverend Roberts stopped doing video."

A jovial guy, Bill had a double-chin and curly blond hair that made him look softer than I figured he saw himself. Right from the start I'd pegged him as one of those types who's learned all the shortcuts to getting things done. They're workhorses, and no corp could get anything done without them, but contempt for the bureaucracy barred them from ever getting into the power structure.

"You look tired. You feel okay?" he asked.

I shrugged. "Went to the 'Dogs game last night."

"Extra innings?"

"Yeah." I smiled. "Oh, wait, you mean the game. No, just eight and a half. Mackelroy caught one on the warning track in center, then threw out the runner from third on a one-hopper to end the game. It was great."

Bill sipped his soykaf. "Good, good. We'll have to take in a game some time."

I nodded. "Yeah. Let's do it when we're on some errand for old TAB and we can get them to spring for a 'business lunch.' "

"I like it." He gave me a conspiratorial wink, then looked up and nodded. "The wicked witch of the paycheck is watching, so I'll get back to my workstation. If you need anything, just let me know."

"Thanks, Bill."

Left to my own devices, I had to figure out what I was supposed to do. I really had no idea what Kant's duties had been, and even Frid had been fairly vague. As nearly as I could make out, Kant was part troubleshooter, part confidential courier. Even when I called up a log of things Kant had done in the past two weeks, it looked like most of his time had been spent sitting on his hands.

Fully aware that idle hands are the devil's playthings—a concept that I was certain Ms. Terpstra detested—I pulled a blank manila folder from my desk drawer and placed the employment and location policy agreements I'd signed the previous day into it. I labeled the file "Wolverton, Keith" and stuck it behind the Wolcott Trucking file.

Feeling fairly satisfied with myself, I noted, to my chagrin, that I had another two hours to kill before the lunch wagon arrived outside. I looked at the stack of datachips on the corner of the desk, but all of them dealt with statistics, math, and probability modeling, so I just couldn't bring myself to pop one of them into the computer. Making a mental note to have Valerie get me games that would work on this monster, I started exploring the Interactive Building Directory.

By the time the telecom beeped and saved me, I'd succeeded in memorizing the names and divisions for all TAB employees A to J in the building. "Keith Wolverton here."

"I have good news and bad news for you." Dempsey was one of the few people who sounded better on the telecom than in person. "What's your pleasure?"

Seeing Ms. Terpstra glowering in my direction, I raised my voice a bit so she could hear. "Well, Doctor, will the patient live?"

"Mr. Kies is in no danger, beyond those expected for a man in his line of work. Whatever symptoms he thought he had, he was mistaken."

"And the bad news."

"No one's out to ace Wolf, but there's five thousand nuyen on your head, Mr. Wolverton."

Someone wanted Keith Wolverton hit? Why? He didn't exist forty-eight hours ago. "Your source was impeccable as usual, I assume?"

Dempsey grunted out a laugh. "The grieving widow was spending the five hundred nuyen down payment to blot out the memory of her late squeeze. Closed casket ceremony, you know."

"At least they could go for a shorter box and save money." I drank some more of the soykaf. "You have a name for the patron of this poor departed soul?"

"Are you sitting down and alone?"

I looked at the monitor and saw a message presenting itself to me, letter by letter. "Only my very wonderful supervisor, Ms. Terpstra, reminding me that I should not be taking personal calls via the wonders of binary magic."

"Probably safe, then. The name William Frid mean anything to you?"

I suddenly wondered if soykaf could cover the taste of arsenic. I assumed I would find out shortly. "Rings a bell. Thanks. Dempsey."

"No sweat, chummer. Tell me, is your Ms. Terpstra heavy-set, first name Agnes?"

I shrugged. "Hit on the first, and an 'A' for a first initial on her nameplate. Why?"

"No real reason." I could see Dempsey smiling like a fox in some dark telecom booth. "Heard that was the handle she'd adopted. Always wondered where she'd ended up after the Mitsuhama embezzlement scam. Watch your paycheck."

"Got it, Dempsey. I owe you big time."

"You'll be hearing from me."

"Anytime, bud, anytime."

I broke the connection and glanced over at Bill's cubicle. Braving the harsh look on Ms. Terpstra's face, I walked over there and crouched down at Bill's side. "Bill, I need some help."

His smile slowly died as the seriousness in my voice got to him. "Sure, Keith, what is it?"

I shook my head. "Not here. It's personal. I'm new in town, and there was this woman last night..."

He patted me on the shoulder. "You're right, not here. C'mon."

He led the way past the dragon lady to the men's room. We quickly checked the stalls for lurkers, then flipped the lock. Leaning back against a sink, Bill smiled with mild amusement. "Now, what's the problem?"

I shrugged. "The problem is that this woman is upset because the man you hired to kill me got dead himself in the attempt." I filled my right hand with Stealth's pistol. "That almost ruined my day. Now explain to me why I don't want to ruin yours."

Bill's eyes grew wider than the bore of the pistol he was staring at. "No, no, no, you have it all wrong."

"That's correct about one of the two of us." I tore the loop-towel across the back part of the loop and started pulling it down in long lengths.

His blue pupils rolled around like a chalk-mark on a cue ball. "What's that for?"

"You're going to wrap it around your head so the brains don't splatter when I shoot you." I let my smile die except for a nervous twitch at the corner that convinced him I meant business. "No need to make the janitor's job any tougher."

"Oh God, oh God, oh God." Frid dropped to his knees. "I don't want to die."

"Good, then tell me everything you know about the elves and TAB."

"What?" He looked at me with absolute terror in his eyes. "What are you talking about?"

"The Ancients."

"Who?"

"Damn it!" He flinched as I swore. "Why'd you want me killed?"

"I didn't want you killed. I just wanted you, ah, roughed up." His thick lips quivered in a way that told me he had to be telling the truth.

"Offering someone five thousand nuyen to rough me up is a bit much."

He looked crestfallen. "How was I supposed to know? I went down to Damian's and offered a guy five grand to do a job, then I gave him five hundred and the copy of your picture I got from security. I just wanted you put out of action for a week or so."

I frowned. "I'm still waiting for a 'why' here, chummer."

"Because I wanted your job. Kant gets all sorts of courier jobs, and he gets bonuses." He looked down at the floor and clasped his hands in an attitude of prayer. "You have to believe me."

"No, chummer," I said, tossing him the towel. "You have to convince me. What do you know about Kant's courier actions?"

"Oh, God, you're from Auditing, aren't you?" Frid wilted, and his shoulders slumped forward. "Kant said he dealt with shadow projects."

Shadow projects. Anything a corp wanted to do without the shareholders or the government knowing about it. Projects that never showed up on the books, but got money funneled to them through fake projects and promotions. Given all the interlocking directorates and vertical integration within the corporate world, tracking down the source of funding for almost anything was impossible. For shadow projects, it was that much more so.

And funding a war against the Ancients definitely sounded like a shadow project to me.

"Okay, Bill, let's take this slowly. Kant made three courier runs recently. One was on the twenty-third of last month. This month he did one on the seventh and the other on the twelfth. Enlighten me."

Sweat poured from his forehead and down his face. "I don't know."

"You'll look good in a turban, you know."

"Keith, I don't know. Honest, I don't."

I dropped down onto my haunches and parked the derringer a centimeter or so from the tip of his nose. "You've got two strikes against you, you weasel. You figured you'd get Kant's job and his bonuses, and you still think you can swing some sort of deal out of this..." I paused to let him consider how much his greed might cost him. "Well, chummer, you can. I only care about that one job. It involves elves and only local travel."

I tapped his nose with the gun. "Now what'll it be? True Confessions, or die knowing that whatever you had for breakfast was your last meal."

"Oh God, oh God, oh God. Ah, ah..." He screwed his eyes shut. "I don't know for sure, Keith. All those jobs went through Ms. Terpstra. Please believe me."

I'd seen enough men crumble in my time to know Frid's marshmallow center was leaking through all the cracks in him. He had to be telling the truth, which meant I had a new nut to crack. I wouldn't have thought Ms. Terpstra capable of running a shadow project, but with Dempsey's cautionary tale about her, anything was possible.

"Okay, Bill, this is the way things go down. You're going home sick, right now." The man nodded like a child promising Santa he'd be good. "If I find you've been lying to me you can consider our little talk here as the opening scene of the worst nightmare you've ever had." I slipped the gun back into my pocket. "Get out of here."

Back in the office, I leaned forward on Ms. Terpstra's desk. "Agnes, I really need to know who asked you to give courier jobs concerning the demise of the Ancients to Mike Kant."

Ms. Terpstra's head jerked around as if I'd gaffed her in a gill and yanked her from the Sound. "Mr. Wolverton, I have no idea what you are talking about. How dare you address me in such a familiar manner?"

I gave her my best I-know-lots-you-don't-want-to-have-known smiles. "Is it that Tucker and Bors has a better retirement policy, or did you just tire of the Mitsuhama corporate grind? Audits after an embezzlement can be so tedious, don't you think, Aggie?" From the sour look that answered my question, I realized whoever had her running a shadow project was using the same or similar blackmail evidence to keep her in line.

"You play well, Mr. Wolverton, but you will meet your match." She gave me a cold smile. "Benbrook, Sidney M."

"Benbrook?" I frowned as I tried to remember his entry from the directory. "Benbrook is in Marketing! Why would Marketing have a shadow project?"

"Mine is not to wonder why..."

"Yeah, what you do is steal and fly." I shook my head. "Thank you for your help, Ms. Terpstra. You make me proud to be a TABbie."

Sidney Benbrook looked exactly the way you'd expect someone with that name would. The Interactive Building Directory showed me a tall, cadaverously slender man with dark hair so thin that when he combed it from right to left over his scalp it could have been deciphered by a barcode reader. His deeply set eyes remained hidden in shadow and, along with his corpse-like pallor, accentuated the impression that he had died late in the last century.

As I entered the darkened sanctuary of his office, I knew, almost immediately, that no matter how benign or un-salesperson-like he looked, he was at the core of the problem with the Ancients.

Benbrook sat in a big padded chair centered on a raised dais at the end of a narrow canyon formed by walls of computers and other electronic equipment. Little amber and red lights flashed off and on across the faces of the machines, enclosing him in a star field with constantly shifting constellations. Cables crisscrossed the area behind him and one snaked out from the tangle to jack into his skull behind his left ear.

Like a spider aware of a fly's careless tread upon its web, Benbrook swiveled his chair around toward me as I entered the room. I had not tried to be particularly quiet, but his reaction unnerved me. His head came up and his torso came around instantly, but his eyes took their time in focusing down on me.

"You're Sidney Benbrook?"

"I know that. Who are you?" His voice came out as a harsh croak, as if he was entirely unused to speaking to another person. "I did not send for you."

I'd seen other wireheads who were tied even tighter to their machines, but never in a corporate setting like this. I held my hands up in the universal sign of surrender. "I'm Keith Wolverton. I'm taking Kant's place. Thought we should be acquainted in case you need anything done."

"Done?"

I gave him my best hey-we're-all-in-the-know-here smile. "Aggie told me Kant did courier jobs for you, all vapor, no flash. She says there's bonus money in it, and she turned me on to the deal for a rounding error. She told me it could be dangerous, but I told her I wasn't afraid of any dandelion-chewers."

"Dande...yes, elves." Benbrook froze—the only motion from his end of the room coming from the computer light show. "I find it disturbing, Mr. Wolverton, that your computer records appear never to have been tampered with. How do you explain that?"

My smile broadened. "You can figure I've made a career of keeping my nose very clean, or you can assume that I came across Kant's action independently, and decided I'd like to milk the cash cow myself for a while."

"Tucker and Bors takes a dim view of extortion, Mr. Wolverton."

"I said 'milk' not 'slaughter.' You've been devoting significant resources to destroying a certain population of elves. If you happen to know someone who's paying for elven scalps, I might know people who would be willing to create a supply to satisfy that demand."

"You small-minded bigot. Elves and scalps and bounties are not important." Benbrook's eyes reflected the flashing computer lights around him. "Do you think these people might be able to get rid of the Ancients?"

I frowned. "You have me confused. You said scalps aren't important, but you want someone to 'get rid' of the Ancients?"

"That is correct."

"But you don't mean 'get rid of,' as synonymous with kill?"

He frowned, which was rather scary, given the gangrenous pallor of his skin. "I mean it as in move, dispense with, create a decreased population concentration of."

I shrugged. "That says kill to me."

"Whatever!" Fingers clicked and clacked across an illusory keyboard. "I need to affect a ten percent reduction in the elven population of the Denny Park zone by the end of the fiscal year. Is that possible?"

Denny Park marked the southwest edge of the territory the Ancients claimed as their own. Their recent battle with the Meat Junkies was over a piece of turf to the west of that area. That zone was one of the least habitable areas in the Seattle elven enclave, but it was the Ancients' stronghold.

"Possible, yes, but that will be a very tough block of ice to salt." Something was not adding up because I wasn't hearing Humanis Policlub rhetoric coming at me. In fact, Benbrook had actually accused me of being anti-elf. "If you don't care how I get rid of the elves, why do you want that particular piece of real estate?"

His right hand rose from the arm of the chair and, with index finger pointing down, rotated slowly to indicate I should turn around. As I did so, a huge display screen slid down from the false ceiling, flickered to life and shared computer graphics of Seattle with me. As I watched, the image swooped lower, like a helicopter sailing down through vector-graphic canyons. As it headed north from downtown it hit a block of solid green: the Ancients' turf.

The image dissolved into a series of numbers. They scrolled past fairly quickly, but I caught bits and pieces of things. It looked to be a cost comparison between two programs, and then it shifted over into a point by point comparison of population. Outlined in red, and pulsing in time with my heartbeat, I saw the approximate number of elves living in the Denny Park area of Seattle.

I turned back. "I still don't get it. Why are you paying to have elves scragged?"

"It's obvious." Benbrook stared at me as if I was an idiot. "Demographics."

I remembered the datachips in Kant's workplace, then stared at Benbrook unbelieving. "You're killing them because of numbers?"

The red pulsing light burned off and on in his eyes. "Those are not just numbers, Mr. Wolverton. They are the very lifeblood of this company. Those numbers affect our bottom line. That means those numbers determine how much we can pay you and how much you get in your pension plan and what your profit sharing statement will look like. Those numbers are the most important numbers in the world."

Though to look at him I'd not have thought it possible, Benbrook rose from his chair and pointed a scarecrow finger at me. "You will forever be doomed to be nothing but a slave chip in the engines of industry if you fail to understand how important those numbers are. On the right, you have the demographics and psychographics of the group the North American Testing Agency uses to test market our products."

His shoulders hunched and his hands rubbed together like those of a miser aching to fondle credsticks. "They determine what we produce, when we produce it, what it looks like, what it tastes like, what it smells and feels like, and how much we can charge for it. The shift of a percentage point or two in the approval rating for a product can cause us to retool a factory or to scrap a line altogether. NATA's test group is a fickle mistress whom we labor to please, yet pay whether our results satisfy or anger."

His eyes went to the screen. "I will free us of our dependence on NATA and their group. The Denny Park District is identical to their area except for one thing. We have too many elves. Once I can eliminate enough of them, we'll have our own captive market here. I can create a division that will perform like NATA, and we will wrest the dataflow away from them. Our costs will be a fraction of what they were for research, and we can charge others for using our group, which will reverse a negative cash flow in my division."

I shook myself to clear my head of his missionary message. "You want to kill elves so you can taste-test chocolate bars in the sprawl?"

"Crudely put, but I believe you have a grasp on reality."

"Oh, I've got more than a grasp on reality, chummer." I pointed back toward the flashing red numbers. "You're trying to lower the river when what you need to do is raise the bridge!"

He shook his head. "I tried that. I paid the Ancients to take more territory outside Denny Park. It would have created a more even distribution, but they failed."

"No!" I slowly started drifting toward his silicon altar. "Have you seen what TAB did on Westlake?" Benbrook paused as if unable to remember the project or unable to comprehend why I would mention it. "That was the construction division. They are not my concern. Irrelevant."

"Very relevant, Mr. Benbrook." I channeled the Old One's growl of outrage into my voice. "You are seeking to destroy something when you could make it all so much better. You are blowing a perfect chance to do more than just develop one new division."

His hawk-stare bored in at me as he slowly sat. "Explain."

As he called my bluff, I panicked for a half-second.

The Old One came to my rescue as he translated all the demographic statistics into his own view of the world. Suddenly I saw Seattle as it must have been before men set foot on the continent. The Old One and his brothers knew where the deer would drink. They knew what plants would flower or bear fruit when—attracting animals for the hunt. Had it been in their power, they would have created more tree stands to keep their animals safe in the winter and more meadows to feed them in the summer.

"It's fairly simple, really," I said. "You can rebuild sections of the Denny Park area. Encourage people who will even up the demographic mix to move in. You'll have your own little population from which to draw focus groups. You can have your own stores where you can test product placement. You can employ some of the people and raise or lower their income to levels appropriate for whatever you want to test. You can create your own little world, and it will pump out endless streams of data for you to analyze, all the while saving money."

His face had begun to become positively animated as I started to talk. I thought I almost had him with the "streams of data" line, but something changed. The light in his eyes died. Settling his angular, skeletal body into his chair, he became an electronic spider again.

"Projections show the cost of building up that area will be more expensive than wiping out the Ancients."

I drew the pistol. "Factor in the cost of your own funeral."

He slowly shook his head. "Employee contract, page two, section six, paragraph three prohibits one employee from threatening another with deadly force."

"I quit."

"Now that I think of it, your suggestion has some merit."

I nodded solemnly. "Those expenses can be charged back against the fees of clients who use your market testing. And you can make the changes through the construction divisions, guaranteeing the head of that division a tidy profit on the construction work, while the work is done at a below market rate for you."

Benbrook's head started bobbing in time with music that I could not hear. "Yes, that could work. As you said, I would have focus groups and store fronts to test product placement." His eyes flicked up at me. "These people would have children, and I would have to educate them, correct?"

"You better believe it."

"Excellent. We diversify into children's products."

I winked at him. "You build schools and sports facilities. You improve Denny Park and..."

"And we create sports leagues for employees. We get them exercising, which will cut health insurance costs. And they will all be wearing clothing they buy from us that has our trademark names emblazoned on them."

"Now you're cooking."

He stopped hearing me. "And we create Brandname Loyalty Indoctrination Centers. We inculcate the children in the ways of only buying our products. We can wire every home for closed-circuit televisions that will display our ads..."

His eyes started to glaze over orgasmically, so I cocked the pistol and brought him out of it prematurely. "Hey, Sparky, you also have to pay the Ancients to patrol the area so no one can infiltrate it, right?"

Benbrook hesitated, then nodded. "We can get them uniforms..."

"Do you really want to see what they would do with uniforms?"

"No, perhaps not. Plausible deniability can cut liability." His eyes went blank for a moment, then he smiled. "Yes, I think this has a higher profit potential because of the retail sales and the information development angles. It will work."

"Good for you." My eyes narrowed and became the same silver shade as the wolf's-head pendant I wear at my throat. "Listen, Moses, there's only one more thing you have to do before you can lead your people to the promised land."

"And that is?"

"You want to adjust the environment of a profit center because the psychographics are set to take it into a negative growth curve." I gave him a smile that was all mayhem and arson.

"That sounds unsatisfactory. I'm sure, in return for your service here, I can do something about it." His hands hung in space as if poised over the keyboard. "Explain."

I smiled. "Ever heard of a place called Jack O's Lantern?"

I breathed in and got a nose full of noxious vapor that convinced me someone was burning tires for warmth in the middle of the Jackal's Lantern. Of course I couldn't see that far into the place, but I felt happy enough that I was willing to stumble blindly toward the back. Lucky for me, a blond waitress named Pia saw me groping about and slipped her arm through mine.

"The elves said they were waiting for you, Wolf." Despite the black makeup turning her face into a nightmare pumpkin mask, the smile she gave me made my socks roll right up and down. "I can be softer than she is, and I'm much prettier than he is."

"No disputing that." I returned her smile. "It's business with them, darling."

"All work and no play will make Wolf a dull boy."

"And you're the whetstone that will sharpen me up?"

"We can rub our bodies against each other and see." She laughed lightly as we reached the back of the bar. "A Henry Weinhard's for you, Mr. Kies?"

"In the bottle, no glass." I slid into the booth across from Sting and Green Lucifer. "Anything for you?" Sting shook her head and Pia vanished into the billowing cloud of smoke. Green Lucifer wrinkled his nose, looked around, then snarled at me, "Why did you demand we come to this dump?"

"I wanted to see you in your natural habitat." I glanced over at Sting. "Here's the deal: TAB is going to rebuild some housing in your turf and generally upgrade the Denny Park area. They'll pay you to keep things under control. The new housing will go half to folks already there, and half to people they bring in."

As Sting considered what I had told her and Green Lucifer practiced his "I'm mean and nasty" look on me, Pia arrived with my beer. I saw she'd written her number on the napkin she put beneath the sweating bottle and I gave her a wink. I twisted the cap off the bottle with my left hand, drank, then set the bottle down again and frowned at Green Lucifer. "Well, pay her."

He blinked his big elf eyes at me. "What?"

"And tip her well, too. I'm a big tipper."

Pia smiled and gave me a wink. "Thank you, Mr. Kies."

Green Lucifer became obstreperous. "If you think..." Sting nudged him with an elbow. Grimacing, Green Lucifer pulled out a couple of credsticks and started to sort through them for one sufficiently big enough to pay for my beer. A light cough from Sting added a pair of twins to it and all three ended up deposited on the tray Pia carried. With a broad smile and a nod of thanks to Sting, Pia retreated from sight.

I drank a bit more. "What do you think?"

Sting's eyes narrowed into lifeless amber wedges. "Do you think the deal will be honored for a long time?"

I shrugged and my left thumb traced the letters of my name in the table. "If they invest in the project as they are supposed to do, yes, they will stay there for a long time. If not, we'll know soon enough to forestall more trouble of the type you've been through. It's chancy, but if Raven thought it was going to blow up in our faces, he wouldn't have asked you to meet me here. Is it a go?"

Sting nodded.

"Good." I started to smile and feel proud of myself, but Green Lucifer went and spoiled it. His face scrunched up as if he were about to throw a temper tantrum, but then the expression eased everywhere except around his eyes. "And now the minority report?"

"I just want one thing from you, Kies." He hissed the last letter of my name like a snake. "Who was behind the plot to kill us?"

I shook my head. "Not part of the deal. You hired us to stop them, not mount them on a trophy wall."

He sneered at me. "You needn't worry, we'll do our own killing."

"Hey, Greenie, this is the real world." I let the Old One growl through my throat as I rubbed my right hand over my silver wolf's-head pendant. "Any of us with Raven are willing to do wetwork, but not to salve your ego. So, chummer, you've got what you've got."

"What I've got is an anti-elf racist protecting more of the same." He balled his fists and hammered them on the table, nearly upsetting my beer. "We've had people dying out there. We've had elven blood running in the streets. Someone has to pay."

My eyes started a slow shift from green to silver, with the black Killer Rings circling the iris. "Someone is paying. TAB is paying a wergeld that will make things better for your people."

"Tell that to the dead."

My right hand contracted into a fist. "I've seen the streets run with blood, chummer, and I've leaked my fair share into them, too. It's damned easy to call for blood when you aren't going to be the one shedding it. And you can't tell me, Greenie, that a single death at TAB will make life better for those who live in Denny Park."

He started to reply hotly, but Sting stopped him. "Your deal is acceptable and, if TAB upholds its part of the bargain, we will let the matter drop." She glared at Greenie, and he nodded his head as much as his stony rage made possible. "We are indebted to you and Raven and even your friend, Dempsey."

"Raven will send you a bill," I said, smiling, "and you probably already have a message from Dempsey waiting for you at your crib."

I used the bottle cap in my left hand to scratch a tenth line beneath my name, then snapped Green Lucifer's head back with a right jab. He bounced off the rear of the booth, then his forehead dented the table just before his unconscious form slid beneath it.

"I, on the other hand, consider us even."

DESIGNATED HITTER

ONE

The pitch came screaming in at 153 kph, but the black man's bat whipped around yet faster. With a bone-breaking *crack*, the baseball shot away like a satellite planted on top of an Ares booster rocket. I watched the white pellet sail off on its ballistic arc through the Seattle Kingdome's still atmosphere. It dwindled and disappeared over the top of the Dominion Pizza sign out at the 131-meter mark. The centerfielder just waved at the ball as it flew by.

I clapped appreciatively as the hitter left the batting cage. "Damn, Spike, that was a shot. One thirty-one and it cleared the fence clean."

Jimmy "Spike" Mackelroy smiled broadly. "Yeah, I got good wood on that one." He flipped the bat around and thrust the knobby end toward me. "You should take some cuts, Wolf."

I choked out a gasp-laugh. "I don't think that would be such a good idea, Spike. The last time I hit a ball I was using a broomstick as a bat and we were playing on asphalt, not this fancy astroturf." I toed the plastic grass with my right foot. "Besides, your pitcher's throwing them faster than I like to drive, and his curve practically pulls a U-turn out there."

Spike draped a massive arm across my shoulders and steered me toward the batting cage. "Practice is almost over, and there's no one in the Dome here who will laugh at you." He slapped me on the back. "You're in a uniform. You might as well do some hitting."

As much as I wanted to protest that if I was hitting I couldn't be keeping my eye out for trouble, the little kid inside me desperately hungered for the chance to step up to the plate. "All right, you've got a victim. You aren't recording this, are you?"

"Wolf, I wouldn't do that to you?"

As I shucked the navy-blue Seattle Seadogs training jacket[1], Jimmy got me a batting helmet. "Strap this on. You're not chromed, are you?"

"Nope. The only chips in me are the nachos we had for lunch."

Handing me the helmet, he flipped a switch on the back that started a little green LED blinking. I pulled the helmet on and noticed the faint green glow tinting the full faceplate. The helmet had been fashioned of high-impact plastics and didn't feel particularly heavy, even though I knew it contained batteries to power the faceplate.

"Wolf, take a look at this." Jimmy picked up one of the baseballs that had squirted under the batting cage's canopy. He held it under a small lamp built into the batting cage. As he rotated it slowly, I saw a purplish grid play like faerie light over its white horsehide. On the helmet's faceplate I saw a nearly life-size simulacrum of the ball, complete with grid, track along with the ball's movement.

"The helmet tracks the ball?"

Jimmy nodded and slowly stood. "Up there, in the roof, there's an ultraviolet light projector that provides the illumination for the grid to show up to our eyes—or, in your case, on the helmet's faceplate. In the case of most jacked hitters, the helmet would interface with the hitter's biosoft and send an impulse that would direct his swing to connect with the ball. In your case you'll get a projection of where the ball will be, but you have to use your own judgment as to when to swing."

I heard some laughter and looked over toward the bullpen. The pitchers had gathered to watch me, no doubt certain they'd see someone yet worse than themselves at the plate. In the two days I'd been around the team, they'd given me something of a wide berth, which I didn't mind. The last thing I needed was a bunch of practical jokers trying to give me a hotfoot while I was trying to figure out how the team was being sabotaged on their pennant run.

Just before I stepped into the batting cage, I looked up at the mound. The practice pitcher had been shooed away by a tall, stocky player with a pug nose and broad grin.

I turned back to Jimmy. "You guys have been planning this, haven't you?" I pointed toward the mound in an imitation of a gesture my pitcher had once made famous. "I may not be the world's greatest baseball aficionado, but even I know Babe Ruth had a hot hand on the mound."

Jimmy shook his head. "Don't worry. Ken's not wired from those years."

---

[1] I had actually planned to refer to the Seadogs as the Mariners in this portion of my memoirs, but the word-processing software Valerie set me up with seems to be determined to avoid use of the word "Mariner."

Babe plucked a ball out of the basket behind the mound. "C'mon, Wolf, they never let me pitch. You aren't afraid of me, are you?"

I let a low growl rumble from my throat as I dug in on the left side of the plate. "I just hate southpaws, that's all, Babe."

He reared back and threw.

The helmet picked up the ball as it left his hand. In an instant the computer dropped a box around it, then drew a line straight from that original box to a point low and tight across my knees. A series of green boxes then plotted the course of the ball as it actually came in. The direct line readjusted itself as the ball began to break, but by the time I'd seen and tried to digest all the information, the pitch thudded into the batting cage.

Up on the scoreboard someone toted up a strike. Giggling sounded from the dugout, and the outfielders slowly started trotting in. Babe beamed and armed himself with another baseball.

"Don't let it get to you, Wolf." Jimmy's voice soothed some of my embarrassment as I tightened my grip on the bat. "Just relax. When you see the first line, take a cut. You'll get a piece of it. The helmet is tough for all of us."

"Yeah, but you get paid to do this."

Babe's second pitch came in, and I knew I'd seen that track before. I stepped into the ball, but I didn't quite manage to get all of my bat on the carbon-copy pitch. My hit popped straight up, then shot back down as the ball ricocheted from the cage's steel skeleton. I jumped back and dodged it.

More laughter from the dugout started my cheeks burning anew. A second strike appeared on the scoreboard and someone triggered a computer graphic showing a cartoon figure swinging and missing big-time. One of the pitchers flopped over onto his back as the breeze from my cut reached him.

"You do not have to tolerate this, Longtooth," the Old One snarled in my head. *"Let me give you my quickness and strength. Then you will show them."*

I shook my head. Ringing the practice field, four watcher spirits monitored the area for magic. For me to invoke the Wolf spirit in a real game would result in my being ejected from the league forever. Here, in practice, it would attract unwanted attention, and it had been agreed upon earlier that such a thing was not a good idea.

I held my hand out to Babe and backed out of the batter's box. "Ever have a desire to burn one down the third-base line into those clowns?"

Jimmy chuckled under his breath. "Yeah, back in double-A when I was starting out. Pitchers can be hell on you because they're out in the bullpen without adult supervision most of the time."

"I know. When I was out there earlier, they were teaching me how to spit."

"Now there's a skill for the Fifth World." Jimmy hooked his fingers through the netting on the cage. "What would you do if Babe was shooting a gun at you?"

"I'd shoot him back."

"Same dif here, only the bullet is bigger and you're sharing it with him."

"Gotcha." I reached up and turned the helmet off. "I think I'm set now."

"Go get 'em." Jimmy waved at the outfielders to back up. "Longball hitter stepping up, boys. Get on your horses."

Babe wound up and delivered a solid fastball. It came straight down the pipe and I swung all the way through the ball. I was late on the swing, so the ball hooked out into foul territory, but it was a long way out in foul territory. That surprised Babe because his next pitch came in high, leaving the count at 1 and 2 on the scoreboard. "Wolf, this'll be his curve. Tight, golf-shot it."

Just as Jimmy predicted, Babe's curve arced in and broke down. I stepped out and snapped the bat around, connecting rock solid. The ball exploded off my bat and passed just above Williams' glove as the third baseman leaped up at it. Beyond him it skipped off the turf and tucked itself into the corner of the outfield.

Behind me Jimmy chuckled. "That's a double for sure, maybe even a triple. You've got good wheels."

"You're being generous."

"Never going to fit undercover, Wolf, if you don't brag a bit."

"Just taking my lead from you, Jim."

With the rest of his pitches, Babe kept me honest, but I got pieces of more than I missed. As he began to tire and I got into my rhythm, stroking the ball felt really good. Finally, as we both agreed it was to be the last pitch, I pointed toward the outfield. "This time I'm serious."

Babe laughed aloud. "Yeah, you and every other curb-climber. No mercy, Wolf."

"Asked or given, Babe."

Because I'd begun to hit his curve, he came straight at me with a hard fastball. I saw him release it at the top of his arm's arc and I knew in a split-second that ball would be jetting fat and happy through my strike zone. Pushing off with my left foot, I strode forward. Cranking the bat around, I knew the ball was going places.

It was—like right into the backstop as my bat missed it by the same margin Christmas misses June.

With my bat pounding the turf as my swing spun me around, I dropped to my knees. Looking up, I saw even Jimmy holding his sides to stop chuckling. "What the hell was that?"

Babe jogged down from the mound and laughed with a low, sinister voice. "Just a reminder, kid. We're the pros in this league, and you're just a promising amateur." If not for the impish light in his eyes,

I'd have figured Babe was mad at me. He slapped Jimmy on the arm and headed into the dugout.

I slowly regained my feet and brushed my knees off. "That ball broke like a Ferrari on Pothole Road." Jimmy nodded and kicked some of the balls back out toward the mound. "Yeah, well, Babe was just having some fun with you."

"What was that pitch?"

He kicked a ball toward me and I noticed that dirt clung to part of it. "Babe gave you a spitter."

I swore. "And what do *you* do when somebody pitches you one of those?"

"Miss like you did..." Jimmy shrugged. "Or hit it on the dry side."

Even though I'd not worked up much of a sweat, the shower felt good. I would have lingered, but Jimmy and I had dates for the evening, and the woman I was seeing considered punctuality next to cleanliness in the way of divine attributes. As I was definitely considering dedicating a temple or two to her, I knew better than to keep her waiting.

A tall, beer-bellied man with a lopsided smile tossed me a thick white towel as I stepped from the shower. "You went after the spitter. 'Sa nasty pitch." He pounded his own chest proudly. "I'zz able to hit that one."

The man's slightly slurred speech and the partial paralysis of the right side of his body made me uneasy, but I returned his smile. "You're a better man than I, in that case."

Jimmy left the shower and fielded the towel line-drive easily. "That you could, Thumper. You could hit that spitter like it had been in the desert for years." He jerked a thumb at me. "Wolfgang Kies, meet Al Grater. He used to play under Ted Williams for Seattle about ten years back."

My smile broadened. "Yeah, okay, I remember now. You were playing Williams' 1947 season back in '39, weren't you? I actually saw you play. You hit a double, a triple, and a homer in that game."

"The Thumper, 'sme." His brown eyes watched me carefully. "'Sa good year."

The ragged scar tracking back through his black hair on the left side of his head reminded me of what had happened to him. In the 2040 season he'd been hit by a pitch that, as it turned out, had fractured his skull. He remained up at the plate and hit the next pitch out of the park, but collapsed rounding third. The brain damage hit him as hard as a stroke. The Seadogs management tried to put him back together, but could not, so they let him work around the Dome.

"It was a good year indeed." Babe Ruth draped an arm over Thumper's shoulders. He pointed a fat corona's glowing tip at me and grinned. "That was the year I entered the team's AAA Coastal League franchise, and the last year I ever swung at a spitball." Jimmy rubbed his towel through his closely cropped, kinky black hair. "You had to throw that pitch because you knew Wolf would have hit anything else you threw at him."

Babe winked at me. "True enough. A little seasoning, Wolf, and you could play Wildfire Schulte or Footsie Marcum."

"Thanks, I think."

Jimmy rested his left hand on my right shoulder. "Might want to rethink that, Babe. Wolf isn't wired and he turned the helmet off. He was hitting you all by his lonesome."

Babe blanched a bit, but his jocularity only vanished for a nanosecond. "I'll get someone to get me my '16 statsofts[2] and then we'll give him a real workout."

I nodded. "You're on." I turned to Jimmy. "We'd best get moving. We don't want to be late."

Jimmy fastened his towel around his slender waist. "I hope you're right about this woman you've got me meeting. I hate blind dates."

I frowned. "It's not really a date. Just drinks and maybe dinner. Wouldn't do that to her or you."

Babe seated himself on the bench by our lockers. "Big night? Where are you going?"

"It's a new place." I grimaced. "It's called ParVenue."

Babe smiled wryly. "Oh, I think you'll love that place, Jimmy. Thinking about asking the boys upstairs to get me a membership there as my next signing bonus."

Jimmy grunted, but I was unsure if he was still uneasy about having a blind date or if something about the club Valerie had chosen irritated him. I looked at Babe and Thumper. "If you two want to come along, I think my connection can get you in."

Babe shook his head. "Not me. Seattle's governor wants the Sultan at some reception she's tossing tonight."

"Thumper?"

Al shook his head with a herky-jerky motion. "'Sa not for me. 'Sides, I got work to do around here. I'm changing all the burned bulbs in the scoreboard. Want it right for when we beat the San Diego Jaguars."

"Another time then." I opened my locker as they left Jimmy and me alone. I tossed a wink at the picture of Lynn I'd taped to the inside of the door—just keeping with my cover, mind you—and pulled on a pair of khaki slacks. The polo shirt I tugged on over my head was

---

[2] Statsofts are what they call baseball activesofts. They're just like normal activesofts in all respects, save that they carry with them a bit of a personality overlay—much the way an activesoft of Hamlet for some actor might carry with it data on how the role was played by this actor or that in the past. Depending on the rev of *Hamlet* you run, you can be Gibson, Branagh, or Olivier.

navy blue and had the team's logo emblazoned on the right breast. Sheathing my feet in a pair of nylon Armani-Nike[3] power trainers and pumping them to snug completed my outfit, then raking a comb through my hair finished my preparations.

Jimmy took a sidelong glance at me and whistled. "Look lots better now than you did in the batting cage."

I jingled the keys of my car at him. "And we'll both look better in the Fenris."

"Then lead on, my friend."

The short tunnel from the locker room brought us directly to the parking lot beneath the stadium. Off to the right, the Fenris lurked like a piece of primordial darkness. All smooth and sleek, it reflected none of the garage's meager light because of a radarbane coating Doctor Raven had sprayed on it. Time seemed to slow as you approached the car, but I figured that was relativity in action because the car looked like it was doing light speed when it was sitting still.

The Fenris even impressed Jimmy. "'Fifty model, with a twelve-cylinder engine, right?"

I nodded. "Seventy-five hundred klicks on her and still not a dent."

Jimmy ran a hand gently over the top. "Doc Raven must pay very well."

I smiled and keyed open my door. The automatic locks snapped open and Jimmy settled into the passenger seat. "Actually this was a gift from a friend, but Raven has been known to be generous." I smiled openly. "You can bet Ms. Lacy-Mitsuto will pay very well if I can solve your little problem here."

"You find out who's been trying to sabotage our drive for the pennant, and money will be no object."

I punched in the ignition sequence, and the dozen cylinders beneath the Fenris' hood started hitting like Murderers' Row. The vehicle's headlights rotated up into position and I shifted the car into gear. "ParVenue, here we come."

Again irritation flickered over Jimmy's face, but I didn't know him well enough to guess what the cause might be. He controlled it, and forced himself to relax. "Hey, Wolf, that was nice of you to ask Thumper if he wanted to join us."

---

[3] Active wear for the chic. I actually prefer Gucci-Puma sneakers myself—despite the Old One's protests—but part of the licensing deal with the team meant we got this stuff for free, which meant I didn't mind slumming my way into it.

"No big deal. He seems like a nice guy. I thought he'd like some time away from the Dome."

Jimmy frowned. "He probably would, but I don't think he can exist away from the Dome or the circus environment. He's in deep."

"Like Babe?"

"No." Jimmy shook his head solemnly. "Ken Wilson is in deep by choice. Sure, the Seattle organization planned to draft Babe Ruth and use him, so they wanted someone like Ken whose physiology matched the Babe's right down to length of thumbs and space between the eyes. Ken was groomed to play Babe Ruth since Little League, so making it to the show is the fulfillment of a dream for him."

Coming out of the Dome's parking garage I waved at Thumper, then steered toward downtown Seattle. "Wilson's lucky—he looks enough like Babe Ruth to be his clone."

"He didn't when he started." Jimmy began to scowl. "The man's had more plastic surgery than many elf wannabes. Ken's in deep because he chooses to be in deep. He lets the statsoft ride all the time, and he wears the Babe's identity like a mask."

"I take it, from your tone of voice, you've got a problem with what Ken does?"

Jimmy waved me off. "Not really a problem, but a difference of opinion. Look, when I started playing ball, I was just like you. I played in the streets with the kids from the neighborhood, then I graduated to Little League on a team sponsored by Renraku. My father is a district manager for them and the corps take care of their own. A scout saw me, and I got pumped into the Seattle organization, of which Renraku owns a big chunk."

From outside, street lights strobed pinkish highlights on the ebony of Jimmy's nose and forehead. Humanoid shadows scuttled through the darkness surrounding Fourth Avenue South as we shot around the Renraku Arcology. Try as I might, I couldn't make out any signs of where the helicopter had crashed during the Night of Fire, but I'd have expected Renraku to clean up fast, so that didn't surprise me much. By the same token, I knew the area of Westlake where I'd seen action that same night had long since been patched up by Tucker and Bors, so the power of corps to heal their wounds was never in question in my mind.

Jimmy's lips peeled back from white teeth in a grin laden with irony. "I really love this game. In fact, I have it written into my contract that I can play in pick-up games whenever I want to—unlike others whose playing time is all tied up by contract."

"Having your father as a suit in the corp hierarchy must help."

"Yeah, it has its advantages." He stretched, placing his palms flat against the dashboard. "Ken stays statsoft-operational all the time because he really wants to be Babe Ruth. Whatever personality Ken originally had has been smothered by his statsoft. Me? I realize that baseball is my life right now, but it won't be forever. I only let a statsoft ride when I'm on the field. Other than that, I'm Jimmy Mackelroy."

I nodded. The Old One, the fragment of the Wolf spirit lurking in my brain, likewise had to be segregated out of my life. Yes, his power and abilities gave me, through magic, what Jimmy got through wired reflexes and cybered eyes. Still, the Old One, with his wild wishes for combat and killing and blood, brought with him a dark side that I could not let run riot. Like Jimmy, I could not let the Old One control me, or I would lose my personality and end up hurting many people.

As those thoughts coursed through my brain, I looked out and saw a nearly full moon flashing through the picket fence of skyscrapers in downtown Seattle. The Old One's howl echoed through my mind. *"Beware, Longtooth, with the moon comes my power. You retain control for now, but invoke me and I will show you the true way of the warrior."*

I shivered, and spoke to deflect my thoughts away from the path blazed by the Old One's whisper. "So why is Thumper different from Ken Wilson?"

"Ken has a choice, Thumper doesn't." Jimmy's brown eyes narrowed as bitterness entered his voice. "Al had Ted Williams riding him when his skull was fractured. The brain damage was extensive, and the doctors initially thought he'd never be more than a turnip suitable for organ-harvesting. His sister agreed to pull the plug on him, but she demanded he be allowed to die as Ted Williams. League officials agreed, and returned the statsoft to him. That brought Al out of it, though through rehabilitation his personality integrated with that of the statsoft, creating the composite personality of Thumper.

"The corp meat-mechanics refer to him as the first AI in a wet chip. Bastards."

"Amen to that." I whipped the wheel around and pulled into the semi-circular drive in front of the ParVenue. "We're here."

An ork valet opened my door and helped me out. "Be nice to my car and I'll be nice to you," I told him with a smile. He glanced up at me, surly, until he met my eyes. The dark ring surrounding my green irises zapped a little respect into him.

"Yes, sir. Not a scratch, sir."

I nodded happily. What's the purpose of having Killer Rings in your eyes if you can't make use of them? A howl from the Old One rose from the depths of my mind, but I stifled it. *Not this time, you old tick hound. Nothing and no one to fight here.*

The ParVenue Club had some fairly unique architecture. The drive led to a simple three-story brown-stone façade, much like the one Doctor Raven used as his headquarters. The prefab granite looked suitably weathered to give the building an air of antiquity, and the copper awnings glowed green in an advertisement for building fossilizers. In a high-speed, low-drag world where a venerable genealogy means respectability and virtue, this building came off like an old-money family with a virgin daughter.

The door elf, nattily attired in a long, scarlet wool coat with gold braid, smiled cautiously as Jimmy and I approached his station. "Good evening, gentlemen." He turned the word into a title that implied his pleasure at seeing us, though his tense stance and sour glance belied his words.

"Evening, yourself." I gave him a hey-everything-is-cool-here-chummer smile. "You'll want to verify our memberships?"

His tension eased just a microvolt. "Yes, sir, I am afraid I must." He reached back and touched a brick with a white-gloved hand. A panel slid up and the hole in the wall extruded a blocky lucite sheet. I smiled and pressed my right hand to it. A light passed under it and back, then the scanner beeped verification of membership.

The elf smiled. "Very good, sir. And this is your guest?"

I speared the man with a questioning glance. "Guest? Mr. Mackelroy is a member." Winking at Jimmy, I waved him forward.

The door elf paled—which is quite a feat for an elf anyway. "I am afraid you might be mistaken, Mr. Kies. He can enter as your guest, but..."

Jimmy hesitated and the door elf looked stricken. "Trust me, gentlemen." I smiled. "Mr. Mackelroy is a member."

"Wolf, I don't know about this," Jimmy murmured.

"Don't worry, Jimmy. Just imagine you're running Jackie Robinson's statsoft."

Jimmy pressed his hand to the printscanner, and the elf didn't hide his surprise at the affirmative *beep*. He smiled as sheepishly as an elf can. "Welcome to ParVenue, chummers." He swept the door open and smiled. "Locker room is to your left. Your lockers will be in berths four and seven. I've made sure they're upper units."

I stabbed a credstick down into a discreet socket beside the door and zapped him a five-nuyen tip. "'Preciate it, chummer. Don't let the corporators get you down."

"Slot and run," he said with a laugh, then let the oak and glass door slide shut behind us.

As we entered the locker room we saw a single bank of twenty-four lockers facing us. Two of the lockers in the upper row, in slots four and seven, withdrew back into the wall. It left the row looking like some gillette's broken grin for a moment or two, then new lockers slid into place. We both exchanged glances, then shrugged and located our appropriate lockers by the little laminated name plates slotted into them.

I opened mine, then sat down hard on the bench. "Oh, Val, what *have* you done?"

"Do we have to wear this stuff?"

"Dress code." I groaned. "Your clothes will fit perfectly. Valerie is pretty sharp, but her taste runs a bit odd."

The ParVenue, being the latest word in virtual country clubs, demanded that its patrons attire themselves appropriately when on the premises. This meant I exchanged my polo shirt for a navy one of a lighter weight and pricier designer label. Over it went a yellow cardigan sweater of a hue I've only seen in snow. The knickers that replaced my pants matched the sweater in color and fastened tight right below my knees. My blue and yellow plaid socks got tucked beneath the knickers, and my pseudo-golf shoes were a merciful black without any spikes.

"I'm not wearing my cap," Jimmy growled.

Oh yeah, my cap was a tam that matched the socks. In silent agreement with him I sent it flying like a frisbee into a wastebasket. "Comes a point when a man just has to put his foot down."

I swung my locker door closed, giving Jimmy his first full look at me. "Wolf, my mother used to dress her poodle in that type of outfit."

I growled at him. "Hold your arms out at your sides and in those red togs you'll look like the poodle's favorite fire hydrant."

"Point taken. Hope these women are worth it."

I caught a glimpse of myself in a wall-mounted mirror. "I'm beginning to doubt it, but let's not keep them waiting, just in case."

As strange as it may seem, Jimmy and I were not the oddest-looking individuals at the club. The corridor leading from the locker room to the bar and restaurant had a glass-walled section that let us look into the huge warehouse-like structure onto which the front façade had been grafted.

Jimmy paused and stared out at the people gathered there. "Just think, if they were bees, how much honey they'd be making."

I nodded at his apt analogy. Honeycombed stacks of small golfing stalls rose from ground to ceiling. On the bottom two levels the stark white rooms had golfers fitted with simsense helmets. Little mechanical ball-setters placed golf balls on tees or appropriately angled sections of astroturf. As the players swung through the balls, they blasted them into nets at the other end of their golfcave. One guy, at the far end of the row, endured a driving shower and buffeting winds produced by the chamber as he sought the absolute most in sim-golf experiences.

Just above them golfers also wore simsense helmets, but hit no balls. They still swung their clubs with wild abandon, and one man snapped a putter in half and tossed it down into the net protecting the floors below. Other golfers went through the motions of delicately chipping a shot onto a green, and one man stood with driver in hand, desperately waving at an imaginary ball to get over the imaginary trees and onto the imaginary green.

The top level had smoked-gray caps on the hexagonal rooms. Up there, golfers were pulling down simsense data directly from the ParVenue's golf course database. These did not need the challenge of weather and balls and perfect posture or square groove clubs. They played solely in their minds. For them the challenge was besting golf courses in places dreamed up by madmen and physicists and modeled on the fastest decks available. They might play two holes on the front nine from the Sea of Tranquility, then shift to a course imagined for the blazing surface of Venus. Changes of gravity and density of atmosphere were their enemies.

I saw one golfer on the lower level miss his shot and twist around before falling to his knees. "Do they have spitballs in golf?"

Jimmy shrugged. "I dunno. Maybe that was a water hazard."

I smiled and led the way to the bar. We passed two soaking wet guys who were swapping stories about playing the club's simulation of the Burning Tree course during Hurricane Felicia and I spotted our dates immediately. Of course I didn't know any of the half-dozen men watching them from the bar and surrounding tables, but I gathered neither did the women, and they liked that situation just fine.

I smiled at Lynn Ingold and gave her a hug and a kiss as I reached the table. She'd braided her copper hair, and the braid dangled down the front of her white blouse to the tip of her left breast. Her pert nose and quick smile combined with bright green eyes and a scattering a freckles to make her seem full of elven mischief from back in the days when that didn't mean gunfire and magic. The top of her head came up to my nose, and my arm fit around her shoulders as if we'd been designed as a set.

"Jimmy Mackelroy, this is Lynn Ingold, and that is probably your greatest fan in all of Seattle. Valerie Valkyrie, meet Jimmy Mackelroy."

Val is normally quick-witted, and I expected a verbal jab for my introduction of her, but she was awestruck enough to just ignore me. Like Jimmy, she was of African-American descent, but her blue eyes and café-au-lait complexion suggested a liberal dose of other things in her bloodline as well. She wore her brown hair pulled back into a ponytail. Taller than Lynn, but with the same slender, long-legged figure, she was sufficiently gorgeous to make the Pope reconsider his vow of celibacy.

In fact, if not for the barely noticeable jack behind her left ear, she'd have been the picture of the sort of fashion model Jimmy dated, according to the tabloid trid.

Jimmy took her right hand in his. "I am very pleased to meet you, finally."

That shook Val out of her trance. "Finally?"

Jimmy smiled. "Section seven, row five, seat twelve. You've got the whole box, paid for and all. Everyone on the team has been curious, but the team's deckers can't find out who you are."

Val blushed and sat down. "Oh, that, well..."

"Jimmy," I said, nodding toward Valerie. "She's the reason we're members here. Could your father's deckers do that?"

"No, I don't think they could." His smile broadened as he glanced from Val to me. "I guess now I'm going to owe you a favor."

"Excuse me?"

Jimmy smiled sheepishly. "Remember when we met you said you'd owe me a favor? Well, introducing me to Ms. Valkyrie here fulfills that and then some. Oh, and dinner and drinks are on me—the team had a pool collected for the first man to learn her name."

All of us laughed, easing a bit of the nervousness Valerie clearly felt. It struck me as funny because I knew she was bold enough to deck her way into even the most secure of corporate databases without even a hint of anxiety. With other deckers, the problem would have been just trying to interface with something that wasn't silicon-based, but Val's never been a social disaster. She was really taken with Jimmy, and almost paralyzed because of it.

Lynn clearly sensed the same thing in Valerie and took the conversation initiative before any silence could become awkward. "Jimmy, I've never been able to get Wolf to tell me how you actually met. I know he's helping you now, but I gathered you've known each other since before that."

Jimmy nodded easily and leaned forward onto the table. "You remember the night when the gangs all went nuts and blew up that apartment complex?"

Lynn nodded. She knew of it in the same way that almost everyone else in Seattle did—by what she heard on the trid and read in the newsfax. This meant she had no idea about my involvement in the events of that evening. As she's a pacifist who never seemed too interested in trying to find out exactly what I do in working with Doctor Raven, I never felt inclined to give her a blow-by-blow description of what had happened that night. Not that I repeated stories of that night all that often—describing almost dying leaves something to be desired.

"About a week later, at the Dome, I saw this guy leaning against my car. I wasn't getting a clean read off him, but he didn't seem overtly dangerous. He introduced himself as Wolf and asked if I'd be willing to make a personal appearance at a pizza place downtown." Jimmy shrugged. "I almost referred him to my agent to blow him off, which is what I normally do."

Before Jimmy could continue his story, a man who had managed to create a fashion atrocity within the strictures of the club's dress code sauntered over to our table and lightly slapped Jimmy on his shoulder. "Jimmy Mackelroy, isn't it?"

Jimmy nodded and shook the man's proffered hand. "And you are?"

"Phil Knobson. I own the Mitsu dealership over in Bellevue. Ace Mitsubishi. Heard of it?"

Jimmy thought for a second, then shook his head. "Sorry, but I put most things out of my mind during the season, you know?"

"Yeah," the man replied automatically as he waved a woman over. Her outfit matched Phil's, and I started looking for a phone to call the haute couture police. "This is my wife, Maggie. Maggie, this is Jimmy Mackelroy. I've told you about him, right?"

Maggie nodded, her blond perm as stiff as an acrylic spider web. "Phil, he never misses your games."

"So, look, Jimmy, I'm thinking we can do some business. You come down to the shop, we cut an ad or two, and I make you a sweet deal on a new car, you know?"

Jimmy stood slowly, continuing to smile as he towered over the salesman. "I think that's worth talking about, Phil, but right now I'm here with my friends, you know."

"Sure, sure, I gotcha. Look, why don't we all go to dinner? My treat." Phil glanced at the rest of us, then looked back up at Jimmy.

I let the Old One's dislike of Phil and his plastic wife bleed into my voice. "Actually, we were going to be dining outside the club, Phil. A private party."

Phil didn't get my message, but his wife did and gently tugged on her husband's shirt. "Honey, let's let these nice folks get back to their party, okay?"

Phil looked at Maggie as if her suggestion was a wild pitch, but when he glanced at Jimmy, he saw Jimmy had blasted it out of the park. "Yeah, okay, well, look, can I call you?"

"Just call the team office and they'll direct you to my agent. She arranges all those things." Jimmy shook Phil's hand again. "I'm sure we can work something out."

"Right. Have a good night, folks."

As they departed, Valerie shivered. "When I get home, his credit rating will die."

Jimmy smiled. "If you can do that, I can guarantee you a lot of business from the other players on the team."

Lynn raised an eyebrow. "That doesn't happen very often, does it?"

"More often than I'd like to admit, I'm afraid." Jimmy shrugged and jerked his head in my direction. "When anyone approaches me, I have to be thinking, 'What does he want me to buy? What's in it for him?' That's really tough, especially when it's a kid wanting an autograph, because dealers are known to use kids to get players to sign holopics they later sell for big nuyen. Most of the time folks are just nervous and genuine, but there are clunkers in the bunch."

Lynn covered my left hand with her right and gave it a squeeze. "So what did you think Wolf wanted when you first met him?"

"He was different. None of this fake camaraderie or an apologetic 'You don't know me, but...' He just introduced himself and asked, explaining he'd already told someone else I'd do the signing. Most folks would have then tried to play on my sympathies, begging me to get them off the hook. Wolf just said, 'If you're willing, great, if not I'll have to think of something else.'"

I grinned sheepishly. "You remember it better than I do, I think. I seem to recall some stammering on my part."

"No, man, you were cool." Jimmy chuckled lightly. "Instead of wanting something from me, Wolf was giving me a chance to do something nice for someone. I asked him what was in it for me, and he just smiled like he is now. He said he didn't have much, but he'd owe me. I got the feeling that being in his debt wasn't a bad thing at all."

Lynn gave me a peck on the cheek. "It's not been for me."

Jimmy smiled, then nodded to me. "At least he treated me like a human being. Too many players get tightly identified with the players whose StatSoft they use. I guess it's like trid actors being identified by their roles instead of their true names. For the guys who like that, it's great—Babe being a fine example of that. For the rest of us, it's a pain."

Lynn frowned. "I guess I don't understand why you have to use statsofts when you play."

Valerie's eyes brightened. "It's really not that hard to follow, Lynn. Back toward the end of the twentieth century, baseball started slipping in popularity. A devastating players' strike and a number of betting scandals rocked the game. Because players and managers were betting on games and seen as grossly overpaid, fans started deserting. Baseball officials reacted, taking serious steps. For example, one of the greats, Pete Rose, was banned from the game and initially barred from election to the Hall of Fame because of gambling. Baseball also tried expansion, inter-league play, and radical realignment to bring the fans back, but it only slowed the slide. They needed something to reverse it and that need, coupled with two other things, set up the current system."

Her earlier nervousness banished as we got into a discussion of baseball, she laid out the thinking behind the current system like a professor lecturing from her dissertation. "When the world changed and magic came back, and with the rise of bioware and cyberware, the potential for rigging games really spiked. Something had to be done to combat that eventuality. At the same time, sabermetricians had managed to reduce the game to a stack of stats, and with the proper program you could produce a box score that would be very close to what the true outcome of the game would be."

Val held her left hand open, palm up, then made the same gesture with her right hand. "At roughly the same time a great nostalgia for baseball hit. Old-timers' games and replays of old championship series became very popular. The film *Field of Dreams* and its holovid sequels made lots of money. Suddenly the corps that owned baseball got a great idea."

She brought her hands together, her fingers interlaced. "The Hall of Fame produces statsofts for all the players who ever played the game. Teams bid for the services of players in certain years of their careers—guaranteeing a statistical level of performance—and the teams play. It's possible to have Babe Ruth from 1916 pitching to himself from 1927, for example, and that makes for a very exciting game."

Lynn shrugged. "But that could be done with a computer simulation. Why do they need players?"

Jimmy nodded. "Good question. They use us mules because we can get broken, which introduces an element into the game that a computer simulation can't really cover."

"Even so, aren't the outcomes preordained—statistically speaking?" I gave Lynn's hand a squeeze. "They would be except for players like Jimmy here. He's a Legacy player."

"What's that?"

Jimmy hesitated, and Val answered for him. "There are some players in the annals of major league baseball who never had the chance to play enough games to provide a solid statistical base to make them a good player. The teams bid a lot of money for the headline players, like Babe Ruth and Tom Seaver, then fill out their roster with lesser known players. Legacy players come after that, and their identities are kept secret. That injects more chance into the game, and allows folks to guess at who their favorite players are."

She reached over and gently slapped the back of Jimmy's hand. "Last year I thought you were playing Luscious Luke Easter from 1953, but this year, I don't know. This season you could be Red Lutz in 1922 or Bobby Lowe from 1894."

"Good guesses all." Jimmy smiled at her, and I saw Val blush. "Luke Easter was a great player. I'd like to think, *if I* were playing him, I could do him justice."

So would management, and that was the basic problem I'd been asked to help solve. The team wasn't playing up to their averages. Everyone was off their statistical average and even though a few players, like Jimmy, were doing better than they should have, the overall effect was to take the edge off Seattle, and that spelled disaster in the upcoming pennant battle with the San Diego Jaguars.

Jimmy leaned forward and brought his voice down into a conspiratorial whisper. "Look, this place is making my skin crawl. Shall we get out of here?"

"Sure. We can catch something to eat down the street."

Jimmy's face brightened. "You know, I'd just as soon head over to that pizza joint on Westlake you talked me into visiting."

Val looked slightly stricken. "The Dominion place across from the Jackal's Lantern?"

I waved her concern *off*. "Don't worry, Val. The prevailing breeze blows from Dominion toward the Lantern and not vice versa." I stood and pulled Lynn's chair out for her. "How did you get down here?"

"Val gave me a ride."

Valerie smiled as Jimmy held her chair for her. "Lynn, why don't you go with Wolf. I'll drive Jimmy, if that's okay with you?"

"I'd be delighted," he replied to her and I had no doubts he would indeed.

TWO

I arrived at the Dome late in the afternoon the next day because of the night game. I found Jimmy already there and dropped to the bench in front of the locker I'd been assigned. "Jimmy, thanks for going out last night. Valerie is on cloud nine, or so I was told when Lynn called me after talking to Val."

"Good. She was a lot of fun." He smiled pleasantly. "She drove me back to my place and we talked for a long time. She knows baseball and a lot more, too."

I pulled my street shoes off and set them beside the spikes in the bottom of the locker. "I was directed to communicate to you, through means subtle but effective, that Val would be willing to go out with you again."

He nodded. "Yeah, I'd like to see her again, too. Did you manage to get Lynn back to her apartment in the tower before her folks called Lone Star?"

I shook my head. "They called, but I have a friend at Lone Star who intercepted the report, calmed them down, and gave me a call on my car phone." Lynn and her parents work for Fuchi, and share a family suite of apartments in one of their corporate towers downtown. Because she is an only child and because the corp encourages close familial ties, her parents tend to worry a bit. I get along well with them, but come the witching hour, her mother gets anxious. "Lynn said her mother wanted to know if we had a nice time, what with the evening being so short and all."

I pulled off my leather jacket, then shrugged my way out of my shoulder holster. As I turned to hang the Beretta Viper-14 beneath the jacket in my locker, my right shoulder popped audibly. Jimmy looked up and I worked my shoulders around, eliciting a similar pop from the left shoulder. "Batting practice left me stiff."

Jimmy waved Thumper over. "Wolf, take off your turtleneck and that Kevlar vest. Thumper, work some of that Atomic balm into his shoulders."

"Relax, Wolf. Relief's here."

I pulled off my shirt and vest as Thumper dipped his index finger into a squat white jar of red gel. It came out with a big gob pungent enough to make onions weep, and the Old One started howling because of the way it smelled to him. I did my best to ignore his whining and just let myself luxuriate in the warmth as Thumper worked it deep into my shoulders and neck. "Man, Thumper, that's great."

Jimmy smiled, then nodded at a grizzled dwarf bearing a black case. "Time already, Coach? We got a couple hours yet before the game."

The dwarf shrugged. "The league's got someone here to go over things, so I expect the whole process'll take longer." The dwarf reached over and bent Jimmy's right ear down, exposing the chipjack set into his mastoid bone. From the case he drew a small chip and slotted it into the jack with a *click*.

Jimmy let his head droop forward for a moment, then he hummed faintly while the chip coach moved on toward the ork[4] who played third base.

I glanced back at Thumper. "What's Jimmy doing?"

"Warm-ups. Letting the software blend with the wet-ware. Transition's not easy all the time."

"Right. I should have figured." Activesofts become active the second they're inserted into a chipjack, but to assume that every user has instant or perfect command of them is absurd. If that were true, all golfers could slot and run Tiger 4.2 and smoke their friends. Fact is, though, that the wetware side of the equation is full of variables, and unless someone is able to focus himself and integrate his physiology with the activesoft, he won't get the most out of it.

To use the activesofts, all players had to be chromed. Some went all out, getting their eyes done and, like Ken, altering their appearance to look like a player of old. Others, like Jimmy and Thumper, took a more conservative approach. Fiber optic cables had been worked into Jimmy's optic nerve bundle and implanted in his eyes so he could get the data presented by the batting helmet. His wired reflexes and muscles would then respond accordingly and hit or miss in a statistically appropriate manner.

The advantage to the conservative approach was that it left Jimmy and Thumper looking entirely normal. I'd known plenty of gillettes who reveled in the alien look their mods gave them, but not

---

[4] There was a time, of course, when metahumans weren't allowed to play baseball, but that sort of prejudice pretty much ended fast when folks realized elves made great pitchers and having an ork blocking the plate made running through him something that didn't always work. Dwarfs and trolls, of course, weren't allowed to play because of strike zone problems, but they had their own spring and fall leagues respectively, and drew decent crowds.

everyone wants to be a chrome-king. I suspected having another person ride them during a game was disorienting enough for some that being reminded of it when not on the field was preferable.

Jimmy blinked his eyes, then covered a yawn with his hand. "Sorry about zoning on you there, Wolf, but I had to put my playing face on. I'm going to Verification. When you finish dressing, meet me there."

"Right."

Thumper slapped me on the shoulder, then went off to minister to another player. I hung my clothes, including my Kevlar vest, in the locker and started putting on my uniform. Leaving my vest off did not please me, but kevlar isn't commonly worn beneath a uniform[5] and the Seattle club bosses didn't want me giving out any hints that something was wrong. So far, the attempts at sabotage had been subtle to the point of being nothing more than vapor, so the danger quotient was low on this job. Otherwise, Doc Raven would have sent Kid Stealth in to bat clean-up.

Spikes, even the short ones for use on turf, feel weird on the feet when walking across cement. They lacked traction on the wet part of the floor where Babe walked out of a cold shower, naked except for the water sheeting off him and the pouches under his eyes. He sniffed the air as he walked past me, then drifted in toward the lockers, gently calling out Thumper's name.

Before I could get to software verification, Bobby Kane, the short, squat team manager, pulled me into his office. "Wolf, I want you to meet Palmer Clark. He's with the League's Office of Verification. Mr. Clark, this is Wolfgang Kies."

Clark stood a centimeter or so taller than me, and where I tended toward being lean and wiry, he still carried a fair amount of muscle. "Very pleased to meet you, Mr. Clark. I remember when you played here in '43. Even though you were playing for Cincinnati and against us, well, I was one of 'Charlie's Hustlers' out in right field. You were great."

"Thanks." He smiled painfully enough that I guessed the last thing he wanted to deal with was a gushing fan, so I sobered up. "The club informed the Commissioner they had brought in an independent troubleshooter, and we applaud their initiative. I wanted to meet with you just to stress the importance that nothing about this be leaked to the outside world. Not a word of it. If any hint of scandal got out concerning our system, well, that would be the end of all of it."

"Wolf's the soul of discretion, Mr. Clark."

"I'm sure he is, Bobby, as is this Raven person he works for. Most impressive, the record they've racked up. I just need to be sure they understand the extent of our need for secrecy. This whole

---

[5] The exception being road trips to New York, of course.

problem is utterly vexing, and I appreciate the help, but baseball must come first."

From the expression on Clark's face and the tone of his voice, I began to get a read on him and what his words really meant. "Look, I'm not here to grandstand or step on your toes. I'm just going over stuff and asking questions because everything that's obvious to you guys isn't so obvious to me. I'm just an interested observer, nothing more. And I won't say a thing about any of this—not only do I work with a baseball fan who would make my life miserable if I destroyed the game, but I've become friends with folks like Jimmy and Bobby, and I'd rather not hurt them either."

"Good, just so we understand each other." Clark's expression lightened. "Now what can I do to help you?"

I hitched for a second, my mind blanking as it sorted through a million questions. I started to backtrack through my short-term memory, then came up with a general query. "Jimmy's in Verification. Mind giving me a datadump on that process?"

Clark smiled as if I'd served up a fat curve with the bases loaded. "We use a simple, helmet-like device that flashes ultraviolet signals in through the player's eyes. His scalp, facial, and ear muscles react in accordance with the pattern sent to them, as it is interpreted by the statsoft. We read the electronic activity of those muscles and match them against the expected response. If there is a variation from the expected response, we test further. If the statsoft is bad, we lock the player up with a coded message, then pull the software he's loaded. That's verified, and if it's been tampered with, the player is out and the team dealt with if the modifications have enhanced the player at all and they are to blame."

"I take it that doesn't happen very often?"

Clark shook his head confidently. "The system is foolproof, so no one even bothers to try anymore. At least they didn't. This is why it's so vital we find out what's happening now, because the slippage in performances could jeopardize Seattle's playoff hopes."

"Got it." Despite the urgency in Clark's voice, I sensed a distancing between the two points in that statement: he wanted to know why Seattle's players were slipping, but he really didn't care that they were. Seattle had never been one of the strongest draws in the game. As far as merchandising went, they really bit; which was why the team's faux franchise stuff did so well. The San Diego Jaguars, for example, had a much better logo and better-looking uniforms that brought lots of added revenue for the team and the league. Clark, looking at things from a league perspective, wanted to stop the tampering, but perhaps only after things got to the point where Seattle would finish behind the Jags on their way to the pennant race.

I gave Bobby and Clark a smile. "I'll keep my eyes open, see what I can see."

Clark nodded solemnly. "Good. We need to stop this before any real damage is done."

Sitting in the dugout had me full of all sorts of conflicting emotions— all of them good and crawling through my brain like toddlers wanting to be in the front seat of a car. Lining up on the third base line for the national anthem was a real kick, especially with Valerie and Lynn sitting in Val's box and waving at me. I didn't see myself on the Megatron screen out in center, but I knew I could the replay of the game later at home. Being there was a thrill, the fulfillment of a dream I never really knew I had. Just knowing that something I might do on the field would rivet the attention of thousands of people all at once, well, that's really heady stuff.

Ken's always slotting the Babe Ruth statsoft began to make more sense.

Technically speaking, I *could* enter the game. Because we were in September, the teams carried an expanded roster, and they had me on the active list to explain why I was practicing with the team and why I'd go on the road with them when we went to play for the Coastal League Pennant. The actual chances of my playing were nil, of course, because I couldn't really hit and, even if I *did* get my glove on a ball, I didn't know enough strategy to know what play to make where. I had, however, paid close attention and mastered all the signs, so I had a vague idea what was going to happen in the game[6].

We were even with the Jaguars, and if we could get ahead of them, we'd have home field throughout the series, which would be a great advantage. We were up against the Portland Lords—our downcoast nemesis. Even though they were at the bottom of the league, they were thrilled at the idea of playing the spoiler. On the mound they had an elf who was slotting Rosy Ryan, using his stats from the 1923 New York Giants. Rosy had given us trouble earlier in the season, and tonight was no exception.

The seventh inning came and went with no score on either side. Our pitcher, Pete Weatheral, was playing Nomo from '03 and had a two-hitter going. Ryan had a five-hitter and hadn't been scored upon because of some great fielding by his third baseman. Bottom of the eighth Ryan began to tire, so Bobby Kane had someone pinch-hit for Weatheral, with one out and one man on. Sacrifice moved our runner to second, then our leadoff guy hit a double into the gap in right center, scoring the runner. Next batter up hit a worm-burner to third, and the hitter was thrown out at first to retire the side.

---

[6] Actually, Val had told me I'd better do at least that much, and I didn't see giving her any reason to be angry at me as a survival trait.

Our 1-0 lead evaporated with a single and a homer to lead off in the top of the ninth. That left us down one after our reliever struck out one batter and walked the next, then caught out the fourth man in a double play. We were really lucky to get out of that inning so easily, and we all knew it.

Bobby Kane stalked through the dugout, clapping his hands. "We have a chance to win this one in regulation, men, so let's do it. Babe, you're up. Jimmy, you're on deck. Nothing fancy, just get on board and come home, got it?"

Babe winked at Bobby and donned his batting helmet. "Better put it out, Jimmy. I don't want to have to run fast to score."

"Yeah, just get on, Showboat."

I smiled as Jimmy came over to the bat rack and selected his bat. "You're handling the pressure well."

Jimmy shrugged. "Can't let little things get to you."

"Winning's a pretty big thing, isn't it?"

"Yeah, but the details are all small. For example, you check the scoreboard recently?"

I glanced out at it there in center, beneath the Megatron screen. Save for a single, burned-out bulb, everything looked fine, then I saw that the Dodgers-Jaguar game had ended with the Dodgers winning by a run. "We take this game, we have a full game lead going into the game on Monday night."

"Yeah, that's one thing." Jimmy settled his helmet over his head and his voice became muffled. "Their pitcher is another."

The Lords had put an ork on the mound, and the scoreboard reported he was slotting Fat Freddie Fitzsimmons from the 1939 Brooklyn Dodgers. The stats displayed weren't all that great, but Freddie had won about three times as many games that year as he lost. Since he dropped the last two games he'd played for the Lords, statistically speaking, he was due for a win.

I frowned. "Ruth ever face Fitzsimmons in real life?"

Spike shook his head. "Careers overlapped, but Ruth was mostly American League and Fitzsimmons was entirely National. Only place they could have faced each other was in the World Series, but they missed each other by a year. That's what's so sharp about how the game's played now—greats and near greats can face each other again, to decide what might have happened once upon a time."

Kane spat brown juice into a corner. "Ruth would have creamed him. Fitzsimmons never did well in series play."

"Let's hope that's true, statistically speaking." I watched Babe stalk toward the plate. He had the tight little walk down and seemed as natural there as the shouts of hotdog vendors and the smell of popcorn in the park. A couple of Lords' fans—standing out easily in their kelly green and teal jerseys, yelled insults at Babe as he gently tapped dirt from his spikes with his bat.

"Fat suet-sack, you couldn't hit if they delivered the ball on a tray!"

Ken smiled the way Babe Ruth would have, then pointed his bat toward center field. That brought a cheer from our fans and derision from the Lords side. Then Ken set himself, drew the bat to his shoulder, raised it a bit, and waited.

Bobby swore and kicked the bench beside me. "No! No, no, no! Of all the stupid..."

"What?" I looked at Jimmy, but he just pointed at the Megatron. It showed Ken's face as big as could be and his eyes were plainly closed. "What's he doing?"

Jimmy shook his head. "It's how he shows contempt for the pitchers."

"It's how he shows contempt for the manager." Bobby spat more tobacco juice into the corner. "Fine to do when we're a dozen runs ahead and he's hitting into a stat curve, but now?"

Jimmy shrugged. "Gotta believe, skipper."

Kane growled. "I believe I'm gonna kick his butt over the fence if he strikes out."

The first pitch came in and Babe swung at it. He didn't get all of it, but he got enough to foul it off into the stands. He smiled serenely and got set again, then took a pitch that came in high. A second pitch was outside, and he didn't go for that one either, which puzzled me. *How does he know?*

The Old One growled deep within me. *"It is his nature to know, Longtooth. As you know when trouble comes, he knows what is good and what is bad."*

Somehow I doubted that. "He must be peeking."

Jimmy turned and winked at me. "Doesn't see much through those lashes of his, but sees enough."

The fourth pitch came in and Babe nailed it pretty hard. It skipped off the infield between short and third. The left fielder picked it up and threw to second, but Ken had barely rounded first and danced back to the safety of the bag. There he raised his hands and accepted the adulation of the crowd, tossing his batting helmet to the first-base coach and pulling on his uniform cap. He continued to smile and wave, then turned toward his image on the Megatron, doffed his cap, and began a bow complete with cap flourish.

He never straightened up from the bow and instead plowed face first into the infield dirt. Laughter started as if this were some joke, then his body twitched as if he'd landed on a high-power cable. He flopped over onto his back, his cap flying from nerveless fingers. Froth formed at the corners of his mouth, then another seizure shook him, and he lay still.

Bobby and our trainer streaked from the dugout and joined the first-base coach standing over Ken's body. Bobby turned and waved urgently to the dugout, sending our chip coach scurrying onto the field, then from the bullpen I saw a golf cart with a stretcher coming out. The dwarf chip coach pulled the statsoft from the chipjack, causing Ken to convulse one last time, then the trainer and Bobby lifted Ken onto the stretcher. The chip coach traveled with him off the field.

Bobby came jogging back to the dugout and pointed at me. "Take off your jacket, Wolf. You're pinch-running."

I blinked at him. "*Me?*"

"You."

"But—"

He waved me out of the dugout and draped an arm around my shoulders. "Look, you're fast, you can run the bases."

"So can anyone else."

"Yeah, but you're not being ridden by some byteghost." I felt a chill run down my spine. "What are you talking about?"

Bobby shivered. "I've seen that reaction one time before, in the minors. Someone had hacked a statsoft and that's what happens to the player when he's running bad code."

"But Ken went through verification."

"Right, something else caused the failure. Don't know what, but until I do, you're running for him." Bobby slapped me on the back. "Chance to live a dream, kid. Don't let us down."

"Nothing fancy, I remember."

"Well, that was for Babe. *You* I need in scoring position. Watch the signs and do what the coaches tell you to do."

I stripped off my jacket, tossed it into the dugout, and ran over to first base. The public address system announced, "Now pinch-running on first, Keith Wolfley[7]." Had it not been for two wildly enthusiastic female voices, the singsong mantra of the hot dog vendors would have drowned out the cheer that went up for me. I got on first and smiled at Red Fisher, the first-base coach. "What advice you got for me?"

The grizzled old man narrowed his eyes. "Don't get out."

"Do my best." I took a little lead off first, slightly emboldened by the fact that Fitzsimmons had his back to me. I saw Bobby wave me out another step and heard Red growl, "It's called a lead for a reason, kid. Edge of the carpet."

I centimetered my way back out there, then jogged back to the sack after Fitzsimmons delivered a ball to Jimmy. I smiled at the first baseman, but he just spat at my feet. As the pitcher set himself again, I took a lead.

---

[7] That's the name they had me play under because it had parts close enough to my real name that I'd catch it, and it fit on the back of a jersey real easy.

Even though only 27.43 meters separated the bags, second base looked a full light year away.

"I can give you warp speed, Longtooth."

I snarled at the Old One, and resolved never again to fall sleep in front of the trid when watching reruns of old shows. The Old One's grasp of technology faded about the time man began to make tools out of something other than stone, but occasionally he latched on to make-believe stuff. Someone once said that any sufficiently advanced technology is indistinguishable from magic[8], and proof of that was the Old One fully accepting as real the technobabble science pedaled as entertainment by the media. Of course, he thought of those shows as "Shamans in Space"—they were chock-full of special effects he saw as magic—but the ratings folks never asked his opinion anyway.

A quick yip from the Old One warned me a half-second before I saw the pitcher step off the rubber and begin to turn toward me. I pushed off with my right foot and dove back to the bag. Dirt sprayed up into my face and my hands felt canvas as above me I heard the *pop* of the ball in the first baseman's mitt. A split second later, the first baseman slapped me across the head with the ball, the resulting *thud* all but drowning out the umpire's call of "safe."

I suppressed the Old One's urge to bite the first baseman and stood slowly, always keeping in contact with the bag. I brushed some dirt off my shirt. "Fitz has a nice move to the bag."

The first baseman sneered at me. "Ear still ringing?"

"Yeah, but I've got call forwarding." I took one step off the bag. "I'll take it at second."

"Right, pal." The Lord shook his head. "In your dreams."

My dreams, your nightmare. Bobby flashed me the sign to steal. At least, I was pretty sure it was the sign to steal. It made perfect sense— on second I'd be in scoring position, and I did have good wheels. In fact, the only thing that spoke against my stealing second was that I'd not stolen a base since before my age was in double digits.

I almost expected my life to flash before my eyes at a moment like that, but I got nothing quite so serious. What did happen was that every conversation I'd ever had with Valerie concerning baseball ran back through my mind. She was just full of pithy bits of baseball lore, including the very applicable, "You don't steal on the catcher, you steal on the pitcher." I took another step worth of lead, then, as Fitzsimmons started to throw, I was off.

My vision kind of tunneled in on the bag. I saw the second baseman cutting in toward it, raising his glove to grab the catcher's throw. I could feel my spikes like talons, digging into the carpet. My legs pumped, my arms swung. I could hear my heart pounding in

---

[8] Raven said that was Arthur C. Clarke, some old guy who wrote way back when, back when they used ink and stuff.

my ears. I watched the base, prepared to dive beneath the second baseman's tag, and I even grinned at the prospect of sliding head first.

Then I heard the *crack* of the bat, and a rising roar from the crowd. Nothing quite as clean and crisp and pure as the sound of a wooden bat catching all of a ball and then some. I saw a bit of blurred white to my left, then turned my head to the right and picked up this tiny pellet getting smaller and smaller by the second. It arced high through the Dome's darkened upper reaches, then rocketed down, over the wall in dead center.

Fireworks shot up from behind the scoreboard and the Megatron, exploding brilliantly. Below, the scoreboard's graphics likewise put on a light display. The fireworks cannonade fill the Dome with red, green, gold, and blue sparks that drifted down as the Megatron showed a replay of Jimmy's hit. As the explosive echoes of the fireworks died, the pulsing cheers from the stands washed out over the fields, and I found myself howling with delight.

I made sure to step fully on second, third, and home, then turned to welcome Jimmy home. He slapped both of my hands, then we butted chests and started laughing as the rest of the team collapsed in toward us. An army of hands and arms reached past and around me to congratulate Jimmy.

I managed to slip back out of the crowd and felt curiously alone as the team amoeba moved toward the dugout and locker room. I was as happy as anyone with the win—the Seadogs were as much my team as they were anyone else's—but I wasn't really part of the team. Yes, the run I'd scored helped lift us past the Lords, but I felt like I was poaching. I hadn't earned a place there, I didn't have a right to celebrate the way the rest of them were.

Yet being there, alone, was not the same as being lonely. I held myself apart not because I felt I wouldn't be welcomed, but because I didn't want to intrude. They had a camaraderie born of their battles the way I did with Raven and Stealth and Tark and Val; even with Zig and Zag. I respected what they had too much to want to impose myself on it. I was happy for them, happy for what they had done and happy to have contributed to it, even in a minor way. That was fine for me.

I drifted into the dugout as the last of the players squeezed into the tunnel back into the locker room. Bobby Kane stopped me with a hand on my chest. "Your attempt at stealing second..."

I winced. "I got the sign wrong, right?"

The manager shook his head. "You read it right, but that sign meant you could go if you wanted to. We needed you in scoring position, but I wasn't going to force you to go." He brushed some dirt from my jersey. "You got heart, kid. Sometimes, with all these wired guys muling for math-ghosts, it's easy to forget that's what's needed for playing this game."

"Thanks." I gave him a quick smile. "Any word on Ken?"

"Took him off to the hospital. He should be okay, but they'll want to balance out his electrolytes, get him some rest. Given that we've got the Jags coming in, and the nonsense that passes for Ken's lifestyle, having him bedridden for two days is a good thing."

"True, but he'll be vulnerable there. I'll call Raven. He can take a look at him and put some protection in place." I narrowed my eyes. "Assuming this was an attempt to take him out of more than just this game, I don't want to give whoever did this another shot."

"Amen to that." Bobby slapped me on the back. "Hey, Wolf, just in case no one else thinks to say it, thanks. And welcome to the show. You scored a run, you're a statistic now."

"Sure, someday someone will be using me as a Legacy player."

We both laughed and I headed into the locker room. I peeled off my uniform and hit the showers. I parked myself under a nozzle back in the corner, not out of any sense of modesty, but because that was far enough away from the entrance that random cool breezes and giddy players with towels spun into rat-tails couldn't easily get at me. The hot water felt good and even the Old One stopped growling when we heard the occasional *snap* of a towel and the resulting yelp of pain.

After much too short a time, I came back out and toweled off. A low growl and a shot of silver eyes kept a couple of jokers away from rat-tailing me on my way to my locker.

I dropped down on the bench next to Jimmy and started dressing. "Nice shot."

"Thanks." He smiled at me. "Sorry to rob you of your stolen base, but when you went, Fitz hurried his delivery. Came in a bit higher than I like..."

"Not that you could have noticed from the hit."

His grin broadened. "Yeah, I suppose. I did kinda nail it, didn't I?"

The pure, unadulterated joy in his question brought a big smile to my face. I nodded and tightened my Kevlar vest. "I'd bet one side of that ball is squashed flat."

"Maybe. All that counts, though, is that we won. Best the Jags can do now is tie us and we have a playoff to move into the pennant series."

"I'll slot that and run any day." I pulled my turtleneck on. "I'm thinking of heading over to see how Ken is. Want to go with me?"

"I was thinking of doing the same thing, and was going to take Thumper—he said he wanted to go." Jimmy jerked a thumb in the direction of the media office. "I have to go talk to the newsleeches, which will take a little while. Thumper's off changing a bulb in the scoreboard—he says it's bad bulbs we're getting, or a bad socket needs replacing. He wants things perfect for the Jags."

"All right, I'll round Thumper up, and we'll head over there after you get away from the media frenzy." I glanced at my watch, then slid it onto my left wrist. "I need to call Raven anyway. Twenty minutes?"

Jimmy nodded. "Works for me. If I'm not out by then, come in shooting."

"Full-auto." I finished dressing by pulling on a pair of jeans, and then some steel-toed boots, the right one with a slender stiletto sheathed in it. I shrugged my shoulder holster on, then pulled on a leather jacket over that. In my only concession to team spirit I wore the team cap, twisting the brim around so it covered the back of my neck.

I headed out into the network of internal corridors that allowed staff access to every nook and cranny of the Dome and found a public telecom. I briefed Doc on what had happened. He said he'd head out to the hospital immediately and make sure someone was with Ken around the clock. I asked him to exempt Val from that duty and, laughing, he said he would. I said I'd see him at the hospital, hit the Disconnect, and started looking for Thumper.

I asked around among the clean-up crew if they'd seen Thumper, and I was pointed in several different directions. None of those leads panned out, so I headed for the scoreboard, which is where I should have been going in the first place. After a couple of false starts, I found the passageway to the area behind the scoreboard and hurried along it. With the game over and the crowds clearing out, the lights had been reduced by half in the corridors and only a third of them still burned on the field. The air conditioning systems that handled the playing area and pretty much everything save the locker rooms had likewise been shut down, giving the Dome a warm closeness that made it easy to remember we were really just standing in a big hole in the ground.

As I came into the area behind the scoreboard, everything looked normal. The space had been shaped into a little amphitheater used to store rakes, shovels, a turf roller, and seats waiting to be repaired. The black outline of the rear access hatch to the scoreboard and the Megatron indicated it was open, but I expected that. In the dimness at the base of the scoreboard I saw the six short, organ-pipe style mortars that shot fireworks into the sky for a home run. A chair sat next to them, but it had been knocked over onto its side, and I saw something half-hidden by the mortars.

In an instant, I called upon the Old One to give me his senses. As my nose opened up, I caught a heavy whiff of blood and a hint of Atomic Balm. I also smelled a couple different colognes, and started to reach for my Viper.

A piece of shadow moved to my right. The truncheon my attacker wielded arced down fast. I tried to move with the blow, but was too slow. It caught me at the base of my skull and would have dropped me cleanly, but the bill on my cap absorbed some of the impact. I crumpled to the left and rolled a bit, ending up on my back, with my throat exposed.

Given the phase of the moon and my being somewhat stunned by the blow, this was not the best position I could have ended up in. The Old One immediately determined that I was in jeopardy and already defeated, since I'd left my belly and throat vulnerable to attack.

With fierce disgust echoing through his howl, he exerted himself, filling my limbs with energy.

"I will save us, Longtooth."

I had all I could do to prevent him from warping me into a wolfoid monster, which meant my control over my actions wavered. The Old One spun me around and lashed out at my assailant with a foot. We managed to trip her up—the Old One snarled about fighting a woman—but the way she bounced up from the trip told me she had more wire in her than the sprawl power grid, and that she had to be slotting KillaKarate 2.3 activesofts, Black Belt edition.

Unfortunately for her, there really aren't that many katas dealing with the fighting style Man-Who-Fights-Like-Wolf. The Old One bounded me up from the ground and drove me at her very quickly. She brought her hands up in defense, but I just lunged forward, my mouth opening for a bite that would crush her windpipe. Not having a muzzle, I knew that wasn't going to work too well, but the Old One didn't care. He jammed my face in at her throat, which meant I got her chin in my left eye, but her jaw did snap shut.

She fell back and managed to flip me over a hip, but I rolled into a crouch that kept me well below the sidekick she snapped at my head with her right foot. The Old One again lunged me forward and we went for her left leg. I got a mouthful of synthleather and hamstring, but, more important, managed to knock her off balance and to the ground. She landed on her belly and the Old One popped me up into a pounce. I landed on her back, with my knees hammering her kidneys and my hands mashing her face against the floor.

A kick to my ribs from her partner picked me up off her and sent me flying. I would have howled, but the kick knocked the wind out of me. I landed hard and rolled, but he came in at me and clipped me with a kick to the head. That twisted me around and dumped me by the mortars.

And into the pool of Thumper's blood.

His blood covered me, and the Old One went berserk. Here someone I had identified as being in my pack lay dead. My mission had been to protect him and the others, and these attackers had killed one of the pack members. This was not a crime—the Old One had no sense of criminality—this was just an offense, an aberration. It was something that violated the way of things, and all reality cried out for things to be set to rights again.

And set them to rights again the Old One would do.

Though the Old One had often lent me his senses, never had I seen things so clearly through his eyes, as I did now with our attacker closing with us. I saw the man coming in—a simple gillette, nothing special—as a collection of weaknesses and dangers. The flashing feet, the gloved hands, these could hurt us, but they could be avoided. I ducked my head beneath one kick, then, on all fours, leaned away from another. The gillette pulled back, preparing for a new flurry of blows, dancing around to cut me off from his partner, allowing her to recover, and further cutting me off from any avenue of escape.

Had I been a man, thinking like a man, that would have disturbed me. Had I been thinking strictly like a man, I would have pulled my Viper and drilled both of them, but the Old One had called the tune and he was leading, so all I could do was follow.

The Old One proved to be a master of the predator waltz. In his first attacks he directed me as he would have directed a wolf, having me fight as a wolf would. Now he shifted things, using my advantages to account for my shortcomings. While his inventory of my shortcomings would max countless chips, the one thing he does like about me is that I have a weapon he does not: a hand. Moreover, that hand comes equipped with a thumb and can be made into a fist.

The Old One launched me at the razorboy in what I would have classed as a bull-rush, but he howled away the notion that we were employing the tactics used by food to defend itself. I caught part of a kick on my left arm, then was inside on my foe. The Old One slammed my right fist into the gillette's groin. The man wore a cup, but the sheer ferocity of the blow compressed tender bits and surprised him. My head came up, crunching into his jaw, then the Old One stabbed my left hand into the man's throat.

The gillette gurgled and lurched into the shadows. I leaped for him, catching him on the right flank. He clutched his throat with both hands, so I levered his elbow up with my right hand and knifed my left hand into his armpit. My right knee came up, smashing into his stomach, then my left fist hammered down on the back of his neck. He grunted and rolled into the shadowed corner of the room.

I heard his partner get up and begin to stumble off, running, but the Old One did not turn in pursuit. He already had his prey and wanted a kill. His resolution to finish the gillette came powered with the outrage he felt over being trapped in the Dome, in this building that was, like the gillette, entirely against nature. This was a place where men sought to denature Nature, holding it captive to their whims, for their amusement. And this, too, was a hubristic aberration that demanded correction.

I pounced on the man and pummeled him, then felt the Old One make a final bid for power. He used the scent of blood, the whimpers of the man I sat astride, and my memories of Thumper as a bludgeon to shatter my control over my body. I tried to fight him, but a quick, backhanded blow by my foe caught me in the face. It surprised me more than hurt me, but it loosened my grip and the Old One ran wild.

I heard my bones snap with gunshot reports as the Old One remade me in his form. He was, in his mind, not denaturing me, but *renaturing* me, making me over into what I should have been.

Arm bones became truncated and muscle protoplasm flowed to new points of insertion. My hands tightened and knotted; my nails thickened and narrowed. Pain spiked up and down my jaw as my teeth grew, and my face crunched as a muzzle began to protrude from my face.

The Old One made me lunge at the gillette's throat, but I snapped my teeth shut well shy of the intended target. *He is not prey you would kill and eat.*

"He must die, for he is unnatural!"

That, you mutt, is human thinking, not your *way! You don't kill for sport.*

"Men do. Kill him!"

Men may, I do not! I re-exerted control, stopping the transformation shy of where the Old One wanted to take it. With a quick backhanded slap, I stopped the gillette's strugglings, then rolled off his chest and sat with my back to the wall. I had control for the moment, but I could feel the Old One gathering his strength to contest me, and the stink of blood helped him. Thumper *was* dead, and part of me cried out for revenge, but that was too simple for the situation that killed him.

Somewhere in the dark passageway back into the stadium I heard a *thwok*, then the razorgirl came tumbling back into the small enclosure. A half-second later Jimmy entered the enclosure, a bat in his hands. "Wolf? Thumper?"

I tried to answer him, but the Old One growled.

Jimmy turned toward the shadows, raising the bat.

The Old One took that as a threat and tried to make me lunge at him.

I gritted my teeth, locking my jaw shut, and refused. "Go. Away. Jimmy." My voice came in a harsh croak, with lots of growl worked in and around it. "Go."

"He, too, is unnatural, Longtooth. He is as bad as this place."

But he is my friend. I shaped my will into a stick and poked it at the Old One. *You tried to play at man's games, and you lost.*

"It will not always be so, Longtooth."

One game at a time.

Jimmy lowered his head slightly, trying to pierce the darkness that shrouded me. "Wolf, is that you? Are you okay?"

"It's me, Jimmy. I need you to go away." I had to force the words out through my throat. "Call security. Thumper is hurt bad. Dead, I think. These two did it. Go. Now. Please."

"Are you hurt?" Jimmy took a half-step toward me. "You look... different."

His eyes have been done, he can probably see me. I didn't know if his optical mods included low-light vision, but the shadows would only hide me if he stayed back. "I'm going to be fine. *Please,* just go. I'll catch up and explain. Get Thumper help."

He nodded. "'Kay, if that's what you want."

"Thanks."

Jimmy turned and ran away down the passage, and the Old One relinquished his grip on me. I felt all the agonies of my body returning to normal, but I refused to cry out. Torturing me that way was beneath him, but the Old One had been thwarted, so he didn't care. Grumbling like some guttercur, he retreated inside me and lurked like a hangover.

I shivered, then stood unsteadily. I might have been deep in the bowels of a building that mocked nature, covered in the blood of people who had denied their own nature, but at least I was myself again.

And, for the moment, that was a win.

THREE

As wins went, though, it was rather costly. Thumper's death nearly gut-shot the team. His enthusiasm had kept everyone loose, his gentle words had dispelled the negativism that could prolong a slump, and his sense of humor reminded everyone that since baseball was really a game, they should have fun out there. To have him killed stunned everyone, and at such a crucial point in the year, that could easily have spelled doom for the team.

Oddly enough, Ken Wilson helped turn that sentiment around. Against doctor's orders he left the hospital and came to the team meeting after Thumper's death. He looked around at those gathered and delivered a succinct and powerful eulogy.

"Each of us," he said, "knows who we are inside. I'm not Babe Ruth, you're not Matt Williams or Pee Wee Reese. When we step away from the game, when we retire our statsofts, we will be someone outside the game. Thumper devoted his whole life to baseball, and became a person who literally lived for it. And now he's died for it. He died making sure everything would be perfect for us, for our game against the Jaguars tomorrow. Our duty, our debt to him, demands that we make that game as perfect as he made this place for that game. You know, you all know, he's still here, watching us. Well, I'm not gonna let him down."

As Ken spoke, I felt an upswell of emotion, and could see the same shining from the eyes of the other players. I knew they bought into it wholly and completely, but that's because they didn't have a full understanding of how Thumper had died. Palmer Clark had taken immediate charge of the investigation and had clamped a lid on things very quickly. All the media learned was that Thumper had been engaged in some routine maintenance duties when he'd had an accident, struck his head, and died.

The truth was not nearly so neat. There was no denying that the two gillettes had killed him, but there was nothing to connect them with the team's subpar statistical performance. I was not a party to any interrogations, but from what Clark told me, the two of them were being fairly tight-lipped. They had a history of catting—burgling—various and sundry corporate apartments or places where VIPs installed their extramarital lovers. They hit spots where they figured folks would not want much attention paid and would have valuable items hidden. Clark figured they had been hiding out preparatory to breaking into the Dome's luxury boxes, Thumper surprised them, and died in the ensuing struggle.

I couldn't dispute that idea, and cautioned myself against trying to make a pattern where none existed. It seemed to me, though, that if Thumper had found them hiding, they could have made up some excuse and gotten out of there. Moreover, they were wired and skilled enough to have taken Thumper down without killing him. The only reason they had for killing him was if he'd seen something he wasn't supposed to see. Though he might have been killed accidentally, they should have vacated the area the moment he went down, not hung around.

Still, the security force and I had looked around and couldn't find anything out of the ordinary. I didn't like it, but the accidental death theory seemed to be the easiest one to explain all that was happening. Normally that's enough for me, but I was pretty sure there were some dots that weren't getting connected, and if I could find them, I'd be able to figure out what was really going on.

My general feeling of uneasiness had been heightened by a bit of distance between Jimmy and me. He definitely was putting his game face on during practice, concentrating a great deal. He told me that he'd just wanted to help that night, and had come looking for me when I'd not been in the locker room after his media conference. He'd headed for the scoreboard area because that's where he thought Thumper would be. He literally ran into the woman as she fled, swatted her back into the battlefield, and then wanted to help me.

As he told me this, I could hear the hurt in his voice that I had asked him to leave. I really wanted to tell him *why* I'd asked him to go, but letting someone know you've gone feral and are likely to tear his throat out is really not the way to seal a friendship. I explained to him that with bodies and the like, I was trying to protect him from scandal or anything that would hurt the team. That *was* my job there, after all.

He seemed to accept that explanation, which isn't to say he believed it. After that we drifted apart—able to share jokes and all, but it wasn't the same as before.

Given all the other pressures on him, I didn't see any reason to make an issue out of it. And explaining things would have required me telling him my secret. While I knew I could trust him with it, learning it was something that had already killed too many of Raven's aides in the past. With Thumper's death to show that folks were playing for keeps on this one, putting that burden on Jimmy wasn't something I was going to do.

I spent most of my time with the pitchers. I played a lot of catch and received *advanced* instruction in the proper methods of spitting. Chewing tobacco and compost have a lot in common, and you only swallow tobacco juice *once,* which is ample inducement to learn how to spit it as far away from you as you possibly can. Very quickly I switched to chewing gum and got to spitting with a degree of accuracy that I figured would impress even Kid Stealth[9].

In this kind of story about baseball, I'm supposed to note that the day of the big game dawned bright and sunny, full of promise and hope, but you wouldn't believe that. This is Seattle, after all, where they print pictures of the sun on soymilk cartons just to remind folks what it looks like. And our game was in the Dome, at night, which means the most cogent comment on atmospherics is that the roof wasn't leaking in any inconvenient places.

The same could not be said of the team. We were leaking and leaking badly; but we were leaking numbers. San Diego did have an elf with Tom Seaver riding him. He was using the 1971 stats, during which Seaver had a 1.76 ERA and 289 strike-outs. He kept blowing the ball by our guys, or messing them up with off-speed pitches. Those few guys who did make contact all grounded out. Going into the later innings, we were all aware that Seaver had pitched four shut-outs in '71, but had only thrown three so far this year.

The mood in the dugout began to sour, despite guys turning their caps inside out and wearing them backward—anything to start a rally! I felt frustrated in the extreme because there was nothing I could do in the dugout or on the field to help the team. The Old One snarled at me to convince Bobby to put me in.

"I have seen enough of this game, Longtooth. I can make you fast to catch the rabbit-ball, and I can let you club it to death as well."

The image of my trying to take a bite out of a pitch coming in high and tight made me wince. *Sorry, Old One, not your game.* There was no way I could explain to him that if any of the etheric sensors here caught me employing magic, we'd forfeit the game. Being on the roster had given me the access I needed to get my job done, but it also placed a limitation on me.

I dropped down on the end of the bench as we went out into the field at the top of the eighth. I started running over things in my mind, looking at them anew, trying to see if there was anything I'd missed. We all knew tampering was going on somehow, but the software was

---

[9] Never did show him how well I spit, however. I kept thinking he might get his tongue swapped out for some cyberthing that would allow him to spit venom like a cobra, if he ever thought of it. (If he hasn't already done it!)

being verified by the league before each game, so it was clean. And it wasn't like the players were picking up a virus on the field...

Or was it? What I knew about computers and the way they functioned could be put on a chip and still leave terabytes open, but I did know some of those great, ancient, hoary, old statements that had gone from being glib to trite. The eldest among them: Garbage in, garbage out. Based on what Jimmy had told me when he convinced me to hit, I knew players actually did get data fed into them during the game. It allowed them to track the ball when pitched. Pumping other data into hitters would be a simple way to knock their performance off the statistical curve.

But what's the input device? I glanced from the hitter out to center field. *The scoreboard, with that single, burned-out bulb!*

It hit me like a hammer. Ken Wilson should have gone down at the plate, but he got up to bat with his eyes closed. It was only when he was taking bows that he saw the scoreboard and the signals put him down. And Thumper had been out there changing a burned-out bulb, which wasn't burned out at all, but set up to flash instructions in the ultraviolet light range. Even if folks in the stands or other players noticed it, if it wasn't flashing a code that did something to their statsoft, they'd be unaffected, and would have no reason to remember it.

I blew a bubble with my gum and jumped a bit as it popped. The two catters hadn't been waiting for a chance to rob luxury suites, they'd been making sure the proper bulb was in the proper socket on the scoreboard. Thumper surprised them and they killed him. *Which means that bulb is what's keeping us down.*

I got up and started running into the clubhouse. This is not easy to do in spikes. I crunch-clacked my way down corridors, then skidded around corners and scrambled like a cartoon character to get up speed for my next dash. I heard the muffled roar of the crowd as we got San Diego out and started to come to bat. *Now or never.*

I bounced off the corridor wall leading to the scoreboard area and dashed into it. I saw Palmer Clark waiting by the entrance and realized he'd heard me coming, which gave him time to set up for my arrival. His right hand fell fast and the muzzle of his gun hit me solidly on the neck. I went down hard and would have been unconscious but for my aborted attempt to stop running when I saw him. My cleats had slipped out from under me, already dropping me to the ground, so the blow didn't hit as hard as it could have. Still, I bounced once and rolled up into a ball against the wall where I'd lurked in the shadows two nights earlier.

From my position there I could see several things, the first and foremost being the Ares Predator in Clark's right hand. The muzzle looked like the south end of the Alaska oil pipeline, and I really had no desire to be catching what it would be pitching. Up beyond him, just past the edge of the Megatron, I saw one of the smaller video display units set high above the seats on the third base side. It showed Jimmy warming up and stepping toward the plate.

Clark smiled. "Just as well you're here. I'd planned on framing you in the tampering scandal once I heard you were working with the team. You engineer this point-shaving deal, you get caught, and get dead."

"That's what I get for slotting Shoeless Joe Jackson, right?"

"You should be so lucky." As Jimmy stepped into the batter's box, Clark pointed a rectangular remote control sort of device at the scoreboard. I saw no receiver for it, but from where he stood he angled things down past the fireworks tubes, so I assumed it was hidden from my view. "There, that should do it."

On the screen I saw Seaver rear back and throw. Jimmy took a wicked cut at the ball, but missed it cleanly. He twisted around and hit the ground. He stayed down for a second, then shook his head and stood again. The umpire called for time while Jimmy backed off and brushed dirt from his clothes.

I smiled at Clark. "He's tougher than Ken."

Clark shrugged. "What happened to Ken was not very subtle, but was necessary as a show of what can be done. This evening, the effects have been more gentle."

"Use me, Longtooth. We will get the gun away from him and stop him."

I shook my head and rubbed the back of my neck. I still hurt from the clubbing and wasn't certain I could concentrate enough to summon the Old One's help. Moreover, I still knew that if I did so, the game would be lost, I'd be dead, and Clark would be free to continue doing what he was doing.

A second pitch came in and Jimmy started to swing for it, then held up. The ball grooved straight down the middle, and the umpire yelled, "Strike."

Clark smiled. "One more pitch and your boy strikes out. The anguished cries of thousands will be enough to drown out the shot that kills you."

"Think so?"

Clark composed his face into a mask of serene civility. "Count on it."

The wind-up.

The pitch.

I gave Clark a spitter.

The little pellet of gum came in like a hanging curve. He stumbled back from it and batted it away with his left hand. Disgust curled his upper lip, and he was about to snap something at me, when he heard a sound that stopped him.

The *crack* of a bat on a ball.

Funny thing about being that far out in center field. On the screen I saw Jimmy swing and connect, but it was a second or so before I heard the sound of the hit. Clark half-turned to look at the screen I was watching, and completed his turn about the time the ball cleared the fence.

I don't think anyone noticed that only five of the six mortar tubes sent fireworks exploding over the scoreboard. The one that hit Clark entered his back, lifting him up off the ground about a meter or so, and spinning him around. As he came back to where I could see his face, I caught a hint of horror and agony in his eyes, then he vomited green fire. His body somersaulted once, then hit the ground and flopped a lot until greasy gray smoke rose from his back and mouth.

"Longtooth."

I rested my head back against the wall and closed my eyes to let that image fade to black. "Yes?"

"I see why you like this game."

I saw Jimmy about a day later. I was leaning against his ride and smiled as he came walking over. "Never got a chance to tell you, that was a great dinger yesterday."

"Thanks." He glanced at the ground, then put his satchel down and folded his arms across his chest. "They told us some of what was going on. They said Clark had extra code inserted into the statsofts that wasn't picked up in the verification process. Said that allowed him to code orders for us and load them in through the scoreboard."

"Right." I shook my head. "Should have guessed what was going on all the way along. The only folks outside the league who benefited from the statsoft situation are gamblers. They can run the stats and figure out how a game should end up, then adjust odds accordingly. Doing what he was doing, Clark showed he could skew those probabilities big time."

"Think he was betting on the games?"

"Possibly. Apparently he still slotted one of the Pete Rose years he used to play." I shrugged. "No gambler will admit to taking his bets, but I think he was after something bigger. I think he saw Rose as being victimized by gamblers, and wanted to avenge him. By showing he could skew the results, he was in a position to blackmail gambling concerns, and get payoffs from them to do nothing."

Jimmy nodded, but the stiffness in his posture didn't ease. "Funny how letting someone else ride you can get you mixed up."

"Generally why there's only one personality allowed per body." I smiled, but Jimmy didn't return it.

"They said you got to Clark before he could zap me with his thing. Analysis of the code he broadcast said I would have struck out, not hit a homer."

"Really? They didn't tell me that."

"Is what you told them the truth?"

I shrugged. "Truth is open to a lot of interpretations. The only truth I care about was the round-tripper you notched in the eighth. It gave us the win, puts us in the pennant hunt."

"But you know."

"Your secret? Yeah, I know." I nodded slowly. "When you didn't strike out, I saw the surprise on Clark's face—for all of a second—and I realized we're a lot alike. What you see now is the real me, but what you saw the night Thumper died, that's part of me, too. A secret part of me. Not even Val knows about it, nor Lynn. It's me when I'm being *natural.*"

I smiled up at him. "You're a *natural,* too. You're not what people expect. You may load the software so it can be verified, and you've had that much work done on you, but you're not using wired reflexes to hit or field. You're just you."

Jimmy's face hardened. "Ever since I was a kid I was in love with baseball. It's a game for kids and folks who can still take joy in the things that kids take joy in."

"Instead of those who slot Kidjoy 1.3?"

"Right, exactly." He snorted a little laugh. "I saw baseball as a game for people, not machines, and my father agreed. He works for the company that owns the team, so he's been able to *adjust* all the records that show how much work was done on me, and the league thinks I'm just like everyone else. But I'm not. Now you know my secret, so my career is over."

"And you know mine." I gave him a quick grin. "I'll trust you if you trust me."

"That's it?"

"Is there something more I should want?"

"I think so. I mean..." Jimmy ran a hand back over his close-cropped hair. "Whenever I thought about what would happen when someone learned my secret, I figured they'd want money. Baseball makes billions."

I stepped forward and clapped him on the arms. "Yeah, but like you said, it's a game for kids, and those who can still take joy in kid things. Consider me a big kid. I've got no use for money. I'd rather have a friend."

"Yeah, kinda more precious than money, isn't it?"

"It's a supply and demand thing, I think."

Jimmy stooped, picked up his bag, then draped an arm over my shoulder. "So, pal, food?"

"And women?"

"Works for me." Jimmy smiled and tossed me a wink. "Nice to know I have a friend who thinks of everything."

FAIR GAME

ONE

It looked like the prayers hadn't helped after all.

The mouth of the alley didn't boast much of a crowd. The onlookers had all seen a dead body before. As this one had all its parts and wasn't anyone famous, the gawkers had nothing to stare at. The fact that most of them were allergic to the strobing blue lights on top of the Lone Star cruiser knifed across the sidewalk and shining its headlights on the manmeat also helped thin the rabble. No one lingered in my way as I crossed the curb, squeezed by the cruiser and into the alley.

The ork cop looked up at me, raindrops streaking white in the headlights' glare. "Know him, Kies?" Harry Braxen blinked and narrowed his eyes against the warm rain. "Take a good look."

I didn't need more than a second. His pink eyes staring up at the gray Seattle sky, the albino looked more like a wax statue than the remains of a human being. His white hair had been sheared into a mohawk, and the rain failed to wash the glued spikes down. His lips had never been that colorful, but their unhealthy blue blended nicely with the grayish pallor of his skin and the mist coming in off the Sound.

"You knew him too, Braxen. You saw him in the Barrens the day Reverend Roberts did the martyr dance." *The same day I told a little boy to say his prayers so the albino would be okay.* "His name was Albion. I don't think he had a SIN."

Braxen made a note in a small notebook. "Any guess why he got it?"

"Why?" I shook my head and reached instinctively for the silver wolf's-head pendant at my throat. "Not a clue."

"Determining how he got it is simple," offered my shadow.

Inching forward to squat down on birdlike titanium legs, Kid Stealth pulled aside the wet newspaper pages covering Albion's windward flank. He revealed a hole in the side of the kid's washed-out Maria Mercurial t-shirt. Despite Braxen's weak protest, Stealth used his metal left hand to rip the t-shirt open and point out the bluish hole in Albion's chest. "Entry wound, .30-06 with a light bullet and light charge. Stressed copper jacket, I would assume, designed to fragment on impact." Stealth cranked his head around to look at Braxen. "Most of the kid's blood will be in this lung. He got hit, started bleeding, and ran himself to death."

Braxen nodded, but made no notes. He and I both knew that if Stealth—one of the world's experts on innovative means of rival-retirement—pointed it out and it concerned death, he wouldn't be wrong. "What kind of gun?"

Stealth's foot claws grated slightly on the cement as he straightened up again. "Customized rifle. Long barrel to maximize accuracy and muzzle velocity. Good work."

The cruiser's headlights made Braxen's tusks stand out against his swarthy flesh. "You do the work?"

"I'm not a toy maker."

"Wasn't a toy that killed this boy, Stealth."

Stealth shrugged as if to say "have it your own way." He jammed his hands into the pockets of his trench coat and sat back on his haunches. The headlights left him a silhouette except for the reddish lights burning in his Zeiss eyes.

I knew from the set of Stealth's shoulders that he wouldn't be saying anything more to Braxen. "Harry, your forensics people will verify what Stealth is saying."

The ork cop shook his head. "No, they won't. No autopsy for this one."

"What are you talking about? It's a suspicious death, isn't it?" I glanced down at Albion's body. "You need an autopsy for your investigation."

"*What* investigation, Kies? This kid's got no SIN. He doesn't exist as far as the system is concerned. He isn't even a statistic."

I wanted to grab him, but two things stopped me. The first was the realization that Braxen was absolutely correct. Without a System Identification Number, neither Albion nor any of the other denizens who lurked in the shadows of the sprawl had any official existence. Schools wouldn't take them, hospitals wouldn't treat them, help centers ignored them.

Well I knew, for I myself had grown up without a SIN.

There was no way the system was going to investigate the death of someone like Albion. Had he been an elf or ork or Amerind, his own folk might have taken an interest in him. Lone Star, however, was a private corporation hired to keep the peace in Seattle, not to clean up after some murderer who got careless when dropping his trash.

The second thing that stopped me was Braxen's tone. For all of his being a cop, Harry Braxen wasn't like most of the blue crew. He'd grown up in Seattle and, as an ork, knew all about discrimination and the callousness of the system. He'd known who Albion was the instant he'd seen him, but he had probably called me down to identify the body to get me interested in the case.

"Spill it, Harry. I don't like standing in the rain."

Braxen squatted next to the body and I dropped down beside him. Kid Stealth's shadow hid both of us and Harry kept his voice low enough that only Albion and the Murder Machine could hear us. "Could be this is the fourth body I've seen dropped like this. Two gillettes down by the docks and one dreamchipper up in Belmont. She was the first and we got some datafiles on her before they lost her body. Files were dumped."

"She have a name?"

"Athena Neon is what I filed her under. She had a neon rose tied with a yellow ribbon tattooed on her butt."

I nodded slowly. "It went down the same way?"

"Identical, except for maybe one detail." Braxen reached out and turned Albion's face to the left and then to the right. "Can't tell with him, but the other three had all lost a lock of hair. One of the gillettes was a guy I'd popped the month before. That was how I first noticed it—his rat-tail was missing."

In the back of my mind the Old One—what I call the slice of the Wolf spirit lairing in my psyche—started to growl. I felt the hairs on the back of my neck prick up. "No other links?"

Braxen shrugged. "You know sometimes us cops keep 'hobby cases.'"

"Ones you work on in your spare time, right?" I smiled. "I have a list of women like that."

Harry nodded. "Well, these killings were a hobby case of mine, but my files are gone, just flat vanished. Someone with mondo-juice hit my corner of the Matrix and wiped them out."

I straightened up. "You gonna call a meat wagon for him?"

"Unless you think Salacia and her people want to make arrangements for him." Braxen looked down at the kid as a wind-whipped plastic bag molded itself to Albion's face. "The kid should have stayed where he was safe."

"Amen," I said to that, knowing that to find out what happened to Albion, I'd be going places that weren't even in hailing distance of safe.

TWO

Stealth and I retreated deeper into the alley as the morgue van arrived. The attendants zipped Albion into a body bag glistening with rain. Harry supervised and handed the driver a card. Then he got into his car and followed the van away, taking his headlights with him and leaving us in the dark.

I turned to Kid Stealth. "He's gone. Give me what you've got, because I know you're dying to have me show him up."

Stealth answered me in a flat monotone. "Doc Raven will be back from Tokyo tomorrow night. We can give him the scan, let him decide what to do about this."

"Stealth, let me do some legwork first." I pointed to the place where the rain had begun to darken the lighter outline of Albion's body. "The trail will get cold."

"The killer will be back." The red lights in Stealth's eyes bloated and shrank. "He's a thrill killer."

"What?"

"This is his recreation." Stealth looked at me for a moment, looked away, then nodded. "The bullets you use in your Viper[1]..."

"Silver, drilled and patched with a silver-nitrate solution to make them explosive."

"Why?"

I hesitated. Kid Stealth hadn't been around during the Full Moon Slashings, so he didn't know what Raven and I had run into back then. I'd developed the bullets to deal with that mess and I'd kept using them since, just in case. I sensed in his question, however, not so

---

[1] The nice thing about carrying and using a gun as old as the Beretta Viper 14 was that under most current laws, antiques weren't really considered "weapons" for concealment purposes. Me, I never saw the allure of these newfangled guns full of computer components and all. Go ahead, rely on Windows Sniper 4.0 if you want to, but I prefer not to need software patches when I'm in a firefight.

much a desire to know the history of my bullets as to understand the thinking that went into producing them.

"I had them done that way so they would maximize shock and destruction. Bullets are meant to kill, and I wanted mine to do the job well."

Stealth studied me for a moment before answering. "The bullet used on Albion was designed to make him *die*. Back before the Awakening, before magic came back to the world, there were people who would test their hunting skills by using a bow and arrow to take wildlife." Stealth held his hands before him as if visualizing what he was describing. "Bows are uncertain. Because an arrow might not cause enough damage, innovative arrowhead designs were created. One type had three or four razored edges that spiraled around the arrowhead like the edges on a drill-bit. It was called a bleeder, and was designed to chew up as much of the animal's insides as it could, while leaving a blood trail for the hunter to follow."

The Old One howled angrily in the back of my mind. "Stealth, you mentioned a stressed copper jacket with a light bullet and light charge. You're saying Albion was shot with the ballistic equivalent of a bleeder?"

"His wound was non-midline."

I frowned. "It still killed him."

"No. The rifle used was more than capable of putting a shot through someone's eye at a range of at least two hundred-fifty meters. Albion was wounded by design."

"What killed him, then?"

"He drowned in his own blood. He was coursed to death."

"Coursed?"

Stealth nodded and—wonder of wonders—for once the Old One agreed with him. Unbidden, the Wolf spirit lent me his heightened senses. The night vision made everything much clearer in the alley, but that wasn't the sense the Old One wanted me to use. My nostrils twitched and, amid the noxious odors of rotting garbage and thrice-scorched radiator fluid, I caught a very sharp scent.

The Old One forced me to savor it. *A large canine, Longtooth. It was here and marked the territory of its kill. It did as its master commanded. It is much like the Murder Machine to whom you speak.*

"A cyberpup ran Albion down?"

Stealth nodded. "Foot spurs scraped the wall over there when it lifted its leg to mark its hunting ground."

"Custom rifle, custom dog. This guy must have some serious nuyen to be dropping on his pastime." I shook my head. "If what Braxen said is accurate, he's dusted four. Not likely to stop—as you said, a thrill killer."

"A dilettante." Stealth looked hard at me. "You will pursue this before Raven returns?"

A lingering sense of guilt concerning Albion slowly stole over my mind. He'd been angry when I last saw him, and had stalked off into the night alone. That had been months ago, but part of me thought his death was my fault. I knew, realistically, that was nonsense, but I couldn't shake the feeling.

"I knew him. It's personal."

Stealth extended his left hand, the metal one, toward me. "Give me some cab fare."

"I'll drop you at Raven's before I head out."

"Give me ten nuyen."

I dug my hand into my pocket. Could Guinness ever check it out, Kid Stealth would surely make its datachip of World Records in ten different categories—all of them lumped under the Homicide heading. I pulled a credstick from my jeans pocket and handed it to him.

"I want to see a receipt and my change back," I added. Stealth might have had more unsolved murders to his credit than Elvis had imitators, but if I didn't give him a hard time, he'd be insufferable.

Stealth took the stick and disappeared it into a pocket. "Wolf, this one plays at death."

I nodded. That was about as close as Stealth would ever get to telling me to be careful. He ascribes a lot to the "a word to the wise is sufficient" school of caring for other folks. Given that the last time he tried to show concern over my fate he shot me in the back, the verbal message did seem more friendly. "I'll keep you posted, I promise."

Without so much as a nod, Stealth turned and withdrew into the alleyway. I didn't turn to watch him because the Old One tries to make me laugh at Stealth's cyberbunny hopping gait. In terms of lethality, doing that strongly resembles sucking on twenty packs of nikostix a day for longer than I've been alive. The other reason I didn't watch him is that Stealth was likely to cut up and over to Seventh by using those miracle claws of his to scale a building. Getting my knuckles bloody as the Old One tries to prove we can do that too is really annoying.

The Old One's sensory gifts did come in handy as I directed them back toward the street. As I walked in the general direction of where I'd left the Fenris parked in another alley, I heard someone sobbing. Tears aren't all that uncommon in the sprawl, and more than one Samaritan has been lured into a headache by thinking he was rescuing a woman in distress. In this case, however, the sob wasn't coming from a voxsynth chip, but from the throat of a little gamin of a girl slumped against the alley wall.

The rain had soaked her hair, and made it clump into stringy tendrils about as skinny as her arms and legs. She wore a clear plastic raincoat that ended somewhere between her neon-green hot pants and her argyle knee socks. Her blouse matched the shorts in color and ended just below her breasts to show off a flat stomach. It also showed off her ribs. As she looked up at me with hollow, red-rimmed eyes, I couldn't help wondering if she was an anorexia poster-child.

I gave her a smile I hoped wouldn't threaten her. "How long have you known Albion?"

She blinked as I said his name. "You knew him?"

I nodded. Glancing up and down the street, I spotted a diner where I'd eaten before without dying. "C'mon, let's get out of the rain." I reached for her arm, but she retreated away from me.

"No way, chummer. I may be griefin', but I'm no flatliner."

I held my hands up and kept them open. "Okay, bad start. My name is Wolfgang Kies. I knew Albion, and I'm going to find out what happened to him. If you want to help, it'll make my job easier."

She watched me warily, then nodded. "'Kay. Albie mentioned you. I'm Cutty."

I pointed to the diner, and she nodded. "How long you and Albion been together, Cutty?"

She cut across the street like a zombie hungering for a bumper-kiss. She never noticed the squealing brakes nor did she acknowledge the curses shouted at her. I let the Old One growl at anyone who vented his wrath on me and that generally calmed things.

Once across Blanchard, Cutty headed into the diner and dropped into a booth like a rag doll suddenly stuffed with lead shot. The waitress frowned at her, but I gave her one of my "this could be your lucky day, darling" smiles and she relented.

"Soykaf for me. Milk and some soup or something for her, okay?" The waitress snapped her gum, then turned and sang out our order to the ork working the kitchen.

"Third time's the charm. Cutty, how long were you playing house with Albion?"

Her head came up, and I saw a spark of life in her brown eyes. "A month, I guess." She blinked twice, then frowned. "This is October, right?"

"November, but who's counting?"

"Oh, two months, then."

"Gotcha." I'd last seen Albion on a very warm July night, which put him with her within six weeks of leaving his friends in the Barrens. "He was cool during that time? No problems?"

Cutty nodded. "Like ice. Did some boosting, you know? His thing was fixing stuff, though, and he used to patch decks together before folks would fence them. Made him sort of legit, you know? Then folks started recommending him to others, and he fixed lots of stuff."

"I get the picture." And the picture I got was a dismal one. I'd been hoping Albion had gotten himself in solid with some group or gang or specific place that might narrow my area of inquiry. If I had to track every cracked or heisted deck he laid a screwdriver to, I'd be looking for his killer long after Kid Stealth rusted away to nothing.

The waitress arrived with our food, and Cutty stared at the clam chowder with the same look of horror you'd expect if the waitress had regurgitated it right there at the table. She looked at the milk as if the waitress was Lucretia Borgia. I compensated for this by regarding the steaming cup of soykaf like it was the Holy Grail and the waitress as if she was the Madonna. Clearly, though, the waitress thought of herself as a different sort of Madonna, and I realized the kind of music we could have made together would have beat Gregorian chanting by an ecclesiastical mile.

"Drink, eat. You need the milk to strengthen your bones and the soup will put some meat on them." I appropriated a bit of her milk for my soykaf, which suddenly made her possessive about the food. I feigned offense, which seemed to please her somehow and made her eat. "Albion didn't have any steady killtime, did he? Anything that would have made him a candidate for a toxic lead dump?"

She nodded as a droplet of chowder rolled down over her pointed chin. "Just started a caper at the Pacific Northwest Huntsman's Club. Got it through a person he did some fixing for. Steady work that didn't cut into his side biz. Didn't need a SIN for it."

That last bit would draw Albion like a flame draws a moth. Albion fiercely defended his independence, and wanted nothing to do with the system. Like all those who scurry in the shadows, he dreamed of being as big as Mercurial some day, but the chances of that were slimmer than Cutty here. What he didn't know—what few of us without SINs did know—is that it's easier for the society to destroy you than it is for them to even notice you.

"That's a place to start. Do you remember who gave him the job?"

Her wet hair flew back and forth as she shook her head. At least I think she shook her head, but I couldn't see any of her face around the edges of the bowl as she tipped it up to drain it. The bowl came back down and a plastic sleeve came away from her face smeared with the last of the chowder. "Don't remember." She looked over toward the counter and licked her lips as she eyed a stack of frosted doughnuts.

I'd seen bricks with a longer attention span than she had, but I put it down to her being in shock. Our waitress returned and brought with her the doughnut tray. Cutty selected two big chocolate-frosted fat-pills and I passed, so Cutty took a third in case I reconsidered. I paid the bill and the tip while Cutty watched the credstick vanish almost as hungrily as she'd looked at the doughnuts.

"With Albion gone, what are you doing for money?"

She smiled at me, her eyes growing vacant. "For fifty nuyen I'll do anything you like."

"Yeah?"

She nodded solemnly. "Anything."

"You got it." I pulled out my slender cash supply—figuring she'd find the bills easier to use than a credstick—and laid down two twenties and a ten. "You said anything, right?"

Cutty licked at the frosting in a way she hoped was suggestively erotic. "You pay, piper, and you call the dance."

"Good." Had I a necrophile's taste for skeletal women, I might have come up with something truly inventive for her to earn my money. As it was, I had a more sinister plan in mind. "For this fifty nuyen, you're gonna sit here and wait for an elf named Salacia to come see you. She was a friend of Albion's before you knew him—just friends, not lovers. Tell her about him." I got up from the booth. "Stay with her and the rest of Albion's family, and let them know what happened to him."

Cutty looked up at me and shook her head. "Albion always said you were a weird chummer, but one he could trust. He didn't trust many."

"You'll wait?"

She nodded sadly. "I'll be with Salacia, and then you can tell me how Albion's story ends."

I left Cutty in the diner and headed back to the Fenris. Though he's not much on technology, even the Old One likes the Fenris. Low and sleek, angled except where the flat black body curves neatly around a wheel well or back around a bumper, the car looks like a wedge sharp enough to split the sky from the planet at the horizon.

Even before rounding the corner of the alley I pulled out the remote for the antitheft system. Because this section of town wasn't that bad, I'd set it for only one chirp, with the defenses on Stun. As the car came into view, I tapped the control and got a single chirp back in response as I deactivated the security system. From behind the car two startled kids jumped up and started running down the alley.

Their laughter made me believe they'd been up to mischief and little more, but caution made me check the rear of the Fenris. Two big old rats, the fat kind that feast in dumpsters, lay twitching on the ground. The kids had been amusing themselves by catching the rats and tossing them against the Fenris' body. The resulting shock had left the rats half-dead, but served as a practical lesson to warn the kids off messing with my ride.

The Fenris whisked me through the Seattle streets. The radar-bane coating Raven had sprayed over the car's surface made it reflect less light than the rain-slicked street. I cruised around, checking my six for folks following me. When I saw it was clear, I made for Raven's place and used the car phone to call Salacia at the house in the Barrens.

One of the other kids who lived at the house answered the call. Sine said she'd get word to Salacia, and they'd pick Cutty up quickly.

"Good," I told her. "But the girl's in shock. Maybe you can do for her what none of us could do for Albion."

She agreed, and I hung up as I guided the Fenris into Raven's underground parking garage. The automatic door shut behind me and locked tightly. I climbed out of the Fenris and locked it, then put the security on two chirps and set it on Mangle. Anyone stupid enough to break into Raven's place deserved all the surprises he could handle.

I went from the garage straight into the basement computer room. The sanitary white of the walls and tiles is a shocker at the best of times, but it seemed almost dreamlike after the rainy Seattle evening. The same could be said of the room's sole occupant after an evening spent with Braxen and Kid Stealth.

Valerie Valkyrie covered a yawn with a slenderfingered hand. She still looked radiant from having met Jimmy Mackelroy, the *enfant terrible* of the Seattle Seadogs[2]. Actually I think the radiance came from helping him through the trauma of Seattle's loss in the series, which beat the hell out of how she'd moped last year until spring training. Though she'd lost her heart to him, she still had a smile for me, and I returned it with interest.

"Good morning, Ms. Valkyrie. Are you up early or up late?"

Heavy lids half-hid blue eyes. "After thirty-six hours, that sort of question hardly matters." She glanced back at the deck and the datacord that usually fit snugly into the jack behind her left ear. "Another marathon Dementia-Gate session. I could have gone longer, but Lynn said she wanted to leave the game so she could rest up for your date tomorrow night. You getting serious on her, Mr. Kies?"

"That date's tonight, Val, after the sun comes up." If it weren't for Valerie's café-au-lait complexion coming to her through genetics, she'd have looked as pale as Albion. "You have seen the sun this month, haven't you?"

"Nice dodge, Wolf." She smiled and killed another yawn. "You here from the Committee For the Production of Vitamin D, or have you got a job that's beyond your meager computer talents?"

"Meager?" I frowned as I pulled off my black leather jacket and tossed it onto one of the white leather chairs sitting in a corner. "I know how to turn one of these things on and off, you know. Meager, sheesh."

She gave me an exaggerated nod. "Sure you do. What do you need?"

---

[2] Valerie took it as a personal victory that Jimmy referred to the team as the Seadogs in Matrix chat she set up for him, despite the trouble it could have caused him. Granted, only a few of her closest friends were present, and the one transcript of the chat came bundled with a virus that did nasty things, but it was a victory for her nonetheless.

"The Pacific Northwest Hunting Club lost an employee tonight. You pulled a file on him back when we went after Reverend Roberts. You remember Albion?"

"His file was a null. Burkingmen had some anecdotes about him. He was working at PNHC?"

"So I understand. A member recommended him. I want to know who that was and something about him."

"Is that all?" Valerie rolled her eyes. "Look, Wolf, no jack."

I stuck my tongue out at her, but she'd already started beating out a harsh staccato on her keyboard. I left the room and mounted the stairs to the first floor. In the kitchen I grabbed two cups of 'kaf and exchanged a series of uninformative grunts with Tom Electric. He had his eyes glued to a Bookman and was doing his best to upload some self-help book into his gray-ROM. "Annie's coming back to town, eh, Tom?"

Grunt and nod.

I looked at the container that had carried the book chip. *"All I Need to Know to Understand Women I Learned In Catholic School?* You sure that's gonna help you?"

Hopeful grunt and emphatic nod.

I shrugged and carried the dual mugs of soykaf from the room. Tom's ex-wife comes to Seattle every six months or so, whether Tom's recovered from the last visit or not. I wondered at his choice of scanning material because Annie struck me as about the most un-nunlike woman I'd ever met. Then again, I couldn't rule out the possibility that she'd found a convent out there that catered to macrobiotically nourished, politically correct, archeo-feminist, neo-retro splatter-metal enthusiasts with bipolar disorders.

Valerie silently forgave me for taking so long when I handed her the brimming mug. "Got your prey."

"It was that *easy*?"

"No, love, I'm that good." She shook her head, her thick brown braid flopping from shoulder to shoulder. "What does Lynn see in you?"

"She knows, deep down, I'm just a real sensitive guy." I gave her a crocodile smile, then leaned against a mainframe cabinet. "Who is he?"

"She. Selene Reece is her name. She's a great granddaughter of Harold Reece. He was a newspaper tycoon before the Awakening. He diversified and left everyone a lot of money. She's a black sheep of the family, the illegitimate daughter of a granddaughter who used a lot of recreational chemicals at a time when it was thought LSD could keep one from goblinizing."

I nodded. Orks and trolls usually bred true, but some folks in the general population are tagged with "monster" genes. They tend to kick in around puberty, causing embarrassment somewhat greater than having your voice crack or your face break out. In essence, their whole body breaks out, and they shift from being normal human kids to orks or even worse.

It's not pretty and usually very confusing. There are plenty of orks who don't make it through the transformation with their psyches intact. There are even more con artists making a fortune selling everything from sugar pills to votive candles to prevent kids from undergoing the change. While kids might not fully understand the problem, their parents do and will do just about anything to avoid the humiliation of having a child "run away."

"This Reece recommended Albion to the Club as a hire? I have a hard time placing Albion and his porcupine coiffure in that kind of place."

Val shrugged and sipped her soykaf. "Cheap thrills for the elite without having to go slumming. The club's computer didn't have any record of his employment, but the tailor who made his uniform still had a copy of the employment record. Selene Reece is listed as his sponsor."

"Checks with what Cutty told me. Where is Reece now?"

"You're expecting a lot in exchange for a kafcup. Tom Electric would have brought me doughnuts."

"I owe you. Do you know where she is?"

Valerie nodded her head. "According to the club schedule, she's up in the Yukon. She won a lottery, and is going after a snow moose. Won't be back for a week."

I smiled widely enough that Valerie knew I was getting myself into trouble and wanted her to set it up. "Can you crack back into their computer to confirm a dinner engagement for me with her there, tonight, about six? Make it look like it was on, then got scrubbed by the lottery win."

She looked hard at me. "You're seeing Lynn tonight, Wolf."

"I know, I know." I set the mug on top of the computer. "Set the dinner thing for six. I meet Lynn at eight. I just want a chance to look around. I'll be in and out, fast. I want to reconnoiter so I can report to Doc when he gets back."

Valerie drew in a deep breath, then let it out slowly. "I suppose, but if you stand Lynn up, you'll regret it."

"I wouldn't dream of it, Val, honest."

"Good." She smiled wickedly. "Because if you do, I'll make sure you're on every boiler-room investment house hot list from now until the collapse of Western civilization."

THREE

This is the part of the story where most narrators would mention that they slept fitfully and had prophetic dreams about the past and future melding together. I'm supposed to tell you all about the dreams, using cryptic terms that will confuse you until things come together later. It's the way you know the stuff you're reading is *art*.

I've got no dreams to share. That doesn't mean I didn't dream, mind you, but just that I don't want to share them. From the second my head hit the pillow in the spare room Raven allotted to me, I dreamed of Lynn. The dreams might have been prophetic—in fact, I was hoping they were—which explains why I'm not going to share them.

I had fully intended to sleep until the sun was so far over the yardarm they'd have to use a satellite link to communicate, but Stealth whooshed and creaked on into the room I use. My eyes came instantly open, but my Viper stayed under the pillow. No sense in wasting a bullet on a target that could have taken an Exocet hit without denting his hide.

"No new toys to show me?" I sat up in the bed and let the frivolity drain out of my voice. His armor is even better against humor than it is against bullets. "What's up, Stealth?"

"Valerie Valkyrie says you're asking about the Pacific Northwest Hunting Club."

I nodded. "Albion had a job there for the past week. He was recommended by a member. I thought I would check it out this evening."

Stealth remained absolutely still for a moment. He didn't so much as breathe, which he really didn't need to do anyway. To help in the assassination work he used to do before he became claw-abled, Stealth traded a lung lobe for an internal air tank with a slow-release oxygen system. Saved his life once—gave him enough time to free his feet from a block of cement at the bottom of the Sound.

At last, the Oracle spoke. "You will be armed?"

Stealth lives by that fragment of wisdom that says, "There is no problem so large that it cannot be solved by the suitable application of plastic explosives." He proved that, both in his professional and private life. In fact, to get out of the cement block, he blew the lower parts of his legs off. That's why, when we do have casual conversations, I don't tell him about hangnails or hernias.

"Actually I expected this to be a soft recon. I have to meet Lynn later..."

"Ms. Ingold."

"That's the one. She doesn't much like guns—she's still hinky about the grunges who grabbed her, so I thought I'd travel light."

"I see." He froze for another second, then turned and started out of the room.

"Hey, Stealth, wait!"

He slowed and looked back over the shoulder at me.

"My change from the cab?"

His Zeiss eyes blinked at me once, then he turned and left.

Stealth's silent departure didn't bother me as much as it might have someone else. He's weird enough that if having him owe me money meant he would try to avoid me, I could live with that. Then again, for all I knew, he had gone off trying to figure how to give me change in bullets of differing calibers.

The Old One gave me a salutary yip as I looked in the mirror at the results of a shower, shave, and the suitable application of sartorial accouterments. I appreciated the sentiment, but I'd wait for Valerie's opinion before deciding whether I was comfortable with my choices. Not that I was that comfortable in the clothes—neckties and nooses have more in common than both starting with the letter N.

Valerie gave me a full 1000-watt smile. "Oh, Wolf, if I had an icebreaker as sharp as you, I'd be in the Aztechnology database and gone running on a kiddie-deck. Double-breasted blazer of blue, good choice, gray slacks, dark socks, white shirt, TAB tie, nice, and the wingtip shoes." She gave me the hairy-eyeball. "You fixing to make this date *real* special?"

I winked at her. "Val, every date with me is special. And the answer is no, I'm not handing her some gold-bound ice. We're having dinner with her great-aunt from St. Louis." I wanted to toss another wisecrack out at her, but the well was dry. Thinking about Lynn and me and the future required so much brainpower that it didn't leave me enough idle cells to keep coming up with smart remarks.

Val gave me a hug and told me to transfer it to Lynn, noting, "You're on your own after that, jack." I gave her a peck on the cheek and specifically told her *not* to pass that to Jimmy Mackelroy from me, then headed out into the garage. I disarmed the Fenris from outside its effective range, then took it roaring out into the Seattle night.

The rain had vanished, and the dark sky looked clear and a tad crisp. I found the Pacific Northwest Hunting Club on the first try and parked down the block. Two chirps from the remote left it on With Extreme Prejudice, which would be more than enough to keep the local footsponges from mistaking it for a bar, bathroom, or king-size bed.

I managed to wrestle the double-breasted jacket's internal button into its hole by the time I reached the awning extending out over the sidewalk. A doorman waited at the top of the stone steps and opened the door for me without comment. Up another flight of steps and a left turn brought me to the club's foyer, where a large man greeted me with a smile. "Yes, sir?"

"Evening. I'm Wynn Archer. I'm supposed to be dining with Selene Reece." I nervously glanced at my watch. "I'm early."

Dark clouds of confusion spread over the man's face. "Ms. Reece has no dinner reservation tonight, sir. Perhaps you are confused as to the evening?"

I shook my head and let my smile tell him I knew I was right. "Wednesday the twenty-seventh. I've been looking forward to this for two weeks."

He held up a hand. "Just a moment." He disappeared behind a curtain and I heard the *click-clack* of a keyboard. I knew Valerie had managed to mess up his records when the sound of key-pounding got louder.

He returned with a smile on his face. "I'm afraid there has been a mistake, sir. Ms. Reece apparently did have reservations, but they were canceled when she went out of town on an urgent trip."

"Are you sure? Perhaps I should wait in the lounge until we see if she makes it. I'm sure you understand that she would have canceled with me if she didn't expect to be here."

The host started to tell me the lounge was only for members, but I'd stuck him on the horns of a dilemma. If he gave me the bum's rush, he could end up embarrassing a member because her plans didn't happen to include informing him of her comings and goings. He took another look at me and must have decided I looked harmless.

"We would be happy to have you wait in the lounge. You do understand, of course, that it is for members only, so..."

I nodded. "I shall wait at the bar and not bother anyone."

His smile told me we had an understanding and I wandered into the bar. Dim and subdued, it featured dark wood panels and rich leather upholstery. Given the identities of the few local celebs I recognized, I figured the club must charge enough in dues that the decorations were probably realthetic. Even the peanuts in the bowl at the bar looked like dirtfruit instead of vat-droppings.

I ordered the house brew, and discovered that a mug of it set me back more than Stealth's cab ride. It tasted pretty good, but not *that* good. I consoled myself by looking at what the others were drinking and guessing at the number of digits in their bar tabs.

I ordered a refill from the bartender and tried to begin a conversation with him, but he sped off to deal with other patrons— the ones who looked like big tippers or like they were there with someone else's spouse. Before he could return to the styx where I was sitting, someone tapped me on the shoulder.

"Mr. Archer? I understand we're having dinner together this evening?"

I turned around and found myself looking up at a woman who surprised me in many ways. Had I been standing she would have come within a centimeter of being as tall as me. Powerful shoulders tapered down to a slender waist and shapely legs that indicated a serious interest in athletics as opposed to milder "shaping" workouts. Her face showed signs of an arctic tan, and the makeup she used carefully blended away the white skin around her brown eyes. Her black hair, which was cut boyishly short, hid her ears and aptly bordered a sharply angular face. A pert nose and full lips made her beautiful by anyone's definition, but the fire in her eyes made her *challenging*.

I offered her my hand. "Pleased to meet you, Ms. Reece." I figured I could go one of two ways at this point, either making her think we both had been deceived, or I could play it straight. As she took my hand in a firm, dry grip, I decided honesty was the best policy. "But I'm not Wynn Archer. My name's Wolfgang Kies." I gestured to the empty stood beside me. "Please, join me. I can explain the reason for my deception."

She watched me for a moment, reflexively squinting her left eye as if she were sighting down a rifle barrel at me. "I like someone willing to shift tactics when the opening gambit fails. You have five minutes." She released my hand after she slid onto the stool across from me and ordered a gimlet from the bartender.

I remained silent until he had withdrawn, then idly drew an A in the moisture ring on the bar. "A young man you recommended for work here was killed last night."

"The albino, Albion. I heard." She sipped her drink, then set it back on the bar. "I learned about it early this morning when I checked my computer system. I returned from the Yukon immediately. While updating my schedule, I saw the dinner notation and came right over. Do you know who killed him?"

I shook my head. "No, but I knew Albion, and I know people who will be sorry he died. I want to find out who did him, and you're about the only lead I have."

"I see." She dipped a finger in her drink and raised it toward her mouth. A droplet hung from her nail like venom from a scorpion's sting, then she licked it off with a flick of her tongue. "Albion repaired the stereo in my Mako and asked me to mention him to my friends. I did, and a couple suggested I get him a job here."

"I guess I'm missing the connection." I popped a peanut into my mouth. "Why would you want a mohawked street punk working here?"

Selene crossed her legs. Her outfit, a dark green silk blouse under dark green blazer and tight black skirt, left a lot of leg for me to look at as she did so. "This Club is for individuals who are adventurers. We dare go out and challenge Mother Nature in her wondrous and magical splendor."

She pointed through the doorway back toward where a gallery of holopics showed images of members with creatures they had killed. "The membership thrives on traveling to exotic places, seeing exotic things..."

"And killing them?"

"Among other things." She half-shut her eyes and studied me over the edge of her glass. "We're thrill-seekers."

"So bringing a piece of Seattle streetlife into your club is a thrill."

"You're edging toward asking if I think Albion was chosen as prey by a member of our group." She toyed with the stem of her glass, slowly turning it so the light glowed off the liquor's legs. "We live for danger."

I watched her face closely. "And stalking Albion through the concrete world that is his natural habitat wouldn't be dangerous?"

"We may be the ultimate predators, but we're not murderers. Bringing someone like Albion in here is importing some of the danger from the streets, yes. He's not what we normally expect to see here, so he was a curiosity." She clasped her hands together over one knee. "For a while we maintained a cheetah and a Bengal tiger here before certain Creature Liberationists started to threaten us."

The Old One howled in the back of my mind. "I can imagine them seeing this as a Temple of Death, no problem."

"But they do not know what we truly do, for this is also a Sanctuary for Life." She laughed easily. "Between this club and all the animal freedom groups combined, who do you think has spent more money providing habitats for the endangered and threatened species out there?"

"Is this a trick question?" I frowned. "They do."

"No, they do *not*." The skin tightened around her eyes. "The area where I went hunting a snow moose, for example, is all a private preserve purchased and maintained through this club. Our members, either through the club or on their own, have placed acres and acres of threatened wetlands and forests into park systems, both public and private. Did you realize that since the latter half of the twentieth century, it's been the hunters and the licensing fees they pay that has guaranteed wildlife management and, in many cases, actually allowed the animal population to exceed that of colonial times?"

I sat back and did my best to look contrite. "No, I did not realize that."

"It's true." She casually waved her hand toward the other patrons in the bar. "Our membership is also involved in many philanthropic projects right here in Seattle. Part of that is reflected in our willingness to employ someone like Albion."

"Do you think someone took this 'preserve' idea too far with Albion and killed him?"

"I certainly hope not." She leaned forward and I brought my ear close to her mouth. "In a place like this, there are always rumors of someone having hunted the most dangerous prey. Liquor dreams and vaporware, but it is possible someone decided to make them real. If they did, I'm responsible because I brought him here."

I leaned back and took a pull on my beer. I knew from Stealth's description of the weapon that killed Albion that commissioning it would have required the sort of money that someone in the Pacific Northwest Hunting Club certainly would possess. It also struck me as absolutely possible that a member could have decided that harvesting a little two-footed quarry in the city beat freezing in Alaska to bag a rack of antlers. Of course, the one thing I knew that she did not was that Albion was only the latest in a series.

"These stories ever center on one person here?"

She looked up and didn't even try to hide her surprise. "No, not that I know of." She took a sip. "This is very disturbing." She concentrated, her dark brows arrowing down toward the bridge of her nose. "Come with me, and we will discuss this with the Director."

I glanced at my watch, then shook my head. "Can't. I'm meeting someone. Albion's not going anywhere. This can wait for a day or so."

She nodded, then stared down at her glass and the liquid still left in it. "Are you free tomorrow night? I can arrange for us to meet with the Director then." Her expression sharpened and her nostrils flared as she watched me out of the corner of her eye. "You will be my guest tomorrow evening for dinner."

I waved the offer off. "Not necessary, Ms. Reece, really."

"I insist." Her smile warmed and warmed me. "You intrigue me. You bluff your way in here, then admit your deception. You are different from most."

"Exotic?"

"Challenging, Mr. Kies. I'd advise you to accept my invitation. Anyone here can tell you that, as a hunter, I am relentless."

"So I am in your sights?"

She eyed me very frankly, and the Old One started a low growl in the back of my head. "You are too imaginative to be a literalist, Mr. Kies. I find pursuit more thrilling than a kill, and my taste in men does not run to corpses."

I caught the invitation in her voice, and the warning that whatever happened would be on her terms, and her terms alone. "Seven, here?"

She took up my left hand and gave it a squeeze. "Twenty-four hours, then."

I nodded and gave her a kiss on the cheek. As I walked away from the club, Albion became a ghost. Learning who killed him had become immaterial as a reason for my willingness to meet Selene Reece the next night. She knew it, I knew it.

Wolf season was open.

FOUR

Wolf season almost closed again because Lynn's great-aunt Sadie tried to get me into a captive breeding program. "Oh, Wolfgang, you are such a gentleman. You two make a lovely couple. You'll have wonderful children—they'll be smart and handsome."

Luckily Lynn fended off her aunt's comments, which left me time to deal with the Old One. For some reason, he'd joined forces with Sadie, and spent most of the evening divided between complaining that my prime rib was too well done and praising Lynn. *"This is the bitch for you, Longtooth. Her eyes are bright, her ruddy coat is long, and she is cunning. Your pups will be strong and have sharp teeth."*

I was sure Lynn, who had once mentioned a desire to breastfeed children, would love that last bit. Fortunately, Sadie later started talking about the twenty-two cats who lived with her, which cooled the Old One's opinion of his ally. Even so, through the rest of the evening, he yipped encouragingly any time Lynn did anything he felt should make me proud.

The dreams I had enjoyed earlier in the day did not turn out to be literally prophetic, but they functioned perfectly in an allegorical sense. Lynn and I, after we dropped off her great-aunt, spent some time wandering through the market, laughing about what her aunt had said. As Lynn doesn't know about the Old One yet, I didn't tell her his comments, but I let my laughter batter him into grumbling retreat. That was good, because we later retreated to my apartment and engaged in activities that would have had him yipping encouragement to Lynn on a nearly incessant basis.

Lynn woke me up early—the hour on the clock wasn't even close to double digits—then showered and headed off to work. She normally didn't spend the full evening with me because she shared a corporate suite with her folks. With Aunt Sadie using her room, the Ingolds chose to believe Lynn's story that she would stay the night with a friend.

She asked if she'd see me later, but I told her Raven was coming back into town and I had something to do. Because we'd met in the course of Raven, Stealth, and me saving her from kidnappers, she has a vague idea of what I do. Given that I was planning to meet Selene later, I decided that not clarifying my plans was a good thing.

I crashed for another couple of hours, then got up close to noon. Deciding I needed a new suit for the night's adventure, I dressed quickly and headed out. The Old One's grumbling started to give me a headache, but I managed to ignore him and it. Hopping into the Fenris, I headed downtown and started a walking tour of the haberdasheries.

After a few false starts, I settled on a French-cut black suit with double-breasted blazer. The tailor who measured me for alterations asked if I would be "heavy" or "thick" while wearing it, but I shook my head. Wearing a gun or a Kevlar vest was not in order for dinner at one of the city's most elegant clubs. I picked out a tie and shirt to go with the suit, then had lunch and a beer at Kell's while the tailor worked on the alterations.

As night began to creep close, it brought with it a sense of impending doom. Normally I would have put it down to Stealth being in the vicinity, but I suspected that Lynn and Selene were at the root of it. As I thought things over, I could see myself speeding in the Fenris toward a cliff with a nasty drop-off. A cloud of dust obscured what was behind me, and I had the distinct feeling that it hid an equally devastating drop.

I knew I loved Lynn and I hoped she felt the same way about me. I had never fallen so hard for a woman, nor had I ever lasted as long with one. Most women decided I was trouble and gave me walking papers before things became serious. Getting rejected like that *did* hurt, but we usually managed to part on friendly terms, which helped take a lot of the sting out of it. Besides, plenty of other women were willing to offer me solace, so I'd learned to live within the myth that someday I'd find the woman meant for me.

Now that day had dawned and I found it more terrifying than most of the gun battles I'd lived through. In those instances, the worst that could happen was that I could die. In this situation, I could end up *living*. I'd have responsibilities and obligations. While Lynn was more than worth all that, a huge chunk of me saw my window on freedom snapping shut.

Enter Selene. She and Lynn were of the same species and gender, but the similarities ended there. Selene was very attractive and aggressive. Being pursued by someone so powerful and desirable was one hell of an ego-steroid. I was staring at a future imprisoned with one woman while Selene Reece stood there handing me a "*Get Out of Jail Free*" card.

The Pacific Northwest Hunting Club was downtown, and not that far from the Fuchi corporate tower where Lynn lived, so I parked the Fenris in an alley about four blocks from the club. I set the anti-theft system at three chirps, figuring that the alley would keep down the number of injured bystanders. Pocketing the remote control, I set off for the club.

The heavy-set gentleman who'd ushered me to the bar the night before was again at his station. He smiled when he saw me and beckoned me to follow him. "This way, Mr. Kies. Ms. Reece has already been seated."

Selene slipped out of the corner booth as I arrived. She wore a cerulean blue chemise with hair-thin straps under a darker blue crepe du chine jacket and matching pants. She offered me her hand and I kissed it, bowing slightly as I did so. She laughed and we both sat down.

The maitre'd offered me a menu, but I shook my head. "I trust your judgment, Selene."

She smiled and ordered a magnum of champagne and raw oysters for an appetizer. "For the main course we will have the venison steaks, rare, with mushrooms and wild rice."

"Very good, madam."

As he withdrew, she looked at me carefully. "I trust you like venison."

I nodded. "Get it yourself?"

"No. The last deer I shot was a year ago, and I gave some of the meat to another member. He is repaying the favor." Her smile grew. "I didn't get the oysters myself either, but I trust you'll enjoy them nonetheless."

"I'm sure I will."

Our champagne arrived, and she sat back to sip from her glass. "You are even more fascinating than I thought, Wolfgang. Until I did some research I had no idea you were associated with Richard Raven. From what I learned, you've hunted enough to be a member here."

I shrugged. "I bag vermin, mostly. Doc keeps me around for amusement value. And my friends call me Wolf."

"You are too modest, Wolf." Her voice lingered over my name, and the prospect of her becoming an intimate friend made me smile. "From what I understand, a number of the local street gangs consider you quite dangerous."

"I gather, Selene, that various species of big game think of you in the same way."

"Touché. We are a pair, it seems, evenly matched."

I raised my glass in a salute. "To being a perfect match."

"Indeed."

The rest of the evening went from there to become quite hot. We both drank more champagne than we should have, but we stopped at silly on our way to being drunk. We engaged in a war of innuendo and double-entendre that promised much for the night until the maitre'd came over and informed her that the Director was in his office.

She became serious with that news, then broke into a giggle when the maitre'd walked away. "I suppose we should take care of business before we *get down* to business, yes, Mr. Kies?" She looped her purse strap over her left shoulder and slid from the booth.

I nodded almost soberly. "Indeed, Ms. Reece."

I followed her from the dining room and up some stairs. We passed down a corridor that took us beyond the room below and ended at a double door. As we approached, I heard a *click* and the doors opened for us. Without a second thought, I walked into the dark room.

Before I could even begin to ponder why the room was so dimly lit, fire ignited in my spine. I heard a faint crackling sound and agony convulsed my body radiating out from a spot between my shoulder blades. I tried to turn, but given that my equilibrium had succumbed to the alcohol and the electricity running through me had clobbered my muscles, all I managed to do was drop hard to the floor.

Selene hooked a toe under my chest and flipped me over onto my back. In her left hand I saw the stunner she'd used on me. She hit the switch, letting a jagged blue energy line spring to life between the two electrodes on one end. My body jerked reflexively and pain neurons fired again just for the heck of it. She watched me and slowly began to smile.

"Forgive me for this."

I thought, at first, she was speaking to me, but I was wrong. From my perspective on the floor, everything looked very tall. This included the horseshoe-shaped high-bench that ran from one corner of the room to the other. Seated behind the bench, in tall chairs with split oval tops and silhouetted by the backlight, a dozen members of the club looked down at me.

Suddenly, a light from above and behind a chair flashed on. It illuminated the snarling face of a mounted bear's head. "I have an inquiry," a man with a deep, wheezy voice called out.

"Yes, Brother Bear?" Selene said, bowing her head. When she spoke a light flashed on behind an empty chair. It illuminated a huge, translucent snake that I thought just might have been a Central American moon python.

"I believe, Sister Snake, you have already hunted a street ape this month."

"Valid point, Brother Bear, but this one is special. He is a threat to us, but he is likely the greatest challenge any of us have known. Also, because of the chance of discovery the other night, I was unable to obtain a bloodlock. Because of the rules, I do not really have a kill credited to me."

Another light flashed on, revealing the head of a sable unicorn with an ivory spire twisting up and out of its skull. It was located at the keystone position in the semicircle. "Sister Snake is correct. This one is hers to hunt."

"Thank you, Grandmaster." Selene dropped to one knee and gave me a second jolt of juice by pressing the stunner to my chest. I defibrillated up into the air and back down, then lay there like a gumby-chiphead.

She kissed me hard on the lips. "Nothing personal, Wolf, but it's the hunt. I know you'll be leagues better than Albion."

She stood and took a step back. I heard a *click* and the floor dropped away from under me. I started sliding downward headfirst, something that did not make me very happy because I still couldn't control my limbs. As the slide cut into a downward spiral, my dinner started to come up on me, with the oysters leading the break for freedom. The champagne, being stirred up in my stomach, started gathering for a belch that increased my desire to vomit.

Suddenly, the slide ended. When my shoulders hit the canvas padding I did an involuntary somersault and landed flat on my stomach. I bounced once and abandoned the fight against my stomach. When I landed again I puked up everything I'd eaten, from dessert to the peanuts I'd had at the bar the night before.

I tried to fight the dry heaves, but they had an ally working from inside my head. *"Yes, Longtooth, purge yourself of the poisons. Let me fill you, let me help you. We will find this bitch who is hunting you and we will slay her."* Visions of flashing fangs and bright blood filled my mind as the Old One encouraged me.

"No," I wheezed. Kicking weakly, I managed to push myself away from my now liquid diet. Then I somehow pulled myself far enough from the puddle to put my right hand down and lever myself over to the wall of the small room into which I'd been dumped.

I dragged my body toward the wall and sat with my back to it, wiping my mouth on the back of my sleeve. I spat several times, trying to cleanse my mouth, but I only diluted the acidic taste. I let my head rest against the wall and I closed my eyes for a moment. *So, this is what it's like to be a deboned chicken.*

As much danger as I had faced in my time with Raven, this had to be absolutely the worst. The alcohol had worked wonders with my think-box, though throwing up would help curb further damage. The stunner had reduced my muscles to rubber, though they were coming back. That left me in a dark box while somewhere out there a woman with a fancy rifle was preparing to turn me into an endangered species.

Hell, if she had her way, I'd be extinct.

Under similar circumstances on other occasions I'd at least had a few advantages. There was my belt buckle with a homing device I could activate in an emergency, but tonight I'd worn the new belt I bought to go with my suit. I'd also left off my usual kevlar vest for the evening. Ditto for my gun, which I hadn't figured I'd be needing.

"Those are artificial, Longtooth. You do not need them when you have me."

"I need them when someone is shooting at us. For all you've done for me, the only thing you're not good at is dodging bullets."

I heard him howl in protest, but we each knew the other was right in some ways. His speed and extrasensory abilities would help me enormously if I was going to survive. He wanted me to attack, but I wanted his skills to let me do only one thing right now—run for the Fenris. With his speed, Selene had no chance of keeping up with me. "Give it to me, Old One. Your speed, your eyes, your ears, and your nose."

"As you wish, Longtooth, but outside. This place stinks with the fear of others."

That came as no surprise. As the Old One strengthened my body, I found my muscles responding more or less properly to conscious commands. I wasn't in any condition to perform microsurgery, but walking and chewing gum at the same time weren't beyond me.

With the Old One's eyes, I saw the faint outline of a square on the wall away from where the slide entered the room. I crawled over to it and pushed it open. It locked up in place and showed me a three-meter drop to an alley. *Great. Get outside, get my bearings, and make a run for the Fenris.*

I went out through the hole feet first and dropped into a crouch as I hit the ground. The cool night air helped clear my head. I loosened my tie and undid the top button of my shirt so I could breathe easier. The Old One's olfactory prowess kicked in, and I couldn't get Selene's perfume, which made me feel better. I turned my back to the wind and saw the lights on top of the Fuchi tower.

I knew where I was.

So did Selene.

The bullet nailed me in the chest about ten centimeters below my left nipple. It spun me around, smacking me against the club wall, then threw me into a pair of overflowing garbage cans. I landed on my left side, doubling the grinding agony I felt in my ribs. I heard a hissing sound and felt like something inside my lungs was doing everything it could to claw its way out.

Scrambling to my feet, I sprinted down the alley and ducked out into the street. I headed away from the Fenris for a block before I realized what I was doing. At that point I ducked into another alley and kept a dumpster downwind.

I reached around my back and could feel that the bullet had not exited my chest. I pulled off my tie, fighting the pain that came with each breath, and looped it around my chest. Then I dug out my wallet from my back pocket and tore from it a small plastic sleeve used to protect holopics. This one just happened to be filled with one of Lynn. I smiled, slipped it inside my shirt, and pressed it over the hole in my chest. I tightened the tie to hold it in place, and the hissing sound stopped.

That turned out to be fortunate, because it allowed me to hear the distant sound of an animal loping after me. *Cybercur!* Imagining a beast that could carry an armored car off in its augmented jaws, I panicked. Adrenaline coursed through me, and my heart pounded like the pistons in an over-revving engine.

The Old One took over with a calm rationality that mocked my fear. He instantly assessed the situation and knew that I could not fight. I could barely run. He knew the shredded and collapsed lung in my chest would not help me, and that if I sought to evade the creature tracking me, my wound would kill me.

For once we agreed, and he sent me out into the night. Though I was there on the run and I remember it, I remained detached. I remember leaving that second alley and vaulting a speeding Ford Americar. I landed on both feet in the middle of the street, took a half-step back to avoid the leading bumper on a Mercedes 920 XL, then spun around and hopped on the running board of a Pierce Arrow landau reconstruction.

After a block of free ride the Arrow's driver started going for an Uzi, but the Old One snarled at him. He kept his hands on the wheel and his eyes on the road for another block, then I jumped off and sprinted down an alley. Out on the far street, I cut toward the Fuchi tower and into the alley that hid my Fenris.

The Old One headed me straight for it, but I re-exerted control and stopped. I pulled the remote control from my pocket and disarmed the anti-theft device. Smiling, I took one step forward, then staggered and leaned heavily against the car as pain lanced from the wound through my chest. The world began to go dark at the edges.

Keep a clear head!

"I can master this beast, Longtooth. I have watched you do it often enough," the Old One said.

No chance. The Old One considers Vehicular Manslaughter a recreational activity. *Just rest for a second, then I'll...*

I heard a growl, and it took me a moment to realize it wasn't from the Old One. I looked over and saw a huge animal at the mouth of the alley. The glow of street lamps traced the silvery claws mounted to the tops of its paws. Twin pistons hissed as the monster opened its jaw. I saw that its teeth had been replaced top and bottom with a razor-steel strip that included spikes where its canines had once been. And instead of eyes, I saw two red starbursts that went nova as the thing looked at me.

Slowly I turned around and worked my away back around the edge of the Fenris. Looking at the chromed dog over the top of the car, I kind of wished I'd been driving a car big enough to wall off the alley. *No, I had to go for fast and flashy. Val always said this car would get me killed.*

The dog lowered its head and sniffed the ground. He took a step forward and the black fur on its spine came up. A shiver rippled through its muscles and shook it right down to its stubby tail.

The Old One growled a challenge and I couldn't stop him. I voiced the howl and the dog's head came up. I hoped, for a second, that *canis chromus* would run off, but it didn't.

"It can smell Death on you, Longtooth. I am sorry."

The dog loped forward, then came straight at me.

I pushed myself back off the Fenris and hit the remote control. As the Hitachi hound leaped over the car's nose and landed on the roof, four chirps sounded. Before their echoes died, I hit the ground on my back and the Fenris' defense system kicked into overdrive.

I saw the dog in silhouette for a second before all its fur spontaneously combusted. It flashed over, blackening the chrome as the putrid gray cloud drifted up. Then I noticed that the red dots in the eyes had dilated to different sizes as the dog's muscles convulsed. Spraying battery juice and chips against the alley wall, the left side of its head suddenly exploded outward, spinning the cybermutt around and toppling it off by the passenger side of the car.

I lay back for a moment as a cough punched pain through my chest. Hitting the remote control again, I disarmed the Fenris and crawled toward it. I reached up for a door handle, but the trim burned me. I sank my right hand into the sleeve of my jacket and tried again, this time successfully prying the door open.

I started to pull myself into the Fenris and was far enough gone that I didn't even consider what I was doing to the interior. I did know I couldn't drive, but the cell phone would let me call Raven or Val or Stealth and get me some help. Bracing myself with my left arm against the floor, I straightened my legs and grabbed for the phone.

Selene's kick to the back of my knees dropped me to the ground. I twisted around and sat half-upright against the car. I hugged my left arm against the aching hole in my chest and looked up at her. I tried to say something smart, but a cough cut in and hijacked my throat.

"You did well, Mr. Kies. You should have died long before this." She looked over the hood toward the steaming mound of dog flesh and metal over by the alley wall. "And you cost me Cerberus. That wasn't nice."

I half-smiled despite the rifle tucked under her arm. "I suppose you know this means I probably won't be having dinner with you again."

"That was a consideration," she said and her smile made me remember why I'd wanted to have dinner with her in the first place.

"Had you been anyone else, I might have not decided to hunt you." She licked her lips. "Pursue, yes, but not hunt."

My vision began to tunnel slowly. "Lone Star has a file on your activities, you know."

"No it doesn't, Mr. Kies. One of our board members is a major Lone Star stockholder." Her rifle swung into line with my heart. I didn't care what Stealth thought, it didn't look much like a toy from my vantage point. "The game is over."

Selene crouched down and brushed hair away from my forehead. She dug her left hand into her jacket pocket, then brought out something that briefly flashed silver. Her hand returned to my head and I heard a *click*.

Through the shadows I saw her draw away holding a lock of my hair. "You make me glad I didn't get my bloodlock from Albion."

The cell phone started to ring. "Mind if I get that?"

"Go ahead, if you can," she said as the world went dark. "Even if help were on the way, you'd be dead before they found you."

The sound of another bullet being jacket into the chamber of her rifle was the last thing I heard.

FIVE

I discovered, upon wakening, that reincarnation had to be true.

I felt like a retread.

Fearing the worst, I opened my eyes and found myself lying in the bed I used at Raven's headquarters. I tried to take a normal breath but something tight was constricting my chest. Lifting the blankets I saw bandages wrapped around me. I also noticed an oxygen tube held tightly beneath my nose and a plasma bag running fluid in through the needle stuck into my right arm.

"It was clean, Wolf."

I dropped the blankets and saw Raven standing in the doorway. He's taller than me, and broader, but not in a steroid mutant kind of way. He just looks tall and muscular, an Amerindian Hercules from the tips of his toes to the top of his head. He has the copper skin, long black hair, and high cheekbones to make the image stick, too.

In fact, only two things ruin it. The tips of his elven ears poke up through his hair, which is the only clue to his race. An elf built like Raven is decidedly rare, and Raven is rarer still. His eyes bear that out.

They always manage to look straight through me. They're dark, like chips of obsidian, but they have these funny lights in them. The best way to describe it is that he's got a bit of the aurora borealis trapped in there. The lights are blue and red and I like to think they flash in time with Raven's thoughts, which means they're always moving very fast.

I nodded and gave him a smile. "Did you do your stuff to my ribs?"

He folded his arms across his chest and leaned against the door jamb. "The bullet had pulverized approximately twelve centimeters of rib and micro-perforated your lung. You were in shock and were not stable, so I decided not to crack your chest. I was left no choice. I used magic to re-inflate your lung and knit the bone shards back together. The IV is to get fluids back into you." Color rioted through Raven's dark eyes. "Your natural healing process is fast. You should feel better in a couple of days."

Raven is the only other living person who knows all about the Old One, and the reference to my natural healing process told me the Old One had been at work. *"I will have you healthy soon, Longtooth. I did not need his help."*

I threw the blankets off, then pulled the sheet around me and sat up. The room swam, but I steadied myself against the footboard before I could collapse. "I have to get up, Doc. I know who killed Albion. I know why. Can't wait. More people will die."

I felt his hands on my shoulders. "Valerie traced your location after the Fenris sent a call out to inform us about the attempted theft. While I was trying to call you, she learned you were dining with Selene Reece. The club tried to erase the record of the date, but she caught it. Reece has dropped off the edge of the earth. She'll lay low. We've got time to get you healthy."

I shook my head. "No, it's not just her. It's all of them. They've been taking turns." I looked up into his eyes. "They own a chunk of Lone Star. I need your help."

I swear Raven looked back through my eyes and reached some sort of communion with the Old One. I felt the Wolf spirit's vitality surge through me. Doc took my right arm and eased the needle out of it. "Whatever you need, my friend."

"Good. First clothes, then back-up." I smiled as I heard the Old One howl in my mind. "Then it's our turn to hunt."

Raven put the call out for help. Tark and Kid Stealth didn't answer, but Tom Electric and Zig and Zag did. Sporting some body armor and my MP-9[3], I was sure the lot of us could have taken on the world and gone the distance.

Tom ended up driving Raven's Rolls, with Iron Mike Morrissey in the navigator's seat. His partner, Tiger Jackson, rode in the back with Raven and me, starting sullen and getting more so every time I referred to his partner and him as Zig and Zag.

Raven agreed to the plan I laid out as we rode through the night. "I concur, Wolf. Mr. Jackson and Mr. Morrissey will hold the top of the stairs while Tom secures the front door. You and I will deal with the club's Board of Directors." Doc nodded solemnly as I jacked a round into the MP-9's chamber. "And I'll let you do the talking."

"Good." I looked at the big black gillette across from me. "Any questions?"

---

[3] I'd like to say I stuck with the MP-9 because it was an old friend, but the fact was, I really wanted a cannon. Unfortunately, given how I was feeling, a gun with only a few working parts was all I could handle.

Zag nodded. "This hunting club has lots of wheels. If things get ballistic, are we clear to spray up the place?" I was set to nod yes, but Raven shook his head.

"I'm hoping we don't have to end up shooting. As Wolf has aptly pointed out, we only have confirmation of one member actually murdering anyone. We just need to let the Directors know that their new prey is never in season here in Seattle." He looked at me. "Right, Wolf?"

I frowned, which brought a smile to Zag's face, then nodded. I agreed only because wanton murder wasn't really my style. I'd shoot Selene without a second thought, but I didn't know who else in the club had been cap-bustin' on society's ciphers. Purging their membership would only bring heat down on us and it wouldn't hurt them at all. What would hurt, and what Valerie was doing from her haunt in the Matrix, was deducting a healthy "consulting fee" from their club account—including the cost of burning and burying my suit.

Tom double-parked us, and Iron Mike covered the doorman. I winked at him as I went by. Wearing a black leather jacket, jeans, and combat boots, I wasn't really dressed for the club. The MP-9 *was* stylish, which is why I gave the maitre'd a good look at it. "I'm here to see the Board. Are they still here?"

He nodded and opened his mouth to speak, but no words came out. I eased the gunmuzzle's pressure on his bow tie and he swallowed to make sure his throat still worked. "You can't go in there. They're in executive session."

"Always seen myself as executive material," I barked at him. I stepped past and he tried to grab me. I heard a *thump*, then a sigh. I glanced back at Tiger and saw him tuck away a sap, then headed up the stairs. Tom Electric sat himself on the maitre'd's stool and pinned the man to the ground with an AK-97.

Zig and Zag took up positions at the top of the stairs while I led Raven deeper into the building. With a kick I splintered the lock on the boardroom door and boldly strode into the center of the room. I did remember the trap door and used the hall light spilling into the room to avoid its outline. All around me I saw hunched silhouettes leaning forward.

"Sorry to be interrupting, Brothers and Sisters. I never got to thank you for your hospitality before." I sketched a careful bow, ending it abruptly when my rib began to ache. "When I was invited to dinner, I hardly expected to become the center of attention."

The Grandmaster's sable unicorn kill became illuminated as he spoke. "What do you want, Mr. Kies?"

"I'm wondering how I get a bloodlock off a chrome-dome like you." I arched an eyebrow at him. "If I off you, do I get a chair on your board and have your ugly mug perched behind me?"

Brother Bear took offense at my tone. "You have no right to be here. Leave at once."

I swung the MP-9 in his direction. The single shot I let off passed just over his head, between the wings of his chair, and exploded the bear's head. "Damn, shooting high. That happens after you've had a hole blown in your chest."

"Your attempt at humor is not amusing, Mr. Kies." The Grandmaster sat back in his chair. "I can understand your anger. Will fifty thousand nuyen show you we're sorry?"

"Fifty K is a nice sum for the first installment, but I'll give you a break." I shrugged easily. "One time deal: you give me the money and you stop the hunts."

"Policies of this club are not your concern." The Grandmaster leaned forward. "If you are threatening us with war, you will find yourself on the losing side."

Raven came up on my right. "Will we?"

The Grandmaster nodded slowly and the other silhouettes aped him in silence. "We have the weapons and the money and the power to destroy you. You are nothing. No one will notice if you die. We offer to enrich you and give you your life. Do not press your luck."

"Luck is not part of this equation." Raven shook his head resolutely. He kept his voice low, but it still filled the room. "You are huntsmen and pride yourselves on having mastered the most dangerous creatures on the planet. You study your quarry. You track it and you take it." Raven's eyes pulsed with fire. "This time, though, you have been stupid, and all the material things you have will not afford you victory."

"Is that so?"

"It is. You hunt the SINless because they are insignificant. Within the shadows of this city, life is cheap and you know it. You think this makes you invincible because no one cares about your prey." Doc's eyes sharpened. "You would get more of a fight to protect the rights of rats to live in a tenement than you would to defend the lives of people like Albion."

"You make my case for me." The Grandmaster's head came up. "Those people are nothing. They mean nothing. We know it, those ignoble beasts know it. Their lives are worthless."

I saw where Raven was headed, and his nod let me pick up the fight. "You're right, their lives are worthless. That means we can hand a gun and fifty nuyen to any of them along with your picture. See, the only thing you don't have going for you is numbers. There are more of them than there are you, and even if your security is good enough to pick up sixty or seventy percent of their attacks, you'll still be maggot-munchies."

I let out a chuckle. "And, hey, when they learn you're going to be hunting them anyway, we won't even have to pay them. If we offer a prize, they'll pay us for a ticket in the martial lottery."

The image of a bazooka-toting biped Bambi battalion shooting back at them did not thrill the membership in the least. "Doc, do you think we can get an all-night printer to start turning out hunting permits on our way back across town?"

"We can use the phone in the Rolls to start things going."

The Grandmaster sat back. "If these hunts that you allege to be occurring—but which we have never admitted taking place—were to stop..."

"And a schedule of reparation payments were made to the survivors of these hunt victims," Raven added.

"Quite. If this were to take place, then you would see no reason to take action?"

Raven nodded. "A list of persons and amounts to be paid can be in your computer by tomorrow. If you agree to meet it, I would consider the matter closed."

"Done."

Raven looked over at me. "Is that satisfactory to you, Wolf?"

"'Cept for one thing, yeah, very satisfactory." I looked up at the Grandmaster. "When you next see Sister Snake, tell her we still have a date." I jiggled the MP-9. "Tell her it's flak-vest optional."

As we headed back down the hallway and picked up Zig and Zag at the top of the stairs, I tried to figure out how I'd find Selene Reece. With her money and the connections the club afforded her, she could be hiding literally anywhere in the world. After today, she'd know I was still alive, and would dig her hidey-hole a little deeper.

And if that didn't make things tough enough, she'd know I was after her. Given her skills as a hunter, I had no doubt I'd be facing the most dangerous prey. Oddly enough, that did not concern me as much as I thought it would. The very fact that I could make a run at her meant she wasn't infallible.

Stepping into a warm rain as we left the club, I turned to Raven. "I won't make the mistake she did. When I do her, I'll make sure she's dead."

"I am certain that is what she intended to do with you, Wolf." Raven nodded at the shadows near the Rolls. "I don't believe she got that chance."

Stealth opened the Rolls' boot and shoved a rifle-case into it. He slammed the lid down with his flesh and blood hand, then stepped up onto the sidewalk. He said nothing, a flesh and chrome monument.

"Selene Reece is dead?"

The Murder Machine nodded once. "I'd heard rumors of a club that hunted people for sport. I decided discovering it needed to be more than a project of leisure."

I shivered at his cold, mechanical delivery. "You learned I was going to the club last night. You found me in time to kill Selene."

"300 meters, .600 Nitro-express, night scope, no rest." Zag shivered. "Impressive shot."

I swallowed hard. "Thanks for the freebie."

"Amateurs kill for free." He popped open a compartment on his metallic left arm and tossed me a blue silk sachet tied with a lock of black hair. "I am a professional." Through the silk I felt some coins[4] making up change from the ten nuyen I'd given him two nights before. From the second he'd seen Albion's body, Stealth had known what would happen. That was why he'd insisted I give him the money and why I'd had a guardian angel following me, waiting...

I looked up at him. "Was I your bait?"

"You were my patron."

I nodded, ignoring the growing ache in my ribs. Slipping the knot from the silk, I poured the money into my pocket. I offered Stealth back his trophy, but he shook his head.

I tossed Selene's hair into the gutter, and as the rain washed it toward the sewer I realized that no matter how much of a predator you figure yourself to be, you can always be someone else's fair game.

---

[4] Yeah, coins are archaic, but Stealth knows I don't handle new guns well...

IF AS BEAST
YOU DON'T SUCCEED

ONE

When you come right down to it, there's no easy way to tell the woman you intend to marry that you're a werewolf. If I'd been a hit-man for the mob or had worked clean-up for yakuza enforcers or had even been a poacher out in the Tír, I could have told her straight out. I would have taken Lynn's hand in mine and said, "Look, there's something you should know about me. I've done some bad things in my life, but that's all ended now."

That would have been easy. The confession, some tears, some hugging, some kissing, and an "I'll marry you, Wolf," would have all followed one after the other. Not that I'd gone this route before, but I knew it would have worked. Women seem to find honesty seductive—probably because there's so damned little of it in the courting process. Besides, I had it so bad for Lynn I couldn't let myself even think about her rejecting me.

But that was in the case where I confessed being a mass murderer or something just as bad. Being a werewolf, on the other hand, was much worse[1].

Lynn would try to understand, and I knew that for her a try was as good as doing. Her parents would be decidedly more difficult to

---

[1] Pretty much every pundit who ever posted an opinion to the altweirdtblks.shapeshifier news groups has noted that there are no such things as werewolves. And Raven had told me that I'm really just blessed by the Wolf spirit—so blessed that a chunk of it is subletting a portion of my cerebral cortex. Fine. But if you ask anyone on the street what they call someone who becomes a wolf under the full moon, "someone blessed by the Wolf spirit" isn't the answer you'll get.

sway. In an instant I saw Lynn's parents inviting me to dinner and the effect my little revelation might have. "That's nice, dear," Blanche Ingold would say politely. "Does that mean we shouldn't use the good silver?"

Phil would have a use for the silver and probably wouldn't have that difficult a time finding the bullet molds or a gunsmith to do the trick for him. I liked Phil, and he liked me, but he'd still be at the door with a gun to keep me away from Lynn. I couldn't blame him, really. No man wants to think about having to paper-train his grandchildren.

My telecomm beeped, rescuing me from the nihilistic and depressing spiral my thoughts had spun into over the last two hours. I swore when I saw it was only a piece of email from Raven. I'd wanted him to stay online so we could discuss the message I'd sent him earlier. I decrypted his message by hitting two keys and read it as the words scrolled up the screen.

> *Wolf,*
>
> *Kid Stealth, Tom Electric, Tark, and I are taking Valerie Valkyrie and heading up to Oak Harbor to probe a bit more deeply into Mr. Sampson's background. Uncertain when we will return. I would heartily encourage you continue to see Lynn Ingold, as we would not want another attempt to abduct her.*
>
> *We will discuss the matter of your message upon my return. I am glad you are happy, my friend.*
>
> *—Raven*

As I read the message I found myself of two minds, the two at war with each other. I was a bit piqued that Raven hadn't asked me to go with him on the investigation. I am, after all, his longest surviving aide, and I've got talents that all the cybernetics built into Kid Stealth and Tom Electric combined can't equal.

More important, I'd brought the Sampson matter to his attention in the first place. The Halloweeners, a street gang that controlled what had once been my old neighborhood, were never much of a threat to anyone beside themselves. This proved especially true after the Night of Fire a couple of years ago when the Weenies had been taken down, hard. It had taken them over a year to get back up to strength, and then they had to fight to reclaim their turf.

That fight had been going poorly, which was no great surprise because Charles the Red was still in charge of the Weenies. Then this huge guy, with long blond hair and arrogance dense enough to stop bullets, showed up and started giving orders. Chuckles accepted his demotion graciously and, after getting out of the hospital, started backing Mr. Sampson in his effort to retake Weenie turf.

I'd never been on good terms with the Halloweeners, and Charles the Red thought of me as the person responsible for destroying the gang. I knew that wasn't the whole truth, but letting Charles imagine it was kept him away from the others who had broken the Weenies. I had Raven backing me, which meant Charles growled a lot, but didn't bite.

Then Sampson showed up, and the Weenies started being a lot more aggressive. Raven decided to see what he could do to discourage them, and thus had begun the investigation of Mr. Sampson. Apparently something had turned up to link Sampson to Oak Harbor and I was glad Raven was following up on the lead. Still, getting left behind made me feel like I was being punished when I hadn't done anything.

I stopped for a second. *Wolf, sending Raven that message this morning can hardly be considered* nothing.

The message had said that I'd decided to ask Lynn to marry me and, for that reason, I felt I had to sever my connections with Raven and his crew.

I smiled as I reread Doc's suggestion that I continue to see Lynn. Short of having me trussed up and hauled down to the southwestern deserts that had spawned him, Raven knew he couldn't have kept me away from her. It pleased me to see that he took real joy in seeing that I'd found the happiness he denied himself.

The alarm on the telecom went off, and I realized I was going to be late if I didn't get moving. With the stroke of one button, I zapped the message, then retreated to my bedroom. I stood there, staring at the clothes hanging in my closet, and shook my head in dismay. If haute couture ever discovers Kevlar, I'll be doing turns on Paris runways. But though I was amply supplied for playing the well-heeled soldier of fortune, I had virtually nothing to wear that could be described as *normal*.

I shook my head again. *That's because you* are *a soldier of fortune, Wolfgang Kies. For the past eight years you've worked with Raven in his battle to keep the chaos of the Awakening from swallowing up what's left of humanity. You and the others have helped hold the line that keeps normal people safe from magical monsters and technological monstrosities. There's nothing wrong with being a warrior, and your clothes have allowed you to survive dressing for the part...*

I finally settled on a pair of jeans Lynn had cajoled me into buying on our last outing—so I'd have some that had more fabric than holes, she said. The gray t-shirt I selected had two advantages: it was clean and it was woven of Kevlar. Though I didn't expect trouble, I'd not become Raven's longest-living aide by being completely stupid. Lastly I chose my black leather jacket to wear over it, even though it had a red and black raven patch on the left shoulder.

Having solved that problem, I hit the shower for a quick, somewhat bracing scrub-down. I had a devil of a time trying to wash my back and actually gave up after not too much effort. As long as

I was going to be confessing things to Lynn, I figured I could add needing help with that little job, and see if she'd offer assistance.

That tactic *had* worked before.

I toweled myself dry and found myself standing before the mirror, doing the obligatory, double-X chromosomally-challenged person's flexing and posturing. I'm not as tall as some men, but taller than most. I have a lean, muscular build that had prompted a few folks— the aforementioned Charles the Red being one—to think of me as easy pickings until we tangled. Brown hair covered my torso front and back, yet it couldn't hide the myriad scars that crisscrossed my flesh. Each one reminded me of some adventure I'd had with Dr. Raven— and even a few from before I hooked up with him.

A fairly recent scar, a puckered, pink dot with a line bisecting it right beneath my left nipple, stood out because the chest hair around it hadn't fully grown back in yet. I'd gotten that scar from a bullet shot at me by a big-time hunter who wanted to bag a human. She'd gone from hunter to hunted—if one can say that maggots actively hunt— and her compatriots curtailed their poaching of human targets in one of my most recent adventures with Raven.

Scars. They meant I'd survived. No one could say I hadn't given better than I got in all these adventures, but something inside of me was weary of it all.

There'll come a point when you don't live long enough to scar.

I forcibly turned my mind away from maudlin thoughts. I dressed quickly and headed out of the apartment. At the door I hesitated and almost tucked the Beretta Viper[2] in my waistband, but I knew Lynn would hate it. Not wanting to give her any reason to be even slightly displeased with me, I left the gun on the foyer table and went out into the cool autumn afternoon air.

I set off at a leisurely pace, and tried to keep my mind clear of any matters vexing or bothersome, but that wasn't as simple as it might seem. I tried to think of Lynn—which was easy—but my thoughts quickly veered off into the vortex from which Raven's message had diverted me.

Maybe I could ease into it... The next time we go shopping I'll just pick up some dog biscuits or flea and tick shampoo... I laughed at that thought, but a sinister thought followed close behind.

Dr. Raven knew my secret—he'd helped me conquer the darker, savage, wolf side of myself before I could cause too much damage. Through Raven, I'd learned of the Wolf spirit dwelling within me, and because of Raven I was able to use the wolf's strength and speed as other warriors used cybernetics to enhance their abilities in combat.

---

[2] Despite the vaunted opinions of some, carrying even an old gun like the Viper 14 is better than going unarmed.

In enabling me to gain control, Raven had very definitely saved my life, sanity, and soul.

Valerie Valkyrie, Raven's newest aide, knew nothing of my affliction, nor did Tom Electric or Plutarch Graogrim, even though the three of us had worked together for the last several years. Kid Stealth probably did have some idea that there was something special about me from the time when he was stalking Raven's crew, but he'd never mentioned it. Jimmy Mackelroy had a vague idea about me being *different,* but I knew his secret, so we were even and, even more in his favor, he wasn't really inquisitive about my peculiarities.

The others who had learned the truth about me were the real reason I wanted to find a way to leave Lynn in the dark. The Silicon Wasp, Robin Carter, and Mr. Stilts were all members of Doc's entourage who'd known my secret. Each one had taken the secret to his grave, and there were simsense starlets whose careers had lasted longer than my friends did once they knew. I knew it was only coincidence, but learning that secret seemed about as safe as drinking a plutonium cocktail. Though I should have taken heart in the fact that Raven had survived the longest of all, somehow I harbored the fear that knowing the truth had killed the others.

As much as I wanted to share my secret with Lynn, as much as I wanted to share my life with her, I didn't want to add any more pain to her life. I'd sooner have shot myself than cause her any hurt. And, of course, being male and in love meant I knew there was a solution to the problem somewhere. All I had to do was find it and use it to keep Lynn safe.

I'd met Lynn through my association with Dr. Raven. Etienne La Plante, one of the larger pieces floating to the top of the cesspool that is Seattle's underworld, fancies himself a commodities broker. Whereas legitimate folks are content to deal in grain, simsense chips, or other such staples, La Plante goes in for more exotic merchandise. Arms trading and narcotics are his bread and vegemite, but he makes his profit moving bodies through white slavery rings. Pretty women, or men, for that matter, can fetch a premium in the penthouses of the corporate towers around the world.

La Plante's henchmen—orks with brains smaller than your average lug nut—had kidnapped Lynn to provide La Plante with merchandise to soothe the ruffled sensibilities of an angry client. After Kid Stealth had discovered La Plante had something special going down so, he and I and his buddies, the Redwings, hit an old resort complex called The Rock. We ran into something a bit nastier than we'd expected, but Doc Raven showed up in time to prevent Stealth and me from adding our names to the list of deceased aides.

After we rescued Lynn, Raven and I took her back to the apartment she shared with her parents in the Fuchi tower. She was still pretty out of it because of the drugs La Plante had used to sedate her, but Raven pronounced her fit and said all she needed was lots of sleep. I volunteered to stay in case of any more trouble—to the relief of her parents—and spent most of the next thirty-six hours holding Lynn to keep the nightmares away while she slept.

All in all that wasn't incredibly different from similar things I'd done for other victims of Seattle crime. It sounds smug to say that I'd gotten used to people being grateful and looking to me as some sort of savior, but it's true. You have to get used to it because the connection always ends. There's always another person with a problem, or another mystery that needs solving. I'd been through the same thing dozens of times before.

Only this time it was different. This time it involved Lynn—and involved me getting involved with Lynn.

I looked up and found myself at the corner of the small strip mall the Fuchi folks had put into the ground floor of Employee Tower Number One. I winked at the two woman greeters stationed on either side of the door, then hurried across the crowded lobby to the small bakery that employs the whole Ingold family. I waved at Phil as he poured 'kaf for a couple at one of the rear tables, then caught his daughter as she threw herself into my arms. I hugged her tight and kissed her, then set her down and stared at her, scarcely believing she was truly there and really did care for me.

Lynn wore her burnished copper hair pulled back in a ponytail that hung all the way to her shoulder blades. The top of her head came up to my nose. The scent of her perfume brought back pleasant memories of intimate moments that threatened to make me blush. Her broad smile and pert nose accentuated the lively twinkle of her green eyes, and the sprinkling of freckles across her cheeks made her seem happier yet.

She wore jeans and a red-checked shirt with complementary kerchief that meant she was going to try to talk me into going to a neo-Western dance club. After the Ghost Dances had killed so many people and prompted others to go native, things concerning America's Wild West had been downplayed. Time breeds a certain amount of contempt, and this neo-Western club called itself "Oklahoma." Everything had been styled after an ancient musical, which meant the men wore shirts made of tablecloths from Italian restaurants and every other vidiot packed a six-gun with a low-grade laser triggered by revolver blanks.

Blanche came out from the back of the shop and smiled when she saw me. She and Phil both looked happy and content and perhaps a bit proud that their only daughter was seeing someone from Dr. Raven's band of heroes—mind you, that's not as good as someone from the corporate boardrooms, but it beats most of the gillettes running around the streets. Their occupation had made both of them plump as gingerbread people, but I've always distrusted anorexic cooks anyway. They'd invested the last twenty-five years in their daughter, and their love for her showed plainly on their faces.

I shook Phil's hand as he came over. His grip, a bit dry from the flour coating it, was strong nonetheless. "Afternoon, Mr. Ingold, Mrs. Ingold. How are you?" Phil mumbled something I didn't quite catch as Blanche distracted me. Staring at her daughter as only a mother can when trying to remind her to do something, Blanche's gaze flitted to me, then back to Lynn. I frowned. "What's going on?"

Lynn glared at her mother as only a daughter can do, then looked up at me and sighed. "My parents are celebrating their thirtieth anniversary next week, and they wanted to make sure I invited you to the party, *which I would have done a bit later.* They also want you to extend the invitation to Dr. Raven and your compatriots."

Blanche unconsciously clasped her hands together in an attitude of prayer and crushed them to her ample bosom. "That Dr. Raven, such a nice, ah, man."

I suppressed a laugh. Raven is a rare commodity—a Native American elf who's physically big enough to bench press the tower. He's also devilishly handsome—a fact that had not been lost on Blanche Ingold or many of the other women he's met. That was one of the reasons I'd studiously avoided having Lynn renew her acquaintance with him.

Phil looked over at his wife and sighed. "I hope you get that Kid Stealth to come. I've still not thanked him for saving my little girl."

I felt the shiver run through Lynn. Her father put it down to memories of her ordeal, but I knew it came at the mention of the Kid's name. Lynn's very much a pacifist, and Stealth, well, I think he considers violence some sort of performance art. His openings are a splash, and only close after the coroner uses a lot of sutures.

I gave Lynn a reassuring squeeze, then addressed her parents. "I'll see what I can do. Raven and the others are out of town for a while. I hope they'll be back in time for your party. We'll let you know if they can make it."

Lynn's father laughed. "They can come even if they don't call ahead—Blanche, she always makes too much food for parties. I can remember a time…"

Lynn slapped me playfully on the stomach. "That's our cue to leave." She kissed her father on the cheek, then grabbed a jean jacket and brown paper bag from her mother. She kissed Blanche and made her promise not to wait up.

Blanche gave her an extra little hug, then let her go. "Be careful. I worry, even though I know you're in good hands."

I slipped my left arm around Lynn's slender waist and guided her through the lobby. "I take it from your outfit you want to go to that saloon you like?"

She gave me an impish smile. "You're not much of a detective for all the work you've done with Dr. Raven."

I shrugged easily. "He just keeps me around for heavy lifting and comforting damsels in distress." I narrowed my eyes and tried to figure out what nefarious plan she had brewing in her mind. "If there's a mystery here, I can't solve it. Don't tell me you've been hired by the Yamaguchi-gumi to square dance me to death!"

Lynn shivered eloquently. "You know, my love, that *I* know how much you hate Oklahoma." She glanced back over her shoulder at her parents. "However, *they* don't know that. I thought perhaps we might catch a bite to eat, then just retire to your place..."

"Well, my back does need washing..."

"My specialty."

"Maybe *you* think so..."

Lynn blushed and smacked me playfully on the arm.

The awkwardness of her sharing living quarters with her parents had been dealt with before through similar subterfuges. Because her parents had been employed by Fuchi for all of their adult lives, they got a sizable apartment in the employee tower, and it came with cleaning services and child care that made it possible for employees to devote themselves fully to serving the company. The bakery and other company shops provided anything and everything else the employees might need, and children were encouraged to remain at home—especially if they decided to work for the company, as Lynn had.

For a moment my mind drifted back to my younger days on the streets. Born in a tenement with no state or corporate official there to register me, I started early in life as a shadowrunner. No official records existed of Wolfgang Kies, which meant I was free of harassment by the city unless I attracted their attention. It also meant I could never integrate myself with numbered society—like the Fuchi folks—because I didn't officially exist. Whereas legitimate and tracked citizens had a myriad of safety nets built into the system to keep them alive, shadowrunners had to slip through the cracks.

Heading down to Pier 59 and the Aquarium park with my arm around a beautiful woman, I looked at the city in an entirely new way. Sure, it was the same, dreary gray sinkhole of concrete. Yeah, street toughs with more chrome than your average kitchen still lurked on street corners and in shadows. They still had the hollow, haunted look of despair in their eyes that they would die with—and that I had worn until not so long ago—but it just didn't seem to matter to me anymore.

Shadowrunning is fine when your life is a dead end, but when you can see a future, it just seems like a childish game.

The Wolf spirit inside me spoke in a harsh whisper. *"A warrior who views war as a game is a warrior who will not see death when it comes for him."*

We reached the park and walked to the benches beyond the area where the local wireheads had jacked into the public access systems. Those with datajacks installed, like Lynn or Valerie Valkyrie, just plugged themselves directly into the game tables. Others rented electrode rigs from a ramshackle kiosk to do the same.

Two kids were playing some variant of chess in which holographic pieces battled each other—they attracted a small crowd that cheered when a piece died a particularly grisly death. Others did their own things, oblivious to spectators. One guy who wore his purple hair in a spiked mohawk with piglet curls fore and aft seemed familiar, but I couldn't place him immediately. He amused himself by projecting images of city officials and hapless sheep into diagrams from an online edition of the *Kama Sutra*. I recognized what he was doing as I had once similarly amused myself on summer days of my misspent youth.

Lynn sat on the bench and opened her bag. She took out an old crust of bread and broke it into small bits. She tossed them out in a haphazard pattern at first. Then, as birds congregated she sowed her crumbs in a way that kept the bigger birds back from where the smaller ones came to feed. She gave me a hunk of bread and frowned disapprovingly as I tossed a large piece halfway between two monster blackbirds.

"Wolf! You're supposed to break it up into smaller portions!" Her pronouncement came as if it were one of the laws of the universe that I'd missed somewhere in my meager schooling.

"You want to run that by me again, with the help files active this time?"

She rested her hands in her lap, which prompted one bold sparrow to light on her knee and pick at the crust she was still holding. She laughed, then composed her face and turned to lecture me. "You have to use small bits because, as my mother taught me, birds that fly away with your food in their mouths take your prayers to heaven with them." She nodded once as if that answer explained everything, then started scattering crumbs again.

I opened my mouth to ask a question, then stopped. Over the years I'd been with Dr. Raven I'd had the gaps in my knowledge of the world filled in, for the most part. Ever since the Awakening—when magic again appeared in the world—the God Lynn and her family worshipped had lost lots of ground. Still, with all the things I'd seen in Raven's company, and even though I seriously doubted her God existed at all, I couldn't discount the possibility she was right. Weirder things had happened.

"Sorry," I muttered. "I just can't resist watching two dinosaurs fighting over bread."

Lynn rolled her eyes to heaven and tossed a little novena to a wren. "You're not going to try to convince me that birds were once dinosaurs again, are you?"

I quick-scattered a rosary's worth of crumbs in a wide arc, then brushed my hands clean on my thighs. "I double-checked all that stuff I mentioned last time. *Deinonychus* is the name of the dinosaur that had a wrist joint that looks the same as the wing joint in the *Archeopteryx*, and the *Archeopteryx* has feathers and wings, hence is seen as the first bird. See, dinosaurs and proto-birds had this common ancestor in the Jurassic period..."

She frowned. "Why would I remember *deinonychus* as a word?"

I shrugged. "It was a particularly bloodthirsty carnosaur. It ran fast and had this nasty, sickle-shaped claw on each of its feet that it used to disembowel..." As I hooked my right hand over to represent the claw, I saw her pale just a bit, and suddenly I realized why she knew the word.

I reached out and hugged her to me. "I'm sorry. Forgive me."

She kissed the side of my neck. "Nothing to forgive—you didn't mean it."

But I did it anyway. Lynn had first heard the word *deinonychus* when I clarified why Kid Stealth ran with such an odd gait. During her rescue she'd seen only glimpses of him and never got a good look at his titanium legs. She'd actually seen more than she knew, and put the weirdness down to the dope in her system. When I explained how Stealth had chosen legs styled after those of a *deinonychus*, she asked me to stop, but she still dreamed of him for the next couple of nights.

She pulled away from me and set about feeding the dinosaurs again. Her smile returned and she passed me another piece of bread, but I shook my head. "Lynn, there's something I have to tell you about me..." I faltered. After seeing how she reacted to the mention of Kid Stealth or anything that might remind her of violence, there seemed no easy way to tell her about the true Wolfgang Kies.

She brushed her hands off and cupped my jaw in them. "Wolf, I know you've been forced to do things you're not proud of. I know you've killed people and things while working for Dr. Raven, but I also know you did that to help others, like me. I cannot and will not let that drive a wedge between us—that's a decision I made the first time I agreed to go out with you."

She pressed her fingertips to my lips to stop me from saying anything. "I know you, perhaps better than you know yourself. I know you're a good man, a strong man, and I know I love you. There is nothing you could say that would change that or make me think any less of you."

I sat there stunned for a moment or two as I realized the true depth of her feelings for me. Somehow I'd assumed there was no way she could feel the same way about me as I felt about her, but that proved to be a fallacy that exploded with the greatest of ease. Still, she didn't know about my lunar mood swings, and that revelation would sorely test the strength of her convictions.

I started to speak, but something caught my attention above and beyond Lynn's head. Two hollow-eyed kids came around the corner of the trode kiosk, then ducked back when they saw me. Alarm bells immediately went off in my head because even though they'd washed off most of the jack o' lantern makeup the Halloweeners affected, their jackets were black and orange—Halloweener colors.

"Are you done feeding the birds?"

Lynn immediately caught the concern in my voice. "What is it?"

I looked around and saw more potential Weenies loitering in the background. "Gangers. I don't like it."

She sighed with exasperation to cover her nervousness. "Wolf, this *is* a public park. They have the right to use it."

I nodded. "True enough, but this just doesn't feel right."

Again she tried to play it light. "I think you just want to get me back to your place ..."

I stood and held my hand out to help her up. "No denying that. Why don't you scatter the rest of the bread in one huge papal audience, and let's get out of here. We'll keep it natural, as if nothing's wrong..."

"Wolf, you're scaring me." She crushed the bag, then up-ended it and let the crumbs spill out. "Let's go, if we must."

The fear in her voice gave way to anger. I knew it wasn't directed at me exactly, and I immediately focused my reaction to it on the Weenies who had started to follow us. At the same time I wanted to kick myself for having left my Viper behind[3]. The situation that appeared to be shaping up was not one in which I wanted to be unarmed.

The Wolf spirit's voice echoed through my head. *"You need not be weaponless, Longtooth. Embrace me and I will deal with your enemies."*

"No!"

Lynn looked back at me. "What?" Despite her fear, I saw her concern for me reflected in her green eyes.

I shook my head. "Nothing important." I glanced at the forest of gray buildings at the landward end of the pier. "I'm not sure if we're being followed or not, but there's a quick way for us to find out."

She hesitated for only a second. "Lead on."

I guided her toward the crosswalk as if nothing unusual was happening at all. The Weenies stayed with us, but lurked at the back of the crowd gathering to cross the street. I worked us toward the curb, then pulled her into the street. "Run!"

---

[3] See, I wasn't kidding, was I?

The irate honking of horns and the squeal of brakes drowned out any shouting from the other pedestrians as we dashed into traffic. Lynn let her fear run riot and the adrenaline made her nimble and oh so quick. She cut around the front of a Ford American and between two Honda minivans while I vaulted a silver Porsche Mako. The driver shook his fist at me through the windscreen, then went white as a bullet shattered the safety glass.

The next two silenced shots went high, but I saw them hit the Sumitomo Bank building. Adrenaline lending wings to my feet, I caught up with Lynn and grabbed her right hand in my left. Without warning I stopped and swung her around into the alley behind the bank, then I paused and made yet another in a long line of mistakes. I turned back to see who was pursuing us.

The lead grunge snapped two shots off with his silenced Ingram Mk. 22 before another Mako—this one white and sporting a dorsal fin telephone antenna—took him like its namesake would take a swimmer on an Australian beach. The lower portions of his legs whipping around like nylons on a clothesline, the ganger bounced from the hood to windscreen, then up over the top of the car. I'm not sure where the antenna caught him, but it looked crimson to me as the car continued through the intersection.

One of the two bullets peppered me with concrete shards and lead splatter as it hit the wall near my head. The other one hit me square in the ribs and spun me back into the alley. I ricocheted off the opposite wall, then sprawled unceremoniously on stinking bags of garbage.

Lynn dropped to her knees and reached out to me, then her hands recoiled in horror to cover her mouth as she saw the bullet hole in my jacket. "Oh, God, you're shot!" The blood drained from her face and I sensed she wanted to run, but refused to give in to her panic. "I have to get help—"

I held a hand up as my body once again let me breathe. "Wait...I'm battered but not bloodied." Gingerly I opened my coat and the .45 caliber slug slid across my t-shirt and to the ground. "See, no blood, no foul."

It heartened me to see the relief in her eyes. I saw no reason to mention that the bullet had broken at least one of my ribs and that if the Weenies got any closer with their guns, my t-shirt wouldn't stop their evil intentions, much less another bullet.

I took her hands in mine and gave them a squeeze. "Go further along the alley. Duck down behind that big dumpster there. I'll be along in a second. There's something I have to do."

"I don't want to leave you here all..

"Just a second, babe, then I'll be with you. Trust me."

As she headed back down the alley, I worked past the pain and reached inside myself. Deep in my heart I touched the Wolf spirit. The

Old One hauled himself up into a sitting position and looked at me disapprovingly. The red rebuke in his eyes found allies in the scarlet shadows rippling over his black form.

Even before the Old One had a chance to speak, I cut him off. "I need your strength and your speed and your senses, and I need them now! I have no time to debate you. *Now*!" Without waiting for his acquiescence, I pulled myself out of the self-imposed trance and smiled as the world reordered itself in accordance with my new perspective.

Despite the fetid garbage surrounding me, I could still smell the lingering trace of Lynn's perfume and the fear it helped mask. I heard the sounds she made as she ducked to safety, and the sounds of the rats in the dumpster behind which she hid. More important, though, I heard the asthmatic wheezing of a Weenie running toward where he'd seen me fall.

In an instant—the broken rib a twinge of pain to be ignored—I was on my feet and had flattened myself against the opposite wall of the alley. The acrid scent of gunsmoke burned into my nostrils as the silenced snout of another Ingram Mk. 22 poked around the corner. Without hesitation I grabbed the gun and yanked, pulling the startled Weenie into the shadowed byway. I tore the gun free of his feeble grasp, then smashed its blocky butt against his head. He collapsed without so much as a moan.

Following him came a gillette who'd learned to move almost silently. My first warning of his presence came when the forty-centimeter-long claws built into his right hand telescoped out with a *click*, then whistled as he swung them at me. His cut came waist-high and should have sliced my belly open, but I'd already begun to twist away from him before his attack began. The trio of polished steel blades shredded the right flank of my jacket and razored through the t-shirt and some flesh, but they didn't get enough to put me down.

Before he could turn his wrist around and try to backhand me with the blades, my right hand locked on his hand. I bent his hand inward toward his own chest. Anticipating my move, he retracted the claws and relaxed in preparation for using some esoteric martial art to turn my attack against me. That's why it surprised him when I jammed his fist against his own chest, then smacked the gun in my left hand against his funny bone.

The blow numbed his forearm—and released the claws.

I stepped over his dying body and out onto the street again. The half-dozen gangers and razorboys racing down the sidewalk collided abruptly as their lead elements tried to stop. I stroked the Ingram's trigger twice, sending two three-shot bursts in their direction.

Fortunately for them, and whoever does the workman's compensation filing for the Halloweeners, a heavy-set ork up front absorbed most of the damage. One bullet lanced sparks from a gillette's left-arm assembly and another folded an ork over as it drove his navel out through his spine, but otherwise it left the band unscathed.

Four out of at least ten down, and me with a half-empty mag and busted barrel staves in my chest. Why the hell don't these things ever happen to Kid Stealth?

I ducked back into the alley and looped the machine pistol over my shoulder by its strap. I grabbed both of the men I'd downed and dragged them to the dumpster. Lynn's eyes grew wide enough to fall out of her head, and I suddenly realized that with the silencer on the gun and the way I dealt with the first two people, she had no idea any fighting had taken place.

I dropped to one knee and brought the Ingram to hand again. "I'm sorry I got you into this, Lynn, believe me I am." I nodded toward the bodies. "I need you to go through the razorboy's pockets and get whatever he has—guns, knives, bullets, anything. I'll do the kid. It's our only chance at survival."

She reached out to touch the ragged furrows cut in my coat. "You're hurt."

"Not as bad as I will be if they get you because of trying to kill me." I started to pat the Weenie down, then liberated the spare Ingram magazines in the thigh pockets of his khaki fatigues. "Charles the Red or Mr. Sampson somehow learned that Raven and the others were out of town. They decided to make a move against me. Chuckles has been planning this for some time."

"How do you know that?" Lynn said as she pulled wires and datacords from the dead man's pocket and stuffed them into her own.

I whirled around and pointed the Mk. 22's snout at the alley mouth. A short burst blasted a grunge back over a parked car. "This won't do." I stood and twisted the dumpster so it blocked the alley, then answered her question by pointing at the razorboy and his purple-spiked coiffure.

"He was one of the ones in the park when we arrived. He was jacked into one of the public tables. It's my fault: We've been too predictable—always going to the park before we go elsewhere. He just let the others know we had arrived and the gears started grinding."

Suddenly I felt the alley walls close in on me like a trap. I lunged forward and covered Lynn's body with my own. The bullets sprayed down through the space where I'd just been crouching and, somehow, missed my splayed-out legs.

As spent cartridges tinkled down in a brass rain, I rolled over onto my back and burned the rest of the Mac's magazine. Bullets traced a line up the alley wall and through the street samurai who'd taken the high ground. He pitched back out of sight, his body looking like a piñata filled with cherry Jell-O, and I reloaded the gun without thinking.

Lying there on my back gave me a unique view of the world. From beneath the dumpster I saw a truck turn into the alley. Its tires squealed and smoked as it fought for traction in the garbage choking the alley mouth. As it picked up speed and the obscenities being shouted by its occupants fought over the roar of the engine, I realized the Weenies meant to use the dumpster to smear us into a thin, bloody paste.

Off to my left I saw a sewer grating lurking like a grime-smeared island in the midst of an oily patch of waste water. I leaped to it and single-handedly ripped the grating free. "Lynn, over here, now! Get down in here."

Tears streaking her face, she crossed to the hole and started her descent. The slimy, rusty rungs made the climb difficult, but she moved as quickly as she could. My enhanced olfactory senses sampled the sewer miasma with the relish of a wine connoisseur sipping Sterno. The stink gave me ample reason not to follow her, but the gangers in the truck allowed me no alternative.

"Drop, just drop!" I yelled as I thrust my legs down into the hole. I let myself slip into the darkness as the truck slammed into the dumpster with a horrendous *clang*. My left hand grabbed the top rung and my head slipped beneath street level as the dumpster's leading edge guillotined its way above me. I felt a grinding in my shoulder and a jolt of pain as my handhold stopped the drop short, but I was too intent on other things to worry about injuries at that very moment.

I shoved the Ingram back up toward street level and tightened down on the trigger. Like a bandsaw cutting wood, the bullets ripped along the truck's midline. Just behind the cab, the slugs lanced through the gas tank. Almost instantly the acrid scent of gasoline filled my nose and I let go of the ladder's top rung.

The truck exploded before I completed the five-meter drop to the river of sewage below. I saw a tremendous flash, then felt the thunderous detonation shudder through my chest. The scream of metal twisting out of shape as the flaming truck cartwheeled through the narrow alley sounded like a banshee death-wail and was made yet more haunting by the acoustics of the subterranean sewer tunnels.

I hit water and the bottom one after the other. Fire sparked in my right flank as the water gnawed into the claw wounds. Water hissed as it touched the gun's silencer and evaporated into steam. Gathering my feet beneath me I hauled myself to the surface and stood in the waist-deep river of sludge. As quickly as possible I moved upstream. By doing that I rejoined Lynn and avoided the flaming liquid dripping down in long burning rivulets through the hole above.

I slipped my left arm around her shoulders and tried not to react as she wrapped her arms around my middle and hugged. I failed and she recoiled. Her hands came away bloody. She stared at the black stains on her palms, for the burning gasoline's light was too feeble to give the blood its true color.

She looked up at me as if her world was folding in on itself. "You're bleeding. This water... You need a doctor."

I forced a confident smile onto my lips. "You have that straight. I need Dr. Raven."

She gave me a puzzled look. "But you said he'd left Seattle for a while."

"True, but Raven keeps tabs on things through the Matrix. That's why he took Valerie Valkyrie with them." I frowned. "Unless we get to a place where we can use a deck, we're up a creek without a sewage treatment plant in sight."

For the first time since we left the park, Lynn smiled. She plucked a short datacord from her pocket and I recalled having seen her strip it off the gillette I killed. "Get me to a junction box or public telecom access jack and from there I'm in." She pulled her hair back away from her left ear and snapped the cord into the datajack implanted there. "You've got the access codes—I'm not going to have to cut any ice, am I?"

I hesitated. The access codes and link numbers for Dr. Raven's private commnet were secrets I ranked right up there with knowledge of my particular brand of lunacy. They were the most precious secrets Raven had because if they fell into the wrong hands—read the Halloweeners, Mr. Sampson, or the legion of Raven's other enemies—it would be possible to uncover a whole string of Raven's safehouses and resources. Sure, Raven is far too intelligent to keep all of his secrets online anywhere, but any information gleaned could jeopardize operations I knew nothing about.

Furthermore—and far more important to me personally—giving those codes to Lynn would be bringing her into a world I wanted to save her from. I wanted to shield her from the danger I accepted as one of Doc Raven's aides. By giving her the codes, I would increase her risk. It wouldn't matter to someone like Mr. Sampson that anything she knew would become obsolete the moment Raven replaced the codes—she would become a target for getting at Raven.

She looked up at me and I saw she'd done some hard thinking. "Wolf, if we don't reach Raven, what are our chances of survival?"

I took a deep breath—as deep as my broken ribs would allow anyway—then pursed my lips. "Without contact of any sort, Raven would get suspicious after twenty-four hours, but he probably wouldn't return until after forty-eight or even seventy-two hours." I sighed wearily. "I could hold out that long—hell, with a quick trip to my doss I could even carry the war back to the Weenies."

She looked down at the torpid river swirling around our legs. "Do the odds change when you have me in tow?"

"Somewhat, yeah." Slinging the gun over my shoulder, I cupped her jaw in my hands and kissed her. "I'd take you back to the tower—"

"But they're probably anticipating that, and it would only put my parents in jeopardy."

"My thoughts exactly." I didn't add that we had no way of knowing how long they'd been watching us or how much they knew about where I was likely to go. "I'm sorry I've put you in this danger. If there was any other way—"

Lynn pressed a finger to my lips. "If you were anyone or anything else, Wolfgang Kies, I'd never have gotten to know you. Never regret or deny what you are. It's what I love about you."

I kissed her again. "Well, then, let's find a telecom box and get to work."

Finding a phone junction box was actually easier than I'd imagined, and I immediately ripped it open. The wires inside looked like so much rainbow spaghetti to me, but Lynn recognized things right away. She smiled and snugged the datacord into a slot. In a hushed whisper I gave Lynn the link number I'd been assigned and the access codes, including the one that disabled the pattern checker. I had to do that to verify that I wasn't using the codes or the computer would see an input pattern totally out of sync with my previous access and would sever the connection.

Lynn winked at me. "Don't worry, lover. No one will get those codes out of me. I promise."

"I know," I said, but she was already gone. The smile remained on her face, but her eyes got a glassy look as she jacked in. Her eyes REMed and then I watched her grin broaden, which had to mean she'd gotten into Raven's system. For the next minute she looked utterly enraptured, then her eyes blinked and she returned to the land of flesh and blood.

She stared at me with incredible joy flashing in her eyes. "When I used your codes and gave the system the override, I heard Raven's voice say, 'That's not necessary, Ms. Ingold.' He had a pattern check already built into the system for me! The man's unbelievable!"

I suppressed a smirk. "Yeah, that's putting it mildly."

"I left a message telling him that the Halloweeners were after you and me. I also said you thought you could hold out for seventy-two hours, but any help would be appreciated."

I nodded. "Good. That will get him back, or he'll cut someone loose to help us."

Obviously pleased with herself, and the fact that Raven had gone to the trouble of building a pattern file on her—from data undoubtedly stolen by Valerie from the Fuchi system—she unplugged the datacord and tucked it away in a pocket. "What do we do now?"

I pointed further on down the tunnel. "We'll head toward my apartment, but we'll wait until dark before we go up to street level. At my place I can get weapons and some more suitable clothing for both of us. We'll let your folks know we're going to ground, then we lose ourselves."

Lynn frowned. "Isn't it possible they know where you live and might be waiting for us?"

I nodded. "That's why we wait until dark. We'll scan the situation and walk away if anything is weird."

"Sounds like a plan."

"That it is." I smiled and started splashing my way deeper into the tunnel.

Lynn took my hand. "I think we make a good team—one too good to split up."

"I agree, kid." I gave her hand a squeeze. "The only way we'll part company is over my dead body."

TWO

By the time we'd made our way through the tunnels to my part of town, the cold had soaked into my bones, and I was shivering. I knew, without a doubt, that the cuts in my side were infected. I needed antibiotics and bandages, as well as dry clothes, dry shoes, and the better part of the arsenal I owned. Fortunately, all those things were available in my apartment.

The full moon had risen far enough above the horizon that the ball no longer looked huge. Lynn and I returned to the surface through a grate in a storm culvert one street over from my apartment house. With it still being early evening and the neighborhood being on the peaceful side of residential, not many folks were out and about. I took that as a good sign—in these parts "neighborhood watch" meant folks kept score in gunfights. If no one was out looking around I could allow myself to assume there was no trouble brewing.

Once we made it into the lobby of my apartment house I felt a lot better. I checked the security door down the back hallway and saw it was closed tight. With me in the lead, we ascended the stairs as they angled their way up and around three floors. Each flight had twelve steps, forty-eight steps between floors, and we took each one as if it was our last. I kept looking up and down the stairwell core and saw nothing.

Giddy is the only way to describe how I felt when I reached my door. I was tired and achey and stank like raw sewage, but that was all secondary to the happiness I felt in reaching sanctuary. Lynn clearly felt the same way and even the Old One yipped inside my head to signal his pleasure at returning to our lair.

I keyed the lock, opened the door, and reached inside to turn on the light. I tapped the switch and nothing happened. That struck me as unusual, but not dire. *Blown bulb* I told myself, and stepped into the darkness.

Looking up I saw two red eyes burning balefully about two meters above my eye level. A huge hand closed around my forearm, covering it from elbow to wrist. Suddenly I found myself yanked off my feet and flying through the darkness into the middle of my apartment. As I whirled through the air, I saw the silhouette of a troll eclipse my vision of Lynn.

She screamed, the Old One snarled, and I hit a knot of bodies in the dark. The Old One filled me with strength and dulled my pain. I lashed out left and right, connecting solidly. I heard grunts and groans, then I slipped off balance and began to backpedal in the darkness. Something shoved me, and I exploded out into the night through the apartment window.

"Longtooth, we are falling!"

If you were a raven or a hawk, we could be flying!

Landing precluded further discussion. I faintly recalled something about martial arts and breakfalls. I used one, but broke my left arm instead of my fall. The rest of my body slammed into the ground a second later, the breakfall not withstanding. The impact knocked the wind from me and reduced my left side to one huge bruise.

Pain blazing through my body, stale air burning in my lungs, I lay on my back staring up at the jagged black hole in my apartment window. Lynn screamed again, and I could do nothing. I fought to clear my head and tried to roll up to my feet, but I only slumped back. My left arm hit the ground again, sapping all the strength I had.

"You must get up, Longtooth. They are coming for you."

I can't.

"You must. *You must fight them."*

I'm in no shape to fight anyone.

"Then I must fight them."

NO–!

It was too late. With the full moon in the sky, the Old One was at his most powerful. At these times of the month, the control I can exert over him is stretched thinner than a politician's sense of self-restraint. The Old One no more wanted my consent to what he was going to do than he thought he needed it, but we both knew my concession would make things easier.

Just not the woman, Old One, not the woman.

"I will not harm your bitch, Longtooth, just those who would harm her."

The transformation, when I fight it, is a horrible experience. Now, having given my body over to the Old One, I heard my bones breaking as he recreated me in his image of what we should be. I felt the pain, but it seemed distant—like music heard in the background of a telecom call. I could feel it, and I knew it was pain, but there was not enough of it there to hurt me.

My facial bones broke and jutted out into a muzzle. My arm bones telescoped inward, shortening them so my muscles could exert greater leverage in strikes. My hands became blunt-fingered paws that ended in claws. My feet stretched out and my ankles shifted so my legs took on a characteristic lupine shape. Fangs, elongated ears, and a thick gray pelt completed the transformation.

I had become *his* creature. With the Old One at the helm, concepts like discretion, sanctuary, and ambush were all tossed into a bin marked *cowardice*. The Old One could be as murderous as Kid Stealth, and with two bullets blowing the lock out of the security door that led into the apartment complex's backyard, I felt no inclination to restrain him.

One of the Weenies kicked the door open and light from the hallway splashed out in a narrow stripe down the center of the barren yard. "Hey, Wolf's not here!"

Had I been in control, the Halloweenies would have had a smart remark's worth of warning. The Old One has no taste for humor. He stepped us into the light so they could behold the monster they had helped create, then he set about building an even stronger correlation between learning my secret and premature death.

The Old One doesn't view killing as performance art, but he did leave a number of abstract sculptures in the apartment's hallway and yard. Most were still identifiable as human and, no, not *everything* tastes like chicken. In fact, a couple of the chromed guys tasted like Harley-Davidsons in sore need of an oil change. Regardless, the Old One boiled through them before most had drawn their weapons—which he took as great evidence of his skill, but I put down to misguided orders to take me alive.

The Old One's transformation had not healed the wounds I had taken earlier. While the transformation did fracture bones and knit them back together, the process could only heal the damage it caused. My pelt remained ragged where the gillette had cut me, and I still nursed a broken arm and ribs. His rage and power still pushed the pain away, but even he kept my broken arm hugged to my chest.

We bounded up the stairs to my apartment so quickly we didn't even pause to snarl at some of the neighbors sticking their heads out of the doors to see what was going on. Someone said something about calling Animal Control, but that just made the Old One howl with glee. I saw images of him summoning a grand canine army to storm through the concrete forest of the metroplex, and part of me liked the idea of being Napoleon Roverparte.

Half-man, half-wolf in form, but fully lupine in spirit, we recognized and sorted out the various scents still lingering in my home instantly. The musty smell I knew as the odor of a troll—the tall thing that had originally tossed me about. At once I felt fear and anger: fear because they are purported to be hideously powerful creatures of a particularly malignant bent. The anger came because the troll's scent mixed with and masked Lynn's scent. The co-mingled scent trail led to the broken-out window, showing me how the troll had gotten out of the building while I raced up the stairs.

Beneath the troll's scent I discovered that of another foe, and hackles rose on my back. Charles the Red had been in my domain. He had undoubtedly orchestrated the earlier ambush and this battle under orders from Mr. Sampson. My bestial mind did not concern itself with why Charles had been here, or what he had hoped to accomplish. It only cared that he and the troll had taken Lynn. The Old One demanded that both of them die quickly, and I was ready to taste their blood.

Under the Old One's tutelage, my decisions were easy. Like a gargoyle, I perched for a moment in the moon-washed hole in my apartment's exterior wall, then leaped into the night and stalked my enemies.

Their scent trails died at the street where a vehicle picked them up, leaving me no clear way to follow them. Whereas a man might have been frustrated by this, the Old One was a consummate hunter. He started us loping in a big circle around the apartment house, and halfway through it we cut across a fresh trail containing the acrid edge of extreme nervousness. We followed it like a shark trailing a bleeding fish. I wanted to hurry to catch and destroy the person, but the Old One held us back.

He knew we were following a Halloweener, and as we trailed him I managed to intellectualize what the Old One picked up by instinct alone. The lack of spectators in my neighborhood meant that either nothing was going on, *or* people had been frightened back into their homes. The Halloweeners had obviously stationed lookouts in various places who then tipped Charles and the troll to my arrival. The lookouts took off, their role in the events finished, and I had managed to cut across the trail left by one of them.

We lowered our muzzle to the ground at the entrance to an alley that led to a warehouse. This fact I knew from previous encounters with all sorts of low-life scum. *Yes, Charles is here. Lynn is here.* My heart started beating faster yet than it had before I crept forward.

Through a rent in the warehouse's corrugated tin wall I saw Charles addressing two dozen Halloweeners—including two ogres[4]. Their presence—and the addition of a troll—meant Mr. Sampson had brought some serious power to the Halloweeners. We had no idea what his game was, or why he was using the Halloweeners as a power base, but I got the distinct feeling he wasn't some exec slumming for cheap thrills and a flea bite or two.

---

[4] Ogres are about as rare as hen's teeth, and the presence of two of them meant Sampson had serious juice. I knew that, but the Old One just thought hunting had suddenly gotten very good.

The Old One snarled, fending off my attempt to insert reason into his thought process. *He* had come to kill those who had stolen my bitch. He considered thoughts about *why* the Weenies were present to be a matter for forensics experts to piece together later. He wanted to create a crime scene and rescue Lynn, and he didn't see the need for rational thought in accomplishing that end.

Unthinking—a state in which the Old One operates most comfortably—he sprinted us forward and through an open side door. Announcing me, he howled in a low and cruel voice that brought all of the henchmen around to look at us, and drained the blood from many of their faces at the same time. Charles looked about ready to stroke out and took several steps back away from me.

Only Mr. Sampson, looking self-possessed as he stepped from the small office in the corner of the warehouse, did not seemed shocked or even surprised. He gave me a perfect smile. "Ah, our guest has arrived. Welcome, Kies. Your woman lives."

The Old One bared our fangs, giving me a chance to croak out a sentence. "She'll be the exception to the rule here in a minute!"

The Old One launched us into the knot of gangers and ripped away with ecstatic abandon. My right hand punched through the chest of a Weenie and ripped his heart out. I crushed it in front of him, all before his eyes had informed his brain that I had closed to striking range. I slammed my left elbow against a gillette's face and felt his facial bones crumple beneath my blow. My right paw flicked out again, shredding another man's face. He reeled away, desperately trying to piece together the fleshy puzzle I'd made of his handsome looks.

The Halloweeners had just enough brains to recognize the fluid their buddies were leaking and broke. Charles tried to stem the tide of their retreat, then allowed himself to be swept up in it and carried back toward Mr. Sampson. The ogres, befuddled and surprised, backed away faster than the Halloweeners and took up positions behind their leader.

Mr. Sampson looked at his cowering henchmen, then at the bodies lying at my feet and clapped his hands like a theater patron applauding a virtuoso performance. "Excellent!" Then his face and voice filled with menace. "Golnartac, deal with our guest!"

I never would have forgotten the troll.

The Old One, on the other paw, had decided he would save the troll for last.

Those who would be last were put first, and that put us in a world of hurt. The troll came in from behind and moved with a speed that should have been impossible for such a massive creature. I spun, but only barely got my right arm up in time to block the punch that would have taken my head off. The troll's fist smashed my arm back into my head and I saw stars.

Snarling wildly, I launched myself and buried my fangs in his forearm. My teeth sliced through dry, leathery flesh, but the troll didn't react. I bit harder, hungering for his blood and a cry of pain, but I got nothing. Furious, I tore at the troll, ripping my head to the right in an attempt to take a hunk of flesh out of him.

I succeeded and defiantly spat the mouthful out, but it made no difference. I looked up at the thing looming over me and saw only amusement in its dull eyes. I felt Golnartac's left hand close like pliers on the back of my neck. He plucked me from his arm as if I was an insect. Effortlessly he hurled me across the warehouse and into a shipping crate.

I don't know what was in that crate, but it was a tad harder than my skull. Mr. Sampson's laughter ringing in my ears, I struggled to free myself from the crate. I got to my feet. Then, as the troll eclipsed the overhead lights, his fist surged in and bashed me into unconsciousness.

THREE

You never forget the taste of your own blood, especially when it's bubbling up from inside with each painful breath. Charles the Red pulled his right fist back, then drove it down onto the left side of my chest. My body heaved backward with the impact, as it had with every other punch he'd thrown, lessening the effect of the punch somewhat, but that mattered little. With the two ogres holding me in place, he could make up in quantity what his punches lacked in quality. At least he hadn't popped another rib.

Mr. Sampson tangled the fingers of his gloved left hand in my hair and tipped my face up toward the warehouse's ceiling. "You're making this much too hard on yourself, Kies. Just tell me where Dr. Raven makes his home, and I'll end your pain. If you don't tell me, I'm sure Lynn Ingold will."

I wanted to give him my top-of-the-line nasty stare, but having both eyes all but swollen shut precluded that. I thought about spitting at him, but split lips make it damned tough to pucker. I decided to go with my fallback plan. I had nothing to lose because I knew he never intended to free Lynn or let me leave the warehouse alive.

I let my body sag in spite of the pain that shot into my upper arms when the ogres tightened their grip. My hair pulled free of Sampson's hand and I purposely hung my head in defeat. I let blood and saliva drool to the floor in glistening ruby ropes. I mumbled something in a voice barely audible over the rattle in my chest.

Even as Sampson bent over and asked, "What? What did you say?" I knew what I was about to do was stupid and foolish. I already had at least two cracked ribs, a broken arm, blood seeping from the slashes on my right flank, and my left lung had partially collapsed. I desperately tried to concentrate enough to reach inside and touch the Wolf spirit in me to boost my reflexes and give me more strength, but the burning pain in my chest and the lightning stabbing through me with each breath denied me the willpower to reach the Old One.

Still, no matter how foolish it seemed, I had to do something. I knew, if they continued, I might give up Raven's secrets, but even doing that wouldn't save Lynn. If she was lucky, Sampson would turn her over to La Plante to win some favor with the crime boss. If she wasn't, Sampson would use her to verify what I had told him, and since she didn't know where Raven lived, she'd go screaming to her grave protecting a secret she didn't know.

I couldn't allow that, and not just because I loved her. It was my fault that she had run afoul of the Halloweeners, and it was my duty to get her to safety.

Mr. Sampson brought his head down toward mine as I started to mumble again. Suddenly I snapped my head up, clipping him in the chin with the back of my head. Stars shot through my vision with the blow, but the sharp *click* of Sampson's lower jaw smashing into his upper teeth more than compensated for the pain.

At the same moment I gathered my feet beneath me and shot upward. My right fist came up and around, bashing one ogre's Adam's apple. I tore my right arm free of that ogre's grip, then pivoted around on my left foot. I jammed my right foot into the other ogre's groin. Slipping my left wrist from his grip, I side-stepped to the right as the behemoth collapsed screaming in a soprano voice.

Bloodshot tunnel vision only allowed me a hazy glimpse of the Halloweeners. They looked stunned and shocked, more worried about the fact that Sampson was reeling away with both hands pressed to his mouth than that a barefooted, severely beaten man was loose in their midst.

A heavy hand landed on my right shoulder and latched on with a grip somewhere between that of a leech and a Hoovermatic industrial vacuum. The second I felt the gritty flesh rasp against mine and the railroad spike talons rake my skin, I knew I was in deep trouble. I tried to spin away, but the pressure on my shoulder increased and forced me to the ground.

The troll. How could I have forgotten the troll?

Pinned to the ground on my back, I struggled hard and snorted explosively, clearing my nose of the blood that had caked it since the beating had begun. Instantly the dry, musty scent filled my head and started my sinuses bleeding again. I tried to force my body backward in a somersault motion to kick the troll in the head, but he just grabbed my right ankle in his free hand, then stood and held me dangling like a child.

Hanging there, upside down, I saw a real live troll from a perspective that I hope never to have again. Nearly 3.5 meters tall, the creature looked like something cooked up in an industrial genetics vat. I'm not sure what all they used to make it, but I do know they added ugly until it overflowed. His black mane had been braided into a long queue that snaked down over one shoulder. The dry, dusty part of the troll's scent came from the fact that most of his skin was flaking off like the outer layers of a sandstone onion[5]. His dark marble-like eyes burned with malevolence seldom seen outside the ranks of drill instructors or kid-hating spinster ladies with yappy dogs, and he tightened his grip on my leg just to let me know my assessment was not off the mark at all.

The troll grabbed my other leg and turned me around so I could face Mr. Sampson again. Sampson's kick landed over the fractured ribs and I screamed. A fit of coughing shook me and I tried to hug my chest, but I couldn't find the strength to lift my arms. Blood, fresh and coppery-tasting, coated in the inside of my mouth and ran in slender ribbons up to my hairline from the corners of my mouth.

Mr. Sampson snapped his fingers and the lightweight quack mage he'd had working on me all night dropped to his knees beside me. I felt the warm tickle of a spell ripple over me, and the pain slackened.

The mage looked up at Sampson. "He's bleeding internally. His lung is collapsed and three ribs are heavily bruised or broken. His arm is broken, his nose is broken, and he'll lose some teeth. What do I fix?"

Sampson dabbed at his split lip with a white handkerchief. "Stop the bleeding temporarily. Open up at least one of his eyes. I want him to see what we're going to do next. Charles, bring the woman here."

The mage hit me with the same bargain basement spell he'd used all night to keep me from dying. It plugged holes and patched leaks, but repaired none of the structural damage they'd done to me. It strictly ignored anything that was causing me pain and I knew, with the next kick or punch to my chest, the busted spurs of rib would open my lung up again.

As the swelling around my eyes went down, I practiced my nasty stare on him. "I'll remember you."

The spellworm didn't look impressed. "I've heard that before. I still sleep nights."

Sampson snapped his fingers again and the man withdrew. On their feet again and almost back to their normal, off-green color, each of the ogres took one of my ankles from the troll. They started pulling in opposite directions as if they were planning to make a wish, but a sharp command from Sampson stopped them when they got my legs out at a 150-degree angle.

He nodded and I heard a muffled rumble of thunder as the troll sank to one knee behind me. "Golnartac, despite his size, has an exquisite sense of delicacy. You won't know when, but at any one of a dozen prearranged signals he will hit a portion of your anatomy with a swift, precise blow. He'll only use one finger, but you will find

---

[5] Given his abnormal size and skin condition, there was clearly some serious modification that had been done to him. That, or he ate real well as a child and now wasn't getting enough Vitamin E.

the blows most painful. He may stab a talon through a nerve center, or he may shatter a vertebrae."

Pain sharper than a scorpion's sting lanced through my left thigh. It shot in both directions along my leg and up into my groin. I writhed in agony, prompting the ogres to pull on my legs to prevent me from slipping free. I felt a grinding in my hips, then they let me slip down again.

Sampson smiled in the same way the school disciplinarians had years ago. "You need not endure this agony, Wolfgang. All we want is Dr. Raven. Here we've gone and chased you all over Seattle and put a great number of people to incredible inconvenience, not the least of whom is you. Give us Dr. Raven."

"No 'or else'?"

"You won't like *my* 'or else.'" Sampson looked back to where Charles came bearing Lynn's limp body in his arms. "If you decide to resist me yet, I will awaken her and she will take your place. You will watch as she suffers more trauma than if she fell from the tallest building in downtown Seattle. Give us what we want. She will not be harmed, and your pain will end."

I sighed heavily and tried to ignore the agony in my lower limbs. "This 'your pain will end stuff'—you've said that plenty since I've been here. You can come up with something more interesting, can't you?"

An eye-blink later, it felt like the troll had shoved a molten sheet of glass through my right knee. I cried out in pain and despair. The troll's hoarse chuckle sounded akin to a car being crushed in a wrecking yard and, suddenly, the whole hideous ordeal collapsed in on me. In the past dozen hours I'd been hounded through Seattle, had escaped traps and ambushes meant to maim, capture, or kill me. The troll had defeated me three times, and I'd been worked over by individuals who wanted to see torture made into an Olympic sport.

As the edges of the pain crumbled away, I held my right hand up. "Wait, no more." I took a deep breath. "I give you Raven. You let her free, really free, right?"

Sampson settled a mask of superiority over his features. "You can trust me, Kies. You are but a means to an end, and she is a means to get to you."

I shook my head to clear it. Up beyond Sampson's head I saw something flit through the darkness. I tried to focus and identify it, but I couldn't. I was too far gone to make sense of anything but ending the pain. "You make sure she's okay?"

Sampson nodded solemnly. "She shall not want."

I knew in that instant that Lynn would be auctioned off to the highest bidder. *Fine. That makes this much easier.* "Doc's secret headquarters is in the Anasazi Shipping Company warehouse on Pier 27."

Sampson looked up at the troll. "Overhand blow, shatter his pelvis, then break his spine, one bone at a time. Charles, use the woman as you will, then have Golnartac dispose of her."

Behind me, the troll chuckled with evil delight.

"You're much too trusting, Wolf." Sampson dabbed at his split lip again, then spat on me. "I'll be sure to let Raven know who his Judas was..."

The troll loomed up over me, but as his fist began to descend, the ogre holding my right leg began to jerk and spurt blood from a string of holes linking his navel with his forehead. Crimson liquid sprayed the wall behind him, then the whole of his head above his glassy eyes disintegrated. As he toppled backward, his lifeless fingers let my ankle slip free.

The other ogre, who had increased tension in preparation for the troll's punch, whipped me out from beneath the troll's falling fist. I felt the warehouse floor shudder with the blow, and Golnartac's enraged scream shook the corrugated tin walls like a summer storm. Another screech, this one of ogre-pain, sang out in counterpoint to the troll's cry, and the pressure on my left ankle evaporated.

Suddenly I found myself tumbling and rolling across the concrete floor. I landed on my left shoulder and felt a grinding crackle in my ribs, but I used the pain to force my body to react. Adrenaline flooded through me yet again and dulled the pain. I scrambled to one knee, fists balled, then coughed a wet laugh of triumph and joy.

Kid Stealth stood on one ogre's back with his smoking Kalashnikov still pointed at the ogre he'd blown away. The sickle-shaped claws on his artificial, birdlike titanium legs dripped ogre blood—the other talons just clung on to the dead body beneath him. He'd been what I saw moving through the girders above the warehouse floor, and he'd nailed the one ogre while dropping down to rake his claws through the second.

The troll remained down on one knee, cradling his broken fist to his chest. Above the hand, right over where the troll's heart should have been, rode a red dot. Back by the warehouse's side door I saw the stocky outline of Tom Electric. The laser scope on his armor-piercing rocket launcher twinkled reassuringly at me.

Behind and above Tom four more people appeared. Two were the local gillettes I'd taken to calling Zig and Zag. Also armed with Kalashnikovs, they flanked the most beautiful member of Raven's crew, Valerie Valkyrie. She looked over at me with horror on her face while the two street samurai covered the Halloweeners. Plutarch Graogrim, an ork, moved away from Zig and Zag, keeping his pistol trained on Charles the Red.

I saw Sampson go pale and I knew Raven had arrived. I looked over at Doc as he stepped from the shadows. The blackness rippled off his coppery skin and clung to him long enough to deeply score lines around his muscles. Tall, even for an elf, he looked human because of his extraordinary build and the high cheekbones his Amerind blood granted him. His long, black hair fell down over his leather vest to mid-chest, and all but hid his pointed elven ears.

I like to pride myself on having silvery eyes and a scary stare, but the incendiary look Doc gave Sampson put even my best effort into the amateur category. His eyes burned with blue and red highlights as if an aurora rippled through their black depths. Muscles tensed at the corners of Raven's lantern jaw and the flesh tightened around his eyes.

Raven's voice sliced through the silence like a laser through cheap tin sheet. "You had a message for me?"

Those six words might as well have been .50 caliber slugs for the effect they had on Mr. Sampson. He shook his head violently and cursed. "No, damn it, not here, not now!" His hands flew up and around like snakes writhing in pain, then something flashed and Sampson vanished.

The Halloweeners started jabbering nervously among themselves, but the *click-click-click* of Kid Stealth's talons against the concrete as he ran over to cover them killed their conversation. "I have nothing on IR."

Raven stared at where Sampson had stood as if memorizing all that had just happened. He looked up and over quickly, back along the path Stealth had used to come into the warehouse, then nodded as someone yelped in pain. "He went out the way you came in, Stealth."

The Murder Machine smiled. "A strand of razor wire can cut you bad when someone booby-traps his back trail."

"Time enough to track him later," Raven said, then trotted over to where I knelt. He dropped down beside me and wove a quick spell that cut the pain at the same time it told him what was wrong with me.

"Take it easy, Wolf. Nothing that won't heal in time." He gave me a smile that buoyed my spirits, but it sank into a thin line of concern as I reached out and grabbed his hand.

"Doc, I need some help, now..." I looked over at Golnartac. "I want him..."

Raven looked deep into my eyes. He didn't use any magic, at least no magic I could feel, but he knew what I was thinking. "Wolf, you don't have to do this. Lynn is safe. Give yourself time to heal. You know if I use magic and it goes wrong, or there's a complication, it might stay that way."

He looked over at Kid Stealth. "For him, for any of the others, the possibility of replacing a defective part mechanically is there. For you, for me, that option is not possible."

"You heard Sampson, Doc. You heard what they were going to do to Lynn."

"That was their fantasy, but we've stopped them, my friend. I only deal in realities, and reality says she'll be fine."

"Yes, but I won't be." I pointed at the troll and he sneered at me. "Sampson called a tune, and the troll would have gladly played it. Well, I've got a variation on a theme to teach him."

"This is stupid, Wolf."

"We're here, Lynn's here, because *I* was stupid. I want to spend the rest of my life with Lynn, but to do that I need to know I can keep her safe. He always had an advantage over me, and now we're just about even. I have no choice, Richard. I have to do this."

I saw the lightplay in his eyes quicken. I only called him Richard when it was truly important, but he still did not want to damage me permanently. "Wolf, there has to be another way."

I shook my head. "Don't fix anything. Just kill the pain long enough for me to reach the Old One."

Raven stood and helped me to my feet. "And if the troll kills you?"

My eyes narrowed to silver slits. "Don't worry about it. You only deal in realities, remember?"

As Raven's spell washed over me like a warm, spring shower, I retreated deep into my heart of hearts. I swam through lines of pain that shimmered like heat lightning playing through dark thunderheads, but the spell took me beyond its touch. At times the going was difficult, but I forced myself on, haunted by the knowledge that I had almost gotten Lynn killed.

The Old One regarded me with an eager look of bloodlust on his face. *"Leave it to me, Longtooth. Give yourself to me and I will destroy the troll."*

"No. I gave myself over to you and your powers meant nothing without intelligence guiding their use. I need everything you are, but I must have it on *my* terms, under *my* control."

The Wolf spirit yipped high laughter. *"You are in pain and are weak. What makes you think you can control me now?"*

My anger and outrage at having failed to keep Lynn safe tightened around him like a net. "It is enough that I know I *must* control you. I need your speed and your strength. I need your heart and your endurance. You will meet my needs in my way. You failed, and you owe me the chance to put it all right. It must be a man who destroys that troll, and I will be that man."

The old wolf tilted its head in an attitude of curiosity. *"But you are not a man—you are more."*

I ground my teeth together. "Tonight, I will settle for being just a man."

The Old One sensed my need and my pain. *"Very well, I agree without condition. This is my gift to you, Longtooth Man-warrior."*

The warehouse swam into focus again, but the heightened senses made it all seem as if I had never been there before. I smelled terror from the Halloweeners, and death rising from the ogre bodies. I watched tremors threaten to tear the sellspell medic to pieces as I looked at him. All of Raven's aides looked at me differently than they would have normally—physically I remained the same, but they knew I was not exactly myself.

No, my friends, I am more myself than I have ever been in your company!

I turned and met the troll's evil gaze with an eagerness that daunted the monster ever so slightly. I moved away from Raven and into the center of the warehouse's open floor. I forced my left hand into a fist and bit back a cry as bones ground together in my forearm. Pointing at Golnartac, I waved him forward. "Come here, you. You're mine."

His laughter had the same grating quality as fingernails being raked across a chalkboard. "Little man will make little smear."

The troll lumbered forward, but I struck with a speed powered by my anger. As he swung a ponderous fist through where I had been, I darted forward and drove two punches and an elbow into the muscles bunched above his right knee. My blows crumbled flesh to dust, but the creature's rock-hard muscles absorbed the impacts more efficiently than a black hole sucking in photons.

A roar of outrage started in Golnartac's belly and began to work its way up to his throat. He planted his left foot and tried to pivot back toward the right. I dropped low and spun in the other direction, giving the troll a tantalizing glimpse of my unprotected back. Both his arms swung over my head as a second and third punch missed me, then I sprang up and smashed my right fist into the back of his left hand.

Pain overshadowed outrage in the troll's bellow as my punch further splintered broken bones. Unthinking in his agony, the troll backhanded me with that same hand. I saw the blow coming and rolled with it enough to soak up some of the force. Even so, the swat caught me on the left flank, igniting fire in my chest, and sent me flying across the warehouse floor.

The troll's renewed scream drowned out my groans as I hit and skidded to a stop against one of the ogres' bodies. I rolled to my feet, but as I straightened up I felt something give in my chest. More pain shot through me, and I felt the urge to cough because of the blood seeping into my lung. I remained half-hunched over and gritted my teeth against the pain. Hooking my hands into claws, I waved the troll forward.

Golnartac started toward me, but he limped slightly because his right leg failed to respond as it should. I swept in, flicked a glance at his broken hand, then again directed an attack against his right knee. Jamming my left elbow into the joint, I felt Golnartac's kneecap shift sideways and an agonized roar quickly followed. Exultant, I slipped right and stabbed my right fist upward into his stomach.

The troll reacted to the blow instinctively. His right hand slapped my back and smashed me face first into a wall of rock-hard abdominal muscles. Dazed, I rebounded, but hesitated too long to escape him. Golnartac's right hand closed over my head and he unceremoniously hauled me off the ground.

"Like an egg!" he shouted victoriously as he started to apply pressure.

Pain shot temple to temple, forehead to spine, but I refused to surrender to it. My hands hooked up over the troll's wrist and, despite the tearing pain in my chest, I whipped my right foot up in a savage kick that locked the monster's elbow. Uncoiling my body for a second, I brought my foot up again and this time drove it through the elbow.

When I heard the sharp *crack*, I couldn't tell which had broken, my skull or his arm. Then the vise that had trapped my head slackened. I dropped to the ground and launched another quick attack by driving my right heel down on top of the troll's foot. More bones broke with the *pop* of a gunshot, and this time I knew I was the damager, not the damage.

I heard the troll shriek with pain, but it did not matter to me in the least. The second I regained my balance, I whirled around in a circular kick that blasted my left foot through Golnartac's right knee. The leg bent to the side with a wet, tearing sound. The troll began to flail about wildly, his battle now waged against gravity, not me.

Golnartac lost his fight and began to sag to the concrete floor.

The fury in my heart did not allow me to show him any mercy.

He would have killed Lynn. And he would have enjoyed it.

Emotions gathered in me like a storm. I took two steps forward before the troll had succumbed to gravity's relentless attraction. Defying the elemental force that was drawing him down, I leaped into the air. As the troll's head came into striking range, my right foot flashed up. The ball of my foot hit Golnartac square on the chin, shattering his jaw and smashing ivory teeth into splinters.

Golnartac's head snapped back as if someone had grabbed his long black queue and jerked hard. The thick, corded muscles of his neck stretched taut, thrusting his Adam's apple out like an alien creature fighting to win its freedom. As powerful as they were, even those muscles could not fully absorb all the energy in my snapkick. The troll's neck cracked as a vertebrae crumbled under the pressure.

Head lolling uncontrollably, the dead troll crashed to the ground.

I landed a second later on very unsteady feet. Pure agony told me I'd destroyed my right foot, and black pain exploded in my ribs. For a half-second the Old One let me view my fallen foe, then he, too, abandoned me and I slumped to the floor, unconscious.

FOUR

Leaning heavily on a sword cane that had not seen use since the Silicon Wasp died, I watched from afar as Dr. Raven shook hands with Phil Ingold at the base of the Fuchi tower. The parting seemed amiable, though Phil looked stiff and turned away slowly to walk back into the building. I didn't sense hostility in him, only sadness and resignation.

Phil moved as if he hurt on the inside the way I hurt on the outside.

A fiberglass cast encased my right foot. A similar one sheathed my left arm. Stitches pulled the flesh together on my right flank and bandages helped hold my broken ribs together on the other side. My nose still hurt when I sneezed, and the bruises all over my body had gone from purple to a uniform shade of brown, with jaundice-yellow highlights.

I looked up as Raven came over to me. "You explained everything?"

Raven nodded solemnly. "Lynn is recovered from her ordeal and wants to see you. Neither she nor her mother understand why you won't be coming around again. Mr. Ingold does understand, but I think he feels his daughter's pain at not seeing you now more than he fears what might have happened in the future."

I shook my head. "He sees future danger as hypothetical, but you and I know it is reality."

"Do we?"

"Sampson went after her once to get at me, he'll do it again. Breaking it off with her and getting her a transfer out of Seattle is the only way to keep her safe. We both know that."

"It's not the only way. Stealth would have killed the Halloweeners for pocket change."

"Slaughter of Innocents."

"And we *will* deal with Mr. Sampson." Raven's eyes drew distant and the colors in them swirled into a vortex. "Oak Harbor provided some interesting clues about him, as did his display of magic a week ago. His days as a threat are numbered."

"And in single digits, too." I sighed heavily. "Still, if it isn't him, it will be someone else. The person I would have to be to protect Lynn is a person she would hate."

Raven looked over at me as we walked slowly down the street. "You're saying that as if she's incapable of changing and accepting the risks of life with you would entail. She was more concerned about your injuries than her own. Things might not turn out as you think."

"All dreams become nightmares, Doc, if you don't wake up soon enough." Deep down inside, I wanted to believe what he was saying, but in my heart of hearts I knew I couldn't accept the level of responsibility caring for Lynn required. I'd helped hundreds of people like her, and accepted responsibility for them because I knew that responsibility would someday end. With Lynn it would not, and while a life with her would be glorious, life without her—especially if she died because of me—would be unlivable.

Raven smiled slowly. "When you sent me your message, I rejoiced in it because it told me you were willing to shoulder a burden I have refused to accept. I thought you a better man than me in that, Wolf."

I blinked in surprise. "Me, a better man than you? Realities, Doc, not hypotheticals."

"I was certain then, my friend, and I am certain now that I was not wholly wrong." He laid a hand gently on the back of my neck and squeezed. "Perhaps, someday, we will both be able to work past that final barrier."

"Agreed." I shook my head. "It's kind of funny, though, being willing to care for the whole world, but being unable to do it for one special person."

"It's a nightmare, really, Wolf." Raven shrugged easily, but his eyes burned with intense color. "But if we stick with it long enough, we can push on through to where it becomes a dream again, and the dream becomes true."

AFTERWORD

The stories about Wolfgang Kies and Dr. Richard Raven are surprisingly special to me for a number of reasons. While I've probably written the least about this group of characters—in comparison to my *BattleTech*® or *Star Wars*® work anyway—Wolf and Raven hold a disproportionately large position in the minds of readers. Even in the midst of a *Star Wars*® book signing, I'll often have at least one person ask, "Oh, yeah, are you ever going to do a novel about those *Shadowrun* guys?" And that's years after the magazines and books in which the stories were published have folded or gone out of print.

I first heard of *Shadowrun*® back in March of 1989, when it was being developed. I was in Chicago to talk with the FASA team about designing the *Renegade Legion* roleplaying game, but then Jordan Weisman told me all about *Shadowrun*, filling my head full of all sorts of images and cool things. I returned to Phoenix on a Thursday and couldn't stop thinking about this stuff. For a writer—especially one with an assignment that didn't include *Shadowrun*—that's not a good thing.

About six months earlier, my agent, Ricia Mainhardt, had asked me to put together a bible for a men's adventure series of novels that we could sell. I gave it some thought and though I eventually rejected the idea, some of those thoughts lingered in the back of my brain. I'd decided that I'd write about a band of heroes led by a genius, something akin to Doc Savage and his band of associates. The difference for my group would be that the stories were told from the first-person point of view of one of the aides, much in the same way that Dr. Watson or Archie Goodwin chronicle the exploits of Sherlock Holmes and Nero Wolfe, respectively. That viewpoint allows the genius to be a genius and the reader to roll along for the ride.

That Friday night Liz and I went to Fiddler's Dream—a coffee house in Phoenix where folk singers played. I recall withdrawing into myself, hearing the music on the outside, but being a million miles away. *Shadowrun* had reared its head again, and lots of images flashed through my brain. All of a sudden I saw a Rolls Royce car, but instead of the winged woman on the hood, it had a raven. At that moment I saw the double-R logo beneath the raven, and knew instantly that the car belonged to Richard Raven—Dr. Richard Raven—an Amerindian elf and top-notch shadowrunner.

Raven slipped into the men's adventure framework perfectly, and I knew the aide who would chronicle his adventures was named Wolf. I also knew Wolf was a werewolf of sorts—at least that's what he believes—but I didn't know if that was possible or not in the *Shadowrun* world. It didn't matter—I had two characters in place, and the world as I saw it began to congeal.

On Saturday I called Jordan up at home and asked him some questions about the fictional background. On Sunday, in one ten-hour marathon session, "Squeeze Play" was written. By Monday, I Fedexed it to FASA, making it the first piece of *Shadowrun* fiction written.

This was rather remarkable, especially since the rules didn't exist yet.

By the end of that week I'd written "Quicksilver Sayonara," and by the end of the month the story that became "If As Beast You Don't Succeed" had also been written. All that writing hadn't gotten Wolf out of my system, but I faced the basic difficulty of all writers: if you want to get paid, you have to do things for which folks pay you. I shifted over to the *Renegade Legion* work and Wolf let me go.

That summer, with *Shadowrun*® slated for a GenCon release, Jordan decided we really needed a *Shadowrun* anthology, and he wanted to make it into a braided novel. Between the two of us we created the background, figured out the plot points each story would have to hit, and brought writers together. Jordan chose Robert Charrette to lead off and me to anchor the book. Everyone else was given a plot point to hit in it, and we were off to the races. By GenCon we had the first draft of the anthology put together. All the rough spots were ironed out at a big dinner meeting at Mader's.

My two stories comprise the last third of the anthology. The first, "Would It Help If I Said I Was Sorry?" is not a Wolf story. It is a Zig and Zag story, or Iron Mike and Tiger, as they prefer to be known. The second story is Wolf through and through. "It's All Done With Mirrors" chronicles the events referred to as the "Night of Fire" in this book. Both stories slot into the time frame between "Squeeze Play" and "Quicksilver Sayonara."

After writing the two stories in which a chunk of downtown Seattle was destroyed, I actually visited that city. The trip was a lot of fun. I was especially pleased to see I'd gotten uphill and downhill right—an educated guess based on the location of the ocean.

At that point, it looked as if there would be no other Wolf and Raven stories until there was a novel, which I thought would be great fun. Bob Charrette was given the first three *Shadowrun* novels—as well he should have, since he was one of the game's designers—and I was hoping to pick one up shortly thereafter when ROC began publishing both *BattleTech* and *Shadowrun* books for FASA. My first chance at a *Shadowrun* novel slipped away, however, because in the opinion of FASA's Sam Lewis I was all tied up with *BattleTech*. At that point it looked like I'd be writing one book a year for FASA, and Sam wanted that to be *BattleTech*.

At roughly the same time as that decision came down, the anthology was heading out into distribution. I asked FASA for permission to put "Squeeze Play" up on the GEnie network, in the Games Forum, as a taste of *Shadowrun* fiction to spur sales of the anthology. After I'd posted it, Loren Wiseman of the late Game Designers' Workshop and I were talking in a real-time conference. Loren told me that their magazine, *Challenge*, was open for submissions. I shot back that I was booked solid. Loren said that was too bad because they would have loved to have a story by me in an issue. Fiction, I noted back, was a horse of a different color. (Since *Challenge* had never carried fiction before, I thought Loren was soliciting articles or scenarios.) I pointed Loren to "Squeeze Play," which he downloaded, and inside a week *Challenge* bought it.

I followed quickly by sending them a copy of "Quicksilver Sayonara," which they also took. In the spring of 1990 I wrote "Digital Grace" and *Challenge* took it as well. In the summer, at FASA's request, I wrote the story "Better to Reign" for an advertising handout available at Origins. It introduced the character of Green Lucifer and fleshed out his backstory. Not wanting a good character to go to waste, I followed with "Numberunner," and included in it the character of Dempsey—a character created by Loren Wiseman.

Because of my schedule, it was about a year before I finished another Wolf and Raven story. Ever since writing "Digital Grace," I knew I wanted to return to the character of Albion and have Wolf deal with the aftermath of that story. I had the opening scene in mind, no problem, but I didn't know where the tale went from there. Then, one day when I was fooling around with the Destiny Deck (designed by Dennis L. McKiernan and Peter Bush), I tossed cards out to see where the story would go. The Destiny Deck is great for generating game scenarios and, in this case, the rest of the story just fell into place based on the clues on the cards. "Fair Game" was born, and it was rather big. *Challenge* agreed to take it, and spread it out over two issues.

Early in 1992, it looked as if I'd finally get around to getting a contract to write a *Shadowrun* novel. At Sam Lewis' request, I sent in a proposal for taking some of the short stories as a starting point for the novel and weaving them into one big long adventure. I sat back and waited to hear, but before FASA said anything to me, my agent called with an offer of a contract from Bantam Books for two unwritten fantasy novels, including *Once a Hero*. At that point in time, in my career and in publishing, few better offers could be found. Clutching two birds firmly in hand, as it were, I phoned Sam to tell him I had to let the one bird in the bush go.

Sam said, "So, you're telling me that you're turning down the book we're offering you." Because of my commitment to Bantam, I had to. If I'd only had FASA's offer in hand first, I could have delayed the Bantam work, but such are the complications of the publishing business.

It's at this point that things get a bit surreal concerning Wolf and Raven. In the spring of 1992, Liz and I were invited to be guests at Conduit 2 in Salt Lake City. The Guest of Honor there was Roger Zelazny, a man whose work I had admired for decades. I had hoped to get to know him there—often at conventions the out-of-town guests are thrown together just because of circumstances. While we did get to chat a bit, I never felt we connected, and I ended up rather disappointed in myself for not having made a better impression on him.

In September of that year, Roger came to Phoenix as the guest of honor at CopperCon. The following weekend Roger, Jennifer Roberson, Liz Danforth, and I were all supposed to be guests at Wolfcon in Mississippi. Having been to Wolfcon the previous year, I knew how small and intimate a convention it was, and I knew I'd be miserable if I didn't get to know Roger before we headed out there. I resolved to acquit myself better at CopperCon, and headed off to the convention.

When I walked into the green room to get my badge, Roger unfolded himself from a chair. "Hey, man, great to see you," he said, adding, "Roger Zelazny." Right. Sure. As if I could possibly have forgotten who he was.

I mumbled a greeting and shook his hand. He then said, "A friend of mine sent me some stories you wrote about *Shadowrun*. I really liked them. You have some great characters there."

At that moment two things were confirmed for me:

1. There clearly was a God.
2. Apparently I had made Him happy.

Wolf and Raven allowed me to become good friends with Roger Zelazny. The stories also prompted Roger to ask me to participate in the braided novel *Forever After,* which was one of the last projects he worked on before his premature death. And the story "Designated Hitter" served as a starting point for the story "Tip-Off," which I wrote for Roger's *Wheel of Fortune* anthology.

While I had toyed with "Designated Hitter" a bit through the years, I'd not touched a *Shadowrun* story for awhile when Rodney Knox became the editor of the Shadowrun Fan Club magazine, *Kage*. Rodney asked me if I could write a Wolf and Raven story for him and I agreed to do so, thinking I'd finally finish "DH."

As Rodney's deadline grew close and I realized I couldn't finish the story in time, I pulled up the only completed manuscript I had of a W&R story and rewrote it into "If As Beast You Don't Succeed." The original version is cruder and decidedly darker; but I like the version here much better. "Beast" was run in *Kage* in two parts, and succeeded in killing the magazine in 1994. Very few folks saw both halves, so, for all intents and purposes, there had been no Wolf and Raven stories published since "Fair Game" in 1992.

Despite that hiatus, I kept getting asked about the stories. I tried to interest FASA or ROC in collecting them into an anthology, but anthologies seldom sell as well as novels. (This is why this isn't an anthology. Nope. It's a *braided novel*. The difference, though subtle, is one we all hope makes itself apparent at the check-out counters.) Because of the sales issue, FASA and ROC both hesitated and I forgot about the idea of a collection while I dove into *Star Wars®* novels.

Apparently, others did not forget. When Mike Mulvihill took over as the *Shadowrun* developer, folks asked him about Wolf and Raven. Even out on the Internet I'd see folks occasionally lamenting the lack of a Wolf and Raven novel. At Origins in the summer of 1996, when Mike and I were riding up an escalator and heading off to lunch, he asked me about these *Shadowrun* stories I'd written. I let him know I had nearly a book's worth of stories prepared and that Heyne, FASA's German publisher, was interested in doing a collection over there.

One thing led to another, and you've got the result in your hands. I finally completed "Designated Hitter" for this collection and slotted it into place in the chronology where I had always intended it go. A couple of points were cleared up, some passages edited (or restored from the *Challenge* editions), and the rest is history.

A lot of folks—be they writers, critics, or academics—often opine that a writer's characters are really that writer; and since the Wolf stories are written in first person, it would be easy to assume Wolf is somehow my idealized self. Not true. Wolf gets away with things that would, quite rightly, get me killed. And while I wouldn't mind having his car, I'll leave friends like Kid Stealth and a shadowrunning career far behind, thanks.

One of the coolest things about writing from Wolf's point of view is that my brain starts producing remarks that are a lot more witty or cutting or sarcastic than normal. Seeing things through Wolf's eyes seems to hone my sense of satire and the absurd. It also makes me prone to chuckling at various moments at nothing.

In writing the stories I very much enjoyed how the saga just slowly grew. In "Squeeze Play," you can read what I knew about Kid Stealth as I knew it—I had no idea who or what he was as that story was pouring out into the computer. The rest of Raven's aides have defined themselves as well, not becoming what I want or need to have for a story, but what they apparently were intended to be all the way along.

Lynn Ingold is a great example of this sort of thing. I had never intended to carry her beyond "Quicksilver Sayonara," but she kept showing up. She adds a stabilizing and humanizing element to Wolf's life, which allows him to exert more and more control over the Old One. Since Wolf's life can be seen, in part, as a struggle to control the Old One, that makes Lynn very powerful. The fact that the Old One likes her, and is really only part of Wolf anyway, makes the whole set of relationships there something that might even seem to reflect *Literary Aspiration* on my part.

It's a passing phase, really. But it does go to show that a story is about characters, and even stories set in a commercial universe can have characters who develop and grow. I think a great deal of the positive response over the years to these characters is based not on what they do or have done, what they have killed or escaped or blown up, but on who they are and how much we like or fear them.

So the only other question to be asked and answered is this: will there be more Wolf and Raven stories? There's only one other that's partially complete; the rest are ideas and fragments. I'm sure, someday, Wolf will become restless and force me to finish them.

But, that's what I like about Wolf—you can't keep him down. He keeps coming at you until he gets his way. In the matter of more stories, I'm fairly certain he'll get it.

—Michael A. Stackpole
Phoenix, Arizona
August 1997

ABOUT THE AUTHOR

Michael A. Stackpole, who has written more than 15 novels and numerous short stories and articles, is one of Roc Books' best-selling authors. *Wolf and Raven* is his first *Shadowrun*® book.

Among his *BattleTech*® books are the *Blood of Kerensky* Trilogy and the *Warrior* Trilogy. Other Stackpole novels, *Natural Selection, Assumption of Risk, Bred for War, Malicious Intent,* and *Grave Covenant,* also set in the *BattleTech*® universe, continue his chronicles of the turmoil in the Inner Sphere.

Michael A. Stackpole is also the author of *Dementia,* the third volume in Roc's *Mutant Chronicles* series. In 1996 Bantam Books published *Talion: Revenent,* an epic fantasy. *Rogue Squadron,* the first Stackpole hardcover Star Wars® X-wing® novel, was recently published.

In addition to writing, Stackpole is an innovative game designer. A number of his designs have won awards, and in 1994 he was inducted into the Academy of Gaming Arts and Design's Hall of Fame.

SHADOWRUN TIMELINE

How We Got Here

Pay attention. There's not enough time to cover everything. But if you want to have any chance of understanding the world you'd better know something about how we got here. These are the key events that have made the 21st Century what it is.

1999: The Seretech Decision. During food riots in Manhattan, a Seretech delivery truck was attacked, and security killed 200 rioters. The Supreme Court of the old United States ruled that the security guards were justified in their actions.

2001: The Shiawase Decision. After an attack on a privately-owned nuclear power plant, the Shiawase Corporation argues that they have the right to defend their holdings. The Supreme Court agrees, giving large corporations extraterritoriality, making them sovereign over their own property.

2010: VITAS 1. A new virus emerges and spreads throughout humanity. A quarter of the world's population dies in the outbreak.

2011: The Year of Chaos and the Awakening. The year begins with a portion of the infants born across the world looking like elves and dwarfs of legend in a phenomenon known as the Unexplained Genetic Expression. Later, magic long absent from the world returns in an event known as the Awakening. Ley lines, ghosts, dragons, and more appear.

2012: The Continuing Awakening. Magic continues to spread, and more dragons appear, including the great dragons Dunkelzahn and Lofwyr. Lofwyr goes on to helm corporate giant Saeder-Krupp.

2014: The Native American Nations. Detention camp escapee Daniel Howling Coyote announces the formation of the Native American Nations. Later, in 2017, he helps perform the Great Ghost Dance that unleashes chaos on the world and forces North American governments to accede to his demands.

2015: Aztlan. The nation of Mexico, backed by the company that eventually becomes Aztechnology, changes its name to Aztlan. This becomes the base of one of the most powerful corporations in the world.

2021: Goblinization. Ten percent of the world's population take on the traits of mythical orks and trolls, and these races become a significant presence in the world.

2022: VITAS 2. A second strain of VITAS strikes the world. Another ten percent of the population dies.

2029: Crash 1.0. A computer virus like the world has never seen brings down the entire worldwide Matrix.

2030: UCAS. After losing much of their territory to the Native American Nations, the remainders of the United States and Canada merge to form the United Canadian and American States (UCAS).

2033: The Nanosecond Buyout. A financier named Damien Knight executes a flurry of transactions that, in under a minute, give him ownership of the massive Ares Macrotechnology corporation.

2034: New Nations Emerge. As geopolitical boundaries continue to shift, southern UCAS states secede to form the Confederation of American States (CAS); the large nation of Amazonia is founded in South America; and the elven nation of Tír na nÓg in what was once Ireland.

2035: Tír Tairngire. Following the emergence of Tír na nÓg, a second elven nation, Tír Tairngire, is founded in what used to be the northwestern United States.

2039: The Night of Rage. Anti-metahuman bigotry, which had been brewing since the UGE and Goblinization, explodes in global riots that kill thousands.

2048: Operation Reciprocity. In retaliation for the nationalization of all Aztlan businesses, the largest corporations in the world engage in a joint assault on Aztechnology holdings, causing severe damage but stopping short of destroying the company.

2057: Dunkelzahn's Triumph and Tragedy. In a single year, the great dragon Dunkelzahn announces his candidacy for president of the UCAS, wins the election, then, on the day of his inauguration, is killed.

2061: Year of the Comet. The passage of Halley's Comet wreaks great changes on the world, including mana storms, a UGE-like phenomenon known as the SURGE, the eruption of the volcanoes in the Ring of Fire and other locations, the emergence of a new dragon known as Ghostwalker (who goes on to rule the Free City of Denver), and sightings of the undead-like creatures known as *shedim*.

2064: Crash 2.0. A combination of attacks from the cult known as Winternight and the initial public stock offering of the Novatech megacorporation brings down the Matrix, paving the way for the construction of a new wireless Matrix.

2070: Emergence. Technomancers, who can interact with the wireless Matrix with only their mind, cause a worldwide outbreak of paranoia and fear.

2071: Ghost Cartels. A new drug called tempo sweeps the world, plunging millions into addiction and setting off a massive underworld war.

SHADOWRUN TERMINOLOGY

If you're going to walk the walk, better know how to talk the talk. Here are the essential terms you need to know so you can have a conversation without people staring at you.

astral plane: The dimension of all things alive and magical. Everything living has an aspect on the astral plane, and magic lights up this plane like fireworks.

Augmented Reality (AR): The primary way of interacting with the Matrix, Augmented Reality is a digital overlay on reality that allows individuals to access information and customize the appearance of certain areas. Individual pieces of AR are called AROs (Augmented Reality Objects).

Awakening: Term used to describe the return of magic to the world. Magical individuals and beasts are referred to as the Awakened.

bio-ware: Augmentations to the body that act as new organs.

BTLs: Better-Than-Life chips, chips that provide a sensory experience more intense than reality. BTLs (pronounced "beetles") are tremendously addictive.

commlink: A device used by almost everyone in the Sixth World, it combines elements of a handheld computer, telephone, camera, and other functions.

Corporate Court: A body made up of representatives of the ten most powerful corporations in the world that regulates high-level corporate activities.

critters: Animals that, affected by the changes that have shaken the world, have taken on new aspects and various powers.

cyberware: Augmentations that build machinery into the body to enhance and extend its natural abilities.

face: A member of a shadowrunning team who specializes in interacting with various contacts.

fixer: An individual who arranges contacts and meetings between shadowrunners and Johnsons.

hacker: Someone with a special expertise in accessing and manipulating nodes and the data they contain.

HMVV: Human-metahuman vampiric virus, a virus that causes vampirism in metahumans. Certain strains of the virus have the effect of transforming metahumans so that they resemble mythological creatures such as ghouls and goblins.

JackPoint: A private network of experienced shadowrunners, organized by legendary hacker Fastjack, who gather on the Matrix to share information and tips.

mana: The magical energy in all living things that makes spellcasting and other magical activities possible.

manaline/ley line: A concentration of magical energy; these lines form cris-crossing patterns across the globe.

Matrix: The global electronic network formed by the multitudinous wireless nodes across the world.

medkit: A medical kit, assembled goods for delivering first aid to victims and repairing wounds as rapidly as possible.

megacorporation: A tremendously large multinational corporation that acts as a sovereign power, complete with its own army and internal form of currency. In the Sixth World, the power of the megacorporations outstrips that of national governments.

metahumanity: Term used to describe all humanoid races, including humans, dwarfs, elves, orks, trolls, and others.

Mr. Johnson: The code name used by most representatives who arrange jobs with shadowrunners.

nanotech: Technology that uses microbiology and enhancements at the cellular level to carry out certain tasks. These tasks can include enhancements to human abilities.

PAN: Personal Area Network, the network formed by an individual's collection of wireless devices.

RFID tags: Radio frequency identification tags; common to almost all electronic devices, they broadcast information that facilitates communication between devices.

rigger: Term used to describe a specialist in controlling vehicles and drones.

sarariman: Term for the core backbone of any corporation—the salaried workers whose daily work makes a corporation go. Also known as "corporate drones."

shadowrunners: Independent criminals and deniable assets; people who stay out of the glare of the world and try to make a living in the gray areas.

SIN: System Identification Number. The basic form of identification used worldwide. If you don't have one, whether real or fake, things like opening a bank account or crossing a border will be damn tough.

skillsoft: A program that adds abilities or knowledge to bodies capable of using them.

street samurai: A warrior of the streets, a specialist in various kinds of weapons, and someone you want on your side in a fight.

technomancers: Individuals who can access the Matrix with no equipment, using simply their mind.

trideo: The three-dimensional media in which most entertainment is presented.

WHAT YOU MAY HAVE MISSED

The *Shadowrun* universe has evolved throughout its twenty-year history, and the arrival of the Fourth Edition of the game brought some of the most significant changes yet. If you haven't caught up with *Shadowrun* recently, here are some things you should know about:

The Wireless World: Crash 2.0, the Matrix disaster of 2064, paved the way for the creation of a wireless Matrix. The Matrix is all around everyone now; rather than having to log into it through a cyberdeck, the inhabitants of the Sixth World can interact with it wherever they go. Augmented Reality (AR) overlays much of the world, making the locations' appearance customizable and providing cascades of information. This means data is everywhere, so shadowrunners have multiple opportunities to dig up information they can use to make a buck.

A New Horizon: In the aftermath of Crash 2.0, one megacorporation, Cross Applied Technology, is torn apart and loses its AAA status. Its seat on the Corporate Court is taken by the upstart entertainment/public relations giant Horizon, whose employee-friendly policies and generous outlook seem too good to be true. In other Big Ten changes, Novatech merged with Transys-Erika and renamed itself NeoNET, and Yamatetsu restructured itself into the Evo Corporation.

Shifting Borders: The same strain that changed the corporations affected many nations. The Ute Nation caved to external pressures and became part of the Pueblo Corporate Council; the Salish-Shidhe Council made Tsimshian a protectorate; and earthquakes and floods devastated the California Free State.

Emerging technomancers: Recent times saw the emergence of people who can interact with the Matrix without equipment, using only the power of their minds. These strange and inexplicable abilities set off a worldwide panic.

Underworld explosion: A powerful, extremely addictive bio-engineered drug named tempo shook the world, and the potential profits from it set organized crime groups against each other in an explosive conflict.

Those are the central changes, but at its heart *Shadowrun* is still *Shadowrun*. Fixers still arrange things, Mr. Johnson still waits with an offer, and dragons are something to stay far, far away from.

Made in the USA
Middletown, DE
23 November 2022